THE GIRL
WHO WAS ME
IS GONE

THE GIRL
WHO WAS ME
IS GONE

BY

MICHAEL BROWN

www.penmorepress.com

The Girl Who Was Me Is Gone by Michael Brown
Copyright © 2019 Michael Brown

ISBN-13: 978-1-950586-21-9(Paperback)
ISBN-13:-978-1-950586-22-6(E-book)

BISAC Subject Headings:
FIC031020FICTION / Thrillers / Historical
FIC002000FICTION / Action & Adventure
FIC014070FICTION / Historical / Colonial America & Revolution

Edited by Amy Hawes
Cover Illustration by
The Book Cover Whisperer:
ProfessionalBookCoverDesign.com

Address all correspondence to:
Penmore Press LLC
920 N Javelina Pl
Tucson AZ 85748

DEDICATION

For Holly

ACKNOWLEDGEMENTS

First and foremost, my sincere thanks go to Amy Hawes, novelist of *Aspen Haunt*, who generously gave of her time and efforts to edit this novel, correcting my many mistakes while still maintaining the integrity of my writing style. Without her grammatical corrections and appropriate words for time and location, as well as her overall editing skills, this manuscript would not have been completed in a professional manner. Thank you, Amy. You are the best!

I also wish to thank fellow novelist Ron Sharrow, author of the *Bruce West* novels, and Richard Jones, A. Marco Turk, Marilynn London, and my son, Casey Brown, for reading my first drafts and offering their very welcome comments.

My sincere gratitude and love go to my very patient wife, Holly, who read the first and final drafts and offered her most helpful suggestions.

PRAISE FOR "THE GIRL WHO WAS ME IS GONE"

A young woman escapes from Oliver Cromwell's 17th Century rape of Ireland, only to be abducted and auctioned off as a white slave in Jamestown, Virginia, where she encounters a world of harrowing challenges. A must-read for lovers of romance and adventure.
Ken Koch—Television Producer

A fabulous journey with unforgettable characters in a setting that's seldom explored. If you love romance, history, adventure, and thrillers, this book has it all. A totally satisfying page turner that's impossible to put down!
Ron Sharrow—Author of the *Bruce West* novels

Hugely entertaining, with emotional twists and turns, violent sex and loving sex, and through it all an undying love that perseveres through life-changing hardships.
Jerry London—Director of *Shogun*

Oliver Cromwell, his English army of 12,000 troops, and a formidable train of siege artillery arrived outside of Dublin, Ireland, on August 15, 1649—and Nora's life would never be the same.

PROLOGUE
Dublin, Ireland—September 18, 1649

The icy wind blew across wet cobblestones, stirring swaths of mist as three hooded figures hurried along the dark street. Overhead, a mass of gray clouds shrouded the rising sun while, here and there, fingers of light poked through the mantel, giving off just enough illumination to help the travelers toward their destination.

A gust of frigid air slammed into the trio and sent their cloaks whipping out behind them like the wings of dark angels. Shivering, Nora drew her cape closer, aware that their frantic pace could draw unwelcome attention.

But they couldn't slow down. Every minute counted. Passing an alley, Nora glanced into the shadowy depths. Goose bumps prickled her arms as she imagined spectral forms lurking there. The danger, she knew, was not imaginary. British soldiers were everywhere.

If anyone had told Nora a week ago that she, at sixteen years of age, her brother, two years her junior, and her best friend, Anne would be branded as criminals and wanted for murder, she would have laughed until her sides ached. But now it was not a laughing matter. It was all true, and the danger was terrifyingly real.

"How far?" John whispered as he caressed the handle of the flintlock pistol in his waistband. His other hand gripped a satchel much like the ones his sister and Anne carried. The bags held all their worldly possessions.

1

"We turn right at the next street," Nora replied. "The wharf is two blocks after that."

"I pray the ship hasn't left without us," Anne said.

Nora peered over a row of one and two-story rooftops, buildings that fronted Dublin Bay, where skeletal bones of ships reached up like naked supplicants waiting to be clothed with sails and fed by winds of new and faraway places. She almost tripped when she noticed the crew crawling like monkeys over the rigging of one vessel, busily unfurling canvas that whipped and popped in the wind.

"We have to hurry," Nora said anxiously.

They turned down the block leading to the wharf and began to sprint. Nora could now see Aston Quay and the *Goede Hoop*, the Dutch frigate where they had booked passage. It was a beehive of activity as its crew prepared to weigh anchor.

"That dog of a captain," she said breathlessly as the three of them ran side by side. "He's planning to sail without us."

Da said not to trust the man, she reminded herself, but leaving without us, after Da paid for half our voyage in advance, is outright theft!

Dashing past the final cross street, they had an unrestricted view of the ship. Nora's throat tightened when she saw roustabouts on the deck, removing mooring lines. Two crew members scampered over to the gangplank, preparing to pull the ramp onboard.

"Wait!" Nora yelled. "We're coming."

They must have heard her, as they stopped to look in her direction.

"Wait for us!" Anne called. "We're passengers!"

We just might make it, Nora thought with relief as they ran the last hundred yards.

"You! Nora O'Lalor!" a voice boomed. "Stop! Stop where you are!"

Nora missed a step, almost falling. She turned to look over her shoulder at the side street they had just passed.

"Oh, my God!" John exclaimed.

A troop of twenty English foot soldiers, led by a mounted officer, was double-timing it onto the wharf's cobblestones.

"Nora O'Lalor," the officer yelled, "you and your accomplices are under arrest! Stop and surrender at once!"

Nora's heart froze as the soldiers came to an abrupt halt, raised their muskets, and took aim.

We're going to die!

CHAPTER ONE
One week earlier

Now that the time had come to pack her belongings, Nora stood in her bedroom, pursing her lips and tugging at a curl of long blond hair that had fallen from her bonnet. A life-changing decision had been made for her, one she had no control over.

Am I really going to be leaving home forever?

Ordinarily, she loved to travel, although she had never been farther away from the family farm than Dublin, a distance of fifty miles. On her visits to the bustling city where Da conducted business, she had often sat by the bay and gazed for hours at seafaring ships, imagining that one day she would travel on merchant vessels and explore exotic ports and countries.

Oh, how I had longed to go on a great adventure!

Her mam had often chided her for her daydreaming ways, saying she must have been sprinkled with faerie dust when she was born. Why else would a daughter of hers be having such fanciful ideas?

In spite of Mam's good-natured badgering, Nora had clung to her fantasies as tenaciously as ticks to a hound.

Then, out of the blue, Da had informed the family that they would be emigrating! She had been thrilled—until she learned their destination. Nora rubbed her temples. It was too horrible to think about at the moment, too upsetting.

4

With a heave of her chest, Nora looked around the room, her gaze caressing the keepsakes she would be leaving behind. The bedroom walls that had embraced her since she was born were a warm daffodil yellow, trimmed with lovely white wainscoting and crown moldings. Lace curtains on the windows were pulled back like twin ponytails, offering a view of the barns and courtyard.

The hand-carved, mahogany four-poster bed, an heirloom handed down from her grandmother, was the centerpiece of the room. A whimsical smile curved Nora's lips as temptation tugged at her. *I should just lie down on my feather mattress and forget all about packing,* she thought.

The bed had been her retreat. It was where she had spent hours upon hours daydreaming, when she could get away with it. Her eyes moved to a side table and lingered lovingly upon her collectibles: dolls, figurines, seashells, framed drawings, and other whatnots, all arranged just so.

Yes, she thought, *I love my bedroom and the great antique armoire that impractically takes up half a wall.*

She had barely touched her breakfast, her stomach aching at the thought of leaving the large home she had lived in for the last sixteen years. And while she had always dreamed of living in a big, exciting city, she had to admit that life on the farm had been good. Her da, Henry O'Lalor, was a gentleman farmer and an ex-politician—"ex" thanks to the despotic English. Da grew vegetables and raised sheep and the fastest racehorses in County Leix, formerly known as Queen's County, named for Queen Mary, that old battle-ax.

A fortnight ago, Nora had bidden poignant goodbyes to her friends and relatives at Hanratty's, the local pub where families traditionally gathered to celebrate birthdays and holidays, listen to storytellers, and dance to Irish music. She loved the Trenchmore, a peasant dance that, according to legend, had been passed down from the ancient Druids. Da had sworn that when she was a baby, she had danced an Irish jig before taking her first step. Later, when she had *finally* become a woman, dancing had offered her an opportunity to flirt with young men.

It was a girl's prerogative to flirt—in a ladylike manner, of course.

And now, as the reality of a six to eight-week voyage drew near, in all probability separating her from Ireland forever, tears welled. As much as she had longed for adventure, this trip wasn't at all what she'd had in mind. Now, if the family had been going to Paris or Rome or even Madrid, her spirits would be soaring. But sadly, that was not the case, and there was nothing she could do about it.

The family would be traveling to the absolute ends of the Earth to some backward, uncivilized settlement in the Americas called Virginia. It was in the American Colonies of all places! Wild Indians lived there—savages, she had read, who reportedly scalped, raped, and murdered!

On top of that, Da had firmly stated that she would be allowed only one small satchel in which to carry her belongings.

She opened the armoire and stared at her clothes with dismay. One small satchel! Impossible! Didn't men know anything? Why wasn't Mam speaking up and explaining to Da that women need a wardrobe to travel?

Huffing with frustration, she reached into the rear of the closet, pushed aside pairs of shoes she knew she would never wear again, and dragged out a needlepoint travel bag. Its floral design—a green field with yellow and blue flowers— once so charming, now seemed depressing.

Making a face, she let the bag thump to the floor. "My things will never fit in there!" she exclaimed to the empty room, as a tear trailed down her cheek.

Turning back to the armoire, she bit her bottom lip with even, pearly white teeth. On the verge of a good cry, she considered the gaggle of dresses that clung together like old friends at a going-away party. As she reached out and touched her four favorite gowns, a sob caught in her throat.

These were her most treasured possessions in the whole world.

Nora's grown-up wardrobe had begun to accumulate at the age of thirteen, when her parents had started a tradition of presenting her with a new dress to celebrate every birthday. Each frock had subsequently become a keepsake. Each one told a story.

Almost reverently, she withdrew an emerald-green taffeta gown, her fourteenth birthday present, and brought it up to her chin. She turned to see her reflection in the full-length mirror that stood judgmentally in the corner of the room. The green, her friends had remarked, complemented the golden hue of her skin and her flaxen hair, traits she had inherited from her mam's side of the family. Her high cheekbones, straight nose, and full, curving lips had come from her father. Nora spun around and grinned as the fabric flared out like the wings of a butterfly.

What she remembered most about the evening of her fourteenth birthday was the attention she had garnered from the opposite sex. The same young men who hovered around her friend Anne O'Moore with her melon-sized breasts while Nora pined away with a chest as flat as a flounder, were suddenly taking notice. Her bosoms, which had budded like peonies almost overnight, pressed against the thin fabric of the taffeta.

At first, Nora had been flustered and embarrassed when party guests glanced at her swelling bodice. But when they smiled, acknowledging her entry into womanhood, she began to feel cautiously comfortable with her new figure. As the evening wore on and young men asked her to dance, she had a most exhilarating fourteenth birthday!

Nora laid the green gown gently on the bed and then turned back to the armoire to withdraw an ankle-length golden dress with a low-cut neckline. It had been the sensation of her fifteenth birthday party. With baby fat gone and a new slim, yet curvaceous figure, she had made quite a stir among the guests, and one in particular—Billy Devlin.

Billy was a strappingly handsome neighbor of eighteen years, whom she had had a crush on since the age of twelve. He had taken her aside that evening and, while she was distracted by his beautiful honey-brown eyes, had leaned in and stolen a kiss. It hadn't been her first kiss; a few boys had brushed her lips with theirs. But Billy's kiss had surprised her with its intensity—not to mention the feelings it had aroused. Startled and a bit confused, she had been pushing him away when, quick as a fox, he had slipped a hand inside her neckline and pinched a nipple.

"Like that, do you?" he had asked with a lopsided grin.

Almost immediately, she had felt the crunch beneath her knuckles and, to her surprise, realized she had punched Billy —and broken his nose.

Maybe, she thought, I can part with the gold dress.

Her eyes returned to the armoire and fell upon her sixteenth birthday dress, the one her parents had given her just last month.

She simply couldn't part with the toe-length, cherry-red velvet gown that had been made for her by a seamstress in Dublin. The dress was the epitome of simplicity. Perhaps because of its unpretentious cut, it was the most gorgeous thing she had ever worn. She appreciated the fact that the bodice fit her bosom far too snugly for a cad like Billy Devlin to slip a hand inside.

She pressed the soft material to her cheek and whispered, "I will never leave you."

Tuck and Whiskey, her father's hunting hounds, began to bark excitedly outside, interrupting her reverie. Someone was approaching the house.

Nora moved to the window, where she had a view of the road that wound out of the hills to the family's large, slate-roofed manor house. Peering through a thin veil of rain, she compressed her lips and squinted.

A horse and rider were galloping down the muddy track as if they were being chased by the Devil himself. When the hood on the man's cape swept back, her eyebrows rose. It was Fergus Finney, Da's foreman and old friend. The balding, heavyset horseman abruptly reined in his mount, vaulted from the saddle, and splashed his way to the front door, dread twisting his normally convivial features.

Her breath caught in her throat. Something awful must have happened. Exhaling sharply, she tossed the red gown aside and hurried from the room.

CHAPTER TWO

Nora burst into the large parlor/kitchen and stopped short as her da, tall and elegantly slender for a man in his mid-forties, and agile despite his peg leg, strode over to the foreman who had just entered.

"What is it, Fergus?" Henry asked.

The foreman's chest rose and fell rapidly as he shed a wet, mud-splattered cloak. "I bring sad news, Henry. Terrible news."

"Have a seat by the hearth," Henry said. "Margaret, tea, please."

Nora's mam, an older, slightly heavier version of her daughter, rose from the floor where Nora's two brothers, John, fourteen, and Brendan, seven, had been helping to pack family treasures, including her father's prized books, into stout wooden crates. Mam, whose face had paled, slipped off the russet work apron that covered her long-sleeved woolen dress and moved quickly to the stove, where a teakettle whistled softly.

The household maids had left the day before, having been given severance bonuses, leaving Mam to brew tea, cook meals, and supervise packing for the family's impending journey.

Henry hung Fergus's cape on a hook by the door and led him to the table beside the fireplace, where peat glowed on the grate. For fast friends, the contrast between Da and Fergus was comparable to that of a giraffe and a bulldog. Da had the cultured demeanor of a gentleman. He customarily wore a white linen shirt, black breeches that ended below the knee, and one white stocking above a silver-buckled shoe on his remaining foot. Fergus was short, built like a keg of ale, and his large head held dark, challenging eyes. He wore a farmer's rough woolen shirt beneath a belted tunic that came to his knees, leaving his legs bare. His feet barely fit into his stout shoes.

Henry asked, "It's Drogheda then, is it?"

"Aye." The foreman pulled out a chair and sat. "God save us all. Henry, it was a bloody massacre."

Nora exchanged anxious looks with her mam and her brothers. They all knew of the battle that had been raging for days at Drogheda on the River Boyne. The small, fortified city was two days' journey from the farm.

Fergus continued. "Three thousand Irish lads surrendered on promise that their lives would be spared. As soon as they laid down their weapons, Oliver Cromwell, that scum of the Earth, went back on his word and ordered them murdered. The heads of our Irish officers were chopped off and put on pikes to be taken to Dublin, where they're to be displayed on the town walls. No exception was given to the old, the infirm, women, or children. Babies were torn from their mams' breasts and bayoneted, cut in half. Treacherous butchery is what it was!"

Nora covered her mouth with her hand as a cloud of despair settled over the room. Her mam, carrying a cup of tea to Fergus, stopped by the foreman's side, and Nora could see tears welling in Mam's eyes. Nora's brothers stood mute. John, as aware as she that a great tragedy had befallen Ireland, curled his hands into fists.

Da, whose features had darkened with the telling, asked, "Where did you get this information?"

Fergus took the tea with shaking fingers. "Thank ye, Margaret." A quick gulp later, he answered. "Paddy O'Moore. I found him early this morning, bloody and wounded by the side of the road."

"Paddy?" Nora gasped, immediately concerned for her friend Anne's fifteen-year-old twin brother. "Is he going to be all right?"

Fergus shrugged. "He'd been shot in the side. The bullet's still in there. I pulled him up behind me on my horse and rode him home to his da. Conal O'Moore has mended worse wounds. He may save him. But the sadder thing is that his brother, Liam, was killed in the first hours of battle."

Nora's heart constricted. Liam, Anne's oldest sibling, was dead. She said, "Poor Anne. And her parents!"

"Tis a foul day for the O'Moores and for Ireland," Fergus said. He took another swallow of tea. "English troops are hunting down and killing survivors. And that's not all. Cromwell has ordered confiscation of all properties owned by Catholics and any man who has ever fought against England. As if that's not enough, Catholic children are being picked off the streets, kidnapped, taken from their parents to God knows what end."

Mam shook her head at the hopelessness of it all. "Will there be no end to the thievery, cruelty, and murder?"

"Not in our lifetimes." Fergus turned to Henry. "You're leaving, old friend. How do the rest of us survive?"

"By outsmarting the Anglicans. I'm not giving you ownership of this farm so they can take it away. You and your family must convert and become Anglicans. Hopefully, when times and politics change, you can become Catholic again."

"Aye, Henry. That's a game I can play."

"I would stay and play it with you, but I am tired, much too tired of fighting our never-ending battle. And they know of me."

Her father's words reminded Nora of the day two years previously when Da, a member of the Irish Parliament, had returned home from Dublin. He had brought news that England had issued new, pernicious laws. Catholics would be forbidden to participate in their own government, to own businesses, and to attend mass. Priests were to be expelled from the country, subject to immediate execution if caught. Nora was well aware that the deterioration of freedoms—religious and secular—was the primary reason the family was emigrating.

Fergus glanced at the half-packed wooden crates. "Getting to the docks is a dangerous undertaking. If highwaymen or soldiers see those boxes, they'll rob you and murder you. You'd best travel light and fast, taking only your weapons and a few small bags."

Da studied his foreman long and hard and then turned to his wife. "Fergus is right, Margaret. We must leave the cartons behind. We will take only what we can carry."

Mam stared for a long moment at her possessions and then turned away, her shoulders beginning to shake.

Nora hurried to place an arm around her mam. "It will be all right. Da will buy you new things, anything you want. Won't you, Da?"

"That, I will. Our goods are replaceable. Our lives are not."

Margaret sniffled, wiped her eyes, and said, "Fergus, your family is to have everything."

"Oh, no. No, no. Henry is already giving me the farm. I'll not be taking one thing more."

"Old friend," Henry said, clapping the foreman on the shoulder, "eight years ago, you saved my life after that English cannonball blew my foot off. Now, damn it, allow us to give you a few gifts. At least Margaret and I will know they're in good hands. That means a lot to us. And if you read some of my books—Shakespeare, Milton, Jonson—it wouldn't do you any harm."

"Bah," Fergus sputtered. "Enough of the English. I won't be reading their drivel, but I'll be keeping your goods safe. Write me when you're settled. I'll ship them to your new home."

Nora, who had only been half-listening to this exchange, said, "Mam, Da, I have to leave for an hour or two to visit

Anne. With Liam dead and Paddy wounded, she has to be suffering. I can't possibly go without seeing her."

Her father's brow wrinkled with worry. "It's not safe, Nora."

"Da, I have to go."

"Nora," Margaret said, "listen to your father. It's much too dangerous."

"Please," she begged. "I'll stay off the road. I'll keep to the woods. No one will see me."

"I'll go with her," John offered. "If we take Puck and Lille, the English will never be able to catch us, even if we're spotted."

Nora saw her father waver. Puck and Lille were the two fastest horses in County Leix.

"Please," Nora pleaded. "Da, Anne surely needs me."

"I'll be taking my musket and pistol, Da," John said.

Everyone knew that John, while only fourteen, was one of the best marksmen in the county.

"No, I'm sorry, Nora," Da finally said. "I understand how much friendship means, but I cannot allow you and John to risk your lives. The countryside is far too dangerous."

"But, Da, it can't be that dangerous if you, Mam, and Fergus are riding into Portlaoise."

"That can't be avoided. We must see our solicitor. We're transferring ownership of the farm to Fergus. We'll be home by late afternoon."

Nora's mind raced. Home by late afternoon? It was still morning. She could ride to Anne's and be back within two hours at most. Her stomach tensed. Even to think of disobeying her parents was normally beyond her, but the thought of leaving her best friend in the world without saying goodbye was far too painful to bear.

I simply must see Anne, she told herself.

14

CHAPTER THREE

Only minutes after her parents and Fergus had piled into the buggy and taken off in the direction of Portlaoise, the small village situated on a tributary of the River Barrow, Nora opened the barn door and peeked out. Seeing that the road was clear, she led Puck, her father's splendid black stallion, into the muddy yard fronting the family home. A fine mist fell from the gray sky, tickling Nora's face and prompting her to pull up the hood on her cape. The morning was what Da would call a "soft day."

Suddenly, thunder clapped and rumbled overhead, startling the big horse. Ready for him, Nora gripped the reins firmly as he shied. "Easy, Puck. Easy," she said in a calming voice that belied her own nervousness. "It's just a little noise, is all. You've heard it before. It won't hurt you."

After snorting and prancing a few steps, the stallion settled.

Nora turned to John, who was leading Lille, the spirited chestnut mare, from the barn. Trepidation gripped Nora like the claws of a carrion bird. She knew she was endangering her brother's life by allowing him to accompany her to Anne's house. The possibility of encountering English troops was a real risk.

But, she corrected herself, she hadn't allowed it. He'd insisted! Nora kicked a clod of dirt, knowing she would never be able to change her brother's mind. He was as inflexible as pig iron!

Resigned, she reached for Puck's bridle and brought the horse to a stop before Brendan, who stood by the front door. He had managed to scrunch his face into a pout that would have made her laugh if the trip to Anne O'Moore's were less hazardous. Brendan had wanted to join her and John, but they simply could not allow it.

A gust of wind blew Nora's hood back, pelting her with icy drops that trickled down her neck. With a shiver, she pulled up the cowl, grateful for the men's woolen breeches and hose, heavy knitted sweater, and sturdy boots she wore beneath the cape. She drew the cloak snugly around herself and fastened it in place with its silver clasp decorated with a Celtic cross. The fastener was a gift from Da, who had worn it eight years previously during the Irish Rebellion of 1641. It was in that battle, when Ireland had once again failed in its attempt to throw off the English yoke of occupation, that Da had lost part of his right leg.

John also pulled his hooded cape together, beneath which he wore a woolen shirt and a belted tunic that left his legs bare below the knees except for a pair of leather boots.

At John's insistence, Nora carried a musket in an oiled leather sheath, along with a pistol, which she had wedged into her waistband. A powder horn and a pouch containing lead shot were secured to her belt.

"I want to go," Brendan insisted, wearing the expression he used when he didn't get his way.

Nora's heart went out to him. "I'm sorry, Brendan. It's best if you stay here and protect the house."

"The house doesn't need protecting."

"I'm sorry. The truth is, it's simply too dangerous. Da and Mam would kill me if I brought you with us."

"They'll kill you anyway when I tell them."

He's right, she thought, even as she tried to reason with him. "You've never been a tattletale, Brendan. I'm hoping you won't start now."

"I might."

"No! You are not coming with us. And that's the end of it."

Brendan stamped his foot, turned into the house and slammed the door.

"He'll get over it," John said. Holding Lille's reins, he sidled up to Nora and leaned down, cupping his hands. "Leg up."

She placed a foot onto his finger-laced palms and was hoisted onto Puck's saddle. Sitting astride as always, without deference to social mores, she gathered the reins as John leaped onto Lille's back.

As she held fast to Puck's reins, the stallion began to prance with barely contained impatience to be on the road. She waved to Brendan, whom she could see peeking out between the curtains on the front window. "Bye, little brother."

Brendan yanked the curtains shut.

Nora turned to John, who was struggling to hold the mare in place. Like Puck, Lille sensed a ride.

"Ready, John?"

"More than ready," he responded. "Both of us."

A shrill squawk suddenly cut through the mist.

Nora flinched. John's hand flew up in defense as a black raven shot out of the overcast sky, diving directly at them. The raven swooped by so closely that its obsidian eyes momentarily stared directly into Nora's, chilling her to the bone. Seconds later, the bird had disappeared as though it had never existed.

"An omen?" John asked with a frown.

She shivered. It certainly seemed like one. But, she thought, I'm not going to admit that to my brother.

"I don't believe in omens," Nora said with false bravado, and before she could change her mind, she added, "Let's be off."

Nora dug her heels into Puck's flanks, and the large stallion surged forward, followed by the mare. Sister and brother trotted out of the farmyard, churning up great clumps of mud.

CHAPTER FOUR

Paddy O'Moore's face twisted in torment. "Ahhhgh!"

Anne whimpered, wiping tears from her cheeks as her father, Conal O'Moore, both doctor and farmer, performed surgery on her twin brother. His right side bore a bloody hole where a musket ball was stubbornly lodged. Anne stood beside her mother, Keela, holding onto her arm.

Her father wiped sweat from his brow and, once again, using a thin blade and a pair of forceps, attempted to extract the elusive lead slug.

Paddy squirmed on the cot they had dragged out from the ground-floor bedroom and placed in front of the fireplace, where smoldering peat reddened the hearth. The family had been in mourning since yesterday, when they had received news of the death of their eldest son, Liam, at the battle for Drogheda. Only hours ago, their neighbor's foreman, Fergus, had brought Paddy to their front door, wounded and soaked through from the rain.

Paddy had told the family of the tragic circumstances that had befallen Drogheda. Soon after English forces had attacked the fortified Irish-held city, Liam had been shot through the heart. Paddy had buried his brother in a shallow grave, fully intending to bring Liam's body home for a proper burial in the family church's cemetery after the battle. But the opportunity had been lost when Cromwell's overwhelming force of 12,000 soldiers, accompanied by heavy cannons, had breached the town's walls and forced the Irish to surrender.

Paddy, who had been knocked unconscious by cannon fire, had awoken under a full moon, covered with debris. Thankful to be alive, he had nonetheless felt a searing pain coming from his right side, and discovered that he had been shot. Grimacing with agony, Paddy had dragged himself from under remnants of the wall and, using his belt, bound the wound as best he could.

Turning his gaze to the moonlit grounds, Paddy had at first seen only lumpy shadows and unfamiliar shapes. As he had begun to focus, his heart practically stopped. Only feet away, the blue eyes of a young woman stared at him sightlessly. Her head had been severed from her body. Lying beside her was the lower part of a man's leg, and then a naked baby girl—the small body sliced in half. Witness to a horrific slaughter, he saw hundreds upon hundreds of butchered, dismembered bodies strewn everywhere! He had vomited then, and been unable to stop until his stomach was completely voided.

Somehow, he had managed to crawl out through a hole that had been blasted in the wall, and had escaped.

As he stumbled for home, bleeding, he had met Irish sympathizers who helped him. It had taken Paddy two days and nights, avoiding English troops, to get to the road where Fergus had found him.

"I need more light," Conal said.

Stepping to the kindle basket, Anne removed a thin, dry branch, which she thrust into the smoldering compost. When the twig caught fire, she reached up to an oil lamp sitting on the mantel. Lifting the glass sphere, she touched the fiery end of the branch to the wick. A second later, the wick blossomed into a ball of glowing amber.

"Thank ye, Anne," Conal said. "That's much better." Her father, a wiry man, adjusted his glasses and manipulated the thin, bloodied blade as he delved into the wound.

Paddy groaned through clenched teeth.

"Hold on, son," Conal urged. "I've almost got a hold on it."

Paddy's hands clenched into white-knuckled fists. "Do what you must."

CHAPTER FIVE

A horse's neigh shrilled from the woods, causing Nora and John's mounts to whinny in response as they trotted along the tree-lined road. Nora's eyes darted nervously to the thick foliage, searching. Gooseflesh prickled her arms when she heard snapping, much like the breaking of a thousand tiny bones, coming from the undergrowth. Something was forcing its way toward them. English cavalry? A large animal? She glimpsed the quick flash of a horse and rider.

"We're being followed," she whispered with alarm.

"English?" John asked.

"I can't tell."

"How many?"

Nora shrugged, her eyes alert. Another rider, or perhaps the same one, appeared briefly, passing an opening in the copse. "Look there, by the elms."

"Oh, shit," John said. "It's Brendan."

Nora huffed with exasperation. "Darn him. I specifically told him he couldn't come."

"Da told us the same thing," John said with a wry grin.

John had a point, but Brendan was far too young to be joining them on what could be a dangerous journey.

She touched her heels to Puck, and the stallion quickened from a trot to a canter. John followed her into the woods. Within seconds, she and John reined in before a sheepish Brendan, who carried a short, small-bore shotgun. It was the same gun she and John had used when learning how to shoot. Da had trained all his children, upon reaching the age

22

of eight, to load and fire weapons. It was necessary for cautious, well-to-do Irish families to bear arms. An armed populace helped diminish recurring theft, rape, and murder by highwaymen and invading troops.

"I said you could not come with us!" Nora scolded her little brother. "You are to turn around and go home immediately!"

Brendan stared at her with an all-too-familiar look of rebellion and remained resolutely silent.

"Did you hear what I said?" she demanded.

Silence.

"Brendan," John said. "Go back. Now!"

Their little brother looked away, ignoring them both.

"All right," Nora said. "Brendan, get down. John, take his horse, he can walk. We'll pick him up on the way back."

Brendan suddenly kicked his mount, riding off through the trees toward home.

Nora watched her little brother disappear and then urged Puck forward. "Come on, John. We're wasting time."

*****

"I have it!" Conal exclaimed. Anne breathed a sigh of relief as her da withdrew the pincers from Paddy's wound and displayed a misshapen .50 caliber musket ball.

"There you are, my boy. Nasty looking thing."

"Sew me up tight, Da," Paddy said through clenched teeth. "I must be leaving."

"Paddy, you should not be going anywhere," Conal said, shaking his head wearily. He lowered the instrument and picked up a threaded needle. "The English have taken Liam. We won't let them have you. You'll rest here for the remainder of the day. Tomorrow, before sunup, we'll take the wagon to your cousins in Kerry. They'll hide you until I can arrange passage for you on a merchant ship to a friendly port."

"No, Da. I won't let you do that. It's too dangerous. I can still ride. I'll be leaving as soon as it's dark. I know the way to our cousins. I'll wait there until I hear from you."

"We'll discuss it in the morning," Conal replied, working with needle and thread.

Minutes later, Da tied off the last suture and covered Paddy's wound with a bandage. "My stitches will hold fast. No worry about that."

Outside, the dogs began to bark. Geese joined in, honking with alarm.

Anne crossed to the window and pulled aside the curtain. "English!" she gasped.

A column of at least twenty muddied foot soldiers were marching into the yard, leading a haggard group of shackled men, women, and children. Chains and iron collars secured necks, looping one prisoner to the next.

"Da," Anne said, "they've taken the DeVoys and the Devlins!"

"Damn them!" Conal responded, hurrying to the window. A moment later, he spun around. "Paddy, you'll have to leave at once. Out the back. Let me help you." He stepped over to his son, who was already struggling to sit up. Da took hold of his legs, swung them off the bloodied mattress, and helped him to his feet.

Paddy stood, wheezing, breathing hard.

"I'm sorry for the hurt, lad," Da said. "You'll take my cape and musket with you."

"Da . . ."

"No argument."

"I'll fetch something to eat," Keela said, and rushed into the kitchen.

At the window, Anne kept her eye on the soldiers and prisoners as they passed by the barn. They would be in the front of the house in minutes!

Da helped Paddy to the back door, where he grabbed his cloak from a hook. Reaching to another peg, he removed a musket, powder horn, and shot bag.

The bloody cot! Anne's brain screamed as she realized the danger it presented. She dashed to the bed and tore the soiled sheet off. Balling it up, she threw it on top of the glowing peat, where it burst into flames. Feeling dizzy, as if the heat from the fire had suddenly consumed the oxygen in the room, she asked, "Da, what do we do with the cot?"

"Leave it. Oh Lord, my instruments!" Conal leaned Paddy against the wall and hurried over to the bed, where the bloodstained surgical implements were in plain view on a small side table. He gathered them up and jammed them into a brown satchel, which he snapped shut and tossed into a cupboard, then ran back to help Paddy into his cloak.

Keela, her face a mask of panic, scurried over to them and handed her son a cloth bag. "Bread and a slice of cheese. Hurry, now! Go with God!"

"Thank ye, Mam. Love you," Paddy said tightly. He kissed her cheek.

Conal thrust the musket, powder horn, and shot bag into his hands. "Primed and loaded. Hurry. Out you go."

"Thank ye, Da." Paddy gingerly hugged his father.

Anne, tears falling, ran over and hugged him gently. "Be careful."

"I will. Love you, Anne. Keep safe."

"Love you, too. Go! Hurry!"

Paddy pulled the back door open and was about to step outside when a voice asked, "Going someplace, Irish?"

Anne's heart stopped. Her eyes darted past her brother to two English officers mounted on large, begrimed horses. Each held a flintlock pistol. Shiny sabers dangled at their sides.

Conal stepped forward to stand beside his son. Before he could utter a word, the soldiers fired.

"No!" Anne screamed as a blur of blood, bone, and brain matter splattered over her.

Da and Paddy, both shot in the head, collapsed at her feet.

25

Keela, paralyzed, stared at her dead husband and son, the backs of their skulls blown away.

Anne screamed and screamed. She couldn't stop screaming.

CHAPTER SIX

"Those were gunshots!" Nora exclaimed as the black stallion trotted alongside John and Lille on the muddy track that wound through low, rambling hills.

"That, they were," her brother acknowledged.

"Do you think it could be a hunter?" she asked hopefully.

"Two shots. Two hunters? Possibly, but I'm betting it's the fucking English."

The O'Moore farm! Nora immediately thought. "I know a shortcut that will take us to a spot overlooking their house. Follow me!"

She dug her heels into Puck's ribs, and she and John raced up a trail that wound its way through a growth of ash and oak trees. A horse and rider suddenly blocked their path!

Reining their mounts to a sudden stop, they stared in shock at—Brendan!

Nora could hardly believe her eyes. You little shit! He had not only disobeyed her, he had somehow actually managed to get ahead of them!

"You pig-headed boy!" she exclaimed, "Damn it, Brendan, we told you to go home! What is the matter with you? Do you want to get us all killed?"

Brendan's eyes fell to the ground. His mouth quivered as he said quietly, "I like Anne, too."

Nora suddenly felt like she was going to cry. Instead, she exhaled. Now was not the time for tears or arguments, not when Anne and her family might be in jeopardy. "All right, Brendan, you listen to me now. You can come with us, but you have to stay behind. If we see any English, you are to turn tail and ride for home. Do you understand me?"

He stared silently. His lower lip thrust out.

"I said, do you understand me?"

"Yes," he murmured reluctantly. "I understand."

"I hope so. Follow us!"

Nora jammed her heels into Puck's flanks. The big horse responded, chewing up turf as they raced along the path, continuing uphill through trees and patches of budding bilberry bushes. Pounding hoof beats told her John and Brendan were following close behind.

Nora's mind whirled. If the English are at the farm, what will I do? What *can* I do? Engrossed, torn by worry and uncertainty, Nora automatically ducked tree branches that clawed at her face with fingers wet from the rain that had recently passed. A flock of birds scattered before thundering hooves, twittering as they took flight, escaping certain death.

Would she and her brothers be as lucky?

*****

Frozen by shock and fear, Anne was trying to comprehend the horror that had just occurred, when her heart seized. The two murderers were dismounting! She screamed and stumbled backwards, past Mother, who stood motionless, her mouth forming soundless words. Anne's gaze dropped to the floor. Her gorge rose. She gagged. Da and Paddy lay motionless, blood seeping around them to form pools the color of red roses.

A deep, mournful wail tore out of her lungs as waves of sorrow and incomprehension flooded her senses. How could this be? It couldn't be real! This didn't just happen. Da . . . Paddy . . . NO! Please, dear God, don't let this be! Please!

The monsters pushed their way into the cottage, grinning lasciviously at her as they stepped over the bodies of Da and Paddy. They came after her. The taller one, a gaunt officer with a captain's insignia on his jacket, had yellow-brown eyes that reminded her of a feral animal. He had dirty blond hair and chiseled, almost feminine features. A pretty boy, her mother would have scoffed. His good looks were marred by his wolfish stare.

Anne gasped. He was using the toe of his boot to move her Da's head.

"Grimes, take a look at this," he said. "Left eye, exactly where I aimed."

"Yer a marvelous shot, ya are, Captain Dice," Grimes said. The captain's second in command, a slovenly lieutenant, raised an eyebrow at Paddy's bloodstained shirt. He leaned down and lifted the garment. Seeing the bandage, he ripped it off to expose the recently sutured wound.

Anne's heart clutched. Oh, Paddy. . . .

"This one's been shot afore," Lieutenant Grimes said.

Captain Dice grunted. "An escapee from Drogheda, most likely."

Anne began to shake. She had no power to stop the shuddering.

She became aware that the officer called Grimes was now staring at her and her mother, who was still motionless. He was muttering meaningless words, in a lewd and licentious manner. He placed a hand on his crotch and, rubbing himself, said, "Captain, I can do with the old hen, as I imagine you want the buxom young'un."

Anne's heart almost stopped as she heard the tall officer reply, "That, I do. Rank does have its privileges, Lieutenant."

The front door suddenly burst open and six infantrymen, having heard the gunshots, rushed into the room, muskets at the ready. Seeing two dead Irishmen on the floor, and that the officers were unhurt, they lowered their weapons and nodded approvingly.

Captain Dice motioned to the deceased and ordered, "Drag this offal out of here." Then those yellow-brown eyes tracked back to Anne. . . .

CHAPTER SEVEN

Galloping to the top of the wooded knoll, Nora and John, trailed by Brendan, reined in abruptly and stared down on the thatched roof of the O'Moore's farmhouse. Their position, hidden in the trees, offered a view of the rear kitchen door and front courtyard, where barking, growling dogs harassed a group of English troopers guarding a line of chained men, women, and children. The captives were half-dressed, shoeless, wet, and shivering in the cold.

"Bastards!" John said quietly as Brendan rode up beside them.

A burst of anger fired through Nora. "Those aren't rebel prisoners. They've taken Irish families from their homes, even the wee ones." She squinted, searching for wounded, but no one appeared to have been shot. Who had fired the muskets? And who or what were the targets? Nora spotted familiar faces among the captives. "I know some of those families! The DeVoys and the Devlins. That's Billy Devlin, the tall one on the end."

"Who?" said John.

"The nipple pincher," Brendan offered.

Nora shot him a look.

He shrugged. "Everyone knows about it."

"Ah," John remarked. "The one whose nose you broke."

"One and the same," she replied with a touch of chagrin. "The O'Moores?" she asked. "Do you see any of them?"

"Nay," John said.

A furrow creased Nora's brow. "What do you think we should do?"

"There's nothing we can do," John replied. "There's too many of them. But take a look at the two mounts tethered by the kitchen door."

Her eyes narrowed as she identified the saddles and tack. "English officers. They must be inside with Anne and her family. John, I have a dreadful feeling."

Voices drew Nora's attention to the front of the house. Peering over the rooftop, she spotted four infantrymen walking from the cottage into the courtyard—carrying two bodies.

"Oh, my God!" Nora whispered. "Anne's da, and her brother, Paddy!"

The soldiers, laughing, dumped the corpses onto the muddy ground and then strolled back to the lineup of prisoners. The family dogs ran over to the bodies, whimpering and sniffing.

"That accounts for the gunshots," John said grimly.

Nora's heart contracted. "Anne and her mam must be in the house. We have to help them!"

John shook his head. "There's nothing we can do."

"There has to be! Think what Da would do if he were here with us."

"Da would save them," Brendan said quietly.

"Yes, Brendan," Nora said, her mouth setting in a hard line. "Da would save them. And we have to try." A muscle in her jaw twitched; her shoulders sagged. Two adolescents and a seven-year-old boy couldn't possibly defeat two officers and a column of infantry. She certainly wouldn't risk John and Brendan's lives with a suicidal attack.

"We should go," John said, his thoughts obviously coinciding with hers.

"I can't leave! I can't abandon my friend! John, think like Da. There has to be something we can do!"

"Nora, going down there would be like kicking a hornet's nest. Those soldiers would be all over us in seconds." He scratched his chin as if attempting to find a solution, but then shook his head. "It's hopeless. We have to go."

"No," Brendan mumbled.

When Nora and John turned to him, he added solemnly, "We have to rescue Anne."

Nora's heart almost burst with love as she saw the determination in Brendan's face. But an inner voice said, Leave now. Save yourself and your brothers! Run, Nora! You don't want to die!

"Oh, shut up," she said.

"I didn't say anything," John protested.

Brendan threw her an odd look.

"Sorry. I was talking to myself."

"Talk to *me*," John said pointedly.

Nora slid from the saddle and unslung her musket.

"What are you doing?" John demanded.

She pulled the waterproof sheath off the musket and discarded it. Aware that her hands were shaking, Nora ignored the tremors and said, "I'm going down there, *alone*. John, you and Brendan are going home."

"Are you daft?" John said. "You'll be killed!"

"Please, go home."

"Who do you think you are?"

"I'm your older sister and I got us into this and now I am telling you to take Brendan and go home." When she saw his eyes narrow and his chin stick out, she added, "Please."

"You can't order me around." John dismounted, whipping his musket from his shoulder.

"John, I don't want you involved! If anything were to happen to you or Bren . . ."

"Save your breath," John interrupted. "I'm not leaving. You have to know that you can't possibly rescue them by yourself. I'm the only hope you have. Listen, Anne's my friend, too. And look at you. You're shaking like a palsied old lady."

Nora couldn't deny the obvious.

Brendan leaped from his mount and held fast to the reins and his small shotgun.

"Oh, no! No, no, no!" Nora said. "Brendan, *you* are going home!"

Brendan wiped his nose and eyed her with quiet defiance.

"Just what do you think you're doing?" she demanded. "This is not a game. You could get killed!"

Brendan lowered his eyes, refusing to budge or even acknowledge her.

Nora bit back a very unladylike curse. Each of her brothers could, at times, be just as stubborn as she was—an O'Lalor trait she somewhat deplored, especially when it came from the male side of the family.

She held Puck's reins out to Brendan. "Hold him. You, young man, are staying here to guard the horses."

"No." Brendan balked, refusing to take the reins.

"Brendan," Nora said through clenched teeth, "there's no time to argue! It's important that you hold the horses. If they run off, we'll all be trapped here and killed. Do you understand?"

He huffed, and then begrudgingly snatched up Puck and Lille's reins.

John said, "All right, here's what I think Da would do if he were here."

CHAPTER EIGHT

Fear as intense as the lust in Captain Dice's eyes propelled Anne backward as he stalked her across the room. Bumping up against a wall, her heart constricted.

Dice's lips twisted as he moved closer, so close she could smell his rank body odor and reeking breath. The canine eyes dropped to stare at her heaving chest. "Buxom little wench, aren't you?"

Anne's mother, who had been standing paralyzed by the dining table, suddenly burst out of her trance. "No! You filthy, horrible devils! You've murdered my husband and my son! You won't touch my daughter!"

Keela lunged for a knife that was lying on the table. Grasping the handle of the six-inch blade, she whirled around to meet Grimes.

Anne's eyes widened. "Mam!"

Keela raised the knife and advanced upon the lieutenant, howling like a banshee. The soldier blanched. He backed off, but not quickly enough. The blade slashed across his belly, slicing open his jacket.

Dice laughed. "You're getting old, Grimes. The bitch almost gutted you."

The lieutenant surveyed the damage to his tunic and shook his head. "Lady, I don't ordinarily kill women, but I will if I must." He drew his sword. "Drop the knife!"

Keela bared her teeth and charged.

The lieutenant parried the blade and swung his saber. It sliced across Keela's throat.

34

"Mother!" Anne screamed.

Keela stood in shock as blood spurted from her almost-severed neck. She toppled lifeless to the floor.

Grimes said, almost apologetically, "I had no choice."

Anne lunged for the knife Keela had dropped. Her fingers had just wrapped around its hilt when Captain Dice's hand clamped down on her wrist, squeezing so hard she screamed. As the blade fell from her hand and clattered to the floorboards, Anne begged, "Let go of me!"

The captain released her wrist, but quickly grabbed onto her hair and yanked backward. Shrieking, she was spun around and slammed to the floor. Rolling over, Anne attempted to regain her feet. A boot smashed into her ribs with a loud crack. "Aieee!" she cried as pain racked through her. She curled up into a fetal ball as the kicks kept coming.

My face! Anne raised her hands to protect her nose and teeth. Crying, she pleaded, "Stop! No more, please! Stop, please!"

"Stop?" the Captain taunted. "I'm just getting started with you, you Irish slut!" Grabbing her ankles, he dragged her across the room.

Anne dug her nails into the planked flooring, wincing as splinters tore into her fingers. In the center of the room, her assailant rolled her onto her back and, panting from his exertions, stared down at her.

Those eyes!

Before she could move, he fell upon her, his buttocks crushing her thighs as he straddled her. Hysteria took hold. She jutted her hips, bucking and screaming, "Get off! Get away from me! Leave me alone, you monster!"

His slap struck her face with the force of a mule's kick. The room faded in and out of blackness. The walls turned and shifted. She felt her arms savagely twisted, pinned to her sides where the officer's knees clamped them like a vice. The slaps continued, slamming across her cheeks, stinging, cutting her lips. There was the taste of blood.

Mercifully, the blows finally stopped. Her eyelids fluttered open. He was staring at her. The mania in his eyes sent cold waves over her. Hands began to claw at her bodice —ripping, tearing. She struggled against him but, with a growing sense of desperation, she knew she was as helpless as an insect about to have the sole of a boot crush it out of existence.

*****

The back door SLAMMED open! John and Nora rushed in, muskets in hand. A surge of bile rushed up Nora's gullet as she saw two English officers with their trousers down around their ankles hunched over Anne and her mother, having their way with them.

"Nora! Help! Please help me!" Anne cried desperately as she struggled beneath the man rutting on top of her.

Horrified, unable to move, Nora watched as the two Englishmen stopped their motions to stare at them with surprise—animals caught in the act of debauchery. The officer, who had the most unsettling eyes Nora had ever seen, sneered and continued to hold Anne down, grinding on her. "Be done here in a moment," he taunted.

Anne screamed. "Shoot them! Please, shoot . . ."

The tall officer slapped further words from Anne's mouth.

The second officer removed himself from Keela, whose dress was pulled up over her chest, and yanked up his trousers. A scream caught in Nora's throat as she realized Keela was dead, lying in a spreading pool of blood.

The officer with the sulfurous eyes grunted, shivered, and then drew away from Anne, who continued to cry hysterically.

"Now that that's over," the captain said, smirking as he buttoned up his breeches, "lower those fucking muskets!"

"Shoot them," Anne moaned tearfully as she gathered her bodice together with one hand while tugging her skirts down with the other.

"I'll take the tall one," John said, breaking Nora's paralysis.

Nora took in a quick breath and leveled the musket at the shorter, heavyset soldier. Her hands were shaking wildly as she asked herself, can I pull the trigger?

The tall officer unsheathed his sword with a *hiss* that chilled Nora to the bone. His partner picked his saber off the floor; its bloodied blade glinted menacingly.

"I ordered you to lower those muskets!" the captain said harshly. "I have twenty men outside. You have no chance against them. Drop your weapons, and I'll let you take this bitch and leave. You have my word as an English officer."

John's musket barked. The tall officer slammed backward into his partner, who, pushing him roughly aside, raised his saber and charged.

Nora aimed . . . and hesitated.

John, who had drawn his pistol, fired at point-blank range. The bullet blew away the stocky soldier's larynx, killing him instantly.

Nora gasped and ran to Anne. Laying the musket against the wall, she helped her to her feet. "Oh Anne. Anne!"

Her friend was trembling, weeping, attempting to hold her bodice together. "Those murdering fiends!" She leaned over, moaning in pain. "My whole family . . ."

Nora's heart almost broke. If only she had arrived earlier.

"Oh, Nora, I want to die," Anne said, whimpering like a wounded animal.

"Nora, we have to go!" John yelled.

Taking Anne's arm, Nora asked, "Can you walk?"

"I *will* walk," Anne replied with tearful resolve.

John ran to the front window and peered out. A dozen or more infantry were running toward the cottage! "We've got to get out of here, now!" He moved quickly to the front door and barred it shut. Dashing across the room, he retrieved a cloak from a peg on the back wall and threw it over Anne's shoulders. "Hurry!" He yanked the rear door open. Turning back for the girls, he suddenly yelled, "Nora, behind you!"

She spun around. The tall officer had risen to his feet, saber in hand! The brass, half-moon-shaped gorget hanging by a chain from his neck had been gouged deeply.

It must have deflected John's bullet, Nora thought.

Wolfish eyes became slits as the officer staggered forward. "Irish cunt!"

Nora whipped the flintlock pistol from her waistband, cocked the hammer, aimed, clenched her eyes, and pulled the trigger.

The detonation was followed by the thud of a body falling.

Nora opened her eyes.

The English officer was sprawled on floor, his face a bloody mess. He was either dead or soon would be.

She'd done it!

The front door jiggled. English voices demanded entry. The door was pounded upon as soldiers attempted to break in.

"Go! Go!" John ordered as he gathered up their weapons, took Anne by the arm, and led her out the back door. "Hurry!"

Rushing after John, Nora stepped into the yard where the officers' horses were tethered to a hitching post. John pulled the reins free and hoisted Nora onto the nearest animal's saddle, then lifted Anne to sit sideways behind Nora on the horse's rump. Anne wrapped her arms around her friend's waist.

"Hold tight," Nora urged.

John leaped onto the second horse. "Go!"

Nora heard the front door crash open. And then, not twenty feet away, two soldiers ran around the corner of the cottage. John pulled his pistols from his waistband, aimed at the men, and yelled, "Back! Or die!" Although Nora knew the pistols had not been reloaded, the soldiers didn't. They fell over themselves in quick retreat.

"All away!" John screamed.

They galloped up the hillside, shredding turf as additional soldiers burst out of the back door and fired after them. Nora flinched as bullets whistled past her head.

Reaching the top of the knoll where Brendan awaited holding Puck, Lille, and his pony's reins, John brought his horse to an abrupt halt and grabbed Puck's reins from his brother. "Brendan, you hold onto Lille. Mount up! We're getting out of here!"

Brendan, having heard the gunfire and seen the action below, shook his head obstinately.

"Did you hear what I said?" John demanded.

Ignoring his brother, Brendan raised his little shotgun. He coolly aimed at the soldiers and shot. Nora knew the birdshot was ineffective at more than a few hundred feet, but that didn't stop her brother from grinning from ear to ear. He had fought the enemy!

"All right, Brendan, good. Now on to your pony!" Nora yelled, struggling to control her mount as Anne held fast to her waist.

Brendan grabbed Lille's reins and vaulted up onto the saddle. Within seconds, Nora, Anne, John, and Brendan were racing away from the O'Moore farm.

Galloping at the head of their party, with Anne holding on for dear life, Nora knew that their lives had forever changed. From this day forward, they would be hunted as fugitives—and murderers.

CHAPTER NINE

Disoriented, Dice took a moment to realize he was lying on the floor. He moved to get up, and fell back as a searing pain burned through his jaw. Heart pounding, he tried to focus. What had happened? The gun. The flash. He'd been shot!

A man cleared his throat. Dice carefully raised his throbbing head. Several infantrymen were standing by the bodies of Grimes and the woman sprawled on the floor in pools of blood. The damned fools were motionless, gawking.

Dice screamed, "Irishh bitchh shhot meee! Shhe's esscapping!" Confused—his words sounded distorted, garbled—he jabbed a finger toward the back door. "Thrreee oof themmm! Gooo! Gettt themm! Shoooot thoose Irrissh ssswine!"

Seeing that the soldiers hadn't moved, he raged, "Affterr themm, Goddd daaamn it! Arrrest themm!"

The soldiers still didn't move.

Attempting to stand, a wave of nausea struck him, driving him to his knees. His face was burning . . . on fire. Dice raised a hand to his cheek; fingers touched ragged, torn flesh! He spat. Blood and fragments of broken teeth hit the floor. "Ahhh!"

Grimacing, he grabbed onto a table and pulled himself up. Seeing his reflection in the wall mirror, his eyes widened in horror. His left cheek was gone—shot away—leaving an open, gaping hole! Shattered teeth, visible clear to the molars, glistened with blood and saliva. "Noooo!" he screamed, causing spittle to spew.

An image flashed before him—the girl, aiming the pistol at him, along with the name the young man had called her—Nora! Nora, you Irish bitch!

He swore a mangled, blood-splattering oath, "I'll fiiind youu, Noora, wheerrevver youu are, wheerrevver you live! I'lll gouuge oout yooour eeyes! Cutt yoour facce intoo pieecees. I'lll Killl youuu, jamm your head onntoo a ppike!"

*****

I'm really in trouble now, Nora thought woefully as she slowed her mount to a walk, leading the small group into the muddy courtyard, where candlelight glowed from the downstairs windows of the family home. Her parents had obviously returned from Portlaoise and, although it was late, they had chosen to remain awake.

Why couldn't they have been asleep, so she would have time to think of something to say in the morning that wouldn't make her out to be as stupid as she was. How was she ever going to explain?

Anne, sensing her friend's anxiety, tightened her arms around Nora's waist. John and Brendan rode close behind. Her older brother held lead lines attached to Puck and Lille.

The rush of fear and shock that had possessed Nora during and after the encounter with the English officers had mostly dissipated. Glancing to the lighted windows, she thought, Da, Mam, you must certainly have known that I wouldn't, that I couldn't, obey you. Would either of you have let your best friend die?

She let out a long sigh. That argument might have worked had she not jeopardized her brothers' lives.

Da's hounds, Tuck and Whiskey, bounded out of the barn barking loudly, as they always did when riders entered the homestead. A ray of light fanned across the yard as Da and

Mam appeared in the doorway, staring at them with reserved expressions.

Well, here it comes. . . . I wish I were someplace else, anyplace else, Nora thought as she reined over to her parents, dismounted, and helped Anne to the ground. Da and Mam studied them for a moment, silently absorbing Anne's presence and the two unfamiliar horses that bore English military gear.

Da's eyes swiveled back to her. "Nora, what have you done?"

"Da, I'm sorry, but I just couldn't . . . I just had to . . ."

Her words were choked off as she read the judgment in her father's expression; his eyes were saying, I am so disappointed in you. If Nora could have melted into the mud at her feet, she would have. She could accept any verbal or corporal punishment and bear it, but the look of disapproval in her da's eyes crushed her heart.

Da said, "All of you, inside."

*****

Da listened to Nora as they sat at the parlor table, lines of worry deepening around his eyes.

Ending her account of their adventure, Nora said, "I am sorry, Da, Mam, but I wouldn't have been able to live with myself had I not said goodbye to Anne. I simply had to go."

"Me, too," Brendan added.

"It was my fault, too," John offered. "I couldn't let her go alone."

"And you would have, Nora, wouldn't you—gone alone?" Mam remarked. "Don't bother to deny it. Do you know how worried we were? You could have all been . . ." Mam choked up, unable to go on.

"I know, Mam," Nora said, feeling guilty yet resolved in the rightness of her decision. "I'm so sorry I worried you. I just couldn't stop myself."

Anne, eyes welling, stammered, "My ma, my da, my brothers . . ." For a moment she couldn't go on, and then she continued. "All dead. Without Nora, I would be, too. She and John saved my life." Anne opened her cloak, exposing the torn bodice that revealed angry red lacerations and purple bite marks on her bosom. "An English officer did this to me, and then . . ."

"Oh, sweet Jesus!" Mam exclaimed.

Da's frown deepened. "Anne, please, tell us what happened."

Anne, rocking back and forth, was unable to speak. A mournful keening came from deep within her.

"I'll explain," Nora said, placing an arm around her friend's shoulders. "There were soldiers at the O'Moore's when we . . ."

"Tell it from the beginning," Henry said.

Nora gathered her wits and said, "We were about a quarter mile from the farm when we heard shots. We left the road and took a trail to the top of the hill overlooking the house. We counted approximately twenty English soldiers in the yard. They were holding a long line of Irish prisoners, chained to one another with no proper clothing or shoes against the rain and bitter cold."

"Prisoners?" Mam asked.

"Yes," Nora said. "The Devlin and De Voy families were among them."

"Oh, my Lord," said Mam, shaking her head. "Our dear friends. It gets worse by the day."

"That's not the half of it," John said. "We witnessed soldiers carrying the bodies of Conal and Paddy out of the house."

Henry cursed quietly. "How were you able to get Anne away?"

Nora said, "We couldn't see Anne or her mother anywhere, so we knew they had to be in the house with the English."

"There were two officers' horses tethered by the back door," John explained.

Nora continued. "We left Puck and Lille on top of the hill with Brendan, and hiked down. The door was unlocked. We readied our guns and John led the way inside." Nora paused. Out of deference to her friend, she made a quick decision to refrain from mentioning Anne's rape.

"I shot the first officer in the chest," John said.

"Jesus, Mary, and Joseph!" Mam exclaimed.

"I then pulled my pistol and put another slug into the second pig's throat, killing him. Unfortunately, the first officer got back on his feet; the musket ball had ricocheted off his metal collar. He would have done us in with his saber, but for Nora. She saved us with a splendid shot."

"It wasn't a splendid shot. I shut my eyes before I fired. I was lucky to have hit him at all. We quickly gathered up Anne, but Keela was dead, murdered."

"Oh, Anne," Mam cried out. "Dear God, save us all."

"The first officer, is he dead?" Da asked.

John and Nora exchanged a look. John shrugged. "We don't know."

Worry furrowed Henry's brow. "Did either of you call the other by name?"

John looked suddenly troubled. "Nora, I believe I did say your name."

Da exhaled. "There isn't another lass with the name of Nora living hereabouts. If the officer you shot survives and remembers your name, the English will soon be paying us a visit, as well they might in any case."

"Damn!" John clenched a fist. "I should have made sure that bastard was dead."

"It can't be helped now," Da said. "All the more reason for our early morning departure."

Mam placed a hand on Anne's shoulder. "Come, dear, we'll get you out of that dress and into a bath. Nora, there's a pot of hot water on. Bring it up with you and start another to boil."

As Mam led Anne from the room, Nora hurried into the kitchen. She took a rag from a side table and used it to grab onto the iron hook inside the hearth. She pulled the large cauldron of steaming water to her and, struggling with its weight, placed it on the floor. Then, picking up a second pot already filled with water, she reversed the procedure. Pausing to catch her breath, she thought: Poor Anne, she's been through so much. To be brutally raped has to be the horror of horrors.

Nora knew what her mam had told her about men and sex—that the first time for a woman was painful. To be savaged by a thug must have hurt terribly, not to mention being vile and disgusting. And then there was the other complication. Anne could have become pregnant. It was possible.

Nora hoisted the steaming cauldron from the floor and hauled it into the parlor, where John was speaking in a lowered voice. "If we had arrived a few minutes later, Anne, too, would have been murdered."

Henry slammed his fist on the table and rose. He strode around the room, his peg leg striking the floorboards as if its point might pierce the wood. Nora knew from her father's dark countenance that he was struggling to contain his fury.

Finally, he spoke. "You said the soldiers had the De Voys and the Devlins?"

"Yes," John said, glancing at Nora. "There wasn't anything we could do for them."

"You and your sister have done more than enough." He glanced from John to Nora. "I want you to know I understand why you had to risk your lives to save a friend. I would have done the same."

Nora felt as if a long-held breath had finally been released.

Henry added, "I am so very proud of both of you."

Lowering the caldron to the floor, Nora ran to her father and embraced him, feeling his warmth, strength, and goodness. Brendan, who stood nearby, cleared his throat and coughed loudly. Fighting back tears, Nora managed to say, "Brendan helped, too. We might not have made it back if it weren't for him holding onto the horses."

Her little brother puffed out his chest. "I held them real tight."

"Brendan," Da said, "you're the bravest little man in the family."

"I'm the *only* little man in the family," he protested.

The shadow of a smile crossed Da's face. "I meant to say you are as brave as any grown-up man I have ever known."

Brendan grinned from ear to ear.

"Now, John," Da said, "I want you to take the English horses to the barn. Inform Fergus where they came from. He'll know what to do with them. I also want you to ask him to gather some farmhands and go to the O'Moore's. Conal, Keela, and Paddy will need a proper burial."

John nodded. "I'll see to it."

"I'll come with you," Brendan said.

John glanced to his father, who acquiesced with a nod and then said, "Children, after supper tonight, I have some vital matters we must all discuss."

Nora exchanged looks with her brothers and raised her eyebrows. What vital matters could their father possibly have to discuss with them?

"Yes, Da," John said, "We'll be home as soon as we can." He and Brendan dashed out the front door.

As the door slammed shut, Nora turned to her father. "Da, Anne has no place to go. What will we do?"

"Don't you worry, Nora. We are not leaving Anne behind. She will come with us. I'll book passage for her on the *Aurora* and we'll all sail to Virginia together."

Nora kissed her father's cheek. "Oh, thank you, Da. You are such a good man." She picked up the cauldron of water. "I'd best get this upstairs before it cools." She hurried out, lugging the pot.

CHAPTER TEN

"I am so grateful to you, Mrs. O'Lalor," Anne managed, red eyes brimming as she gingerly stepped out of the torn, soiled dress and petticoat and let them drop to the floor.

"A nice, hot bath is just what you need," Mam said, pouring water from a teakettle into the small tin tub. She glanced up and almost dropped the kettle. Bloody smears covered the insides of Anne's thighs.

Anne saw her look and nodded miserably. "They raped Ma, too."

"Oh, Anne, I cannot imagine what you've been through. It's evil, so unspeakably evil." Mam lowered the kettle. "But you are alive. And you will mend, dear. You will get better."

"But what will I do?" Anne asked with grief-stricken eyes as she hugged herself. "I have no family in County Leix. My nearest relatives live in Galway and I don't even know if they're still there or if they've fled the country. I have nowhere to go. What will I do?"

"You will always have a home with us. We will be your family. I know we can never take the place of Conal and Keela and your brothers, but we will try to fill the emptiness you are feeling. We love you, Anne. Now, into the tub, my sweet girl. There's a washcloth and a bar of soap on that little table beside you."

Anne drew in a sharp breath as she stepped into the tub and lowered herself gingerly into the water.

"I know you must hurt, you poor dear," Mam said. "I have healing salves for your abrasions. I'll be back quick as a wink."

"Thank you." Anne picked up the cloth and bar of soap as Mam scurried from the room.

Only a moment later, Nora entered with the heavy cauldron. "This should help the temperature a bit," she said as she began to pour steaming water into the tub beside Anne's feet.

"Ahh, yes . . . It hurts and feels good at the same time."

"I'll wash your back," Nora said, placing the empty pot on the floor. She took the cloth and soap from Anne and began to lather her friend's shoulders. "Does the bath help?" Nora asked.

Anne nodded. "The scratches and the bites sting, and I'm sore inside, but the hot water is good. Oh Nora, thank you and your brothers. I'll never forget that you risked your lives to save me."

"I wish we had arrived sooner. Maybe if we . . ."

"Stop! Don't even think those thoughts. You risked your lives for me! We can't go back and change what happened. How could anyone imagine that monsters like that even existed in the world?"

"Those men deserved to die."

"Yes, they did," Anne responded vehemently.

"Oh, Anne! Our whole world is changing. Nothing is ever going to be the same again!" Nora shook her head in dismay. "It's so hard to believe that I actually killed a man . . ." Soaping Anne's back, her hand came to a halt. ". . . or did I?" Images of the shooting flashed before her—The English officer charging, saber raised. She, aiming the pistol, clenching her eyes. The gunshot. The sound of a body falling. Opening her eyes, the officer sprawled on the floor with a bloodied face.

Nora's eyebrows knitted together. Did her shot kill the monster? Was it possible he could have lived? She felt a weight as tangible as a bag of rocks settle upon her shoulders as she contemplated the question. Finally, unable to solve the mystery, she shrugged and went back to lathering Anne's back. Swallowing hard, she attempted to dispel this new fear, which clutched at her heart with cold fingers.

"Nora," Anne said, her voice tremulous. "What if . . . what if I'm pregnant?"

That question had been lurking in the back of Nora's mind, but it would only be answered by the passage of time. "There's little chance of that," she said, hoping to alleviate her friend's worries. "After my parents married, it took Mam two years to conceive. I don't think it happens after just one time." At least I pray it doesn't, she thought.

"I was born just nine months after my parents' marriage," Anne said fearfully. After a moment, she added, "I feel different inside, as if there's something growing in me."

"Oh, Anne, that's just your imagination. It's stimulated by all the trauma you've been through today." Nora rinsed the washcloth. "You couldn't possibly feel anything, anyway. It's much too early."

"I'll never have that monster's baby! I'll kill myself first."

Alarmed by Anne's vehemence, Nora responded with a soothing tone, "You're not going to kill yourself, no matter what. I love you and I simply forbid you even to think about such a ridiculous thing. Now, promise me you will not think about stupid things."

Anne half-smiled. "I promise."

"Promise what?"

She sighed. "Not to think about stupid things."

"Good." Nora wrung out the washcloth and draped it over the side of the tub. "Now, I have something far more pleasant to talk about."

Anne raised a curious eyebrow.

"You are going with us to the Americas."

Anne's eyes widened. "I'm what?"

"Da is paying for your voyage. He told me so."

Anne gulped. "Leave Ireland?"

"Yes. It's much too dangerous for you to stay in this Godforsaken country."

"But, Nora, I could never leave. I have relatives in Galway. I'm thinking they might take me in."

"If you stay, the English will find you and kill you, as well as anyone who might take you in. There's no place in Ireland safe for either of us anymore."

"I don't want to leave."

"None of us do."

Tears welled in Anne's eyes. "But I guess I don't have a choice, do I? I'm sorry if I sound ungrateful. It's just that . . ." She released a mournful wail. Then, wiping her face, she nodded and said, "Yes, yes, I will consider the possibility."

"There's to be no *consideration*. You are going with us, and that is that."

Mam bustled into the room carrying a small jar. "Anne, dear, I've found my healing ointment. It will take away some of the pain and help mend those scrapes."

"Thank you, Mrs. O'Lalor."

As Mam applied the ointment, Nora's thoughts turned inward. What was it Da had said just a few minutes ago? That he had vital matters to discuss with them after supper. What on earth was that all about?

*****

They're taking their own sweet time cleaning their bowls, Nora thought as she sat at the dining table watching John and Brendan slurp down the last of their dinner stew. Anne had long since eaten and gone to bed.

Nora, her empty bowl before her, began to fiddle with a napkin as she eyed her brothers. "John, Brendan," she said impatiently, "can you eat a little faster, please?"

"What's the hurry?" John asked. "Da's upstairs."

"I'm almost finished," Brendan said, wolfing down a mouthful.

Mam brought a tray with four mugs of ale to the table and sat. "Da will be right down." Even though she had only allowed Brendan a half portion, he quaffed it and mimicked Da by following it up with a loud, manly burp.

Ignoring her little brother, who was smiling like a happy leprechaun, Nora said, "Mam, do you know what Da wants to talk to us about?"

"I do. But it's for him to say."

The *clump, clump, clump* of a peg leg descending the stairs announced Da's imminent arrival.

"Here he comes," Mam said.

"Ah, a pint of ale. Just what I need," Da said as he crossed to the table and took a seat. After slaking his thirst, his expression turned serious, more so than usual.

"Nora, John, Brendan," Da said, "you've had a frightful experience today, and I have some thoughts on the matter that I hope will be helpful."

Having garnered their attention, he continued. "Killing a man, no matter how just, is no little thing. In the uprising of '41, I, too, had to kill or be killed."

Nora had heard stories of the Irish Rebellion of 1641. Hundreds of thousands had been slaughtered by the English.

"I am still haunted by the lives I took. Violent death marks those involved in ways that changes a person—ways that you will now have to come to grips with." He paused, his empathetic gaze meeting each of his loved ones' eyes in turn. "The good news is that time does mostly heal, but you'll discover that the past is never entirely gone. It's there in our memories, sometimes fleeting, but at other times it comes back in a rush to haunt us. If it didn't reappear, there would be no grief or sorrow, and no lessons would be learned."

Nora nodded. She hadn't considered any of this yet—perhaps in time. But it was true. Good and bad memories did exist, suddenly appearing with accompanying joys or regrets. Perhaps Da was right—these reminiscences resurfaced so we could profit from them.

"I am mentioning this because, in the not too distant future, you will begin to question today's events as I have certainly questioned my past actions. Killing is, unfortunately, sometimes a necessity—to fight for your country, to save your family, yourself, or your friends. Killing an enemy before he can kill you is entirely justified. I want you to know, *you did right.*"

"I didn't get to kill anybody," Brendan said with a pout.

Henry struggled to hide a smile. "That, young man, is something to be thankful for. Bravery is not always being in the fight, but standing your ground when others would have run. You did well, Brendan."

Brendan jutted out his chin, delighted to be praised in front of the family.

"Nora, John," Da continued, "I want you to bear this in mind. Be prepared for your conscience to question your sense of morality. Being right doesn't stop us from feeling guilty. The ones we had to kill, although they may have deserved it, had wives, children, relatives, and friends. The fact remains—*it was a necessity.* Never, ever, believe you did wrong. That said, I want to say again how proud, how very proud, your mother and I are of all of you. And how much we love you."

"That, we do," Mam added. "With all our hearts."

Nora choked back a sob, unable to speak. She looked at her brothers. John coughed and gazed at the table, his lower lip quivering. Brendan absorbed the caring words quietly. The shootings this afternoon *had* been traumatic, and she really had not had time to digest the enormity of the confrontation. No matter that the men were killers and rapists—they had still been human beings. And one of God's commandments was—thou shalt not kill.

Da, in his infinite wisdom, knew she and her brothers would soon have to face that irrevocable law of God.

Da's words are a precious gift, she thought. He is giving us reassurance, letting us know our actions were just. How sweet and loving it is for Da and Mam to try to soothe their children's troubled souls. John, Brendan, and I have the finest parents in the world!

Nora rose from the chair and crossed to Da. She kissed the top of his head. "Thank you, Da. I am so grateful that you are my father." She turned to her mother and repeated the kiss. "Mam, I love you and Da so much, I could burst. I am so blessed to be a part of this family."

John rose and kissed his parents. "You are the best parents anyone could ever have. Thank you for everything. I love you."

Brendan said, "But I love you the most."

Da and Mam burst out laughing. Despite the ordeals of the day, Brendan had reminded them of the game they had all played when they were little, where each member of the family had vied to win the game of "I love you the most. No, I love you the most."

Mam had tears rolling down her cheeks, and Da brushed moisture from his eyes. He said, "One more thing." He withdrew a lightweight leather belt from a pocket. It had an attached pouch that was flat like an envelope. Coins clinked softly as he placed the unusual item on the table. "This is to be worn beneath one's clothing. At the moment it contains silver and gold, but, as you can see, there is also room for legal documents."

Silver and gold coin? Nora contemplated. What on earth for?

"As a family," Da said, "we have to be prepared for any turn of events. There's enough money here to pay for food and lodging or, in the event we are separated or something should happen to your mother and me, your own voyage to Virginia."

"Nothing is going to happen to you!" Nora cried out.

"Certainly not," John chimed in.

"Nora," Da said, ignoring their protests, "I believe that you, with your pleated dresses, are best suited to wear this pouch under your clothing until we arrive in Virginia. Now, if the unforeseen happens, and it often does, we could become separated. The plan would then be to meet at Running River Plantation. The location is on the James River, twenty-five miles west of Jamestown. Children, this will be our new home. Growing tobacco will be our business venture for the future. We will start anew in Virginia. I have sold all of my business interests to purchase the plantation. The land is good and fertile, so I am told. For generations, our family has built our fortunes with the ownership of land. Land ownership is everything, it's in our blood. Never forget it."

Land is everything. The words resonated through Nora like church bells summoning a flock of believers. Da was right. The earth and ownership of it had always been part of their family's heritage. It had given the O'Lalors status and made them prosperous. Now, with Da's foresighted acquisition of Running River Plantation, he had managed to give the family an opportunity—and a chance to succeed—as tobacco growers and landowners.

"Children, I want you to promise me you will do everything in your power to hold on to the land. It may be difficult at times. Owning a plantation is not easy, but it is the family's future."

"I promise you, Da," Nora said fervently. "I'll never let it go."

John nodded. "We will keep it in the family."

"What if I don't want to be a farmer?" Brendan asked.

Da and Mam exchanged a smile. Da said, "A plantation owner is a bit different from a farmer."

"I want to be a pirate," Brendan retorted.

"You may wish to reconsider that, Brendan, when you're a bit older. A pirate's life expectancy can be rather short." Da pushed the pouch to Nora. "Be careful with this."

"I will, Da," Nora said, picking it up.

Mam rose from the table. "Children, we have an early start in the morning. We're to be up and dressed before dawn. Now off to bed with you. Try to get some sleep before the cock crows."

Nora stood with the others. She glanced at the belted envelope in her hand and felt its weight, thinking, If I were to be wearing this during a shipwreck, I would surely drown.

In spite of the warmth in the room, she shivered. The secure cocoon that had protected her for the first sixteen years of her life was quickly unraveling.

CHAPTER ELEVEN

Captain Dice's eyes tracked the doctor's unsteady hands as the man hovered over him, wielding a curved, three-inch needle threaded with catgut. He grimaced as the point pierced his flesh, snagging the skin on his left cheek where he'd been wounded by the bitch's bullet. The needle came out and hooked another hanging shred. Dice's knuckles whitened as he grasped the side rails on the small cot. After the shooting, he had been brought to the officers' quarters at the English army compound in the small village of Portlaoise.

"Only one, maybe two more stitches, Cap'n," said the fiftyish, gray-haired Irishman who reeked of ale and tobacco. "You're lucky yer soldiers found me. Not many *tréidlia* have me sewin' talents."

Mother of God! The man was a bloody livestock doctor! Dice threw an accusatory glance at the two soldiers who stood by, watching the proceedings.

The taller one, a sergeant, shrugged. "A veterinarian was all to be had, Captain. Our English army doctors are at Drogheda taking care of the wounded. And the village doctor was executed two days ago. He was found treating rebels." He spat on the floor. "A stinking papist, he was."

Dice exhaled with disgust and then flinched as the needle again speared his flesh.

"One more'll do ye," the vet said as he tied off a knot. "I want ye ta know ye be looking right fine. I do dandy stitchin', if I say so meself."

"Gett onn with it, you cod-facced sod!" Dice barked. Moving his tongue to wet his lips, he cringed as a piece of broken molar touched exposed nerves. He sputtered at a memory, spewing blood from his swollen lips, "Thhat Fenian whhore!"

"It's a lass that shot ye then, was it?" the veterinarian asked.

"Quiett!"

The man ignored him. "You'll be able to speak better once the swelling goes down."

"Shuut uup!"

The doctor spitefully jabbed the needle into his skin.

Dice reared his head up, eyes afire. "Eassy, orr I'll haave youu shhot!"

"Shoot a good Anglican? I doubt it, Cap'n," the Irishman said with a confident chuckle. "We're a protected species. You need us Anglicans to run the businesses and farms you're taking from the pox-ridden papists."

Dice grunted, ignoring the man's babble as he relived the horrifying moment the Irish bitch had shot him. *Nora. . . .* The name had been indelibly burned into his brain.

"All right, Cap'n," the veterinarian said, placing his suture materials into a small satchel. "Yer back together again, and it's a handsome job, if I do say so meself. That'll be ten shillings for me stitchin'."

"Lett mee see my faace," Dice said, ignoring the request and the sudden look of wariness on the medic's face. Dice struggled to sit up, but a wave of dizziness dropped him back to the cot. Fighting it, he swung his feet off the cot and onto the floor. As he sat up again, a piercing pain bisected his head. He snarled, disregarding the agony as he attempted to stand. But his legs buckled, and he fell again to the cot. His mouth twisted. Nerves in his jaw and teeth exploded. "Ahhh!" he cried.

"Sir, may we help?" asked one of the soldiers, stepping forward.

Dice waved him back, sucking in a great draft of air to steady himself. As he wiped perspiration from his brow, he was vaguely aware that the vet had left the room without a second request for payment.

Good riddance.

As the throbbing subsided, Dice looked up. The two soldiers were staring at him oddly. Dice raised a hand to his left cheek. He could feel stitches. Wincing, he ran fingers over painfully sensitive sutures and ragged lumps of flesh.

Alarmed, he lurched unsteadily to his feet and moved to the mirror on the wall. His apprehension lessened as he gave it a sideways glance; the magnificent profile, the one that had always attracted admiring looks, was still impeccable. With a guarded sigh, he turned to see the other side of his face—and recoiled in horror.

The left cheek was almost entirely gone! What was left was a series of black, unevenly crisscrossed stitches that had pinched and puckered ragged remnants of flesh. There had been insufficient skin to close the wound, leaving a thin, weeping opening like a second pair of lips that revealed splintered molars and oozing saliva.

Heart thundering, Dice felt his stomach clutch and knot. The scream that erupted from his constricted throat was a cry from the depths of hell.

*****

The sky, dark as a raven's wing only minutes before, had begun to lighten in the east. A misty, bone-chilling breeze swept across the courtyard, piercing Nora's cloak with a rush that raised goosebumps and prickled her skin.

A lot of good my cape, woolen shirt, and breeches are, she thought. They may as well be made of fishnet!

Sitting on the driver's seat of the family buggy, Nora pulled her cape closed, shivering in the early morning coolness as she gazed out over fields and outbuildings. She would miss this all terribly . . . except for the rain and the cold.

Now that the family was actually leaving, it was more traumatic than she had imagined. So many memories.

The geldings snorted and pranced in their traces, shooting frosty vapors into the air, ready to be off. Nora's gloved hands tightened on the reins. "Whoa. Whoa," she said, soothing the feisty animals. "That's it. Easy. Easy."

Da's two hounds trotted over and circled the four-wheeled vehicle, whining. They sensed something out of the ordinary.

Nora felt a wave of sadness wash over her. I'll miss you, Tuck. You too, Whiskey. Will you boys miss me? As if in answer, the dogs yapped and wagged their tails.

Nora glanced over to Da and John, who held Puck and Lille's bridles as they stood in front of the house conversing with Fergus and his wife, Agnes. The farm, Nora knew, would be in good hands, since Da had magnanimously deeded the property to Fergus in return for his years of service to the family.

Fergus and Agnes's sons, Tim and Willy, twenty and twenty-two, rode up on stout farm horses. Both lads were armed with flintlock pistols and Brown Bess muskets.

Mam hurried out of the house and crossed to the carriage, trailed by Anne and then Brendan, who looked grumpy from lack of sleep. She grabbed the railing and stepped up to sit next to Nora. Anne and Brendan climbed into the rear seat.

The hounds, barking at all the commotion, ran over to Da, who reached down and petted them fondly. Nora felt a pang of melancholy. Da would miss the dogs' company, especially in the evenings, when they would curl up at his feet by the fireplace. Da gave them each a last pat, then turned to Fergus and Agnes and shook their hands as he and John bid their farewells to the couple.

Henry and John mounted their horses and reined over to the carriage.

"Keep alert, everyone," Da said. "Fergus has informed me that English soldiers are on the road, robbing Irish folk and shooting those that resist." His eyes were glinting like chips of blue ice as he touched the two flintlock pistols in his waistband and called out, "John, you and I will ride ahead. Tim and Willy, you boys follow the carriage, and keep vigilant."

"Aye," they yelled back as one.

"We're off," Da said as he prodded heels into Puck's flanks. The big stallion charged ahead, followed by John's horse. Nora slapped reins on the geldings' backsides, and the buggy rolled after them.

On the road, Nora turned to take a last glimpse of the farmyard as it receded in the distance. Goodbye, my beautiful home. I will miss you always. Nora's blue eyes finally swept back to the track ahead, alert and wary. If the family makes it to Dublin without encountering soldiers, we'll be fortunate, she thought. But if anyone could get them there safely, it was her Da. And once in the great city, they would find the wharf where the *Aurora* would be docked, and embark on a new adventure.

What will the voyage be like? Nora mused. I've never sailed on a ship before.

She had heard stories of fierce hurricanes in the Atlantic that often sank vessels, leaving no trace of survivors. Would that be their fate, to be lost at sea? And, even if they made it to Virginia, she had read that the country was a wilderness with mosquitoes as large as horseflies, diseases like smallpox and malaria, little food, and savage Indians.

Stop it, Nora! You're scaring yourself. And that isn't helping, as there is no turning back. Admonishing herself for having too vivid an imagination, she tempered her thoughts. Da owned a cultivated tobacco plantation. Certainly, it was located in a part of Virginia where there weren't that many mosquitoes, and most probably the nearby Indians would be friendly. One couldn't run a plantation or a business in uncivilized surroundings and make a profit. One thing of which she was certain—Henry O'Lalor knew how to make money. And unlike Ireland, there were opportunities in the New World for everyone, including young women who could read, write, and do math. She would teach school, keep accounting books, and help Da run the plantation. Then, one day, she would own a plantation of her own.

Her father's words came back to her: Land is everything. Yes, ownership of land is the goal, our future! The opportunities, she thought, outweighed the dangers. If we make it out of Ireland. . . .

*****

Dice's eyeballs ached. The pounding inside his skull was relentless. During the night, unable to bear the pain, he had yelled out. An orderly, standing outside his door to monitor his recovery, burst in. Dice, embarrassed by his outburst, had cursed the soldier who, fearing for his own safety, had backed out of the room. For two days now, the agony from broken teeth and lacerated gums, along with his horrifically sutured cheek, had drained his will to leave the bed. But now, as stirrings of vengeance became dominant, he found renewed incentive.

The door creaked open. Dice's yellow-brown irises, surrounded by inflamed capillaries, swiveled to the officer who had just entered. The man was dark featured, of Napoleonic stature.

"Lieutenant Bruno, reporting as requested, sir."

Grimacing, Dice rose from his cot and staggered to his feet. Dizzy, he cautiously touched his bandaged left cheek and grimaced. Damnable pain! The slightest movement sent knives into exposed nerves in his gums where molars had once resided. He lifted his captain's jacket from a rack on the wall and carefully slipped it on, then turned to the lieutenant. "That bitch who shot me—her first name is Nora." He hesitated momentarily, grunting with the slim consolation that his words were no longer slurred. "I have no knowledge of her surname. She's between fifteen and twenty, and her companion, a younger boy, must live somewhere near the O'Moore farm. You are to search the countryside until you find this Nora. Do not return until you have her in manacles, or information on her whereabouts. Understood?"

"Yes, sir," Bruno replied.

"There can't be that many Noras in County Leix. Ask everyone you meet on the road, go to every farm, visit every damned cottage. She is obviously Catholic. Search church records, births, baptismal certificates. Get going! When you find them, execute the boy, but I want you to bring that bitch back to me—alive!"

"Yes, sir."

"Dismissed." After the officer closed the door behind him, Dice's eyes narrowed into a myopic gaze. He began to salivate as a wild animal might anticipate a kill.

*****

Nora, gripping wet, slippery reins, guided the family buggy toward the narrow passageway of Dublin's St. James Gate. A squawking gull drew her attention to dark thunderclouds pushing in from the sea. We don't need more rain, she thought, thankful for the hooded capes that had protected the O'Lalor contingent from the early morning drizzle as the carriage rolled on. Da and John rode several yards ahead. Tim and Willy trailed close behind.

Passing through the arched stone gate, Nora recalled Da telling her it was one of seven portals that had been constructed in the wall by Vikings, who had settled Dublin over five hundred years ago. The city had been known as Dubh Linn, meaning "black pool"—for what reason, she had never been able to figure out. Perhaps, back then, most of the city had been a swamp. A meandering stone fortification encircled three-quarters of the city, and the large C-shaped bay to the east made up the fourth boundary, giving entry from the Irish Sea.

While the O'Lalors had been to Dublin several times, Nora knew this would be Anne's first trip to the city. She looked over her shoulder at her friend, sitting beside Brendan, who was fast asleep with his head on her lap. In spite of the nauseating odor of garbage and urine surrounding them, Anne's face reflected a feeling of awe. She stared wide-eyed at the passing sights as they bumped over cobblestones still glistening from the last rain.

Good, Nora thought. This was just the distraction Anne needed to take her mind off the horrific events of the past few days.

It had been a two-day trip to Dublin. They had taken side roads, sleeping for a few hours at the homes of friends and traveling mostly at night to avoid English troops. Now, as they wound through the strangely deserted streets heading for Essex Quay, Nora remembered it lay on the east end of the Liffey, the wide, seafaring river that bisected the city and flowed into Dublin Bay. Its fresh waters were deep, lined with quays, where large galleons, brigs, caravels, and smaller vessels from all over the world were moored. It was at these wharfs that Nora had first seen Africans and marveled at the color of their skin, as black as tar. There had also been Asians and Europeans, and all had been speaking in their own languages. It wasn't unusual to see drunks, prostitutes, and poverty-stricken indigents on the streets, but today the number of vagrants seemed abnormally low. Feral dogs, with prominent ribs, slunk along the cobblestones and back alleyways, scavenging for food.

On our last family trip to Dublin six months ago, she recalled, Da had had to vie for space on the cobblestones with horseback riders, carriages, and drays of all sizes and shapes, but today we almost have the streets to ourselves. Why is that? Is everyone hiding from the English who had made Dubliners' lives a living hell since Oliver Cromwell's invasion?

Entering the wharf area, Nora peered down a side alley and recoiled. An older woman, obviously drunk, was sprawled, half-clothed, on the wet lane, oblivious to the rats scurrying over her limbs.

Nora glanced at Anne. The look of wonder on her friend's face had disappeared, replaced by shock and distaste.

Thank God, Nora thought, we will soon be aboard the *Aurora.*

Henry and John, riding ahead, turned onto a wide street that ended at the river's edge, where a long line of quays lined the Liffey. In the wind-churned anchorage, whitecaps frothing like beaten egg whites crested thousands of wavelets as a gusting breeze blew in from the Irish Sea.

"Oh, Lord!" Nora whispered when a squad of English troops marched out of an alley ahead of them and continued on, ascending a gangway leading to the main deck of a huge man-of-war, which bristled with cannon.

Craning their necks, everyone in the carriage looked up at the ship's multi-tiered decks and three masts that towered above every other vessel in sight. Its name, *Sovereign,* was painted in gold against a black background. It was the most impressive ship Nora had ever seen—it must surely belong to Oliver Cromwell himself.

Beside the man-of-war, sailors and roustabouts unloaded cartons of food and munitions, transferring them onto carts. As the buggy clattered over cobblestones, Nora felt grateful that the workers paid little attention to the O'Lalor party.

On her left, they were passing a row of one and two-story buildings that Nora thought resembled odd-shaped faces, with hatched and slate roofs appearing to be either mops of unruly hair or bald heads. Doors were imagined as elongated mouths, and windows, wet from the recent rain, glistened like crying eyes with reflections of the bay. Several older structures, she noted, were half-configured shops in various stages of rehabilitation. Stacks of lumber, stone, and brick lay unattended. Strangely, the sites seemed to be deserted.

Why had half-built structures been abandoned, left to the elements?

A warning in Gaelic was suddenly shouted from an upper window. A second later, slops from a chamber pot splashed beside the buggy, barely missing them and spooking the horses. Nora reined the animals in while Brendan awoke with a startled yelp. Tim and Willy hurled curses at the woman.

"Why do people do such awful things?" Anne asked, wrinkling her nose. "They're smelling up the whole city."

"Because they're too lazy to carry their waste to a pit," Nora responded.

Mam said, "When Da was a politician in the city, before he was forbidden to hold office, he tried to persuade council members to build a sewage system, but they voted the idea down as being too expensive. Now only a few inhabitants have outdoor privies behind their homes and offices."

"Pew," Brendan said, holding his nose. "It smells like dung."

"That's what it is," Margaret responded. "Horse dung, people dung, all kinds of dung."

Brendan began to sing:
"No more pooping on the streets
No more peeing on the walls.
Poop in a can, pee in a jar,
Dig a hole somewhere afar.
No more smells to bugger your nose,
No more poop to splatter your hose.
No more . . ."

"Brendan, please," Mam admonished, interrupting her son. "Where did you learn that awful song?"

"From my friends. Do you want to hear the rest?"

"No, I do not. And I would appreciate it if you don't sing it again."

As they approached a large berth, circling seagulls caught Nora's eye. The sleek white birds with black-tipped wings screeched noisily above Henry and John, who had stopped to talk to a dockhand. A sign nearby identified the mooring: *Essex Quay.*

It was conspicuously empty.

Something is amiss, Nora thought, bringing the buggy to a standstill behind her father and John. Scattered raindrops began to plop on the hood of her cape, prompting Nora to look up. The dark mass of clouds was moving in off the bay. They would have to find shelter very soon.

Da and John reined their mounts over to the buggy.

"The *Aurora* was supposed to be here days ago," Da said. "Hopefully, she'll arrive this evening or tomorrow . . ." Preoccupied, he let his words trail off. After glancing at the blackening, overcast bay and seeing no ships, he added in a voice tinged with anxiety, "Well, we'll have to wait and see."

Nora's heart went out to her father. She knew the pressure he was under in trying to get them safely out of Ireland, especially now that she and John were certain to be wanted for murder.

"Henry," Margaret said, pulling the hood of her cape closer about her face, "we should get rooms."

"Yes, of course. Follow us to the Brazen Head."

In spite of the pending storm and all their troubles, a smile flitted across Nora's lips. The pub and inn, where Da and the family had stayed ever since she was a young girl, was a favorite. Years before, when Da still had both feet, the two of them had danced Irish jigs on a small dance floor before a boisterous crowd. Even Mam and John had joined in; Brendan had been too young.

Those were happier times.

Nora slapped reins on the geldings' rumps and the buggy lurched forward, following Da and John, with Tim and Willy close behind.

Several blocks later, Nora breathed easier as they came upon the familiar two-story stone structure and reined in. It bore the sign:

The Brazen Head
Established: 1198

Da dismounted, adjusted the pistols in his waistband, and passed Puck's reins to Willy. He peg-legged over to the carriage and offered Mam a hand. "We'll soon have rooms and a fire to warm us."

"And a glass of ale, I'm hoping," Mam said as he helped her down.

"As many as you like. Nora, hand your reins to Tim." Then, motioning to the backseat, he added, "Grab your bags. Everyone inside. The rain is really starting to come down."

"Thank you, boys," Mam called to Tim and Willy. "Safe home."

The farmhands nodded and waved as the group hurried inside the Brazen Head.

Henry lingered a moment to give the young men a few silver coins. "Tim, Willy, thank you for your efforts. And keep Fergus out of trouble."

"Aye, we will," Willy said, pocketing the coins. "Thank you, Mr. O'Lalor. We're happy to be of help."

Tim added, "You and the family have a safe trip, sir."

Without another word, the two lads rode off with buggy and horses in tow.

Henry watched after the young men as lightning split the sky, white tentacles casting an eerie glow over the cobblestones and buildings.

Nora, waiting by the front door, opened it as Da limped up to her, accompanied by the rumble of thunder. "Da, what are we going to do if the *Aurora* doesn't show up?"

"That's my girl, always thinking ahead. It's not unusual for a ship to be late. Weather conditions throw schedules off all the time. Even if the *Aurora* arrives tonight, she'll have to stay in port for at least two days to off-load and restock supplies."

Two days! Nora instinctively looked back to the road as rain came down in buckets. There was the possibility—slim, but there, nevertheless—that the English could be looking for her at this very minute. But aside from a soaked mongrel dashing across the cobblestones, the street was empty. There was not a red and white uniform in sight.

That didn't mean they weren't somewhere close.

"Come along, Nora," Da said, opening the door. He must have sensed her distress, for he added as he followed her inside, "We will get through this. When we awake in the morning, the sun will be shining. And hopefully, the *Aurora* will be at the quay. Soon thereafter, we'll be on our way to Virginia."

CHAPTER TWELVE

Fergus plunged the pitchfork into the mound of hay. He hoisted a clump of feed and dumped it into a trough in front of four black and white milk cows corralled inside the barn, then stood back and watched them munch. Although he would miss the O'Lalors, he couldn't help but grin. These were now his cows. He had suddenly become a man of means, a landowner. The two-story house, the farm, and all of the livestock—*his*—a gift from his good friend, Henry O'Lalor.

It had been three days since the O'Lalor family had left for Dublin. Tim and Willy had yet to return, but he knew the journey from Dublin might take longer than usual, especially since the boys had to bring back the buggy and extra horses.

Outside, Tuck and Whiskey barked. Fergus heard horses cantering, approaching the farm.

He tossed the pitchfork aside and strode out through the barn's double doors.

Fergus stopped midstride. English cavalrymen—eight soldiers and an officer—trotted into the yard beneath the gray sky. The hounds circled the intruders, woofing and snarling.

Fergus's eyes narrowed as a short, dark-featured officer, wearing the insignia of a lieutenant, reined his mount over to him. The hounds continued to yap and growl, lunging at the horses' feet.

The officer gestured to the dogs and issued an abrupt order to his men. "Kill them."

Two cavalrymen aimed their muskets.

"No!" Fergus protested. "Don't shoot! I'll call them off. Tuck, Whiskey, down! Down, I say!"

The soldiers hesitated when the dogs stopped barking and lay down.

"I said, shoot them!" the lieutenant demanded.

Two shots rang out. The dogs yelped and rolled onto their sides, pawing the air as life drained from them.

"You bloody bastards!" Fergus said. His hand reached for the pistol in his waistband, but it wasn't there. He remembered he had left it in the house. He glared at the officer. "That was a foul, dastardly deed."

The lieutenant waved the reproach aside. "I am Lieutenant Bruno. I am looking for a young woman by the first name of Nora. One of your neighbors informed me that Nora O'Lalor lives here."

"And I am Fergus Finney," Fergus spat. "There is no Nora living here."

Lieutenant Bruno's eyes swept the farmyard and house. "This *is* the O'Lalor farm?"

"No more. I own the property now."

"When did the former owners leave?"

Fergus was tempted to lie. But he knew the falsehood could easily be discovered and cause more trouble. He answered, "Three days ago."

"I'll assume Nora O'Lalor was with them. Where did they go?"

Fergus shrugged. "They're Catholic. They wouldn't tell me the time of day, let alone where they were planning to travel."

The lieutenant leaned forward. "You're not Catholic, then?"

"Anglican."

Bruno sat back, seeming to relax. "I need to find Nora O'Lalor. She shot an English captain and participated in the murder of another officer. She is a fugitive. Anyone found abetting her escape will be executed. Now, for your sake, think back. The family must have said something to you before they left—perhaps an indication of their destination."

Fergus looked Bruno straight in the eye. "I did hear Henry mention something about Cannacht. I've been told Cromwell has given Catholics a choice, relocation to Cannacht or execution."

"You heard correctly," Lieutenant Bruno said.

Fergus locked eyes with the officer.

The officer added, "You could be lying."

"I have no reason to lie."

"You say you're Anglican. You now have an opportunity to prove it to me . . . or suffer the consequences."

A sense of smugness warmed Fergus's heart. Weeks ago, he'd had false christening documents prepared for his entire family. "Are baptismal papers sufficient?" he asked. "Or do I have to send for the local vicar?"

"Fetch them," the officer responded. "Now."

Fergus bristled at the man's tone. He turned to see his wife, who had been watching them from the front door. "Agnes," he called. "Would you bring out the family's baptismal papers, please? They're in my desk drawer."

Agnes gathered her apron in her hands and, without a word, disappeared into the house.

Waiting for her return, Fergus and the lieutenant turned at the sounds of galloping horses.

Fergus's heart tripped when he saw his sons racing into the yard, obviously alerted by the gunshots. Tim, driving the buggy hard with Puck tied to its transom, followed by Willy on Lille and leading the extra horses, came to a mud-splattering stop before the English. The boys eyed the bullet-riddled carcasses of Tuck and Whiskey. Turning angry faces toward the soldiers, they unslung the muskets from their shoulders and laid them across their laps.

"Easy, lads," Fergus said.

"Da?" Tim questioned with concern.

The lieutenant demanded, "Who are they?"

Fergus felt his stomach tighten. "My sons."

Bruno eyed the young men closely.

"Da," Willy said, "what is this about?"

Bruno speculated, "An empty buggy, extra mounts, carrying two muskets apiece and pistols. They wouldn't have been at Drogheda now, would they?"

Fergus felt a sliver of ice slide down his spine. Heavily armed, the boys looked like rebels. He attempted to explain. "As I said, we're Anglicans. The lads had nothing to do with the fighting at Drogheda. They've been to Dublin, having the buggy's axle repaired. The extra horses and muskets were being shown to prospective buyers."

"It's a crime for Irish to bear arms, Anglican on not," Bruno said. "They appear to be better armed than my own soldiers. Perhaps they were helping the O'Lalor family and their daughter, Nora, to escape." The lieutenant turned to the boys and demanded, "Where have you two been?"

"I told you," Fergus said quickly. "They were in Dublin having an axle repaired and attempting to sell horses."

The lieutenant eyed Tim and Willie skeptically. "I'm beginning to think you may have taken the O'Lalor family to Dublin. Where did you leave them?"

"Lieutenant," Fergus said, "you and your soldiers had best be leaving."

The officer ignored him, staring coldly at Tim and Willy. "Where is Nora O'Lalor?"

"No idea," answered Willy.

"None," concurred Tim.

Bruno grunted. "Mr. Finney, you and your family are under arrest for unlawfully bearing arms and helping criminals escape." He gestured to his men and bellowed, "Arms at the ready!"

Eight cavalrymen unslung their weapons. They cocked their hammers and prepared to shoot.

Lieutenant Bruno said, "Both of you, throw down those weapons or I will give the order to fire!"

Tim and Willy calmly sized up the soldiers. Fergus's heart began to pound. He knew his sons weren't about to allow themselves to be arrested; both knew their fate would be execution.

Raindrops began to pelt Fergus, but nothing could diminish the fire flashing from his eyes—from his soul—stoked by memories of English injustice. There would be no surrender. Not today—not ever! He glanced to his sons, sadness weighing heavily upon him. Only a short while ago, he, Agnes and the boys had been the luckiest people on Earth. And now, he thought, our luck has sunk into the depths of a nightmare.

"I've found the documents," Agnes called as she stepped from the house with Fergus's cloak over her arm. "And your cape, Fergus. It's starting to rain. You'll be needing this, I'm sure."

Fergus took the cloak, immediately feeling the heft of pistols in either pocket. Threading his hands through the sleeves, he locked eyes with Agnes. He could see anguish within, but also bravery and resolution, along with the welling of tears.

She said very softly, yet steadily, "You've been my world, Fergus Finney. I could never have asked for a better man. I love you, dearest one."

Fergus reverted to the intimacy of Gaelic as he told her he loved her. "*Is brea liom tu.*" His heart ached as he wrapped his hands around the pistol grips. "Agnes, *mo shíorghrá*, my eternal love . . ."

Still looking into her eyes, Fergus heard the officer issue an order directed at his sons, "Discard your weapons IMMEDIATELY, or you will be shot!"

Fergus whipped out the pistols, swung around, and yelled, "Go at them, lads! *Erin go bragh*! Damn the Anglicans!"

Fergus, his sons, and the English opened fire simultaneously.

Slugs tore into troopers and their mounts with bloody splats. Tim and Willy were hit. Horses reared and neighed, the whites of their eyes rolling. Lieutenant Bruno fired at

Fergus, striking him in the chest. Agnes pulled a pistol from the back of her waistband and pulled the trigger. The bullet tore into Bruno's right thigh, and his horse reared, unseating him.

Agnes ran to Fergus, who had fallen to the ground. The lads, wounded and bleeding, second muskets now in hand, returned fire, blasting soldiers from their saddles. Tim and Willy were hit again and again. Unmanned horses ran frantically, wounded soldiers screamed and scrambled to reload. An opaque cloud of gun smoke rose above the yard like the fumes from a funeral pyre.

Tim and Willy, bleeding profusely, snatched pistols from their waistbands, aimed, and fired. Two more soldiers fell. The lads drew their second pistols and shot again. Additional soldiers cartwheeled to the ground. Weapons reloaded. The English fired a volley. Tim was hit in the forehead and went down. Willy, shot in the neck, collapsed. Fergus, eyes fluttering and barely conscious, held onto his wife as she keened over him.

With blood running down his breeches, Bruno staggered to his feet and gazed at the carnage. Six of the eight cavalrymen lay dead or wounded. Only two of his soldiers remained mounted. The lieutenant's face twisted with rage. He turned to glare at Fergus and Agnes. "Goddamn you Irish!" Deliberately, he reached for his saber; steel shrilled from its sheath. Bruno stumbled across the yard to stand over Fergus and Agnes.

"You're not Anglican. You are Catholic swine!" the officer spat out, his chest rising and falling. "All you had to do was tell me where Nora O'Lalor went off to . . . and . . . now this."

Fergus was vaguely aware of Agnes moving from his side as she sprang at the lieutenant like a wildcat, clawing for his sword. Bruno's wounded leg buckled, and he fell. Agnes wrested the blade from his hand and raised it. "This is for my family and for Ireland!"

BANG!

A bullet struck Agnes in the center of her chest.

"No!" Fergus cried as the sword dropped to the ground.

Agnes, his love, fell with the weight of sorrows.

Lieutenant Bruno, shaken, snatched the blade up. "Goddamned papist pigs!" The officer limped to stand over Fergus, loathing seeping from every pore.

Bruno raised the sword above his head.

Fergus closed his eyes. . . .

CHAPTER THIRTEEN

"Henry, the plague is here," Robbie Burns said with a heavy voice. "It's come to Dublin."

Nora, Anne, and the family stood in stunned silence inside the entrance of the Brazen Head, staring at Robbie, Da's old friend and proprietor of the inn.

The plague! Fear crawled up Nora's spine. Very few things scared her, but the dreaded disease was one of them. The plague afflicted young and old alike. From what she had been told, the infected came down with coughs and alternating fevers and chills. Painful reddish-black boils appeared in armpits and groins and festered on necks and chests. Skin turned black, tongues swelled. Vomiting of blood ensued, followed by dysentery. These complications led to almost certain death in one to four days after contraction.

"How many people are infected?" Da asked.

"At first, there were just a few cases, and we thought it would pass. But, no, it's gotten worse—much worse. Hundreds are dying every day. Just this week, it took two of my neighbors, a husband and his wife. The man died within twenty-four hours, the woman two days later. I've sent my family north to live with relatives. I'll be following first thing in the morning. Until further notice, the Brazen Head is officially closed. My staff, except for the cleaning girl, has left, and I've evicted the boarders. Henry, I can't offer you rooms, not even for the night, as I can't vouch for the health of the people who last occupied them."

Nora glanced to Da. His face reflected their dire situation. With the Brazen Head closed, the family had no place to stay.

"I am sorry," the proprietor added, "but I must do what I think is best."

"I understand, Robbie," Da said. "Can you suggest alternative accommodations?"

"I'm afraid I can't. The city is scared. No one is taking in strangers. Perhaps you could try the smaller villages outside Dublin."

Da rubbed the back of his neck. "We no longer have any means of transportation. And we must stay close to the quays. We're waiting for the *Aurora*. I've booked passage for the family to the Americas."

Robbie shook his head. "Waiting could be the death of you."

"Even if we found a buggy, the roads aren't safe. I won't bore you with details, but there's a good chance the English are searching for us at this very moment, hoping to arrest and perhaps execute us. We're really in trouble."

The innkeeper appeared thoughtful for a moment, then said. "Wait. What am I thinking? You could use my mother's cottage. It's just up the street. Two small bedrooms upstairs, but certainly adequate. She died last year of natural causes, and no one has occupied it since." He looked to Mam. "Margaret, if you don't mind a year's accumulation of dust, it's a place to stay."

Mam smiled. "Oh, Robbie, dust I can handle. It would be a Godsend! We heartily accept."

"Thank you, my friend," Da said.

Robbie, pleased to have solved their dilemma, motioned to the serving girl, a plump redhead whom Nora noticed had entered the rear of the room carrying two small wooden pails.

"Lily," Robbie said, "over here, if you please."

When she approached, the innkeeper took the containers and turned back to Henry. "Inside is a bit of ham, some cheese, and a loaf of bread that I've had packed for your family. These small buckets will come in handy to gather water from the street pipes." When Da reached into his pocket, Robbie said, "Don't insult me by offering to pay. It's my small way of thanking you for all the favors you've done for me in the past." He passed the pails to Henry.

"You may very well be saving our lives," Henry said.

Robbie withdrew a ring of keys from his pocket. He extracted one and handed it to Da. "This is the key to the door. The cottage is up the hill, on the left. Number six. It's best, old friend, if you leave as soon as possible."

"Yes, you are right," Da said. "Thank you, Robbie. I will never forget your kindness." Da turned to the family. "We must go at once."

*****

"Number six," Da said. "Here we are." He stopped before a modest thatched-roof cottage. He took the key from his pocket and unlocked the door. "Let's see what we have."

Nora, Anne, and the family followed Henry into a dark, medium-sized parlor. Mam quickly pulled open the shutters on the window beside the door. With dim light flooding in, Nora could see the adjoining kitchen with a stone fireplace for heating and cooking. Henry lowered his satchel and the two buckets to the floor, saying, "The bedrooms are upstairs, one for the boys and one for the girls. Your mother and I will make do down here."

"Rats!" Annie gasped.

Two rodents scurried across the floor and disappeared into a hole in the wall.

Nora's skin crawled. She hated rats!

"This place needs a hungry cat," John said.

"And some heat," Mam added, wrapping her arms around her chest. "It's freezing."

"That's easily fixed," Da replied. He reached into his pocket and withdrew two pieces of flint. "John, take these into the kitchen and start a fire. I can see kindling and peat by the hearth."

"Yes, sir." John palmed the flint and strode into the cooking area.

"John, once you have that burning," Da called after him, "go outside and find a rock or a piece of wood to plug up that rat hole."

"Aye," John responded.

"I'll go, too," Brendan said.

"Thank you," Nora said with relief. "The thought of rats in the house would keep me awake all night."

"Nora," Da said, "you and Anne each take a pail and fill them at the fountain. It's just up the street. Be wary. Keep your hoods up, and if you see soldiers, come home straightaway. We can always get water later."

"Yes, Da," Nora replied, relieved to have an excuse to get away from the cottage, since Mam was certain to ask for help dusting and cleaning the rooms. It wasn't that she minded housework. It was just that the thought of coming face to face with a beady-eyed rodent made her skin crawl.

Nora suddenly cocked her head, looking toward the door, which had been left partially open.

Clip clop. Clip clop. Clip clop.

Swallowing nervously, she pushed it closed, leaving a half-inch gap to peer through. Pressing her eye to the opening, she drew in a breath.

A dozen English cavalrymen were riding down the street. As they passed, one of the riders glanced toward the cottage.

Nora stepped back, her heart pounding.

"What is it?" Da asked.

"Soldiers," she whispered, leaning against the door, easing it shut.

Da moved to the curtained window and made a narrow opening in the fabric with his fingers. Peering out, he said, "They've moved on." Turning back to them, he added, "It appears we're safe, at least for now. Girls, the water fountain is at the opposite end of the street, away from the soldiers.

John, now would be a good time to find that rat plug for the wall."

"Aye," John responded as he stood.

"I'm going, too," Brendan said.

"No, you are not," Mam said firmly. "I need you here."

Brendan stamped his foot.

"Brendan, you'll do as Mam says." Da said. He picked up two of the satchels and peg-legged toward the narrow set of stairs.

As John slipped out the door, Nora shivered, finding it difficult to shake off the feeling generated by the appearance of the cavalry. Did the English authorities know the O'Lalor family has arrived in Dublin? she worried. Had someone recognized them as they arrived in their carriage? If so, how long could they remain hidden before they were forced to go outdoors for food, water and information on the *Aurora*?

*****

"Four dead and two wounded!" Captain Dice screamed, his face flushing beet red in stark contrast to the white bandage wrapped around his head. He paced the floor of the officers' quarters as if it were the enemy—to be crushed and stamped out. Whipping around, he shouted, "Plus, three horses lost!"

Bruno stood frozen, reduced to submission by the force of yellow-brown eyes that impaled him like daggers. Two of the Lieutenant's surviving soldiers stood by the door, mute with apprehension.

"And you are telling me," Dice seethed, "this was done by a motley bunch of farmers?"

Bruno swallowed nervously, standing mostly on one foot, favoring his wounded leg. Blood seeped down the side of his breeches, staining them a bright red. He had yet to be treated.

"It was an ambush, Captain," he sputtered. "We were lucky they didn't get all of us, sir. As it was, we rallied and killed every one of them."

Captain Dice strode over to stand directly in front of him. "How many did you kill?"

Bruno squirmed. "Three men and a woman." He hastened to add, "They were armed to the teeth, sir."

"Three men and a woman!" Dice ranted. "This is despicable."

"I do have information for you, sir," Bruno offered desperately. "On the girl named Nora."

Dice's fury abated marginally. "Out with it, man."

The lieutenant exchanged uneasy glances with his men, who stood by the door, and then said, "The girl's family name is O'Lalor. We went to their farm, and it was there that we were ambushed. The family had sold the place and left three days prior to our arrival."

Dice grunted and began to pace, slowly, deliberately. "If the O'Lalor farm was sold, as you say, then the family is running. They, very likely, are going to attempt to leave Ireland. And if they are planning to emigrate, the most obvious port for departure is Dublin Bay."

"That's what I was thinking, sir," Bruno replied quickly.

Dice's tone turned icy calm as he barked an order at the soldiers by the door, "Have my horse saddled. And you, Lieutenant, are to gather a dozen troops. We're riding to Dublin."

"But sir, my leg, I can't possibly . . ."

"Have I not made myself clear?"

"Captain, look at me," Bruno pleaded, gesturing to the bloodied leg of his trousers. "I'm wounded. I need medical attention."

"If you want to keep that leg, you'll wait until we get to Dublin where there are legitimate doctors. All we have here is a damned veterinarian." Dice's hand rose to his bandaged cheek. He flinched as the touch set off explosions of pain. He commanded, "You'll ride with us."

81

"Sir," Bruno responded, on the edge of panic. "I could bleed to death on the way."

"Yes, there is that chance," Dice said callously. "I suggest you find a tourniquet and use it. Get moving, Lieutenant. That's an order!"

*****

"But I want to play outside," Brendan whined as Mam dragged him by the elbow through the door of the cottage. "Other boys are playing outside."

"Look at you, Brendan. You've been splashing around in the rain. Your shoes are soaking wet. I've told you before, you are *not* to go out or you will be punished."

"I'm punished just staying inside," he complained. "There's nothing to do."

"I have an alphabet book you can study."

"I'd rather do nothing," he replied, and coughed.

"Take your wet clogs off and put them by the hearth to dry."

Brendan huffed and removed his shoes.

It was true, there was nothing to do, Nora had to admit as she sat at the parlor table with Anne and John, picking at a few chunks of dried bread, the last of their food. With the exception of the quick walk up the street to fill water pails on the day of their arrival, the girls had spent the past forty-eight hours inside the cottage like cooped-up chickens. Even Mam had given up finding them chores. Every room had been dusted from top to bottom, the mattresses were aired out, the rat holes plugged, and the floors scrubbed so clean you could eat off them. With the exception of Brendan's sneaky forays, Da was the only member of the family who had ventured outside the cottage as he'd walked to Essex Quay the last two mornings in hope of finding news of the *Aurora*.

The berth remained empty.

Thumping from Da's peg leg preceded him as he came down the stairs and crossed to the table. "Good morning."

They all returned his greeting as Mam brought over their last piece of bread. "Not much of a breakfast, I'm afraid, but it's all we have."

Instead of sitting, Da reached for his cape, which hung by the door. "Margaret, I want you to have that."

"I'm not hungry," Mam said.

"Please, just take it," Da said as he slipped on the cloak. "While I was at the quay yesterday, I was told of a new shop that has begun to sell coffee, The Trinity on Powell Street. They say it's become a gathering place where politicians, merchants, sea captains, and locals meet to exchange information."

"A coffee shop, of all things," Mam said with surprise. "I've only tasted it once in my life. It was quite bitter. It will never put tea shops out of business."

"No," Henry agreed. "But it's rare and expensive. That brings in the gentry. I'm going to stop by the shop this morning and see if there's any news on the *Aurora*. If not, then perhaps I'll be able to find us another ship. With this plague and the English military everywhere, it's becoming far too dangerous to remain in Dublin."

Nora perked up at the thought of an outing. "Da, can John, Anne, and I go with you?"

"What about me?" Brendan asked, followed by a coughing fit. After he regained his voice, he added, "I want to go, too."

"You've been out," Mam reminded him. "And now it appears you're coming down with a cold."

"I am not."

"Brendan," Da said. "If you're catching a cold, it's best if you stay inside. If you're good, I'll bring a treat home for you."

Brendan brightened. "What kind of treat?"

"It's a surprise."

Appeased, Brendan grinned like an elf.

"Nora, I don't believe The Trinity is a place for young people," Da said, quashing her hopes. "Besides, the less we all come in contact with strangers, the less chance we'll be recognized or contaminated with this awful plague."

"How do people get the disease?" John asked.

"No one knows for certain," Mam replied. "Some say it comes from vermin, animals, or from other people, or perhaps spoiled food, contaminated water, even the air we breathe. It's best to be safe and stay to ourselves."

"Da," Nora said. "You're going to a coffee house. Won't you be in danger?"

"It's possible, but it's something I must risk. We need information."

"And food," Nora said pointedly, as she thought, I have to get out of this cottage. The walls are closing in.

Da acknowledged her with an understanding nod. "It's come to the point where we must all take risks in order to survive. But if we're smart about it, if we have no personal contact with strangers, I believe we will get through this. While I'm away, John, I want you to take the buckets and replenish our water supply. Nora, I have an errand for you and Anne."

At last! Nora couldn't wait to go outdoors.

Da retrieved a few silver coins from his pocket and handed them to her. "There's an open market a few blocks to the east of us. Purchase enough food to last us for a few days. There's no telling how long we'll be here. Be careful not to touch anyone, and when you return, wash the food and your hands thoroughly."

Nora clenched the coins in her hand, repressing a cheer.

"Make sure your hoods are up," Da warned. "If you see any red coats, walk away as quickly as you can."

Da suddenly looked tired. In spite of his weariness, he forced a weak smile of encouragement. "God willing, we're all going to get through this."

"Amen," Mam said.

"I'll be back early this afternoon." Da turned to the door. "Pray it's with good news."

"Henry," Mam said, "if you see any sign of illness at the coffee shop, please come home straightaway."

Da, acknowledging her concern with a slight smile, stepped out onto the wet cobblestones and closed the door behind him.

Brendan coughed, and then sneezed.

"Bless you," Anne said.

He sneezed again.

Margaret shook her head. "See what happens when you get your feet wet? You have a cold."

"I do not."

Margaret frowned. "Brendan, how do you feel?"

"Good. I feel good."

"You look pale. I want you upstairs and into bed."

"Mam . . ."

"If you argue, there'll be no treat."

"Oh, all right."

John rose from the table and picked up the two empty wooden pails. "I'm off for the water."

"Don't dawdle," Mam said, and then she, too, coughed.

"I'll be quick as a wink." John hurried out, pulling the door shut after him.

Brendan suddenly threw up on the floor.

Mam hurried over and felt his forehead. "Goodness, you have a fever. Let me have a look at you."

"I'm fine," Brendan protested, attempting to wave her away. "Leave me alone."

"Hold still," Mam ordered, taking him by the arm. "Do you have a headache?"

"Maybe . . . a little one."

Nora's hand rose to her mouth, more than a little worried. Mam touched the sides of Brendan's throat and her face paled. She unbuttoned his shirt with shaking hands and pulled it open. Reddish boils circled the lower portion of his throat like an ugly, festering necklace.

Nora gasped.

Anne said quietly, "Oh, no. . . ."

"Dear God in heaven," Mam said in a quivering voice. She closed her eyes for several heartbeats and then said with resolve, "Brendan, let's get you up to bed. Nora, add peat to the fire and set the water that's left to boiling. Then you and Anne run to The Trinity and ask Da to go to the herbalist's. I'll be needing devil's bit and hawkweed."

Nora, always impressed by her mam's knowledge of herbs and her ability to take charge in the face of adversity, couldn't take her eyes off Brendan as she thought, Little brother, please don't have the plague! Unable to bear the thought, she prayed, Dear God, please, don't let Brendan be ill! She raised a hand and made the sign of the cross, unwilling to accept the dreadful possibility. Surely, all he needed was medicine.

*****

"I'm sorry, Henry," Sir Joshua Pembroke said.

Henry O'Lalor, who sat across the table from him, lifted a cup of The Trinity's excellent coffee. Henry had been surprised and pleased to find his old friend at the establishment. He remembered when he had first met Sir Joshua—now white-haired and in his seventies—almost twenty years before, when he had been elected to the Irish Parliament. While they had often differed politically, as Sir Joshua was an Irish Anglican, they had remained friends, even after England had ruled that Catholics could no longer serve in Ireland's government.

Sir Joshua was one of a few brave men who didn't mind being seen with a papist. The elder man continued, "There's been no word on the *Aurora*. One thing I've learned about the shipping trade, nothing ever runs on schedule. But timetables are the least of my worries. I've lost two vessels to storms and another to piracy in the last three years.

Merchant shipping is a terrible investment. My profits barely cover my expenses."

Henry nodded. Sir Joshua was being modest. He and a consortium of Anglican investors had made a fortune in the import and export trade.

"If my partners and I were smart," Sir Joshua continued, "we'd be in business with the likes of that Dutchman over there." He pointed to an expensively dressed, slightly built man whose shoulder-length reddish hair curled around a narrow face dominated by a long nose and cunning delft-blue eyes. Below these were a mustache and beard trimmed in the fashion of the Flemish artist, Anthony van Dyck. He was conversing familiarly with a younger companion who, with similar features, clothes and weapons, appeared to be either his son or a relative. Both men were smoking long-stemmed pipes.

"His name is Jan van der Root," Sir Joshua said. "He's owner and captain of the *Goede Hoop*, or in English, *Good Hope*. It's a fair-sized frigate moored at Aston Quay. And, damn his hide, like many of his Dutch countrymen, he's making three times what I earn on every crossing."

Henry's eyes narrowed as he assessed the weapons fortifying the Dutchman's leather belt: a matched pair of pistols, a dagger, and a rapier, all engraved with elaborate silver and gold scrollwork. Any swordsman who wielded a rapier's thin blade against the heavier saber normally worn by soldiers and seamen must possess an outsized degree of confidence—or foolishness. And Jan van der Root didn't appear to be foolish.

"The man is a dandy, and I'd venture to say a bit of a scoundrel," Henry stated, summing up his appraisal with a degree of distaste.

"Bravo. You always were a good judge of character, Henry. The Dutchman transports anything from stolen goods to opium and who knows what else, but his days of sailing our waters are numbered. Parliamentarians in London are said to be drawing up laws that will soon bar

Dutch vessels from English ports. Unfortunately, it won't put men like him out of business. Sorry for the history lesson, Henry, but sometimes I just feel the need to talk to an intelligent man—a rarity nowadays." He drank the remainder of his coffee and set the mug down. "Listen to me. If you are serious about leaving Dublin anytime soon, Van der Root's *Goede Hoop* is the only ship sailing for Jamestown within the week."

"Regrettably, I may have to talk to him."

"I wish you good fortune, my friend." Sir Joshua pushed his chair back and rose. "I will miss our conversations."

Henry stood and shook Joshua's hand. "I, too, will miss your company."

A fleeting smile crossed the elder man's face just before he turned for the door.

Henry strode over to Jan van der Root's table, where the captain was speaking in Dutch to his companion.

Van der Root looked up when he noticed Henry. "Wat? You want something?"

"I've heard you're sailing for Jamestown, Virginia. I'm seeking berths for my family. There are six of us in all."

Jan waved him off with his pipe. "No passengers."

Henry bristled at the man's dismissive manner, but stood his ground. "I'll pay twice the normal price."

Van der Root's head pivoted. "Ja? Twice?"

"Yes. It's imperative that my family leaves Ireland as soon as possible."

The captain exhaled a plume of smoke. "You rich man, mijnheer?"

"I can afford our passage, if that's what you're asking. I'll be needing three berths."

"Onmogelijk! Impossible!" He added, "Two only."

"I have six people."

Jan waved his pipe. "Niet mijn probleem."

Henry asked for the price of the voyage in the best Dutch he could manage, "Hoeveel kosten dit?"

"Goed!" Jan nodded with approval at Henry's Dutch. "U Nederlands spreken?"

"No, that was the extent of my Dutch."

Jan raised a calculating eyebrow. "You have trouble with schoten haring English pigs, ja?"

Schoten haring, Henry knew, was a familiar Dutch curse that meant *worthless*.

"I hate English," the Dutchman continued. "They want to own everything, the whole world. The ocean is free. They cannot tell me where I can and cannot sail!" The Dutchman drew on his pipe, still studying Henry with a skeptical eye, and then said, "Six people kosten two hundred pounds."

"I will give you fifty pounds."

"Onmogelijk! Go! No more business."

Henry looked to the younger man who wore a mildly amused expression as he repacked his pipe with tobacco. Henry raised the offer. "Sixty pounds."

"Nee," Jan refused, without even glancing at him.

A disturbance at the front entrance drew Henry's attention.

Nora and Anne were in the doorway! They were trying to get in and a burly man in a tavern keeper's apron was blocking them.

"You have to let us in!" Henry heard Nora arguing. "My da is right over there. I have to see him. It's a family emergency."

Henry frowned. "Excuse me," he said to the Dutchmen. He clumped over to Nora and Anne, who were scowling at the barkeep. "Nora, what are you doing here?"

"This oaf won't let us in, and I must talk to you."

The man responded with a gruff, "No children allowed."

"I am not a child!" Nora responded, blue eyes flashing.

"Nor am I!" Anne added just as vehemently.

"Excuse me, sir," Henry said to the man in the apron. "Let me talk to my daughter and her friend. I assure you they will not be entering."

The man growled under his breath, then walked a short distance away.

"Well, Nora," Henry said with measured patience. "What is so important that it brings the two of you here?"

Nora moved close, and whispered, "Brendan is sick. Mam needs devil's bit and hawkweed."

Henry's brow furrowed. "His symptoms?"

"Fever, and he vomited blood." Glancing around, she added in an even lower voice, "He has boils on his neck and chest."

Henry's face paled. "Good God."

A man behind him cleared his throat. Henry turned to see that Jan and his companion had followed him. The two men were barely as tall as Nora, even with three-inch heels on their polished black boots. The Dutchmen were also peculiarly skinny—thin shoulders, arms, and legs, but with odd little potbellies.

Jan and his companion stepped closer, eyeing the girls lasciviously, as if they had just walked into a bordello.

Jan turned to Henry. "Your name, Irishman?"

"Henry. Henry Smith."

Nora exchanged a quick look with Anne, nodding conspiratorially. Da was changing their names to protect them from inquiries by the English.

The captain made a slight bow to the girls. "Kapitein Jan van der Root," he said, introducing himself. He gestured to the youth at his side. "My zoon, excuse me, my son, Pieter Van der Root. And you pretty young ladies are . . ?" The Dutchman stepped closer to the girls and made a hand gesture that all but caressed Anne's ample bosom.

Henry was tight lipped as he made the introductions. "My daughter, Nora, and her cousin, Anne."

"Anne *Smith,* also?" Van der Root questioned, as his eyes flitted from one girl to the other.

"That's right," Henry responded through clenched teeth.

Nora mused, I enjoy the idea of having Anne as my cousin, if in name only.

"Nora and Anne Smith," Jan said in a throaty whisper, his eyes seeming to undress each girl. "Very nice."

Nora, who had resisted the temptation to kick the skinny dandy's shins during his perusal, responded by suddenly arching her shoulders back and thrusting her stomach out to mimic the captain's potbelly.

Jan unexpectedly chortled, enjoying the comparison.

"Ja, erg mooi. Very pretty," agreed Pieter, obviously excited at the prospect of traveling with two striking young ladies. He sucked ardently on his pipe.

Jan turned to Henry. "Sixty pounds, two berths. Pretty girls have zoon's room."

"Vader!" Pieter protested, coughing out a mouthful of smoke.

Jan raised a dismissive hand. "*Goede Hoop* sails tomorrow on morning tide. Pay sixty pounds now."

"No," Henry said as he withdrew a bag of coins from his pocket. "Half now, the remainder when we board."

Irish eyes locked on their Dutch opposites—a glowering conflict of wills.

After a moment of strained silence, Pieter quietly urged, "Vader..."

Jan's nostrils flared as if he intended to refuse the offer, but his stare darted to Anne's bosom once again. Delft eyes flashed brightly with barely restrained lust. "Deal!" He thrust out his small hand.

Henry shook the captain's hand and opened the money pouch, counting out thirty pounds. Dropping the coins into Jan's palm, he said, "The young ladies are off limits."

Jan's gaze fell to the silver in his hand. His fingers closed greedily. "Mijnheer Smith, money more valuable than women." He gave Nora and Anne an appreciative glance. "No matter how beautiful."

With the transaction finalized, Henry grabbed his cloak from the wooden peg by the door.

"Van der Root, we will meet shortly after dawn, tomorrow morning at Aston Quay. Good day." He turned to the door. "Girls, we must hurry."

CHAPTER FOURTEEN

Raindrops, annoying little drumbeats, tapped upon the hood of Nora's cape, reminding her that time was passing at an excruciatingly slow pace. Brendan might be dying! she thought anxiously. What is taking so long?

She and Anne had been pacing up and down the rain-slick cobblestones for twenty minutes, waiting for Da to emerge from the herbalist's shop. They must have trudged by the thatched-roof cottage a hundred times or more. She glanced again at the small sign attached to the front door:

Dermod O'Meara, Esq.

Physician. Surgeon.

Pharmacist. Herbalist.

Ollamh. Poet. Author.

Nora made a fist and pressed it against her breast, attempting to suppress the ache in her heart that had been with her ever since Brendan's symptoms had emerged. The knowledge was overwhelming that he—or all of them—could perish from the plague within a matter of days.

It was clearly possible. Would their bodies be burned in a mass grave—as was customary for those who died from the plague—without leaving any sign that they had ever existed?

Attempting to adjust her state of mind, Nora turned to Anne. "Those Dutchmen, the way they stared at us. I feel like I have to bathe."

"I wouldn't wish to be alone with either of them, of that you can be sure." Passing the sign on the door once again, she inquired. "What's an Ollamh?"

"A healer trained in the old ways. Dermod O'Meara certainly seems well qualified."

Anne's hand moved to the flat of her belly. "Do you think he could tell me . . . if I'm pregnant?"

Nora missed a step. Anne had to be terribly frightened. "It's much too early for a midwife to tell, or even for a doctor like O'Meara. Hopefully, you'll have your time of the month in a few days, and that will be one less worry."

As close friends, each knew of the other's monthly cycles; bodily changes had always been a topic of conversation.

"I am scared," Anne said. "I know I've mentioned this before, but I feel strange, different. My breasts are sensitive, and my lower belly . . . it's like I'm carrying something inside me."

As they walked in silence, Nora's thoughts drifted to a chat she'd had with Mam, when she had asked what it felt like to be with child. Margaret had described the first stages of pregnancy in much the same way. Along with fuller breasts and a new sensitivity, there was a certain inexplicable feeling that couldn't be denied. Unwilling to add to her friend's worries by revealing the conversation, Nora said, "Anne, you were beaten and injured. Certainly that has to account for your feeling different."

"I hope so. I just have this sense . . . I'm so troubled. I don't know what I would do if I . . ."

The *clip-clop* of hooves along with the *clink* of chains scraping cobblestones interrupted Anne and drew their attention to a line of shackled prisoners rounding a corner a short block away.

Nora eyed the column with a growing sense of sadness.

Men, women, and children, manacled, shoeless, and wearing soiled, inadequate clothing, were trudging toward them on their way to the docks. Mounted soldiers guarded their ranks.

Suddenly realizing they could be spotted, Nora said, "We mustn't let the soldiers see us!"

Anne pulled the hood of her cape close about her face.

"Over here!" Nora said, moving into a small alley, pulling Anne after her. She whispered more to herself than to Anne, "Da, please don't come out."

"What did you say?"

"I'm praying Da will stay inside the doctor's cottage until they pass."

"Look! There's Billy Devlin!"

Nora's heart missed a beat. The lanky Irishman walked a head taller than the mass of shackled humanity. Good Lord, Billy and the others must have been forced to walk through rain, cold, and muddy roads from the O'Moore farm where she had last seen them. That was over fifty miles away!

As they drew closer, Nora tensed. Billy's handsome face and arms bore marks of the whip. Red, bloody welts striped his skin. Yet he wore these lacerations like chevrons, heraldic ornaments awarded to soldiers in battle.

She couldn't help but remember a Billy from another time, her fifteenth birthday, and the surprised look on his face after she punched his nose.

Looking at him now, chains on neck, ankles, and wrists, she marveled at the man's confident stride. It was as if he were on his way to a friendly gathering, rather than imprisonment or a firing squad. For a mad instant, she thought, If I had Da's pistols with me, I could rescue him! But as sanity returned, she acknowledged, Too many English. I would only succeed in getting us both killed.

As Billy passed by, Nora was overcome by a devastating feeling of loss. She stepped to the mouth of the alley and threw back the hood of her cape. A breeze caught her flowing blond hair and whipped it about her face.

"Nora," Anne said, alarmed. "What are you doing?"

"Saying goodbye to a friend," she whispered.

Nora's movement had caught Billy's eye. He stopped midstride, holding up the line of prisoners.

Nora raised a hand in farewell.

Billy flashed the lopsided grin she knew so well and added a gentlemanly bow. Nora flinched as his gesture was rewarded with the lash of a whip that cut cruelly across his shoulders. She drew back into the shadows.

The mounted soldier who had wielded the blow ordered, "Move along, you!"

Billy strode on, as if the cut of the lash had no more effect on him than the bite of a mosquito.

Caught between emotions of sympathy and admiration, Nora watched after him with a sense of awe. Billy Devlin's gait still resembled that of a man who didn't appear to have a care in the world.

What a unique fellow. Goodbye, Billy Devlin.

The door to the doctor's cottage opened and Henry stepped out, carrying a small bag. He stopped midstride to watch after the departing line of prisoners and soldiers. Shaking his head, he turned, searching for the girls.

Nora and Anne hurried over to him from the alley.

"That took longer than I wanted," Henry said. "Come along. We must hurry."

Walking at a rapid pace with Da's peg leg clicking on the cobblestones, they listened to his explanation.

"I have the herbs, and something called opium. It's a painkiller Queen Elizabeth imported from India. O'Meara obtained it from a doctor visiting from England. It will help ease Brendan's pain, but it is no cure." He added heavily, "There is no cure."

As much as Nora wished to rush home to help care for Brendan, she knew the family lacked sustenance. "Da," she said. "Anne and I have yet to go to the market."

Henry frowned. "All right. Hurry along. There are food stalls on the next street over. Be extra careful." He looked up to the darkening sky. "It's getting late. Come straight to the cottage after shopping."

"We will," Nora assured him. "I pray the herbs and opium help Brendan."

Henry withdrew one of the two flintlock pistols he wore from beneath his cape and offered it to Nora. "Take this.

Aside from the English, there are more than a few ruffians by the waterfront."

Nora placed the pistol in the pocket of her cloak. "We'll be home before dark."

"Godspeed."

*****

Purple-red clouds darkened St. James Gate as the sun began to dip below the horizon. Captain Dice, his bandaged head encircling a face that was a mask of pain, led a double line of cloaked cavalrymen through the narrow confines of the portal that arched above Dublin's streets. He reined his mount in, slowing the stallion's gait from a steady canter to a much safer walk.

Moments later, Captain Dice halted his troop before the cottage bearing Doctor Dermod O'Meara's identity. Candlelight glowed in the front window.

"Corporal Poole," he called to the soldier who rode alongside Lieutenant Bruno, whose leg had been bleeding steadily despite the tourniquet cinched around his thigh. "Help Bruno down. Lieutenant, are you still with us?"

"Aye, sir," the long-suffering man managed to mutter.

"If anyone can save that leg, it's O'Meara. He's the best surgeon in Dublin. You'll be happy I insisted that you wait for him—if you live, that is. Poole, stay with him. The good doctor may need your help if he has to amputate."

"Aye, sir."

Dice touched spurs to his horse's flanks. "Meet up with us at the barracks."

"Aye, sir." The corporal helped Lieutenant Bruno dismount and led him toward O'Meara's cottage, as the troop continued down the cobblestone street toward River Liffey.

*****

THE GIRL WHO WAS ME IS GONE

Nora and Anne, each carting a sack of groceries, hurried away from the market stalls where last minute shoppers crowded the square. Along with fruits, vegetables, and meat, Anne carried a small jug of cider, which she had purchased as a treat for the family.

Nora glanced up to the sky where dark clouds threatened. "We're just going to make it home before it rains."

"I hope so," Anne responded. "I felt a few drops already."

Hoof beats approached, clattering sharply over cobblestones and spooking a flock of pigeons that took flight, fluttering over the marketplace.

"Soldiers!" Nora warned.

A double line of cavalry was trotting onto the wharf from town center. As the troop drew near, Nora missed a step, almost dropping her groceries. The lead officer had a bandage wrapped around his head—covering the left side of his face.

Nora's blood turned to ice. Good God in heaven, she thought. He's alive!

The officer must have recognized her at the same instant, as he had abruptly reined his horse to a standstill.

Nora's heart thumped wildly. "Anne, that soldier! Come with me. Hurry!"

Nora grabbed Anne's hand and pulled her into the throng of shoppers, explaining as they ran, "He's the officer I shot at the farm. Your rapist! He's here! And he's seen us!"

Startled, Anne threw a frightened look over her shoulder.

The officer was spurring his mount forward, leading the column after them into the marketplace.

Anne screamed as she ran, "Lord save us!"

"You! Stop!" the officer yelled as horse and rider pressed further into the crowded stall area. "Stop at once! Nora O'Lalor, you are under arrest!"

As she heard her name, a deep, gut-wrenching terror spiked through her. He knew her name, knew who she was!

Nora and Anne dashed past stalls, racing deeper into the congested marketplace.

"Clear a path!" the officer yelled furiously, as his horse and column were hampered and blocked by the crush of people. "Goddamn you, move aside! Out of the way! Those women are criminals! Stop them!"

Driven by sheer panic, Nora and Anne continued past shoppers and vendors, the latter of whom had begun closing for the night. The girls raced on, running between customers who were leaving and new shoppers who had just arrived to bargain for the best prices at the end of the day. Nora and Anne careened around crates and past flat-bedded drays being loaded with unsold fruits and vegetables.

The officer's high-pitched voice followed close behind. "Someone stop those women in the brown capes! They are murderers! Stop them!"

The officer's description reverberated through Nora. "Anne, quickly, take your cloak off and bundle it under your arm."

The girls were shedding their outerwear when Nora spotted a congested alley. "We have to split up."

"No!" Anne responded, her face crumpling. "I have to stay with you!"

"Please, don't argue. Listen to me! I want you to run down the next alley on the left. It will lead you toward the cottage."

"I can't," said Anne with terror in her eyes. "I won't leave you."

"You have to do this!" Nora exclaimed, breathing hard. "At least this way, one of us has a chance to live."

The logic must have hit home, as Anne managed, "All right."

"I'll draw them away," Nora said, approaching the alley. "Here," she said, gesturing to the dark lane. "Go, quickly!"

Anne dashed into the alley.

Nora ran on, whipping the flintlock pistol out. She plunged further into the crowd of vendors, handcarts, and wagons that were helping to block and delay the English.

"You! Nora O'Lalor, stop where you are!"

Nora flinched at the nearness of the voice. She scampered behind a row of stalls and, keeping her head low, took off as fast as she could in another direction.

"There she goes! Spread out, cut her off!" the officer yelled. "Don't let her get away!"

Gasping, out of breath, Nora came to a sudden stop by the side of a produce wagon and glanced over her shoulder.

The mounted soldiers were fanning out into a wide half circle.

Chest heaving, drawing in great drafts of air, Nora assessed her situation and quickly surmised their tactic. The maneuver was meant to work like a pincer, forcing her into a smaller and smaller area until there would be no escape. Well, she promised herself, that is not going to happen! Not if I can help it.

Satisfied that she had drawn the troops away from Anne, Nora raced through the milling throng toward the far end of the market. Stopping to crouch behind a stack of crates, she wiped perspiration from her eyes and waited.

A single cavalryman advanced toward her position. When the rider was only a few feet from her, a voice inside her head yelled, *Now!*

Nora burst from cover, waving her cloak wildly. "Yeow! Yah! Yah!"

The soldier's horse reared high into the air, dislodging its rider. Almost before the man hit the ground, Nora was up in his saddle. With the sack of provisions still in hand, she jammed her heels into the animal's flanks, racing off just as a clap of thunder rumbled overhead and rain began to drench the marketplace.

Behind her, she heard the distant voice of the officer. "Shoot her! Kill the bitch! Shoot!"

A fusillade of bullets whistled past as she galloped on through the pouring rain. Within seconds, Nora had guided the mount out of the market and onto the street.

Behind her, an angry, screaming mob gathered around the officer and his cavalrymen, blocking the soldiers who had fired and hit several innocent bystanders.

Racing away through the heavy rain, her heart sank. He knows me, she thought, and he knows the O'Lalors are in Dublin.

She wanted to cry. Just when things couldn't possibly have gotten any worse, they had.

*****

Nora walked briskly along moonlit cobblestones that still glistened from the rainstorm that had passed minutes after nightfall. She guessed it had been almost an hour since she had abandoned the stolen mount to make her journey home. All the while, thoughts of the scar-faced officer had terrified her. She, Anne, and her family were now being hunted, pursued. She had to get to the cottage and warn the family! Crossing an alley, she held her breath as she peered down the shadowy lane, aware that soldiers could appear at any moment.

Had Anne made it safely back to the cottage? She prayed she had, and that Anne had alerted the family to the encroaching danger.

Hurrying down the street, Nora experienced a sudden fright. The buildings were unfamiliar. She was lost! Instinctively, one hand tightened on the sack of groceries while the other clutched the pistol in the pocket of her cape. If Anne has been captured, she thought, this bag contains my family's only food.

A pub door banged open a few feet in front of her, spilling light across the cobblestones. Two men in sailors' regalia stumbled out. They turned to leer at her as she hurried past. She was aware now of roustabouts departing the quays. They had begun to fill the sidewalks once the rain had passed. Some of the men stopped to ogle. One called after her with offers of money for obscene acts.

Nora pulled the hood of her cape closely about her to ward off the unwanted attention.

Turning a corner, she came upon a few scantily clad women lining the street. Opening their cloaks, they flashed naked figures at passing men. Nora realized that these females, some barely old enough to have bosoms, must be Dublin's famous "ladies of the night", women who sold favors for a few shillings and then spent their earnings on gin. What an awful existence, this life of debauchery. She hurried on, clinging to the sack of food, determined, if necessary, to fight for it with her life.

A short distance ahead, globules of light floated in the air, bobbing and dancing in erratic circles like giant fireflies. As Nora drew closer, she could see that burning torches were being wielded by a crowd gathering and milling about in front of a cottage. Nora noticed that a red cross had been painted on its front door. Alarmed by angry voices, she moved to the opposite side of the street. Several men hurried past her, carrying pieces of timber. Others at the small home were nailing boards across the door and windows. Discerning a faint wailing coming from within, Nora pulled back a corner of her hood. Yes, she could hear them now—children crying, and men and women pleading for help, begging to be let out of the cottage. The hair on the back of Nora's neck rose. The occupants were being imprisoned.

"Board it up tight," a man said. "They mustn't escape."

"It's the law. All diseased people are to be sealed in their homes."

"My sister, husband, and three children are in there, but it's too late to save them. We must protect ourselves."

"May God have mercy on their souls."

An icy chill crawled up Nora's spine as she recalled seeing other boarded-up homes in the city. She hadn't understood their significance until now—and now she understood all too well. Fear of the plague was running rampant, causing ordinary people to commit horrific acts in hope of protecting themselves and their families. All those suspected of having the contagion were sealed inside their houses. Either the disease would kill the occupants, or they would perish from thirst and starvation. Entire families had already been entombed.

With an aching heart, she walked on, her thoughts returning to their borrowed cottage. Would her family be boarded up to suffer the same fate?

A short time later, she breathed a sigh of relief as the Brazen Head Inn came into view. She'd made it. She was almost home!

Approaching the cottage, she hesitated by the front door and glanced around. Shadowy figures walked the streets, but there were no English uniforms in sight.

She opened the door and stepped inside.

"Nora!" Anne cried, rising from the table. "Oh, thank God! I was so worried that monster had taken you."

"I'm so happy you're safe," Nora responded with happiness, embracing her friend tightly.

"Nora," John said. "Anne told us the officer we shot is alive and recognized you, and that a whole troop of cavalry chased after the two of you at the market."

"Yes, John. He is alive, and now he knows we're in Dublin."

John digested that news with a frown. "How did you manage to get away?"

Before Nora could answer, Da's peg leg came thumping down the stairs. When he entered the room, she flinched. Da was as pale as death.

In spite of his obvious distress, Da's face broke into a tired smile. "Nora, thank God you're home safe. Anne told us about the soldiers and the officer that you shot. I was just about to go out to search for you, but, well, I'm so happy you're home."

Relieved to see color returning to Da's face, her thoughts turned to her little brother. "How is Brendan? Are the herbs and opium helping?"

THE GIRL WHO WAS ME IS GONE

The slight smile evaporated. "So far, they have had no effect. The opium, mercifully, allows him to sleep. In truth, I don't know if he'll make it through the night."

John added, "Mam has been throwing up."

The food sack slipped from Nora's fingers, thudding to the floor. "Mam, too?" she asked. "How can this be? Only a few hours ago, she was so . . ."

"It came on with no warning," Da said as he ran a hand through his hair. "It's as if a hole suddenly opened up in the earth, and each hour draws us closer to the void."

"Da . . ." She fell into his arms, sharing his misery. Holding onto him, she became aware of his fragility; he was skin and bones. She sniffled back a sob. Da had been wasting away these last few weeks, and she hadn't even noticed!

What an awful daughter I am, she thought, to have been unaware that my father has not been eating and has been worrying himself sick. He's been under an awful strain, leaving the family farm, evading the English, preparing for the voyage to Virginia on a ship that has yet to arrive. And now, Mam's illness!

"Your mother's fever and cysts appeared without warning, and she's vomiting blood." Da's mouth quivered. He took a few breaths to gather himself. "I fear the worst, that Mam and Brendan have the . . ." He couldn't go on.

"No," Nora said, refusing to accept his unspoken word. Tears blurred her vision. "Da, we don't know for certain. Maybe they have bad colds, or the flu, or . . ." Her words trailed off. Just two days ago, everyone had been so healthy! And now, the world she loved and understood was fading away, and there was nothing she could do to stop it.

"I'll go back to the doctor's," she said. "I'll ask for new herbs, medicines . . ."

"There is no cure," Da said. "If there were, I would give my life to obtain it."

Nora turned to stare mutely at the fireplace. The peat was smoldering, on its last embers. Finally, she knew what she had to do, what she couldn't stop herself from doing. "I have to go to Mam and Brendan. They need my care!"

"No," Da said, grabbing onto her arm. "You mustn't go near them. It's too contagious. I don't want to lose you, too. I need you and John to live. For Brendan, for your mother, and for me."

Wiping her cheeks, Nora gazed into her father's blue eyes, once so alive with merriment and now shaded with the same fear that tore at her. "Please," she implored. "Let me go. I have to see them."

"I can't allow it," Henry said, shaking his head. "If you were to come down with the plague, I would never forgive myself."

"Da," John spoke up. He, too, had tears in his eyes as he came to stand beside Nora. "It's our mam . . . our little brother. If they die without . . . without a goodbye . . . We have to go to them."

Da said, "I'm sorry. I won't let you jeopardize your lives. Your mam has asked me to tell you that she loves you more than anything in the world. She also begs you not to come near her. As for Brendan, he is no longer able to speak. Please, I know how difficult this is."

Nora's whole body ached. She felt as if her heart was disintegrating, piece by painful piece. She would never forgive herself if she didn't see Mam and Brendan, she realized.

A sorrowful wail emanated from deep within her. She tore away from her father's grip and dashed up the stairs.

CHAPTER FIFTEEN

Nora burst into the bedroom and stopped short. Her hands flew to her face in shock. Mam and Brendan were unconscious, lying in single beds, their figures partially covered by thin sheets. Brendan's skin was gray-white beneath angry red boils that covered his face, neck, and chest. He was sweating. A frightening gurgle came from his throat. Mam, only hours ago so perfectly normal, was now jaundiced, and covered with identical festers.

Nora inched closer to them. A sob escaped her as she peered down at Mam. How could this have happened so quickly? To see Mam's once pretty face twisted so painfully . . .

A deep, rattling cough drew her to Brendan's side. He was twisting beneath the sheet, struggling to breathe. She reached down and placed a hand on his shoulder. He was burning up.

Dear Lord, she prayed, please don't let Brendan and Mam die. I will gladly trade places with them if you will allow it.

Nora's glance went back to her mam's disease-blemished face. She recalled lessons learned in younger, happier, healthier times. Mam, more than anyone, had taught her the meanings and values of faith, hope, integrity, inspiration, understanding, thoughtfulness, wit, humor, laughter, and love.

Oh, yes. So much love—tempered by discipline, patience, and strength.

A ghost of a smile flitted across Nora's face as her thoughts drifted to times gone by: Mam combing her hair, sewing new dresses, tending to scraped shins and knees, protecting her from bullies, kissing away her tears, and always supporting her when she was in the right, which, she allowed, was more often than not. The memories of Mam giving encouragement and guidance, not only to her but also to John and Brendan, intensified her sorrow.

John entered the room, followed seconds later by Da, who said in a voice filled with sadness, "Children, you mustn't stay here. Please, come downstairs."

"Just another minute, Da," Nora pleaded. She leaned over the bed to place a hand on her mam's arm.

"This is so dangerous," Da said.

John added, "Nora, the infection . . ."

Ignoring the warnings, Nora spoke quietly to her mother, "Mam, please, please don't leave us. You have to get better. I love you, so very much. We all need you."

Mam's eyes fluttered beneath her eyelids, and then opened.

Nora drew back with surprise. Mam was staring up at her with the earnest look of affection that had always made her feel like she was the most important person in the universe.

"My . . . darling." Mam's voice was barely audible. Her eyes shifted to Da and John. "Henry, John, Nora, I love you all . . . with all my heart. But I . . . I am dying. There is nothing that can be done. I know that. Please, for your own sakes, leave me. It isn't safe. Please, Nora, John, go with Da. He'll take care of you. Remember, even when I'm gone . . . I will always be with you. Listen and you will hear my voice. I will be beside you, with you, always."

Mam's eyes closed and a wheezing cough rose from deep within her lungs.

Nora shivered.

Da's hand came to rest on her shoulder. "We must go downstairs."

"Da, I can't leave. What will we do without Mam? Without Brendan? How will the family exist?"

Da simply shook his head.

John stepped close to his brother's cot. "Brendan, little man," he said, teary eyed. "I love you. You always stuck up for me, even when I was an idiot. I couldn't wish for a better brother. I don't want to lose you."

John's shoulders began to shake. Catching himself, he wiped his cheeks and turned to the next bed. "Mam, I love you so! I know I've troubled you at times, many times, and I wish I could have been a more thoughtful son. I am sorry. I am so sorry for all the pain and the worry that I've caused you. I wish I had . . ."

"Shh," Mam murmured as quietly as a baby's breath. She lifted the fingers of one hand while her eyes remained closed —eyes that might never open again. She finally added with halting, barely perceptible words, "John, you and Nora, I am so proud of you both—how you've grown up. Be good to each other. Help each other. Help Da . . ."

John bent at the waist and cried.

Da's hand squeezed Nora's shoulder. When she turned, she saw that he had placed his other arm around John. "We must go downstairs. I don't want to lose any of you. Time is drawing short, and I have urgent matters that we need to discuss."

Hesitantly, reluctantly, Nora stood and gazed down at Mam and Brendan. The parting tore at her as she thought, Mam, Brendan, I'll love you forever.

Finally, Nora forced herself to turn and follow Da and John as they left the room.

*****

"Children," Da said as he led the children into the parlor, "we are in a miserable place now. All we can do is pray for your mother and Brendan, and God will answer us as is His will. But time is of the essence, now more so than ever. There are important matters I must make you aware of." He turned to his daughter. "Nora, you touched your brother and mam. Please wash your hands."

Nora went to a ceramic bowl on a nearby stand, poured water into it from a jug, and using a bar of soap they had found in a cupboard, carefully cleansed her hands.

Da gestured to the dining table. "Now, please take a seat." He turned to Anne, who was in the kitchen area laying the table with bread, cheese, and ale. "Anne, come sit with us" he said. "What I have to say also involves you."

Nora and Anne sat at the table as Da retrieved a leather saddlebag from beneath his chair and placed it before them. Opening the flap, he withdrew an envelope and removed a sheaf of correspondence. Lifting the top sheet, he said, "When Mother and I were with our solicitor in Portlaoise, transferring ownership of the farm to Fergus, I also had this drawn up." He nodded toward the papers in his hand. "My last will and testament."

Nora felt a stab of anxiety. The ability to foretell certain outcomes in the future was a family trait that had been passed down for centuries on the male side—from the Druids, Mam used to say. Da never spoke of these prognostications, but he was more often than not in tune with what the morrow would bring. Thus, the last will and testament.

"This document names Mother as my principle heir. When Margaret dies . . ." His words faded. He had to clear his throat before he could go on. "The estate is to be divided equally among our three children, Nora, John, and Brendan. If any of our children were to die, that share would pass equally to the remaining siblings. If one of the remaining children were to die without an heir, his or her portion of the estate would go to the survivors. If the entire family dies, leaving no heirs, then the estate will be given to the Catholic Church in Ireland, or what's left of it."

He glanced up. "I hope you are in agreement with this." When everyone nodded, he continued. "The entirety of your inheritance, since I've divested myself of my Irish properties, is ownership of the Running River Plantation in Virginia. It consists of one thousand prime acres. Currently, we are raising tobacco on four hundred acres. In the future, the plan is to clear and cultivate the remaining six hundred acres. Tobacco is a very lucrative crop, and you, my heirs, could become wealthy plantation owners. It is now run by my overseer, Malcolm Butler. He is an excellent farmer and businessman, and I would suggest, should anything happen to me, that you retain his services. Mr. Butler knows I have children, so when you appear at the plantation, it will come as no surprise."

He lifted a second document. "This deed proves, beyond a doubt, that I own the land and that you are my rightful heirs. As further proof of identity, you'll remember that last year I had inked imprints of your palms made." Da pulled out additional sheets of paper. "Here are those prints. Rest assured. With these, you will always be able to prove that you are my lawful heirs."

Nora, still reeling from the events upstairs, became aware of what was being left unsaid. "Da, we're not still going, surely! We can't leave Mam and Brendan."

Da took a moment before he said, "The *Goede Hoop* leaves in the morning. And you children will be on it."

Nora couldn't believe her ears. "I, for one, will not be on it!"

"My dear," Da said somberly, "it is impossible for you to stay another day in Dublin, and not only because of the illness. The English officer will not stop searching for you. Going house to house, his soldiers will find you. Then you, John, Anne, all of us, will be executed. It's a certainty if you stay."

Nora's heart sank as she realized the truth in Da's words. He had just negated all the arguments she had been about to propose.

"There simply is no alternative. You, John, and Anne must leave in the morning. I will be staying here until, God willing, Mother and Brendan have recovered, and then we will board the next ship to Virginia." Da did his best to offer an encouraging smile. "So, if all goes well, we will meet again at our plantation in a few months' time."

Nora dropped her gaze to stare numbly at Da's paperwork. She knew her father was right, but that didn't stop the sensation of cords tightening around her chest so forcefully that she couldn't breathe. She also knew that the odds of Mam and Brendan recovering were slim, very slim. Even more hurtful was the probability that if Da remained in Dublin he, too, would probably succumb to the terrible disease. "Da, there must be an alternative, some way . . . Can't we all leave Dublin together and go to . . ."

"I'm sorry," Da interrupted, "but this is not open for discussion." He lifted the last sheet of paper. "This is a receipt for slightly over two thousand pounds, held in my plantation accounts by Malcolm Butler. You will be able to draw on this money as needed for living expenses and to develop the plantation, should something happen to me. Anne, you will always have a place with us, so there is no need for you to worry about how you will survive in the Americas."

"Oh, Mr. O'Lalor, you are so kind."

"Da," Nora began.

"Please, let me finish. The *Goede Hoop* leaves on the morning tide. Captain Jan van der Root has agreed to take you to Jamestown, Virginia."

"But, Da . . ."

"Nora, please. Soldiers will soon be knocking on our door. You simply can't stay here. There is no alternative. I wish there were." Da pushed the family documents to her. "Place these papers in the belted pouch I gave you. Make sure you wear it beneath your clothes at all times until you arrive in Jamestown."

"Da," Nora pleaded, taking the papers, "couldn't we . . ."

He gave her a look that silenced her, then continued, "Because of these circumstances, you children will now have to assume the role of adults."

Adults? While Nora had lately considered herself an adult, she wondered if she and John, only sixteen and fourteen years old, could actually take on all the responsibilities that would be demanded of them. Nora knew part of the answer. As John was still too immature, the challenge would become hers. But was she up to the task?

"It will be difficult," Da continued. "You, in effect, will be children in an adult world. But you are intelligent and resourceful, and even though you may make a few mistakes, you will learn from them. You will encounter good, compassionate people, and you will meet the dregs of humanity. But I trust you will know the difference. I expect you to flourish and prosper. After all, you are my progeny."

So, it was settled, Nora thought with a heart as heavy as stone. When Da made a decision, there was no changing his mind.

He added, "I wish I could be with you on your adventure, to protect you and guide you along the way, but you will do well. I know that."

Nora wanted to wail, to protest, to scream, No! Never! But now was a time when her head must overrule her emotions. Da's pained face told her how he was suffering, how he would miss them, how he loved them, and how he feared for them.

She drew in a breath. She was not going to make things any more difficult by arguing.

She placed a hand on her chest. It is true, she thought, as she felt the beat of her heart. All aches reside within. Will Da, Mam, and Brendan die? Will they be boarded up inside the cottage and suffer a horrible death? What can I do about it?

Nothing.

Absolutely nothing.

CHAPTER SIXTEEN

Nora O'Lalor! Captain Dice pounded a fist into the palm of his hand as he paced up and down the small rectangular room used by English officers to hold staff meetings and issue directives.

"God damn it!" he cursed, directing his wrath at two noncommissioned officers who stood by, watching their superior with noncommittal eyes. "Tell me, sergeants, how did you and your men allow those Irish shake bags to escape? How, for God's sake? We had them surrounded!"

Their silence thickened the air.

He continued to pace, still smarting from Nora O'Lalor's ingenuity. She had unhorsed a cavalryman, leaped onto the man's mount, and made her escape through a hail of bullets.

Dice snapped up a document from the table. It had been acquired from Dublin's Harbor Master. His eyes scanned a list that showed ship arrivals and departures. The only vessel scheduled to leave port within the next two days was a Dutch-owned frigate named *Goede Hoop*. It would sail on the morning tide.

Dice tossed the sheet back onto the table. He doubted the O'Lalors would choose to travel on a ship that, at best, would smell like the bottom of a latrine. But, to be safe, he had ordered two soldiers to stand guard at Aston Quay, where the boat was berthed. He was betting that Henry O'Lalor would wait for the *Aurora*, which had yet to appear. Once that ship did make port, it would restock provisions before taking on cargo and passengers. That would be his opportunity.

113

The door opened and Corporal Poole entered. "Sir, if I may have a word?"

"Yes, Corporal, what is it?"

"Sorry to report, sir, Lieutenant Bruno bled out while undergoing amputation. He's dead."

"Damned fool. If he had attended to his tourniquet correctly, he would still be alive. Thank you for informing me, Corporal."

Poole hesitated, and then added, "I have news, sir, regarding the O'Lalor family."

Captain Dice's eyes riveted on the soldier. "Speak, man."

"Henry O'Lalor visited O'Meara's shortly before we arrived. He was purchasing medicine for a member of his family."

A surge of adrenaline shot through Dice. This new piece of information was pertinent. It meant the O'Lalors must certainly be holed up within walking distance of Doctor O'Meara's office and the marketplace.

He turned to the two noncommissioned officers, who stood stoically beside the corporal. "Sergeants, you have a chance to redeem your pathetic actions of today. You and Corporal Poole are to assemble forty foot soldiers in the commons before dawn. I will lead them on a thorough search of every dwelling between the wharf and Doctor O'Meara's office on Livingston Street. With the exception of those doors marked with red crosses, no living quarters are to go uninspected." Pounding his fist into the palm of his hand, he added, "I expect to flush the criminals from their cozy rat's nest and arrest them by noon tomorrow. Instruct the troops that, under no circumstances is the young woman, Nora O'Lalor, to be harmed. I intend to deal with her personally. Dismissed."

When the soldiers had filed out, Dice turned to a mirror on the wall—the one he had been avoiding. He stared at the bandage encircling his head that concealed his disfigurement. Revulsion and hatred cursed through him, boiling his blood. He clenched his eyes, imagining the horrors he would inflict upon the Irish wench. Opening his eyes, Captain Dice let out a long-repressed breath. He was feeling better already.

*****

Nora followed the flickering circle of flame as it cast shadows over the walls and floor. Da carried the candle through the parlor where she, John, and Anne had slept fitfully. Only minutes ago, he had awakened them, in the small hours before dawn.

Now they followed him to the front door, toting small satchels that held all of their worldly possessions. Nora touched her waistline and felt the slight bulge of the pouch she had strapped on before getting dressed. She felt vulnerable, carrying the family's valuable documents, but the flintlock pistols that she and John had stashed in their waistbands lent her a degree of reassurance.

Nora threw a quick glance to the stairs, and her chest tightened. She couldn't shake the last images of Mam and Brendan when she and John had bid them farewell. She would never forget their feverish faces, the horrible blisters, and the way they had struggled to draw air into failing lungs.

Nora's thoughts fragmented as a cold wind blew across her face. Da had cautiously opened the door and was peering warily into the predawn darkness.

Da, after ascertaining that the street was vacant, said, "To get to Aston Quay, walk past the Brazen Head Inn, then turn right for two blocks and you'll come to River Liffey. The wharf will be straight ahead. Once you've boarded the *Goede Hoop*, ask for Captain Van der Root." He handed her a little bag. "Inside are fifty pounds to keep in the pocket of your cape. I don't want you reaching under your dress to take money out of the pouch to pay for anything until you arrive in Jamestown. Twenty pounds are for you children, for anything you may need, the additional thirty pounds are for the captain. It's his remaining fee for the voyage. Now, don't forget, you are all Smiths now."

Nora responded, "We will remember."

With a final glance outside, he motioned them forward. "It's clear. Off with you now."

Nora embraced her father. "I love you, Da."

"And I, you," he said with a catch in his voice. He kissed her forehead. "God bless. You make me proud, Nora. If you can, keep Running River Plantation in the family."

"I will, Da, I promise. Come as soon as you can." She tore away from his arms and, fighting her longing to stay, slipped out the door.

John embraced his father. "Bye, Da." Too choked up to speak further, he followed his sister.

Nora turned to see Anne give Da a hug. "Thank you so much, Mr. O'Lalor. I owe you my life."

"You owe me nothing, Anne. Watch after each other."

"We will. Goodbye." Anne passed through the door, joining her friends.

As the cold breeze picked up, blowing their capes out behind them, Nora led off. She heard Da's quiet blessing as he whispered, "Godspeed. Keep safe."

*****

Hurrying along the cobblestones, Nora noticed the first blush of daybreak brightening Dublin's rooftops, setting them aglow with a pinkish-orange hue. Passing the Brazen Head Inn, she turned right and led the trio toward the River Liffey. She noted the three tall masts of the *Goede Hoop* as they drew close, and then the entirety of the frigate showed itself, moored in the choppy waters of Aston Quay. Nora exhaled with relief—they were almost there. With the sky lightening, she could make out crew members scampering up and down the ship's rigging like monkeys. A few had crawled out onto yardarms and were unfurling sails. Captain Jan van deer Root and his son, Pieter, were on deck, smoking their pipes and barking orders in Dutch.

A wave of uneasiness swept over Nora as she recalled Jan and Pieter's leering looks at the coffee shop. Then, as sails caught in the breeze and blossomed, popping and snapping, she suddenly realized the frigate was only seconds from departing!

"Oh Lord!" Nora exclaimed. "They're going to leave without us! Run!"

They dashed over the cobblestones, passing the last cross street. The path to the ship was clear.

"You! Nora O'Lalor. Stop! Stop where you are!"

Nora missed a step, almost falling. She turned to look at the street they had just crossed, and her heart clenched.

A troop of English foot soldiers, led by a mounted officer, were double-timing it onto the wharf. "Nora O'Lalor," the officer shouted, "you and your accomplices are under arrest! Surrender at once!"

The cavalryman issuing the orders had a bandage wrapped around his head, covering his left cheek. It was him!

"Run like the devil!" she screamed.

As Nora, John, and Anne raced for the *Goede Hoop,* two soldiers, who had been standing guard at the bottom of the ramp, appeared from behind a stack of barrels and whipped muskets off their shoulders.

"Damn!" John said, drawing a pistol from his waistband.

"If we stop, we're dead!" Nora said, drawing her own weapon. "We've no choice. Run right through them and up the ramp! If they try to stop us, I'll shoot the one on the left. You take the one on the right."

Good God in heaven. What was she saying?

Throwing a quick glance back at the approaching troop, Nora gasped. The officer leading the foot soldiers was now galloping ahead of his men, rapidly closing the distance between them.

THE GIRL WHO WAS ME IS GONE

They had come so close to escaping, Nora thought miserably. And now this. They would surely be executed.

She turned to see the two sentries at the end of the ramp. They had raised their muskets, aiming at them.

Shots rang out!

Blood spurted from the front of the sentries' tunics. They toppled beside the foot of the ramp.

Startled, but without taking time to question their good fortune, Nora led her companions past the fallen men and up the ramp—even as it was being hauled in by sailors and the mooring lines were being cast off.

Nora, John and Anne bounded onto the deck, and stood leaning on each other, gasping for breath. Nora looked to the poop deck. Captain Jan van der Root and Pieter were lowering a pair of smoking muskets.

She was speechless. The Dutchmen had shot the English guards! Why?

Father and son passed their muskets to a pair of sailors and bounded down the steps to the main deck, where they stopped before the trio. Doffing their feathered hats, they bowed in an elaborate gesture. "Welkom aboard *Goede Hoop*," Jan said.

"Thank you," Nora said, exchanging stunned glances with Anne and John. -

The Dutchmen replaced their flamboyant head coverings and the older man, Jan, became all business. Ignoring his new passengers, he barked out rapid orders to the crew in Dutch. The sailors scurried about, unfurling the remaining sails and hauling in lines to draw them tight.

"Captain! Hoy, Captain!"

Nora's attention flew to the bandaged English officer, who had reined his mount to a stop beside the two dead guards where only moments before the loading ramp had stood.

"Captain, reef your sails immediately! I order you with the authority of the English government to heave to at once."

Nora, Anne, and John exchanged apprehensive looks.

Overhead, the large square sails fluttered in the rising wind, and sailors continued to haul in lines, hand over hand. The frigate had already begun to ease away from the quay.

Captain Jan van der Root yelled back to the mounted officer, "Denk je Nederlands spreekt? Ja?"

"No, I don't speak Dutch, you filthy shotten herrings!" the officer retorted. "Heave to at once! You are under arrest for harboring criminals guilty of murdering two English soldiers! Drop your goddamned anchor! Do it at once! Do you understand me?"

Jan jeered back, "As my dear Dutch vader would say, 'Fuck yourself, Englishman!'"

Nora's eyebrows flew up. She exchanged incredulous looks with Anne and John. They shrugged, at a loss to understand the Dutchman's bizarre behavior.

Nora was puzzled. Why would the captain be defying the English over a few Irish youths?

She jumped when Van der Root began barking orders rapidly to his son. Pieter scrambled up the stairs to the poop deck and ran over to one of two short-muzzled cannons mounted on the stern rail, where he waited, pipe gripped tightly between his teeth.

The captain turned to Nora and inquired with a frown, "Meneer Smith? Family?"

Nora realized the captain was asking for Da and the remainder of the family. She thought quickly. If she revealed that Mam and Brendan had been infected with the plague, Van der Root would very probably throw them overboard. "My father had last minute business," she said. "He, along with my mam and little brother, will board the *Aurora* when it arrives."

The Captain stared directly at her, judging her with ice blue eyes.

Did he believe her? What would she do if he didn't?

Finally, he growled, "Cost is same. You bring money?"

"Nora," John said, pointing toward the dock. "Look!"

Nora turned to the quay, where the distance between ship and dock was widening, but much too slowly. The captain was rapidly gesturing to a longboat floating in the water below the pier and yelling indistinguishable orders. He leaped from his saddle and ran with a contingent of troops to the large skiff. They all piled in, with two of them grabbing oars.

Anne exclaimed, "They're coming after us!"

Dear Lord! Nora felt a prickle of fear crawl up her spine.

Despite billowing, snapping sails the *Goede Hoop* was moving at an excruciatingly languid pace.

"Money," Van der Root demanded, completely ignoring the activity at the quay. "You bring money?"

Nora could hardly believe her ears. Why was he standing there like a bumpkin asking for money when he should be preparing for an attack? Huffing fearfully, she produced the small money pouch.

Before she could open the bag, the captain snatched it from her. Greed illuminated his thin, goateed features as he poured coins into the palm of his hand and began to count.

Nora glanced nervously toward the longboat. At least eight soldiers had now clambered aboard. The officer with the bandage around his skull stood at the prow, shouting orders. The men manning the oars put their backs to work, and the skiff shot away from the wharf.

"Captain," she said with growing alarm, "the English . . . I believe they are going to catch up to us."

"Ja, ja," he said distractedly, focused as he was on counting. Finally, he poured the coins back into the bag. Pocketing it, he said, "One cabin, one price. Eighty pounds, ja?"

"No, no! You can't do that. My father reserved two rooms for sixty pounds. He paid you thirty, we only owe thirty more. I want the remainder of my money back," she stammered.

The captain sneered. "One cabin. Eighty pounds. Price go up."

With a timorous glance toward the long boat, she agreed. "Yes, fine then! Take it!"

She felt Anne grab her arm. "Nora . . ."

"Captain," Nora said, attempting to break through the man's nonchalance, "I believe we are about to be boarded."

Van der Root's head swiveled to the skiff. It had drawn to within twenty feet of the stern.

Nora could see the bandaged officer's face in detail. He appeared to be gloating, obviously anticipating his armed force taking command of the *Goede Hoop*. He roared, "Muskets at the ready!" The soldiers raised weapons and aimed directly at them. The officer added with a confident snarl, "Heave to, Dutchman! That—is—an—order!"

Captain Van der Root scampered up the stairway to where Pieter stood smoking his pipe. Stepping to the rail, the captain scowled down on the longboat that bristled with raised muskets.

"Damn you, Dutchman!" the officer yelled. "Heave to immediately, or we will fire! Do you do understand?"

"Ja, I understand, English dog!" Van der Root retorted.

"Sergeant," the officer motioned to the soldier beside him, "put a bullet through that damned Dutchman's head!"

The soldier's musket *BOOMED*. Captain Van der Root's hat flew off.

"Swine!" the Dutchman screamed. He picked up his hat, jammed it back on his head, and grabbed one of two short-barreled cannons mounted on the stern rail. He calmly aimed the cannon at the longboat. "Fucking English! Here is gift from Van der Root family!" He motioned to Pieter, who came alongside of him and upended the bowl of his pipe above the round little powder vent at the base of the gun. Burning embers fell into the hole. Smoke curled.

Nora couldn't believe her eyes. Was the Dutchman actually going to shoot additional English soldiers?

The officer and his men, associating the rising smoke with instant carnage, dropped their muskets and dove overboard. A split second later, the cannon *ROARED*.

A load of shrapnel tore away the skiff's entire bow, immediately flooding the craft.

The Dutch crew yelled and cheered. "Ditcjhland voor ocit!" "Fuck England!" "Prachtig!"

Nora looked on in amazement as soldiers dog-paddled frantically to reach and cling to the floating debris. The Dutchman had actually done it!

"Van der Root is mad," John said quietly.

"Good, Vader!" Pieter said loudly enough for Nora to hear. "Grandvader would be proud."

The *Goede Hoop*, sails blossoming, began to pass Essex Quay where *Sovereign*, the ninety-cannon pride of the English fleet, was berthed. Officers and sailors on the man-of-war's deck, alerted by musket and cannon shots, had rushed to the rails.

Nora's breath left her. That behemoth of a ship would certainly open fire and blow them all to pieces!

She glanced at Jan. He was staring at the *Sovereign*, his eyes glistening with mania.

He had to be insane!

"Now we make grandvader *very* proud!" Jan yelled vehemently. He turned to the main deck and bellowed, "Fire kanon!"

A seaman below repeated the order loud and clear to the deck below.

The *Goede Hoop*'s ten portside cannons *boomed,* one after the other. Thunder rolled across the bay.

Nora, John, and Anne grabbed the railing as the deck beneath their feet rocked violently. Nora had no idea that the frigate would be armed with cannon, let alone primed for battle. Trails of acrid gray smoke swept up and over the main deck, burning her eyes.

They stared open-mouthed at the sight that materialized as the haze lifted. Gaping holes had been blown into the magnificent man-of-war's hull at the waterline. Onboard, naval officers and crew dashed across the decks in shock as water rushed into the splintered openings. The pride of the English Navy had been completely disabled!

Jan, Pieter, and the Dutch crew cheered jubilantly! Several sailors climbed the rails and lowed their breeches, exposing their bare bottoms to the English, as the *Goede Hoop* sailed past the *Sovereign's* bow. Jan yelled, "English swine! England never sink another Van der Root ship!"

Nora glanced back to the shattered longboat. Some of the survivors were splashing about frantically, trying to stay afloat, while others had already grabbed onto floating debris. Her heart jumped. One of the men clinging to the long boat's wreckage had a bandaged head. As she watched, a swell washed away the bandage and, even at this distance, Nora could make out the man's monstrously deformed face.

He was alive!

CHAPTER SEVENTEEN

Dice pounded a fist in the water with venomous fury as he clung to the bow of the half-submerged long boat. All around him, soldiers who had never learned to swim and had no debris to hold onto flailed about, crying for help before slipping beneath the surface to a watery grave.

Dice ignored them. His eyes were fixed on the young Irish woman who stood at the *Goede Hoop's* stern with a group of Dutchmen that hooted and cheered as they sailed past the *Sovereign.*

"Nora O'Lalor," Dice screamed. "You bitch! You will never get away from me! I will find you! I will hunt you down! I am coming for you!"

*****

"That horrid man," Anne said, taking Nora's hand. "He's the devil himself. I pray we've seen the last of him."

"With any luck, the bastard will drown," John said.

Nora felt her heartbeat slowly return to normal. Hope, her elusive friend, began to grow as the threats being spewed by the officer became incoherent beneath the wind-whipped sails, the creaking masts, and water rushing past the hull.

The elements were carrying the *Goede Hoop* further and further away from the carnage. Nora dropped her eyes to the churning sea. Waves rolled by, repetitive and hypnotic, and within minutes, they had washed away the English officer's horrid image and his vile curses.

Squawk! Squawk!

Nora looked up. A flock of seagulls had congregated above, circling, soaring. The breeze caught her hair; blond tendrils whipped about her face. She was finally able to release a long breath. Free at last!

Despite the English officer's threats, she believed the New World was too far away and too immense for him to find her. Nora turned to Anne and her brother and hugged them. "Thank the Lord!" she exclaimed. "We could never have managed without His help."

The wind changed direction and Captain Jan issued orders. The ship tacked to take advantage of the southwest breeze.

Nora's nose crinkled. "Pew!" She waved, as if batting away flies.

"Oh, my God," John said, suddenly looking ill.

"What is that awful smell?" Anne asked, covering her nose.

"Shit," John said, cringing. "It smells like shit."

The scent wafted past them, reeking of feces, urine, and vomit. Nora's stomach surged. She rushed to the railing and vomited. John and Anne barely made it to her side before they, too, retched.

Hanging over the rail, Nora heard Pieter laugh as he stopped beside her on his way across the deck. "You get used to it."

"Used to what?" Nora gasped, barely able to speak.

"Slaves."

Nora jerked up, wide eyed. "Slaves?"

"Ja. Three hundred this trip."

Nora's stomach heaved.

John turned to Pieter, wiping spittle from his face. "This is a slave ship?"

"Ja," Pieter said, and then added, as if to justify his occupation, "We treat slaves well. Feed two times a day."

Anne spun around, her face white. "You're disgusting!" she declared. Then, beginning to dry heave, she leaned back over the rail.

Pieter, looking momentarily ashamed, said, "It is business. Van der Roots are merchants. We buy, we sell."

Nora placed a hand on her stomach, swallowing back another urge to retch. "That's horrible! How can you buy and sell human beings as if they were nothing more than animals?"

"It is biblical," he defended. "Read *Bible*."

"No, it's about money," Nora accused. "You sell helpless men, women, and children for silver. You and your father should be ashamed of yourselves."

"Not ashamed. Make good profit."

"Profit! Is that all you care about?" Nora stared incredulously at him. "Slavery is an awful, sinful business!"

Pieter grunted, giving her a demeaning look that implied her sex would never understand a man's business. Then he walked off.

Nora stared after him, the scent from below ripe in the air. They were sailing to the New World on a slaver! How was it possible? Da would never have knowingly purchased berths on a slave ship. In his hurry to get them safely out of Dublin, he must have booked passage on the only available vessel—without being aware of its human cargo.

Her mind reeled. What conditions are those poor souls being subjected to? That odor was bad enough on deck. How unbearable it had to be below.

A wave breached the railing, spraying Nora with cold rivulets that ran down the neck of her dress. She shivered as the events of the last few days came back with distressing suddenness: the murders of Conal, Paddy, and Keela O'Moore, the rape of Anne, their arrival in Dublin, Brendan and Mam falling ill with the plague. She relived the shock of seeing that the officer she had shot was still alive and the ensuing chase through the marketplace, followed by the heartrending family parting as she left Da, knowing his decision to stay behind would almost certainly be the death of him. Finally, she was left with that last sight of the officer's gruesome face—and his promise of revenge. It was almost too much to bear.

Another wave sprayed Nora, bringing her thoughts back to the present. Wiping her face, she looked over the bowsprit that dipped and rose like a dolphin as the frigate sailed out of Dublin Bay into the Irish Sea. In the *Goede Hoop's* wake lay wreckage, death, and the curses of a lunatic.

The future, she thought, will bring new hopes and anxieties. John, Anne and I are going to Jamestown where we can start our lives anew with our recently assumed identities, which will free us from the threat of English law.

She reminded herself that she no longer had to fear the scar-faced Englishman. He would either drown or be separated from her by thousands of miles. Nor did she fear the extended voyage, with its elements of danger from pirates and hurricanes. But, she acknowledged, she did dread life without her family and with the unknown future that lay ahead in Virginia. How could she and John ever hope to run a tobacco plantation? Even with an overseer's help, it seemed daunting.

Gazing up at the windblown sails, she murmured, "Da, Mam, I don't think I can do this. I'm only sixteen. I don't want to be a grown-up. Not yet. I need to be your little girl."

*****

"Here, use this," Nora said, ripping a piece of material from the hem of her petticoat and handing it to John.

"Thank you," he replied, finally over his bout of vomiting. He wiped spittle from his mouth. His face, she noticed, was as pale as the sails fluttering overhead. John spat over the railing and said, "No one would believe our story if we ever told it."

"It's a miracle we're alive."

Anne asked, "Why would Captain Van der Root shoot those English soldiers and then attack that monstrous warship?"

John dabbed a last bit of sputum from his chin. "The man's either crazy or he has a death wish, maybe both."

Nora had also wondered about the Dutch captain's bizarre actions. "Firing a broadside into an English man-of-war is like attacking England itself! The Admiralty will never stop looking for him. Although, I have to admit, it did end any chance of pursuit."

"Of that we can be thankful," Anne said.

"Are the Dutch at war with England?" Nora asked, and then answered her own question, "No, I don't believe so."

"Ugh!" John pinched his nose. "That stink isn't going away."

Nora nodded to a large iron grate in the middle of the main deck. "It's coming from there. We should move to the other side of the ship."

As Nora led them to the opposite railing, Anne said, "I don't see how those poor people down below can live with that smell. It would kill me."

Captain Jan van der Root and Pieter tramped down the stairs from the poop deck and, beaming proudly, strode up to them. "I save your lives and BOOM, teach English 'respect Dutch shipping.' Ja?"

"Ja," Nora mimicked, having no idea what he meant by "respect Dutch shipping." She raised an eyebrow when she noticed Pieter's blue eyes ogling Anne's chest.

Jan, who had also become aware of his son's fixation, jovially slapped Pieter on the shoulder. "Ja, geode groten."

In response, Pieter said something in Dutch, his hands moving in obvious reference to Anne's bountiful bosom. They both laughed, and then Jan motioned to two brawny deckhands, waving for them to join them. When the sailors were standing by, he nodded to John. "Chain deze benedendeks."

Nora's brow furrowed. What had the captain just said? Chain? Was he telling the crew to chain John?

The deckhands suddenly grabbed John by the arms and began pulling him away.

"Stop! What do you think you're doing?" John demanded, trying to twist away. "Let go of me!"

"Captain!" Nora said with alarm.

"One cabin. Too small for three," Jan said. He flashed a wicked grin and added, "Brother visit Irish friends."

"What do you mean?" Nora demanded, speared by a jolt of anxiety. Did the Dutchman actually mean to have John join the slaves? "I insist you let my brother go!"

John struggled to free himself. "Let go of me, damn you! I said let go!"

"Captain Van der Root!" Nora yelled. "Stop this at once! You can't possibly let them take my brother. He can stay with Anne and me in our room. I don't care how small it is."

Jan puffed silently on the stem of his pipe as the two brutes hauled John over to the steel grate.

John's head twisted aside as the odor hit him. "God, no! Nora, help me!"

Nora started forward but was grabbed by another sailor, who had come up from behind.

"Take your hands off of me, damn you!" she yelled, resisting ineffectually as the man easily held her in place. "Captain, you must stop this at once! You can't do this to my brother! He's a paying passenger!"

Jan removed his pipe. "Ja, I can do."

"Nora!" John struggled at the lip of the hatch. "Nora, help me!"

And then he was gone. Pulled below deck. The grate slammed shut.

"Captain," she pleaded, on the verge of tears. "I demand that you let my brother . . ."

"Ja, ja, ja," Van der Root said, waving aside her protests. "Kom met mij mee." He repeated the words in English as he strode toward the cabin area. "Come with me."

"No! I am not going anywhere with you until . . ." Nora was pushed from behind by one of the brutes.

"Go!" Pieter ordered. "Now!" He motioned to Anne. "Beide! Both! U follow!"

Nora ground her teeth as a sudden thought presented itself. She and Anne were quite capable of picking up the slightly built father and son and throwing them both over the railing. But, she quickly realized, the crew would probably then throw them overboard.

Temporarily defeated, she suppressed her impulse. She took Anne's hand and they followed Captain Van der Root.

*****

Nora scrutinized Jan and Pieter as they celebrated their victory over the English. They were singing what seemed to be a Dutch seafaring song as she and Anne stood quietly by the bookcase in the captain's quarters. Between stanzas, father and son swigged rum and puffed on long-stemmed pipes. Singing out of tune, they strutted like bantam cocks across the thick Persian carpet, passing a series of multicolored leaded glass windows that opened over the *Goede Hoop's* stern. The windows depicted sights of a quaint village bisected by waterways, which Nora surmised was the city of Amsterdam. On a wall, set between a pair of Flemish tapestries, was a built-in bed, covered by rich quilts, and across from it was a large desk that had been bolted to the floor.

Nora pressed her lips into a tight line as the Dutchmen ogled the girls with covetous eyes. Attempting to ignore their untoward looks, she wondered what was happening to John. She *had* to find a way to rescue him.

Jan sidled over to her, interrupting her thoughts. He took a silver goblet from the bookcase and showed it to her. He said proudly, "Flemish, fifteenth century."

"Very nice."

"Ja, we Dutch, we live geode, ja?"

"Ja," she said, humoring him.

"*Goode Hoop* was flagship of Van der Root fleet, until I'm forced to convert to slaver." Jan's countenance had darkened with his last words. He drank another slug of rum, tapped ashes from his pipe into a large seashell, and continued. "Van der Roots owned three—*three*—good ships, now only one. Goddamn English sink Vader's grand schooner last year." His face twisted into an ugly mask. "Six months ago, they sink my brother's frigate. Family, crew, all murdered! Why?" He peered at her with icy eyes. "I tell you why! English Parliament draft law. Dutch, Spanish, Portuguese ships *forbidden* to trade in free ports! English dogs forbid us. Impossible! They don't own seas! They attack our ships on sight! But I outsmart them. I fly Italian flag and sail under their noses. Ha! Goede, ja?" He quaffed the remainder of his rum and began to pace. "Now you see why I help you Irish. I smash England good, not for you, for me." He whirled around to stare at Nora, the watery blue eyes unreadable. He finally said, "You owe Van der Roots your lives. You repay us, ja?"

Nora traded an uneasy look with Anne.

"Ja," Pieter chimed in, setting his pipe down on an ashtray. "Ja, you ours now."

"Captain, you did save our lives, and for that we are very grateful. But we do not belong to you, or to anyone else."

Jan moved close to her, so close she could smell the reek of rum, tobacco, and sweat. When his eyes dropped to her midriff she pulled in her belly, but the effort did little to hide the pouch secured beneath the folds of her dress. Jan's eyes flickered curiously, he placed a hand on her waistline and began to grope. "Wat is dat?"

Nora's pulse quickened. "My private things."

"Take dress off."

"I will not!"

Jan stepped back and withdrew his rapier. The *hiss* of steel as it came free of its sheath sent shivers through her.

Then Van der Root pivoted to Anne and pressed the last six inches of the razor-sharp blade on top of her ear.

"Stop!" Anne exclaimed. "What are you doing?"

"No move!" Jan ordered Anne. Then his eyes flicked back to Nora. "Dress off or ear off. Choose quickly!"

The Dutchman's gaze bore into her.

Nora swallowed and nodded. She began to unlace her bodice with trembling fingers. After untying the top, she reached down, gathered up the hem, and slipped the dress off over her head, letting it fall to the carpet. She stood before the captain in a white cotton petticoat with the pouch in plain view, secured around her waist.

"Wat is dit?" the captain asked.

Unwilling to answer, she stared defiantly at Van der Root.

The captain sheathed the blade.

"Nora," Anne said. "I am so sorry."

"You," Pieter pointed to Anne. "Dress off!"

Anne's bottom lip trembled. Then she crumbled as she, too, began to undress. Within a minute, both girls stood nervously in their underclothing.

Pieter came up to Anne and patted down her torso, taking liberties as he searched for hidden valuables. Finally, he said, "Niets," repeating it in English. "Nothing."

Captain Van der Root pointed to Nora's pouch. Wiggling his fingers, he ordered, "Give me."

"This is my property. You have no right to it."

"I am Captain. I have all rights. Give, now." Jan placed a hand on the hilt of his sword for emphasis.

"You are a beast!" Nora reluctantly unstrapped the belt and threw it at the captain.

He caught it and opened the bag. Looking inside he said, "Wat is dit?"

The Dutchman extracted her father's documents and inspected them. While she knew the legal papers were worthless to the Van der Roots, she also knew that without them she and John would never be able to prove they had a valid claim to the Virginia plantation.

The captain scowled. "English words! What they say?" Apparently, he was unable to read the English legalese.

"Those documents are not valuable, but they are sentimental to me," Nora said. "Please, may I have them back?"

"No," he said, stuffing the papers back into the pouch. "I hold for safekeeping."

Jan opened his desk drawer and placed the belted canvas pouch inside. Then, turning to a recessed wall cabinet, he retrieved two glasses and filled them with to the brim with rum. As his gaze once again fell on the girls, he grinned lasciviously. "Now we celebrate Dutch sea victory over English dogs, and Van der Roots saving your lives, and good fortune to have pretty girls for company, ja?"

"Captain, I am worried about my brother," Nora said. "He should not be down in that awful place with those prisoners, we are paying passengers and . . ."

"Ja, ja, ja," Jan interrupted with a dismissive wave of his hand. "First, we have victory toast, ja?"

"No. First you release my brother."

"No!" he said emphatically. Then he shrugged his shoulders. "Maybe later. First, you be good to me, then we see."

Good to you! she thought. What was this popinjay implying?

"You like me?" Jan asked. His sly smirk reminded Nora of a bearded devil she had once seen in a painting. "You find me handsome?"

Biting back a response that would not have helped free John, she said diplomatically, "You make a handsome figure in your fine clothes."

He preened. "Ja, only finest for Van der Roots. Finest women, too." He leaned close to her and whispered, "I have secret to share. I find you attractive."

"Thank you," she responded. Then, trying not to offend him but also hoping to end his flirtation, she added a white lie. "I am sorry, but, even though you are a fine-looking man,

I am engaged to be married and would never think of inviting another man's favors."

"Bah! I think you change mind. First, we drink, then we play, ja? Later, we talk about brother. You be nice to me, maybe brother go free, ja?"

"Vader," Pieter said. "I like this one." He indicated Anne, who drew back, terrified.

"Don't come near me!"

Pieter gave her a surprised look. "You no like me?"

"No, I do not!"

Pieter looked perplexed. He turned to Jan. "Vader?"

"Rum," Jan offered, suggesting by his tone of voice that alcohol would change Nora's and Anne's attitudes. "Ja. Rum is good. Drink. Then play."

Nora's mind whirled. If we refuse to drink with them, she thought, the captain will no doubt resort to the threat of the sword. He will also keep John in that awful hell hole. What can I do? There has to be something. What would Mam do? Then an idea materialized. . . .

Jan lifted glasses of aromatic liquor and held them out, offering a tumbler to each girl.

Anne waved him off.

"It's all right, Anne," Nora encouraged. "Have one."

Anne flashed her a startled look, then hesitantly lifted a glass. Pieter took one for himself as Jan passed Nora a tumbler.

Encouraged, the captain said, "I make toast. To Dutch and Irish. Good friends."

The men drained their cups, while she and Anne sipped sparingly.

Nora flinched when Jan placed a hand around her upper arm, nudging her breast. He said, "Now, you, me, to bed."

Nora stiffened but then forced herself to offer a comely smile. "I do owe you my life, don't I?"

"Ja, ja," he said, heartened by her sudden change of manner. "Ja, good. Come."

"Nora!" Anne exclaimed. "What are you doing?"

"It's all right," she replied as she sat on the edge of the bed. "I believe the captain is a good man. He is going to help us."

"Ja," the captain replied, picking up a pillow and throwing it at his son. "You use carpet, ja?"

Anne balked. "I don't want to . . ."

"Don't fight him, Anne," Nora said, adjusting covers on the bed.

Confusion wrinkled Anne's brow, but she allowed Pieter to lead her to the carpet.

"Down," Pieter ordered. When Anne lay down, Pieter unbuckled his pistols and rapier and set them aside. All the while, he stared at her almost sheepishly, as if he wasn't sure he was doing the right thing. Lying beside her, he raised a hand to her cheek and caressed it with surprising tenderness.

Nora, sitting on the edge of the small bed, gave the captain her most coquettish look.

Jan hurriedly withdrew his belt of weapons and placed it on the desk. Grinning, he swaggered over to her and began to unbutton his breeches.

Nora felt her heart thumping so hard she thought it might burst.

Jan let his pants drop to the floor. Nora wasn't shocked by the sight of his flaccid member—she had seen many penises around the farm and in the villages, where men pulled out their manhood whenever they had to pee. But his grin did unnerve her as he began to step out of the clothes curled around his feet.

Nora's mind cried, *Now!*

She raised her feet and kicked him in the chest as hard as she could!

Jan's face wore a startled look as he flew backward to land, butt first, on the floor.

Nora raced to the desk.

Peter turned just in time to see her lift both pistols.

Blood boiled through Nora's veins as she checked the firing pans. Yes! Thank God, they were primed. She cocked the hammers!

Spinning around, Nora aimed one pistol at Jan, who was cursing, struggling to his feet, and the other at Pieter, who had frozen as still as a statue.

"No!" Pieter pleaded. "No shoot, please!"

"Anne," Nora said, shaking, barely resisting the urge to fire. "Over here."

Anne rose from the carpet and hurried to her side.

"Now what you do?" Jan growled angrily as he pulled his breeches up. "You shoot us, my crew kill you. That is for certain."

Nora, still trembling, was surprised that she had actually succeeded in getting the upper hand. She said, "We'd be better off dead than being raped by you."

"Not going to rape," Pieter said quietly. "Just want to kiss."

"I make deal," Jan offered. "You give me pistols. We leave you alone. Promise. You have no problem with Van der Roots or crew. I protect you."

"Just like you were going to *protect* us seconds ago?"

He shrugged. "Things change."

Nora thought it over. She really didn't have a choice. But she had to make the best deal possible. "I want my money and documents returned, and my brother has to be freed immediately."

"Ja, I do this." The captain must have seen her look of skepticism, for he added, "You trust me. I am good Lutheran. I pray every day."

"You would have raped us."

He shrugged. "Maybe you enjoy, not bad, I promise."

"You're disgusting!" Nora said. "Besides being a rapist, you're a slaver. That's not being a good anything."

"English dogs force me to be slaver. They cut off trading for Dutch ships. Slaving is only way to recoup and rebuild. I

136

tithe church. I am good man." He gestured sheepishly. "Perhaps little bit weak, but I have honor. I keep word."

Nora absorbed the captain's story and his claim of being an honorable man. She remembered that the English had sunk two of Jan's fleet, killing his father and brother in the process. It was just possible that, except for his carnal tendencies and his despicable trading in slaves, he might be a man whose word was his bond. And he *had* saved their lives.

"As a Christian," Nora began, suspecting she had no choice but to believe there was a moral center in the man that she could tap into, "I want you to swear to God that you will not attempt to assault either of us again, ever. And that my brother can share a room with us."

"Ja. I swear that to God the Almighty."

Hesitantly, Nora lowered the pistols. Jan quickly stepped forward. He pulled the flintlocks from her hands and stuck them into his waistband. As Pieter came up to them, Jan went to a cabinet, opened it, and withdrew two pair of iron wrist and ankle manacles.

Alarmed, Nora demanded, "What are you doing?"

"For you. You see, *I* no trust you."

"I wouldn't really have shot you," she said. "And besides, you gave me your word of honor that we could trust you."

"Ja. I keep word. You be with brother. You share room, very big room with other prisoners." He kicked the manacles over to them. "You wear chains, keep you from mischief. Give time to think."

"Think?"

"About coming to our beds."

"I would die first," Nora said, incredulous.

"Never," Anne added vehemently.

"Chain them!" Jan ordered, motioning to Pieter. "Take them below, find nice place with slaves."

"You lying snake!" Nora yelled.

"I not lie. I promise not to rape. I not rape. I promise you be with brother. You be with brother. I keep word. Now, next step up to you." His blue eyes glinted impishly. "You wish to come back to this beautiful room, sleep in fine feather bed, have wine, good food? Then maybe I consider it, but first you must *beg* to bed me. Ja?"

"You're dreaming," Nora said.

"Ja," he nodded. "I dream in few days you beg for my cock." Chuckling, he turned to Anne. "You, you will beg Pieter to bed you."

"I will not!" Anne declared.

"We see, we see. One week, maybe two, lying in piss and filth, maybe you change mind. Ja?"

Nora quailed. Her eyes flitted to Anne, who was horror-stricken.

Jan raised his eyebrows, amused. "Maybe now you think Pieter and I not so bad, ja?"

"You're worse than the English," Nora said.

He flushed crimson. Her accusation had hit a nerve. He finally said, "I am good man. When you change mind, I give you soap to wash off filth. Then you come to my bed, and I give you my cock. Pieter, too. If we find you pleasing . . ." he paused, like a cat playing with a nest of trapped mice, ". . . you be our hoers for remainder of voyage."

"You are pure evil." Nora spat at him.

"Not evil. Just a man," Jan said matter-of-factly. "You think differently soon. You come begging to be in my beautiful bed. Until then . . ." He motioned for Pieter to put on their chains.

Pieter knelt before the girls and began snapping on ankle manacles. Nora flinched as the heavy iron straps clamped shut, cutting into her flesh. She was tempted to spit in Captain Van der Root's smug face. But the fear of being sent below decks to live in that foul-smelling place gave her pause. Was she strong enough to face the hellish circumstances she and her friend were about to be thrown into? She would see John—that was good—but under vile conditions. Was Jan's prediction correct—that the slave quarters were so dreadful that they would break down her resistance, as well as Anne's?

Scared and uncertain, she trembled as Pieter rose and clamped iron manacles around her wrists.

She was now a captive, no better than a slave.

CHAPTER EIGHTEEN

Nora and Anne stood barefoot on the main deck, shivering as a chill breeze whipped through the loose weave of the knee-length shifts they had been given to wear. A tall, skinny sailor was securing a twelve-inch length of chain from Nora's left ankle to Anne's right, effectively linking them together. As if wrist and ankle manacles weren't enough to subdue them.

Anne pressed manacled arms to her chest for warmth. Nora commiserated. If only they had been able to collect their dresses and underclothes from Van der Root's cabin . . . But Jan had insisted their garments would be too cumbersome to wear below decks, as most of the prisoners wore lightweight smocks and still suffered from the heat.

Nora glanced at Pieter, who was leaning on the railing a few feet away, supervising the proceedings. He was staring at Anne with an almost apologetic look. Pieter wasn't as cruel as his father, but he wasn't much better, either.

Nora looked heavenward. Only hours ago, they had escaped the plague and the English soldiers. And now they were in chains, prisoners of a slave trader!

The deck shifted beneath her feet as the frigate slid into a deep trough. She and Anne had to grab onto the railing to keep from falling.

"Steady," mumbled the seaman as he finished clamping their chains together.

A moment later, the ship shot up the other side of the declivity, its bow crashing through a twenty-foot wave. Spray drenched the deck as the *Goede Hoop* plowed through the Irish Sea like a leviathan.

Dripping wet, shaking from icy water, and feeling seasick, Nora wiped her face and looked over her shoulder. The Irish mainland was gone.

Da! Mam! Brendan! Would she ever see them again?

"Jakob," Pieter said, motioning to a bald bulldog of a man. "Take these two below."

The seaman carried a long-handled whip. It had several braided leather strands with knotted ends. Nora had seen whips like that before. They were fashioned to punish, delivering deep, flesh-cutting lashes. The man motioned for them to proceed to the steel grate in the center of the deck. "Go."

"Anne," Pieter said in an almost pleading tone. "Change mind. Stay with me. I care for you."

"Never," Anne retorted. "You and your father are savages."

Pieter turned and walked off.

"Move!" Jakob emphasized his order by jabbing the butt end of the whip into Nora's backside. "Go!"

"Stop it! I am moving!"

Jakob ushered them forward and called to a deckhand. "Sander." When the man turned to him, Jakob gestured to the grate. "Open!"

The sailor hurried over to the perforated iron hatch and lifted it.

Nora recoiled from the loathsome stench that assaulted her nostrils. Anne raised a hand to cover her mouth. Stomachs churning, they began to gag.

The crew laughed and hooted. Jakob used the end of his whip to prod them. "You go!" he ordered.

Nora balked at the top of the ladder that led down to the stinking compartment. Could she make it down without vomiting again? She thought of her brother in this foul-smelling hole. He had to be suffering terribly. She had to go to him. Inhaling fresh sea air, which would probably be her last opportunity for a while, she said, "Anne, we have to."

"I . . . I can't," Anne said, wiping her pale face. "I can't go down there."

"We can do this. Hold onto me if you need to."

"Nora, I . . ." Anne said fearfully, "I'll die."

"Take the hem of your smock and cover your nose and mouth."

Setting an example, Nora lifted her garment, attempting to preserve her modesty by exposing as little of her bare thighs as possible. She pressed the cloth to her face. "Do this. It helps."

Anne hesitantly followed Nora's actions, covering her nose and mouth.

"Go!" Jakob ordered impatiently. "Now!"

Nora resisted an urge to lash out at the oaf, knowing it would only result in more abuse. Gritting her teeth, she looked into the dark abyss. The odor was repellant, overwhelming. Pressing the cloth tighter to her nose, she noticed that the crew had stopped work to gawk at her bare legs—but she was past caring. She returned her gaze to the ladder and took a hesitant step. When her chained foot landed on the first rung, she said, "Anne, we can do this."

Cautiously, she took another step, which pulled Anne's shackled foot along. Together they hobbled down the rungs, with Jakob following, ready to poke them at any given moment.

Nora stepped onto the floor, and her bare toes sank into squishy, wet muck. Don't even think about what's in this ooze, she told herself.

A dim light from a single lantern that hung on a nail illuminated a small portion of the interior. As Nora's eyes adjusted to the darkness, she could see there was only one way ahead, down a long narrow aisle that bisected the hull. The entire space had been partitioned off. Four roughhewn shelves were crammed with sweating, half-naked prisoners. They lined either side of the narrow walkway. Sounds of scraping chains and agonized moans filled the cavernous space, and Nora knew she was walking into a living hell.

Shadowy figures, smaller than the others, occupied the top planks—children. Below them, on the second tier, lay the women. The two bottom shelves were lined with men. All had their feet facing the aisle, and had been packed together so tightly that they reminded Nora of fish packed in a barrel. Less than three feet of headroom separated the levels. The poor wretches could hardly move, or even sit up.

Long chains had been looped through ankle restraints to iron rings set on posts that secured the prisoners to the wooden planks. The men were the most aggrieved. Being on the bottom, they were inundated with a steady drip of filth from the prisoners above them. They were covered with bloody sores, chafed raw by lying on sodden boards that pitched and rolled with the ship.

Nora's stomach tightened into knots. She could never have imagined such suffering. It was an inconceivable spectacle of horror.

Anne bent over and dry heaved. When she was able, she pointed. "Nora, these poor souls are Irish!"

Yes, Nora thought, as she looked closer at the prisoners. More of Cromwell's doing.

Jakob pushed from behind. "Go! Go!"

Nora stumbled forward, helping Anne along as she searched for a familiar face. John had to be here somewhere.

"Nora O'Lalor, as I live and almost breathe," a rasping voice called. "A social call you're making now, is it?"

She spun around. *Billy Devlin!* He was propped up on his elbows, staring at her as he lay on his backside, sandwiched between two men on the second shelf from the bottom.

"Billy!" she gasped.

So this was where the shackled prisoners from Dublin had ended up! Like most of the men, Billy wore only cut-off breeches. In spite of the vile conditions, he managed to offer a lopsided grin. "You've made quite a name for yourself with the English," he said. "Congratulations."

Avoiding the subject of the shootings she'd been involved in, she asked, "Have you seen my brother, John?"

"Aye. But here I am thinking it was me you'd come to visit."

"Billy . . ."

He huffed with theatrical disappointment. "You'll find him a bit further on."

"Move!" the Dutchman ordered, prodding her painfully in the kidney.

"Easy, Jakob!" Billy said. "You'll be answering to me if you mistreat my lady friends."

"Hou je bek!" Jakob said, ordering him to shut up.

Nora and Anne moved deeper into the belly of the ship. The heat rose and Nora felt perspiration trickling down her sides. It became more difficult to breathe. Plaintive murmurs and groans surrounded them as they passed sweaty figures. A few of the prisoners raised their heads to stare, others ignored them. Then she saw him, on the third shelf, wedged between two men.

"John!" she cried.

Unable to turn or sit, he raised his head. "Nora!" he exclaimed. "Those bastards! How dare they send you and Anne down here."

She flinched as Jakob jabbed her ribs.

"Stay safe, stay brave," Nora said, before being pushed farther down the aisle.

Twenty feet later, Jakob grabbed the back of her shift and brought the girls to a standstill. He pointed to a small space between a group of shackled women on the second tier from the top.

"Up!" Jakob ordered. "Up!"

Nora balked. There wasn't enough room for one person, let alone two.

"We can't fit between them," Anne said, mirroring her thoughts.

"Up!" Jakob raised his whip.

"He's not giving us a choice," Nora said with resignation. "Grab onto the side rail."

They gripped the support and, hindered by their restraints, began the awkward task of climbing to the women's shelf. Nora felt Jakob's hand grab onto her buttocks, touching her indecently as he pushed her upward.

"Damn you!" she cursed.

Jakob reached over to Anne and groped her next, as he lifted her up.

"Stop it, you pig!" she yelled.

The uncouth oaf laughed. He then threaded a long chain through their ankle restraints, securing them to the shelf.

As Nora and Anne attempted to wedge themselves into the space between two women, Nora pleaded, "I'm sorry. I'm sorry."

The women on either side grunted, making an effort to give Nora and Anne a smidgen more room, but there wasn't more space to be shared. Nora and Anne finally squeezed in between the captives. Nora found herself pressed up against Anne's back, while another woman was wedged against her backside. Anne, too, was sandwiched up against the person in front of her.

Nora wiped sweat from her face as she introduced them. "I'm Nora Smith, and this is my cousin, Anne Smith."

The prisoner close behind Nora's ear said, "I'm Mauve Madden, dear. The woman in front of Anne is Bridget Duffy."

Bridget coughed deeply and then said, "I'm afraid we're not meeting under the best of circumstances."

"Sorry to be crowding you like this," Nora said, squirming on the wet shelf.

"Nothing to be done about it," Mauve said. "I have two young ones above us. God willing, we'll all survive our journey to the Americas."

"Nora!" Anne gasped. "I feel like I'm going to suffocate."

The humidity was indeed almost too dense to inhale. Nora attempted to be supportive. "Hopefully, it will get better when it cools down tonight."

"It never cools down in hell," Mauve said.

So much for trying to be supportive.

Bridget said, "We've been in this shithole for a week waiting for a full load of prisoners. Now that we're at sea, I've heard they'll be letting us up on deck two times a day to eat and wash."

"Mauve," Nora asked, "how can the Dutchmen get away with this, treating us like animals?"

"My dear girl, we lost the war. England sells us to slavers like the captain, who in turn sells us to auctioneers in the colonies, who then auction us off as indentured servants and slaves to work the plantations."

"That's completely immoral."

"Be that as it may, 'tis our fate."

Nora closed her eyes. A moment later, she became aware of heavy drops spattering on her hair and face. When the fluid ran past her nose, she gagged. The ooze smelled of urine, feces, and vomit. Her senses reeled at the stench, along with the horror of being shackled and pressed between hot, sweating bodies with barely enough oxygen to maintain life.

Anne's shoulders shook as she wept. Gasping through her tears, she moaned, "God help us. I can barely breathe. God help us!"

Surrounded by wails of suffering, Nora's thoughts drifted. How many of them would die before the *Goede Hoop* reached Virginia? Would she survive? Would Anne and John? And, if they did, what lay ahead? Years of servitude, years of pain?

CHAPTER NINETEEN

Captain Dice clenched and unclenched his fists, struggling to hold his anger in check as he stood before the officer's review board inside Portlaoise's English military compound. The hearing was being officiated by three senior officers: Colonel Henning, Major Thomas, and Major Mills. Searching their faces, Dice identified a mixture of macabre interest and distaste. He was well aware that his mutilated face was repugnant. He also knew that today's review would very probably end his career—there was no place in England's spit-and-polish officer corps for a deformed soldier. He stretched his shoulders in an effort to distract his attention from the acidic burning that ate at his gut.

The agony, he knew, would not be assuaged until he caught up to and disposed of the Irish wench who had degraded him at every turn.

"Captain Dice," Colonel Henning said as the hearing continued. "You lost Lieutenant Grimes at the O'Moore farm. You, yourself, suffered an unfortunate gunshot wound to the face. Then, at the O'Lalor farm, good soldiers died under your command. Lieutenant Bruno later expired from a wound that should have been treated earlier. In Dublin, you not only allowed criminals and murderers to escape, but several innocents were killed by gunfire in the marketplace."

"Colonel Henning," Dice said in a tone that bordered on insubordination. "Those people who were struck in the marketplace were *Irish*."

"Be that as it may," the colonel replied testily, "there is a code of honor among gentlemen. Unless provoked, we do not kill innocent human beings, Irish or otherwise."

Dice's face turned crimson. He countered, "Sir, if I may remind you, Parliament has stipulated that Irish may be killed at any time. In fact, we are encouraged to do so."

Henning's eyes steeled. "I don't need reminding of that barbaric law, Captain Dice. I'm no advocate for Oliver Cromwell. He and his followers espouse hatred and murder, all to take Irish land for themselves and their supporters. Let me remind you of something you seem to have forgotten, one of God's commandments: *Thou shall not kill.* Shooting innocent men, women, and children is a sin and an abomination."

The officers to either side of Henning murmured agreement.

Dice's eyes glistened in thinly veiled defiance.

"Lastly," the colonel continued, "in Dublin Bay, again in pursuit of those same criminals, you, sir, allowed them to escape despite leading a full contingent of infantry. Several soldiers were killed or drowned, and the *Sovereign*, one of England's finest ships of war, suffered a crippling broadside from the Dutch Captain Van der Root, whom you provoked unnecessarily."

Dice responded coldly, "Van der Root's actions were beyond my control, sir. As for the criminals escaping . . ."

"Stop!" Colonel Henning ordered. "We don't wish to hear excuses. It is our consensus that, in respect to your earlier stellar career, you be given an option. You can either resign immediately or return to London and await reassignment to a foreign post."

A foreign post, he thought bitterly. Yes, bury me in a land where I will be forgotten.

He wiped saliva from his cheek, thinking of his options. He didn't have any.

*****

Rivulets of sweat rolled off Nora, pooling on the planks beneath her as she lay curled up against Anne's backside.

How long had it been since they'd sailed out of Dublin Bay? Ten days? Two weeks?

During that time, Nora had watched her friend wither before her eyes as storms pitched and rolled the *Goede Hoop* about like a leaf in a windswept gutter.

First there had been seasickness. Then the always-inadequate food and drink, along with unending heat and unbearable humidity. And the ship's constant motion irritated painful sores on shoulders, hips, and ankles that had no chance of healing. Then Mauve Madden came down with a cold. She sniveled and hacked almost continuously in Nora's ear.

And the rats!

Below decks was alive with rodents, some the size of small cats. They were around at all times of the day and night, chewing and gnawing, and everyone was terrified of being bitten.

Only last night, one of the vermin had come within a foot of Nora's face. It sat and stared at her, waiting for an opportunity to sink its sharp teeth into her flesh. But she had edged closer to the rat and, gathering courage, had whipped her chained wrists out. The iron cuffs had stuck the rodent's head, killing it. It lay dead now, just inches away, its eyes open, staring at her.

When there was a respite to the surging, rolling sea and blustery winds, the prisoners were brought up from below to breathe fresh air and bask in the sunshine. After enduring the ghastly conditions below, it was like climbing the ladder to heaven.

With good weather holding, Nora and Anne were brought topside twice a day in small rotating groups of men, women, and children. During these brief visits, they were fed and given water. Every third day, Captain Van der Root allowed the prisoners to wash accumulated filth from their clothes and bodies with buckets of seawater, while seamen gawked at the females and made lecherous comments.

At first, Nora and Anne had balked at the thought of being naked in front of the Van der Roots and their crew, but the desire for cleanliness quickly outweighed those inhibitions, especially when all of the other females eagerly disrobed. Nora soon discovered there was a degree of anonymity in a crowd.

Pieter was always hovering nearby when the women were brought up. He stared at Anne as if she were a goddess. As the days passed, he tempted her to join him for the remainder of the voyage by offering the comfort of his cabin, quality food and ale, and the return of her dress.

Nora had watched Anne's resistance to Pieter gradually erode, finally coming to a head when her friend missed her monthly courses.

"Nora," Anne said, turning her head so they were eye to eye on the sodden planks. "Please don't be mad at me, but I'm going to go with Pieter."

It wasn't Anne's choice that was so unsettling, but the fact that any argument Nora might have made to counter it seemed to have so little merit.

"I understand," Nora responded sincerely. Morality could be a variable virtue, especially at times like these, when life and death were in the balance.

Of course, there were dangers. Pieter could tire of Anne and pass her off to Jan or, worse yet, to the crew. Or Anne could contract a venereal disease. And pregnancy—well, that might be the case already.

"I'm not as strong as you," Anne said. "I'm not a fighter. Please don't think badly of me."

"I'll never think badly of you. I beg you to be careful."

Anne twisted about and hugged her friend as best she could. "I will be careful, and I'm sure I'll be able to help you once I'm living with Pieter. I can bring you better food, and maybe arrange for you to spend more time on deck. You might even be able to visit with me in Pieter's cabin. That would be so wonderful."

"What would be so wonderful?" Billy asked, suddenly appearing in the aisle beside them. He was filthy, and carried an overflowing slop bucket in each hand.

Anne said, "I'm leaving this awful place."

"Ah," Billy responded. "It's to Paris you'll be going, no doubt?"

"Billy," Nora said, waving off the odor that accompanied him. "Can you please keep moving?"

"Not until I know where Anne is going."

Anne pinched her nose and spoke through her fingers. "I'm going topside to be with Pieter."

"Ah. Interesting."

Mauve Madden began to cough on Nora's back. The woman propped herself up on an elbow. "Billy Devlin, go on with you! I can't stand the stink. Go!"

"Please take those buckets away," Nora pleaded.

"And to think I was once such a popular fellow. All right, all right, I'm on my way." He leaned in close to Anne and added in a conspirator's whisper, "You and I will be talking."

A moment later, he was trundling down the aisle, the containers overflowing, splashing on his feet.

Nora, who had heard Billy, frowned. What was he up to now?

CHAPTER TWENTY

Despite the adversity of her recent life, or perhaps because of it, Anne allowed herself to wallow in the comfort of the mattress as Pieter rolled out of bed, naked as a newborn. The bed they shared was so narrow that she and Pieter had to sleep intertwined—a situation she found far more comfortable than her last accommodations. Yes, the mattress was narrow, but oh, so soft.

Anne pulled covers up to her chin and watched her diminutive, potbellied paramour as he dressed in the first mate's elaborate costume. His silk shirt had puffy sleeves with green, yellow, and red stripes. After fastening the shirt, he pulled on a pair of ebony breeches. He looked over at her as he retrieved a white frilly lace collar and fastened it about his neck. He raised an eyebrow. "Good?"

"Ja, Pieter. Good. You look very handsome."

He grinned as he pulled on knee-high black leather boots.

Anne could not believe that fortune had finally smiled upon her—and in the surprising form of Pieter. She had come to him several days ago. Despite her aversion to doing so, it had seemed a better choice than dying below, on those awful, stinking planks.

Their first night together Pieter had undressed her rather aggressively, and the rough sexual encounter that followed had caused her to burst into tears. Inexperienced in the art of love, Pieter had been taken aback by her reaction. Genuinely concerned, he had asked why she didn't enjoy his manly efforts. Anne, touched by his unexpected thoughtfulness, was moved to explain that she had heard lovemaking should be a good experience for both parties—at least that's what her mother had told her. Pieter had listened attentively and, surprisingly, had then inquired about her life and her experiences. When the gruesome details of the last few weeks poured out, he had been genuinely sympathetic. "We sleep together," he had concluded, "but I wait. I wait for you. When ready, I be gentle."

Two nights ago, she had succumbed to Pieter's patience. They had undressed together and had started with slow, gentle kisses that became deeper as their hearts began to pound. They explored each other's bodies, nipping, touching, squeezing, their breaths shortening as their passions grew in intensity. Anne found herself aroused, and then *Oh, Lord!* even needy—delightfully so.

It had only taken one gentle bedding to open her horizons to the physical joys a man and woman could share. The fear of sex that had haunted her since her horrific rape had fallen away like leaves in autumn. Pieter was loving and kind, as well as absorbed with her in a way that made him all the more attractive.

Did she love him? she asked herself. No. But she did like him—and how he made her feel.

She giggled to herself. The experience had left her with a new sense of wellbeing and satisfaction, and, yes, a growing anticipation of their next romp in bed.

Now, as Pieter strapped on his sword belt, holstered the flintlock pistols he always carried, and put on his large feathered hat, she watched him with an admiration bordering on desire. She felt gratified. It was a welcome feeling.

Pieter opened the door and waved. "Tot later."

"Tot later," she repeated.

When the door closed, Anne ran a hand over her bare shoulders and bosom. Her skin was warm and sensitive and clean. She mused, I would probably be dead by now if I had stayed one more day in that unspeakably loathsome hold.

Her gaze fell upon the tiny tin bathtub sitting by Pieter's desk. Pieter had taken the tub from his father, who he said had never used it.

A bath, that's what she needed. She would ask the ship's cook to heat a pot of water and have it brought to the cabin. Washing with soap and soaking for half an hour would help ease away the nagging fears that plagued her—that her situation was too good to be true, that the rapport she shared with Pieter might be sabotaged by Jan, and that she would be sent back to the dreadful conditions below deck.

After her bath, she would put on her dress, the one Pieter had returned to her. Then, when the female prisoners were brought topside, she would go out on deck. She had a small packet of food she planned to pass furtively to Nora. It was the least she could do for her friend. She was still feeling guilty about having deserted her.

There was a distinctive knock on the door. That would be Billy.

Billy, along with the dour seaman who followed him like a shadow, came twice a day to empty the chamber pot. As the Dutchman neither spoke nor understood English, it allowed them to speak freely.

. . . Which has created my current dilemma, she thought with anxiety.

Anne slipped out of bed, wrapped a blanket about her nude body, and shuffled over to the door. "Yes?" she asked to confirm her expectation.

"Offal collector," Billy announced, "or awful collector, if you prefer."

She couldn't help but grin as she opened the door, allowing Billy, who carried an empty chamber pot, to enter while the guardian lurked behind. As she stepped back to let Billy pass, the blanket caught on the arm of a chair and pulled the fabric down, exposing her!

"Oh!" she said, quickly reaching to untangle the cloth.

"Anne, a bountiful wonder you are," Billy said, catching an eyeful before she covered herself. "'Tis a shame to be giving all that to one little popinjay, when you could be sharing yourself with a fine lad like myself."

"And if I did, that lout in the doorway would tell Pieter, and his sword would certainly do away with your favorite plaything."

"Ouch." Billy scrunched his face and crossed his legs. Then, flashing a quick grin, he picked up the room's chamber pot, substituting it with the one he carried. He whispered, "Well?"

Anne knew exactly what Billy was after. He had been hounding her, playing upon her sympathies ever since she moved into the cabin, until she had finally succumbed, with reservations, and given in to his request. Moving to block her actions from the deckhand in the doorway, she turned and removed an item from a small jar on the shelf and wrapped her fingers tightly around it. A twinge of remorse hit her as she thought of her lover and roommate. "I am so sorry, Pieter," she murmured quietly. She stepped to the door, as if waiting for Billy to exit so she could close it after him.

Billy nodded ever so slightly. As he was walking past her, he paused beside Anne, feigning an adjustment to the chamber pot. Anne glanced over his shoulder to be sure the sailor's field of vision was blocked. Satisfied, she passed the item to Billy—but missed his hand. It fell to the floor with a *clink!*

"Wat is dat?" the guard asked suspiciously as he stepped forward. His eyes widened when he saw the key on the floor a split second before Billy stepped on it.

Snarling, the guard lifted his club and struck Billy over the head.

Anne screamed!

CHAPTER TWENTY-ONE

John, trudging amongst a line of prisoners, stumbled up the aisle. He stopped briefly beside his sister. "Nora," he gasped. "Billy and Anne, they were caught pilfering Pieter's key to our chains."

"What?" she asked, startled, sitting up as much as her restraints would allow.

"Billy was planning a mutiny. He was to release the prisoners tonight and take over the ship."

"Take over the ship?" she exclaimed, her heart beginning to pound at the thought. And then what? Billy could no sooner sail a ship than she could fly to the moon. And she seriously doubted the Dutch, if any were left alive, would volunteer to sail it for him. Billy would have run them aground, and they'd all have perished. Oh, that was so Billy! He was a bletherskate, a cock who crowed to hear himself squawk! Taking a breath to regain her composure, she asked with trepidation, "And what's become of them?"

"We were brought topside to witness the punishment. They were flogged. It was the worst sort of carnage. They were whipped until there was nothing left of them but raw meat and blood."

Barely daring to ask, she inquired, "Are they alive?"

John shrugged. "I can't imagine by the look of them. I heard that the captain plans to throw their bodies to the sharks."

The women to either side of her, having heard John's words, gasped and cried out as Nora clenched her eyes, tears streaming.

"I'm sorry. Nora, I . . ."

"Move on!" a guard barked from the back of the line.

John gave her a sorrowful look as he was dragged off behind the other prisoners.

Billy and Anne dead? Sobs began to rack through her. It can't be! Oh, dear God, no! Don't let it be.

*****

Thirty agonizing minutes later, the female prisoners were brought topside to witness the results of the punishment that had been dealt to Billy and Anne.

"You see?" Captain Van der Root yelled from the poop deck as the women lined up before him. "Look! Look good! Ja? Dutch justice."

Nora's eyes, red from crying, stared up at Anne and Billy, who were strung up side-by-side, hanging from a yardarm. Their figures dangled above the poop deck, suspended from ropes that bound their wrists. Nora's heart constricted as she observed their tortured bodies. Each bore bloody marks from a lash that had shredded what little clothes they had, to expose severely lacerated skin. They resembled carcasses in a butcher shop.

Overwhelmed by sorrow, Nora cried out and ran toward the stairs, only to be stopped by Jan van der Root, who blocked her path. "No!" he ordered. "Back! Stay back!"

"You murderer!" she flung at him. "You terrible, horrible beast!"

"Not beast." He gestured to Anne and Billy. "Not dead."

A rush of relief. Anne and Billy were alive? But they appeared to be dead. Was the captain playing a cruel trick on her? But then she could see they were breathing—barely. "Cut them down! Please, cut them down! Please, Captain!"

Jan van der Root smirked.

"You must cut them down!" she pleaded. "They'll die."

"Ja, kan zijn." He repeated the words in English for her benefit, "Yes, maybe."

"Damn your heartless soul!"

"You no damn me!" Jan retorted. "I hang you also!"

"Don't irritate . . . the little shit," Billy managed to mutter, opening a battered eyelid. "You don't want to be keeping us company."

"Billy!" she said, her heart leaping, "We'll get you down, and Anne too!"

Billy's eye closed as if the effort to open it had taken the last of his strength. A sudden gust of wind barreled into the half-rigged sails, rocking the ship as its bow continued to ram through the rolling sea, causing Billy and Anne to swing from the yardarm like marionettes without a puppeteer.

Nora, holding onto the stair railing for balance, cringed when she saw a smear of blood on the inside of Anne's legs. *A miscarriage?* Anne was so severely wounded, it was impossible to know if the source of the blood was internal or external. Nora's stomach tightened as her mind whirled. Anne and Billy needed immediate medical attention, or they would die! Asking the captain for mercy would be as futile as asking the Dutchman to return her father's documents and gold coin. But, she thought as she glanced toward Pieter, there might be a spark of decency she could appeal to in his son.

"Pieter," Nora said, raising her voice above the blowing wind, "Anne doesn't deserve this."

"They stole my key!" he interrupted bitterly, almost teary-eyed. "They would have released prisoners and mutinied! Maybe kill us."

Nora understood his anguish. He had placed his trust in Anne, only to be betrayed.

"Pieter," she said, "Anne wanted to free her countrymen. I'm sure you would have done the same if the prisoners had been Dutch. She was just doing what she thought was right. Please forgive her. Help her, Pieter. I know you're a good

158

man, and I know how much she cares for you. Please, take her down. Take them both down."

"Mutiny is treacherous act!" Jan van der Root exploded before his son could respond. "We feed to sharks. Ja, Pieter?"

"Ja," Pieter intoned miserably as he grabbed for his feathered hat to keep it from being blown away by the rising wind. Holding onto its brim, he glanced toward Anne and stared at her bloodied figure. His features almost crumbled, but he caught himself. He turned to his father. "Dead prisoners kosten money. Alive—we sell at auction."

A smattering of hope surged through Nora. Pieter was suggesting they keep Anne and Billy alive, to be sold at auction!

The captain's eyelids narrowed, becoming foxlike. She recognized the expression—he'd had had the same look when he counted out her gold coins—greed.

Jan stroked his goatee, then nodded exuberantly. "Goede! Very goede, Pieter. Cut down. Fatten pigs for market, ja?" He clapped his son on the back. "Goede zoon. You think like vader."

Pieter motioned a sailor over and spoke to the man rapidly in Dutch. The seaman drew a knife, placed it between his teeth and scrambled up the rigging to the yardarm that held Anne and Billy. He crawled out beneath wind-whipped sails, and with two quick strokes severed their ropes.

Pieter caught Anne in his arms, while Billy dropped to the deck like a broken doll.

*****

Nora's thoughts were a combination of anger and relief as she sat on the poop deck, holding Billy's battered head in her lap. Billy, you can't die on me, because I'm going to kill you myself! Sometimes I don't believe you have a brain in your skull. How could you possibly involve Anne in your wild scheme? How could you possibly have thought . . . oh, never mind. I will never understand you.

"I know . . . what . . . you're thinking," Billy managed to mumble without opening his swollen eyelids. "But one learns . . . from failure."

"Some men never, ever learn," she responded.

One of his eyes opened a crack. "That was unkind, I . . ."

"Shh," she interrupted, not wishing to hear another word from him. Her eyes followed Pieter, accompanied by Jakob, as he carried an unconscious Anne across the main deck to the prisoners' hatch. Jakob yanked the iron grate open and Pieter, balking at the stink, passed Anne to the burly seaman. Jakob hoisted Anne over his shoulder and stepped down the ladder.

Captain Van der Root had also been watching the proceedings. He grunted with approval as Anne disappeared, and then he kicked Billy. "You go now!"

"Stop it!" Nora protested. "Haven't you done enough damage?"

"Go!" he ordered, administering another kick. "You go! All go below!"

"He kicks . . . like a . . . little girl," Billy murmured, his good eye fluttering as he sat up and struggled to his feet. "I think . . . I can . . . stand."

"The less thinking you do, the better. Give me your arm."

"Cruel . . ." Nora thought she heard Billy mumble. Why am I acting so rude? she wondered. It's so unlike me. The poor fellow is half dead.

Unwilling to pursue that line of thought, she took hold of Billy's arm and helped him up. A groan escaped him as he leaned on her, his open eye centering on Captain Van der Root. Billy spit blood from his mouth and said, "Captain, we'll . . . have to do this again sometime, trading places."

Nora cringed, waiting for another kick. When it didn't come, she realized Jan hadn't understood Billy's jibe. She led him to the stairs.

"Hold onto me," she urged Billy as the ship rolled with a large swell.

"I've been waiting years . . . for you to say those words," he gasped.

"You are irrepressible," she said with a feeling akin to admiration as she wrapped an arm around Billy's chest and held him close, helping him navigate the steps.

She could feel the warmth of Billy's face almost touching hers. If she turned, her lips would brush his cheek. Her pulse quickened as she felt his body pressing against her bosom. Tiny shocks sparked. She missed a step. Catching herself, she released a quiet moan.

"Are you all right?" Billy managed to ask.

"Fine. I am fine," she stammered, then corrected her thought. No, I'm not. What has come over me?

Billy groaned, clenching his teeth.

"You're hurting," she said.

"It's just my soul reacting to your embrace."

"Billy Devlin, I am not embracing you. I am holding you up so you don't fall flat on your face. How can you be half-dead and still be a flirt?"

"I've been called that before, but never by anyone as beautiful as you."

She couldn't help but smile. Billy's words emanated from an irrepressible personality that no calamity seemed to subdue. "You haven't changed at all."

"That's . . . probably not a compliment," he said as they stepped onto the main deck.

She remained silent, although it actually had been a compliment. Optimism in the face of adversity was a trait she admired, but she wasn't going to let him know that. She guided Billy over to the hatch just as Jakob climbed up from below.

Jakob motioned to Billy. "I take."

Knowing they were to be parted, Billy said quickly, "Nora, we weren't born to be slaves, none of us. One day I will set you free. I promise."

Jakob picked Billy up and threw him over his shoulder, ignoring the Irishman's moans as he retraced his steps down into the hull.

Nora repeated the words in her mind. I will set you free. I promise. "I believe you, Billy Devlin," Nora said quietly to herself. "I believe at least you'll try. I only pray that you and Anne live to reach Jamestown."

Nora was well aware that open wounds on a filthy, vermin-infested ship could fester. Both of her friends might die within days, and she could do nothing about it. So much of life was in the hands of fate.

*****

Drip, drip, drip.

Nora eyed the bodily fluids that seeped, drop by drop, from the children's shelf as she lay sandwiched between Anne and Mauve Madden's hot, sweating figures. She thought with certainty that she had never been so filthy in her entire life. Her ankle and Anne's had been relinked by the twelve-inch chain, making it difficult to move without scraping sores that had been rubbed raw on planks that never stopped moving. Taking in a breath, she immediately regretted it. With three hundred prisoners all drawing on the same oxygen, the hold was stifling, and rank with vile odors. She closed her eyes, wondering if the pitch and roll of the sea would ever end.

During the last two weeks, one storm after another had assaulted the *Goede Hoop*. At present, the hull was being pummeled by twenty and thirty-foot waves that tossed the ship about as if it were an eight-foot skiff. Because of the weather, prisoners had been confined to their hellish quarters.

Anne mumbled in her sleep. Her breathing was labored.

"How is she?" Mauve asked.

"Better," Nora responded. "She's getting better."

"Poor thing. That was such an awful whipping."

Yes, thought Nora. Anne's beating had almost killed her. But someone—it could only have been Pieter—had sent curative ointments down to the hold that were helping heal her friend's shredded skin.

Adding to Anne's anguish, she had also suffered a painful miscarriage.

It was God's will, Nora thought.

*****

She had heard little of Billy. The last news was that his wounds had become infected, and that his health was fading.

Don't die, Billy. Please, don't die! she thought.

Prayer now seemed to take a large part of her waking hours. She prayed for Anne, who thankfully slept most of the day. She prayed for her parents and Brendan in Dublin, for John, who had come down with a fever and dysentery, and for Billy, too.

The Van der Roots had steadfastly refused her requests to see John or Billy. Consequently, Nora found herself caught in a dilemma—whether to pray that the Van der Roots would change their minds, or to curse them for their cruel refusals. Cursing was a habit she had never acquired, and one she was not at all comfortable with, but nothing seemed to be as satisfying as condemning father and son.

Damn the Van der Roots!

Damn the chains they'd put on us!

How dare any human presume to place another in bondage?

Damn. Damn. Damn.

I am sorry, Lord, but cursing helps me survive.

Nora raised up on her elbows as Liam, the older man who had taken over Billy's job collecting slops, came trudging down the aisle. Liam spilled more than he gathered, but he did bring Nora fragmented news.

"Your brother," Liam said with a shake of his head. "He's not eating. I'm worried for the lad."

Fearfully, she asked, "And Billy?"

"In a deep sleep. He hallucinates. Feverish." He shrugged. "It's up to the good Lord."

Liam trundled away, mumbling to himself.

Nora lay back on the plank, torn between uttering prayers or curses.

*****

During the next few days, Nora thought conditions couldn't possibly get any worse, but, damn it, they did. I have to stop cursing, she told herself.

Rations were cut in half. Captain Van der Root hadn't brought enough provisions on board for three hundred prisoners and crew. What food there was had become infested with weevils and worms. Rats foraged voraciously, biting and burrowing beneath shifts and breeches, leaving disease-carrying fleas and lice behind. Typhus and dysentery became common. On an average day, six prisoners died, many of them children. Among the dead were Mauve Madden's ten-year-old son and thirteen-year-old daughter. Mauve was grief-stricken, inconsolable.

Billy, hovering between life and death, had little or no chance of recovery, while Anne was gradually getting better.

Early one morning on his rounds, Liam stopped beside Nora. He said, "I am sorry to be the one to give ya sad news, but yer brother passed on during the night."

Nora felt a sudden emptiness, a deep sense of loss, as another part of her soul shriveled and died. "Thank you, Liam," she replied quietly. She settled back on the planks and shook as tears flowed.

Anne, who had been awake beside Nora, comforted her, even though she herself was still suffering. "I am so sorry, Nora. John was a wonderful young man."

Later in the day, Nora, Anne, and several others were brought up from below to witness burials at sea. Nora's throat constricted when she saw John's body, along with an older woman and two children, laid out on the deck in their soiled, tattered shifts—rags that fluttered in the breeze while they remained so deathly still.

Nora stared at her brother's emaciated face, so youthful and yet so worn.

Oh, John, I am so sorry you had to die, she thought. You were too young, and so very special. Thank you for teaching me how to shoot a gun and hunt and fish, and how not to cry like a girl when I got hurt. You were the smartest, bravest brother in the whole world. I will miss you forever. And I will always pray for your soul.

As Pieter read a passage from a timeworn Dutch bible, she continued to gaze at John, reflecting on earlier times when she and her brothers had played together on the family farm in Ireland.

Those had been happy, trouble-free days. How had everything disappeared so quickly? Were Da, Mam, and Brendan alive, or had they, too, passed on?

When Pieter finished his eulogy, a gust of wind whipped across the deck, almost taking away Pieter's feathered hat. He caught it, pressed it firmly onto his head, and motioned to two seamen standing by the bodies. They picked up the older woman, carried her body to the railing, and dropped her over the side. Next, came the children. They, too, slipped beneath the waves, one after the other.

"Oh, Nora," Anne said, "my heart is breaking."

Blond strands whipped across Nora's face as she wrapped her arms around Anne, attempting to gain solace for her aching heart. "I know, Anne. I know," Nora whispered as they lifted John's body, momentarily rested him upon the top rail, and then pushed. John splashed into the sea and disappeared, leaving no trace that he had ever existed.

A quote from one of Da's books popped into Nora's mind. "Ay, but to die, and go we know not where."

Shakespeare? Perhaps. Nora couldn't remember. But it raised the eternal question: Does everything end when one stops breathing, or is there life, some kind of existence, after death? She certainly hoped and prayed there was an afterlife. Otherwise, all of their endeavors, relationships with friends and foes, family and lovers, along with the joys and sufferings in the world were pointless—or cruel—or both.

*****

After the burial at sea, Nora felt despondent for days, wishing that she, too, would be taken. Is life really worth living? she asked herself. Down deep, she knew the answer. Of course it was. But there were times that she was sure God was testing her perseverance.

Her moods rolled like the swells of the sea. She had good days and bad days. But it was her sense of responsibility to Anne—and to her family in Ireland—that reconnected her with her innate optimism. Nursing Anne back to health helped her to cope with the grief of John's passing.

Mauve Madden, since the death of her two children, was slowly shrinking away in mind and spirit. One morning, she didn't wake up. Mauve, Nora was sure, had died from a broken heart.

Soon after Mauve's burial, the weather cleared, and Nora had a new plank mate, Nell Ryan, who simply slid over from her prior position opposite Mauve. Nell was a widow in her fifties, who would exclaim "Hallelujah!" whenever the prisoners were brought topside.

When Nora and Anne were on deck, Nora could see that young Van der Root was still smitten with Anne, and that her friend would have nothing to do with him. Anne had explained that she would never forget that Pieter had stood by and done nothing when she was strung up to the yardarm and beaten almost to death.

The captain, who wore a permanent scowl these days, stayed mostly on the poop deck, smoking his pipe. Was Jan ruing his penny-pinching ways, now that so many of the prisoners had been lost to typhus and dysentery due to his inadequate management of food? That would surely help to account for his perpetual frown.

Billy was nowhere to be seen. Had he died?

*****

Back on the planks with Anne beside her, Nora was staring up at the constant leakage and contemplating the likelihood of Billy's death, when Liam trudged by with his slop buckets. He stopped beside her and announced, "'Tis a miracle, if ever there was one."

"What miracle?" she asked.

"Billy Devlin woke from his deep sleep. He's alive."

Nora's heart leaped. "Thank God!"

"He's been causing a ruckus, and now he's confined below decks for the remainder of the voyage. Weak as he is from fever and whippings, that boy is as mad as a caged alley cat."

Nora grinned. That sounded like Billy Devlin.

"Nora," Anne remarked. "That's the first bit of a smile I've seen on you in a long time."

"I'm happy our friend is going to recover."

Anne gave Nora a perceptive look. "Maybe Billy is a little more than just a friend?"

Was Billy more than a friend to her? Nora contemplated. She shook her head, unable to come up with an answer.

"Nora?" Anne prodded.

"I . . . I find him interesting," she finally allowed.

"It seems to me you find him *more* than interesting."

Nora conjured up an image of Billy's head on the body of a bumblebee. He was circling a bed of flowers, buzzing about in a frenzy, attempting to taste nectar from each bud in a field full of blossoms. Nora half-smiled at her imaginings. "I don't believe he is right for me," she said.

"Be that as it may, he likes you and you like him. I can tell."

"Billy is attracted to any female that will respond to his silly ways, and besides, these are not normal times. There is no sense in thinking about a relationship with a man who is soon to be auctioned off as a slave. No sense at all."

CHAPTER TWENTY-TWO

Nora began to breathe easier as Anne's health improved, even as others on the ship fell ill and died. And while Nora continued to mourn John's death, the pain of his loss, while never going away, lessened a little each day.

A fortnight after the whippings, Anne's scabs were gone. And while the lacerations were still a dark purple, they were well on their way to healing. Nora hoped the scars might fade over time.

As for Billy, Nora gleaned occasional snippets of information from Liam: Billy is still confined to the planks. Billy has almost fully recovered.

At the end of the seventh week at sea, Nora and Anne, along with the other chained female prisoners, stood naked on the *Goede Hoop*'s deck, washing their shifts and themselves with buckets of saltwater. Standing beside them were seventy-six of the original one hundred female prisoners who had sailed from Dublin. Twenty had died from disease, and four others, unable to stand the horrifying conditions aboard the slaver, had committed suicide. Of the original one hundred children onboard, thirty-one had perished.

As the women finished their cleansing routines, the crewmen, who had long ago given up ogling them, gathered the small wooden tubs and set them against the railing for the next rotation of prisoners.

Nora and Anne, hampered by their ankle chains, donned their damp shifts, enjoying the warm breeze that would soon dry the threadbare fabric.

A buzz of excitement had been growing all morning above and below decks, as the coast of Virginia had been spotted on the horizon before sunset the day before. Now, in the late morning, the *Goede Hoop* had sailed into Chesapeake Bay. Nora marveled at the vast body of water lying inland from the Atlantic Ocean. There seemed to be no end to the length of the inlet, which was bordered by the mainland to the west and a peninsula on the east.

Nora's eyes widened as she counted several merchant ships in the distance.

Anne asked, "How did those people get here? How did they cross the vastness of the ocean and find this place?"

"Navigation is all a mystery to me, but, thank God, this nightmare of ours will soon be over."

Captain Van der Root barked an order from the poop deck. "Helmsman, port tack!"

The helmsman leaned into the whip staff, and the frigate changed course. The ship's new destination—a freshwater tributary.

*****

Later, the female prisoners, sitting topside, were finishing an evening meal of moldy bread and watery fish soup.

"That was awful, as usual," Nora said.

"Puke," Anne concurred.

They set aside their empty bowls and rose awkwardly to their feet.

The first thing Nora noticed was a settlement on the bank of the wide river. "That must be Jamestown," she said. She pointed to a group of rustic buildings lining a wharf that backed up to a timber-walled fort that was built in the odd shape of a triangle. Nora saw two large ships that had dropped anchor a hundred feet from the docks. There were also several smaller vessels moored nearby.

Captain Van der Root barked, "Reef zailen!"

Deckhands scampered up webbing to reef the great square-rigged sails that snapped in the wind. Some of the sailors pulled in lines, furling canvas in loose rolls to the yardarms, while others bundled the unwieldy sheets and battened them down with sturdy lengths of cord. Within a short time, only one small sail remained fluttering on the bowsprit. The jib captured just enough wind to keep the frigate maneuverable. Captain Van der Root, who had pushed aside the helmsman, was now manning the whip staff as he steered a course to bring the *Goede Hoop* close to the wharf.

A seaman, balancing a small tray of mugs, staggered up to Nora and Anne. He handed each a cup. "Captain salute Jamestown," he said in halting English. "Blessed tot of rum."

Nora and Anne exchanged amused looks; the man had obviously had a few drams already. After an exaggerated bow, he moved on, passing mugs out to all the women. The indulgences were gratefully accepted by the women, who had clustered together in excited anticipation.

Nora tasted the spirit and wrinkled her nose. "Oh my, this is no treat."

Anne sniffed the rum and blinked; the fumes made her eyes water. "I would throw it overboard, but it might kill the fish."

"Oh, look!" Nora said, pointing over the railing to the bay's clear blue-green water. A turtle, at least four feet from nose to tail, swam unhurriedly beside the hull, only inches below the surface.

"I've never seen such a big turtle in all my life!" Anne exclaimed.

"Look! Look!" Nora added as a school of fish, flashing silvery scales in the sunlight, darted past them, pursued by a stingray.

"Oh, my goodness, a devilfish! This is incredible! So many . . . and they're all so different."

"Beautiful," Nora wholeheartedly agreed. She pulled her attention from the aquatic display to an array of buildings lining the wharf. With the exception of what might be two new offices, the structures were one and two-story wood-framed homes and shops with stone chimneys and bark-slatted roofs.

Beyond the odd-shaped fort, the land was heavily forested and surrounded by swampland. Nora, recalling pictures from her father's books on botany, identified the tall, knobby "kneed" trees poking above the wetlands as Cypress trees. She recognized the towering, majestic magnolias with their dark green leaves and huge white blossoms. She'd seen several specimens in Ireland, which had been imported from China many years before.

Nora marveled at the landscape. It was all so wild and different. It truly was a new land.

As the ship drew near the wharf, she could see shoppers, merchants, clerks, and families, who wore everything from work aprons to suits and dresses, scurrying along a cobblestone lane that was noisy with the clatter of horsemen, carriages, carts, and wagons. At the end of the quay, several ox-drawn drays piled high with barrels waited in line as bare-chested men rolled large casks up a gangplank onto a schooner. The markings on the barrels read: VIRGINIA TOBACCO.

Nora had a sudden thought. Was it possible that some of those barrels contained tobacco from Running River Plantation?

Seeing Jamestown with all its activity brought home the reality that their shipboard nightmare would soon be at an end. She was really here, where her family wanted her to be.

Her thoughts flew back to Dublin. Had Da, Mam, and Brendan survived? Would they be following on the *Aurora* or the next available ship? Dear Lord, she prayed, please let it be so. And John, dear John. How close he had come to seeing this new world!

The crack of a whip brought Nora's focus to a heavyset guard who was yelling and laying lashes across the back of a short, emaciated black man struggling under the burden of an enormous barrel. The African, for that's what she recognized him to be, was the only dark-skinned man among the white slaves. Where had he come from? What was his story?

Looking over the top of the fort's log wall, Nora discerned the square steeple of a church, along with many additional structures. The population of Jamestown was larger than she had imagined. A few hundred people could easily live within the confines of the fortress, and new buildings were under construction everywhere.

One building in particular stood out from the others. It was two stories tall, and built of gray fieldstone. Black shutters framed its windows. A forbidding presence, Nora thought. A flagpole stood before it, flying a pennant with a white background bisected by a red cross—the Cross of Saint George. The colors of England!

In spite of the heat, Nora felt a chill traverse her spine. Yes, she now recalled, Virginia was an English colony.

"Anker!" Captain Van der Root yelled.

The anchor's thick chain rattled through the hawse pipe and the two-armed shank splashed into the bay. A crewman pushed past Nora, crawled out onto the bowsprit, and began furling the jib.

Nora and Anne reached for the railing to steady themselves. The hull's forward motion shuddered to a standstill as the *Goede Hoop*'s anchor held fast, having successfully purchased a piece of earth. All at once, the breeze fell off, and the August heat engulfed them in a warm, misty embrace.

Nora gasped. "Anne, this humidity, it's like we're standing in front of a steaming tea kettle."

"Look at our shifts. They're clinging to us as if it had just rained."

Nora could see their figures clearly through threadbare smocks. "We look rather indecent, if that were possible anymore." She glanced back to the wharf, where men were loading and unloading goods. It was no wonder the men were working half-naked. Jamestown, with its muggy air and wetland marshes, was going to take some getting used to.

"Ja! Ja!" Jan shouted proudly from the helm, admiring his seamanship at bringing the frigate safely to its mooring. He motioned to his son down on the main deck. "Pieter, roeiboot."

Pieter laid his pipe on a water barrel and withdrew a small red and yellow flag from his inside breast pocket. He crossed to the railing, where he fastened the pennant to a line and pulled it upward. The international symbol for harbor service fluttered to the top of the mast.

Nora connected Pieter's action to two men on the wharf who yelled a greeting and then scampered down a ladder to crawl into a long boat. The men raised a pair of oars and began rowing toward them.

Jan van der Root left the helm and stepped down to the main deck. He crossed to the rail to stand by Pieter. "You stay. I go ashore, make arrangements, ja?"

"Ja," Pieter responded.

Nora raised her mug and sipped, barely tasting the stringent brew as apprehension bore into her like a weevil chewing into a wheel of cheese. The captain was going ashore. Most likely the "arrangements" he'd be making would be to sell the prisoners, including Anne, Billy, and herself. Would he return the documents he'd stolen before she was led off the ship? Not very likely. As for the coin he'd pocketed, she knew she'd never see that again.

Her mouth set in a hard line. She had to recover Da's papers! She glanced about. Crewmen were everywhere. Even if they weren't, being shackled to Anne would make any attempt to get the documents almost impossible.

The rowboat knocked up against the side of the hull, and a deckhand threw a rope ladder over the railing. Captain Van der Root climbed down into the boat and was being rowed toward the wharf when Nora spotted Pieter's pipe lying on the step.

Her pulse quickened. She turned to Anne and whispered, "Don't drink any more."

"I have no intention of doing so," Anne replied. "It's awful."

"Move with me," Nora whispered.

"What?"

"Shh." Attempting to act nonchalant, she led Anne over to the water barrel where Pieter had left his pipe. Nora's nose twitched at the fine wisps of smoke drifting up, accompanied by the pungent aroma of tobacco.

She made a furtive search of the deck. Pieter was looking ashore and no one else was paying them any attention. Nora snatched the pipe and quickly hid it by her side.

"What are you doing?" Anne whispered.

"Shh," Nora repeated. Her heart was pounding so hard she was sure it would give her away. "Come with me."

What a stupid thing to say. As if Anne has a choice, she berated herself.

Nora and Anne hobbled over to an open hatch and glanced down. Several bundled sets of sails were stored below.

Nora whispered, "Pour your rum into my mug."

A puzzled look crossed Anne's face, but then she shrugged. "Gladly." Anne emptied the strong-smelling liquid into her friend's cup.

Forcing herself to remain calm, Nora glanced around once more as if she were admiring the view. Satisfied that the crew was occupied with shipboard duties, she again whispered, "Move with me."

Nora and Anne surreptitiously moved closer to the edge of the hold. Standing beside it, Nora tipped the contents of her mug into the hatch.

Rum splattered onto the sails. Even that small dribbling sound gave Nora the shakes. She nervously raised Pieter's pipe, turned the bowl upside down over the hold and, as quietly as she could manage, tapped it against the side of her empty mug.

Glowing embers spewed into the void.

"Pray," she whispered.

"Oh, dear Lord," Anne said almost inaudibly as concern twisted her features. "Shouldn't we best move away?"

"Yes, over to the hallway." Nora started off, dragging Anne along. Linked together, they sidled beneath the overhang that led to the officers' cabins.

A tipsy crewman ambled up and stopped in front of them, holding out a pitcher of rum. "Virginia. Goede, ja? Meer rum. Proost, ja!" he said, suggesting that they join him in a toast.

Nora and Anne raised their cups. While the deckhand filled them, Nora nervously kept an eye on the open hatch.

Nothing.

Then, a wisp of smoke wafted into the air.

Nora drew her lower lip between her teeth. Please, catch fire!

The Dutchman raised his mug. "Proost!"

A thicker curl of smoke followed the first, and a surge of excitement raced through Nora.

"Proost!" the crewman repeated with a frown of irritation.

"Yes," Nora answered, eyes flashing. "Yes, I believe we will. Shall we toast, Anne?"

Anne nodded tensely. They clinked mugs.

The Dutchman grinned happily, "Ja! Goede. Proost!"

"Proost!" Nora and Anne said in unison and then sipped at their rum, eyes riveted to the rising smoke.

"Gezondheid!" the crewman said and staggered off.

"Shouldn't we move further away?" Anne asked nervously.

Before Nora could answer, a yellow-orange tongue of fire burst from the hatch. The ensuing roar of flames momentarily paralyzed the crew.

"BRAND!" a Dutch voice yelled. Then the Irish prisoners cried out, "Fire! Fire!"

Deckhands scrambled to retrieve buckets, calling for help. Prisoners milled about in frightened confusion.

Nora took hold of Anne's hand. "Come along. Hurry."

"Where are we going?"

"No time to explain."

Slowed by the twelve-inch chain fastened to their ankles, Nora led Anne into the short hallway behind them.

*****

Nora threw a quick glance over her shoulder to make sure they hadn't been followed. Everyone was yelling and running about, focused on the fire. She turned her attention to Captain Van der Root's cabin door. Drawing in a nervous breath, she grabbed onto the brass handle and pushed down. The door opened!

"Are we really doing this?" Anne asked incredulously.

"I'm not leaving this ship without my father's documents. I'm sorry I have to drag you along with me."

"I'll do anything to get back at that horrible man," Anne replied in a quivering voice. "After you."

The girls ducked inside, closing the door behind them.

Hurry! Nora's inner voice shouted.

Nora led Anne over to the captain's desk and reached for the top drawer. Please don't be locked. She pulled on the handle, and it slid open. Yes! The belted pouch was right where Jan had left it.

Scooping it up, Nora checked its contents. Da's will and the deed to Running River Plantation were there. She exhaled with relief, then pursed her lips as a new dilemma presented itself. How was she going to wear the pouch without it being obvious under her shift? Jan van der Root had previously noticed the bulge under her dress. It was going to be even more pronounced beneath her thin smock. Damn.

Nora lay the pouch on the desktop and quickly rifled through its contents to see what she could discard. Nothing. Without the documents, there would be no new life in Virginia.

Fighting back tears, she remembered her promise to Da that she would keep Running River Plantation in the family.

She would never break that promise.

Anne glanced nervously at the door. "Nora . . ."

"I know. I know. Let me try something." She quickly spread the documents out on the desk into single sheets. She folded and compressed them, and replaced the flattened documents in the canvas pouch. Better, she thought, looking at her handiwork. She lifted her shift and fastened the belt about her waist. Lowering the garment, she studied the results.

"There's still a bump," Anne said.

Nora reevaluated the bulge. It was smaller, but still obvious to the curious eye. She exhaled deeply and tightened the muscles in her midriff; her stomach became noticeably flatter. "All right, I can do this," she said tightly, holding her breath. "Let's go!"

They hobbled to the door, opened it, and peered out. The short hallway was empty, but on the deck beyond, crewmen were throwing buckets of water down the hatch as flames raged furiously.

Nora and Anne exchanged terrified looks.

Nora suddenly thought, Good Lord, will I be responsible for burning up the ship and killing us all?

The girls watched as several crewmen ran up with buckets of sloshing water and upended the containers into the hold. Flames sputtered and died, producing a thick cloud of smoke. Encouraged, they yelled exuberantly, calling for more buckets. Additional pails arrived and were emptied. When the smoke began to clear, two men jumped down into the hold and, seconds later, were tossing out smoldering pieces of canvas. Others quickly scooped the soaking, charred remnants from the deck and tossed them overboard.

Voices from the hold shouted triumphantly, "Het vuur is uit. Het vuur is uit!"

Nora gathered from the relieved faces around the hatch that the sailors had announced, "The fire is out."

Heart racing, she whispered. "Let's go." She led Anne from the hallway to the edge of the deck.

"What you do?" a voice thundered.

Nora almost jumped out of her skin.

Jakob came bounding down the stairway from the poop deck, carrying his ever-present whip. He stopped before them, blocking their way.

Attempting to rein in her panic, Nora answered as evenly as she could, "We were keeping out of the way."

Jakob's eyes darted to men tossing the last of the burned canvas over the railing, and then tracked back to them. Nora remembered to pull her stomach in and hold it. Jakob glanced to the hallway they had just vacated. His eyes narrowed.

Crack!

The girls jumped. Jakob laughed. He had slapped the whip against his thigh.

Nora quivered as Anne's hand found hers and tightened. The Dutchman, she knew, was a dangerous bully, but he also had the tendencies of a little boy who enjoyed cruel pranks. Seeing their terrified looks, he assumed he had frightened them—and he had. Jakob grinned, then waved the whip toward the prisoners lined up against the far railing. "U go!"

Nora started to exhale with relief but caught herself just in time as she remembered to hold her stomach flat. Hoping her face wasn't turning blue, she nodded to Jakob. Then she and Anne hobbled past the Dutchman to stand with the female prisoners.

"You can breathe out now," Anne whispered.

Nora released a whoosh of air. "Ah, much better."

179

Anne suddenly looked worried. "What will the captain do when he returns and finds out you've taken your belongings?"

"Anne, I'm hoping we'll be off the ship before he discovers it. If not, he might connect the theft to the fire, and then he might just hang us. I'm sorry I dragged you into this."

"You didn't have much choice," Anne answered. "If we hang, we hang together."

*****

Would the captain return and discover the pouch was missing before they disembarked? Nora wondered as she lay on the fetid planks, sandwiched between Anne and Nell Ryan. If so, it wouldn't take him long to suspect that she had started the fire as a diversion so she could take back her father's papers. The more she worried, the louder her heart thumped. He was going to come to that conclusion. She knew it.

The sound of something knocking against the side of the ship suggested the return of the cutter.

As if to confirm her suspicion, Captain Van der Root's muted but distinctive growl resonated through the hull. "Komende aan boord!"

"The Dutch prick is back," Anne said.

A short time later, the iron hatch creaked open. Jakob cursed loudly, "Stinkende hell hold." He climbed down the ladder, his boots squishing into the filth on the floor. There was the rattle of chains as they scraped through restraining brackets. Jakob barked, "Go! Go!"

"What's happening?" Anne asked.

Nora propped herself up on her elbows as male prisoners crawled from their planks into the aisle.

Nora cocked her head. "Listen. . . ."

Oars could be heard slapping water. Faint voices. English voices.

180

Nora felt the hull moving. "I think we're being towed."

"Aye, that we are," Nell confirmed. "I heard the ship will be moored at the docks so they can unload us."

As prisoners trundled past them down the aisle, a feeling of sadness fell upon Nora like a heavy cloak. Most of the Irishmen were limping, coughing, and wheezing. After almost eight weeks at sea, their clothes had been reduced to rags. How many men, women and children had died during the crossing? She couldn't think about that or she would cry.

Jakob was at the base of the ladder, prodding the prisoners. "Go! Go!"

"Anne," Nora said, "once we're ashore, we'll find a way to contact the authorities and inform them that we are free Irish citizens. I'll tell them that the captain stole my money, kidnapped us, and has been holding us against our wills."

"But how do we prove it? Do you think they'll take our word against the captain's?"

Anne was right. No one would believe them. They had no receipts to prove they paid for their passage. If they were to press charges against the Van der Roots, they would have to do so using the surname under which they traveled—Smith—which presented a dilemma. To substantiate her claim of being a free Irish citizen, and to vouch for Anne, she would have to show the authorities Da's last will and testament and the deed to Running River Plantation, which would prove her to be an O'Lalor. Damn! That would surely put a noose around her neck, as the O'Lalors were murderers in the eyes of English law! And, by association, it wouldn't take them long to realize that Anne was an O'Moore and also a fugitive. It was hopeless.

While it was too early for the authorities in Jamestown to have heard of the crimes they were accused of and of their spectacular escape from Dublin Bay, news of the event was sure to arrive on any of the next ships from Ireland.

God in heaven! What was she to do?

An imagined voice, as soft as a gentle kiss, materialized out of thin air. *Nora, hold onto Da's will and the deed to*

THE GIRL WHO WAS ME IS GONE

Running River Plantation. As long as you possess them, you have proof of ownership. When it is safe to reveal yourself as Nora O'Lalor, you will be able to claim your inheritance. But for the present, to remain safe, you must continue to be Nora Smith.

Nora paused, absorbing the message she had just *heard.* Ever since she was a child, Nora had perceived this *inner voice.* It had confused her. Where did it come from?

Mam had explained, "Everyone hears inner voices. Some people are more receptive than others. The ancient Druids called it a gift and claimed it was the dead's way of communicating with the living. But that's all conjecture. What we do know is that *voices* are a part of our intuition. These inner voices also provide us with a conscience, to help us distinguish right from wrong. In the end, it is up to us as individuals to decide whether to act upon these conversations with ourselves or not. A wise person listens, but always questions the messenger."

That was probably as close to an explanation of where the voices came from as she would ever get, although she was certain prayer had something to do with generating these ethereal communications.

Only moments ago, she hadn't known how she could survive in the New World, but now, because of this *message,* she knew there was a future. She had to save Da's precious documents.

"Thank you", she said to the silent voices that had been so supportive in her life, yet were beyond her understanding.

Footsteps sloshed up the aisle, interrupting her musings. "Ah, if it isn't my own Nora Smith as I live and breathe."

She twisted around.

Billy Devlin, trudging forward, was bringing up the end of a line of prisoners. Like the other men, his only article of clothing was a pair of ragged breeches. He flashed a lopsided grin and added, "As pretty as an Irish rose."

182

Nora grimaced at the painful-looking scars covering Billy's torso. "Hardly a rose at all," she responded. "More like a wilted cabbage."

"I'm very partial to cabbage." Billy said. "Once we are on shore, please don't go changing your name."

"Oh, and why not, may I ask?"

"I'll be wanting to find you. 'Tis not for myself, mind you, but for you, as I'm sure you'll be longing to see my handsome face once again."

She almost laughed as she thought, He's presuming I actually give a cat's meow about him. Yet, to be entirely honest, I wouldn't mind casually bumping into him again, only because we were once neighbors. God knows, he isn't the type of man I would ever wish to be involved with romantically. He is, she reminded herself, rude, incurably flirtatious, and much too into himself.

On the other hand, to give the devil his due, Billy is handsome and well-educated, and he does come from a cultured family. But as my grandmother used to say, "Good breeding offers no guarantees. There is always the chance of birthing a blockhead."

Finally responding to his question, she said, "I hate to mention this, but if fate separates us and we never see each other again, I will survive."

"Ah." He clutched his chest melodramatically. "You've broken my heart. All this time, I thought you were mad for me."

Billy was suddenly yanked away, and she was left staring after him with her mouth half open.

Mad for Billy Devlin? He truly was a blockhead!

*****

Nora lay cramped between the sweating bodies of Anne and Nell Ryan, listening to the clanking and scraping of chains as the last round of male prisoners left the deck and descended the gangplank.

Finally, after being confined below decks for most of the day, the women and children were finally going to depart. Nora wanted to shout, "Hallelujah!"

Now what? Would they be taken directly to the auction yards? Further unsettling questions came to mind. Who would be buying them? Would she and Anne be separated? Uncertainty cramped the muscles in her stomach.

Minutes later, chains that had been strung between the women's calves were unlocked and pulled through restraining rings, freeing the prisoners. Jakob slapped the end of his whip noisily against the shelving. "Up! Up!" he ordered. "U go! U go!"

"Gladly," Nora muttered. She helped Anne slide from the shelf into the walkway, where ladies were stumbling and leaning on each other as they trudged toward the ladder. As they passed by, she noticed two women who lay motionless on planks, no longer breathing. Their glazed eyes stared sightlessly into a world that, for them, no longer existed.

"Oh!" Anne moaned as her foot hit a slop bucket, splashing sewage over her feet. Catching onto Nora's arm, she said, "I'll never get this smell out of my nose or my hair."

Washing was a priority for Nora, but certainly not the most pressing one. She touched the bulge beneath her shift. The slim pouch held all of her hopes. Her lips set in a firm line. There would be obstacles to overcome, of that she was sure, but with the help of God, she and Anne would prevail. Her first hurdle would be to win their freedom. How she would manage that was elusive, but she would find a way.

As long as she had a breath of life left in her body, nothing was going to stop her from achieving her goal—to honor the promise she had made to her father, to keep the land in the family.

Somehow, someway, she would claim the family plantation.

CHAPTER TWENTY-THREE

Nora and Anne hobbled down the gangplank. Both of them were relieved that their wrist manacles had been removed, along with the short length of chain that had linked prisoners together in pairs. Each still wore individual ankle cuffs, so walking remained awkward.

Anne stepped onto the wharf and latched onto Nora's arm. "Oh, the ground is moving! Or is it me?"

"I feel it, too. It's like we're still on the ship, rolling with the motion of the sea." Suddenly Nora's eyes widened. "Look." She pointed. "By that building."

"Indians!" Anne exclaimed.

Six natives, four males and two females about Nora's age appeared to be bartering with a local merchant. Nora raised an eyebrow.

Those weren't the primitive, wild savages she'd heard about. They were as tall as any white person, and surprisingly attractive, with slim, mahogany physiques. The men's heads were particularly interesting, shaved on one side, long black hair adorned with eagle feathers and small trinkets on the other. They were dressed in simple breechcloths, and were barefoot.

When the Indian women turned, Nora blinked and looked closer. They were wearing leather skirts—with no tops.

"They're bare-bosomed!" Anne whispered in shock.

"I noticed," Nora said, finding it difficult to take her eyes off the group. "It must be their custom."

The youngest girl's hair was cut very short, while the older one had shaved the top of her head and had a long braid that trailed down her back, made of the surrounding hair. Both males and females wore bracelets and necklaces of seashells, and had multiple ear piercings adorned with freshwater pearls, shiny pieces of copper, small animal bones, and claws. They also exhibited a number of tattoos.

"Do you think they've killed and scalped settlers?" Anne asked.

"I hope not," Nora replied tentatively.

"You two," a guard yelled at them. "Keep moving!"

Nora pulled her gaze away from the Indians. She and Anne followed the line of prisoners across an open stretch of cobblestones and walked through tall wooden gates at the fort's main entrance to the center of Jamestown. Their arrival drew a gaggle of men, women, and children. Some stared curiously, while others ignored them. A group of unsavory males in scruffy clothes moved close to ogle and harass the women. Nora's ears burned at the filthy, obscene proposals that were called out in English and other languages, followed by raucous laughter.

"They're animals!" Anne said with disgust.

"Animals are not profane," Nora said.

"Stay back!" a brawny guard yelled, threatening several men who tried to touch the women. The guard cracked his whip over their heads. "Back, I said!"

The hecklers retreated but continued shouting vulgarities. The prisoners were led across the compound toward a group of three fenced corrals already filled with men and children.

Nora and her female companions were herded toward the empty pen. Entering the women's corral. Nora glanced to a wooden platform just outside the fence. Six feet above the ground, it looked large enough to hold half a dozen people. It had to be where the prisoners were displayed when they were auctioned off.

How long would it be before she and Anne were standing up there? she pondered. Would the horrible, shouting men be the very individuals who'd be bidding for them? Just the thought of being owned by a lecherous dog of a man made her blood run cold.

Entering the enclosure, Nora's nose crinkled at the all-too-familiar reek.

"I'm going to be sick," Anne wailed. "Will we ever get away from the stink of shit and piss?"

Nora, trying not to inhale, spotted the source of the stench—a raw cut in the earth that overflowed with sewage. As prisoners filed past the filth, large black flies rose in a cloud, buzzing and swarming ferociously around them.

"Oh, Lord," Nora exclaimed as she and the women swatted wildly. Several slaps connected, with bloody splats appearing on faces, arms, and legs.

Anne gave Nora an incredulous look when she saw that there were no barriers around the latrine. "Are we supposed to squat out there in the open?"

"We're not going near that putrid bog. We'll dig our own pit and take turns standing around each other when we use it."

Still batting at flies, Nora and Anne came to a standstill in the middle of the pen. Armed men, as many as a dozen, stood outside the railings, keeping a watchful eye on the prisoners.

"Nora," Anne said, casting an eye at the raised platform. "When we're auctioned off, we'll be separated, won't we?"

"Likely so," Nora responded, knowing the odds of them staying together were slim.

"Making slaves of other human beings is the cruelest thing on Earth."

Nora's face suddenly lit up as she spotted Billy. He was standing at the fence, separated from the women's pen by a four-foot path patrolled by guards.

"There's Billy. Let's visit," she said as an excuse to avoid thinking about their probable parting. Nora and Anne shuffled over to the railing.

"Cheers on your birthday, Nora," Billy said, offering his lopsided smile.

Nora's eyebrows shot up. "Birthday?"

"Yes. Today is your seventeenth birthday."

Nora blinked, surprised, and stared into his honey-brown eyes. "How could you possibly know today is my birthday?"

"August first, is it not?" Billy touched his slightly crooked nose.

The gesture made her recall a memorable happening that had occurred a year ago at her sixteenth birthday party, when Billy, a guest, had led her to a corner away from the crowd and kissed her. When he'd slipped his hand down the front of her dress and pinched one of her nipples, she had punched him—and broken his nose! Hence the slightly crooked proboscis. She smiled. "How could I ever forget? You deserved that."

"Perhaps, but you could have hit my shoulder and saved my pretty nose."

"Actually, I think it's an improvement on the old one. But please, tell me how you know today is August first. I don't even know what month it is."

"It's in the stars. All you have to do is look at the night sky, and you'll see the days, weeks, and months. Of course, one has to be intelligent enough to read the heavens."

"Oh, and that would be you, Mr. Intelligence himself." She added dryly, "You've proven that many times."

Billy responded with a self-deprecating shrug. "Nora O'Lalor, or rather Nora *Smith*, we started off rather unfortunately, and for that I wholeheartedly apologize. I can assure you, in spite of my previous ill-mannered reach for your bosom, a very lovely one at that, I want you to know that I am truly a gentleman."

Nora couldn't help but smile at Billy's outlandish attempt at an apology.

"Nora, once you get to know me better you will find that there's much more to Billy Devlin than meets the eye. I believe you might fall in love with me if you give it half a chance."

The gumption of him! But despite Billy's braggadocio ways, Nora had to acknowledge he was charming in a rascally sort of way, like a naughty but loveable little boy. "Billy," she said, "within days we'll be parting, possibly never to see each other again."

"There's no chance of that."

"Really? How can you be so certain?"

"I have the *gift*." He tapped a finger to his temple. "The Devlins are descendants of ancient Druids. We have powers to predict the future."

Containing the urge to laugh, she listened as he went on.

"I want you to know this. I have loved you since the first time I laid eyes on you. You were but a wee lass and I was just six."

Oh, good Lord! she thought. Back in their childhood days, she'd had a crush on Billy, too. Did she dare confess that? No, what good would it do? It was too late. Much too late.

"Wherever you are taken," Billy continued, "I will find you. And I will free you, even if I have to fight my way through an army to make you mine. You see, Nora O'Lalor-Smith, you and I are destined to be together."

"Is that so?" she said.

"That you may count on." He flashed his silly grin and then reached down to pick a sprig off a wimpy little plant. He held it out across the path. "A birthday present."

Amused, Nora reached out and took the offering. Squinting at the sprig, she asked. "What is this?"

"A flower."

"No, it's a weed."

"Look harder, and you'll see what I see—a beautiful flower."

"Uh-huh."

"Now, keep it close to your lovely breast, and every time you see it, you'll think of me."

"But what if all I can see is a weed?" she teased.

"Then you will have broken my heart."

*****

Later, after they had been fed their morning gruel, Nora sat with Anne on the hard ground, eyeing two men who had begun questioning the female prisoners and writing responses on a tablet. The younger of the two, short and middle-aged, eventually stopped beside them.

"Names?" he asked, his full, red beard barely moving.

Nora's breath quickened, but she calmed herself. "Nora Smith."

He scribbled on his pad. "Can ya read an' write?"

"Yes."

"Math? Can ya add, subtract?"

"I can add, subtract, multiply, and divide."

The man's eyebrows rose. "Is thet so?"

"Yes, that is so," Nora replied. She motioned to Anne. "And my cousin, Anne Smith, can also do math."

"Most unusual." Red Beard looked to Anne. "Yer name is Anne Smith?"

"Yes."

He wrote her name down. "A good many of the women can read an' write, but very few do math. Ya'll bring a good price."

"That makes us very happy," Nora said sarcastically.

"It should," he replied, missing the sarcasm. "Ya'll have it better'n most, ya can be sure of thet. A gentleman or a tradesman is sure to buy yer contract."

"What is this contract?" Nora asked.

"It's an agreement you sign that states yer ta work off the debts ya incurred on your passage to Jamestown."

Never mind that their passage was already paid for! Nora thought with a quiet rage.

Anne asked, "How will we know how much the captain has charged for our passage?"

The bearded man said, "That's up ta the captain of the ship ya arrived on. He figures out yer debt an' then sells ya ta an auction broker ta cover his expenses. Thet's why yer here, an' it's how the captain gets his money back, with a bit of profit. Then the auction broker here in the yards sells ya ta pay himself back, with a bit more profit. The man who ends up buying yer contract must bid high enough ta cover these costs, and then ya belong ta him. He owns ya, body an' soul, until ya work off yer debts. It's simple, really."

"How long does it take to pay off these debts?" Nora asked.

"For most, it's between five an' seven years. Others never pay off their contracts, an' are lifelong debtors."

"How can they do that?" Anne blurted out. "It's sinful."

"Thet's the way of it, sinful or not," the bewhiskered man replied.

"When do they auction us?" Nora asked.

"Right about now." As he walked off toward another group of women, he added, "The young'uns go first."

Reeling from the thought of "belonging" to another human being "body and soul" for five to seven years, Nora reaffirmed her oath: I will never be a man's chattel! Never!

She glanced over to the men's enclosure. Where was Billy?

She could see that the male prisoners were also being questioned. Then she caught sight of Billy. He was seemingly taking a nap as he leaned against a rail in the men's pen. As far as Billy Devlin's talents were concerned, she knew he could read and write, but doubted with his flighty temperament that he'd had the patience to learn math. Billy's one weakness, as far as she knew, was his disdain for anyone he thought unworthy of his time, or a fool. And Billy considered most people to be fools. Nora sighed. Billy would probably end up being bought by a landowner and sent to toil in the fields.

"The Van der Roots are leaving," Anne said, interrupting Nora's thoughts as she pointed toward the bay.

Nora looked over the fort's timbered barricade. The *Goede Hoop* had left the wharf. The frigate's topsails billowed in the breeze as it pulled away from Jamestown, headed toward Chesapeake on its way to the Atlantic Ocean. Nora had heard that the Van der Roots were sailing to Africa.

"Pieter saved my life," Anne said quietly.

Nora knew her friend was probably right. If Anne had stayed below decks in the *Goede Hoop*'s filthy, rat-infested hold, it was likely she would have perished. Pieter wasn't nearly as bad as Jan was. She said, "But then, his father almost killed you."

"It was my fault for stealing Pieter's key."

"No! Jan's whippings went beyond normal punishment. The father is a cruel man." Nora felt a degree of satisfaction when she realized the Dutchmen had obviously not discovered she had taken back her da's documents. "Anne, I was raised to never wish ill on anyone, but it would bring a smile to my lips if the good Lord were to strike Jan van der Root's fat head with a lightning bolt."

CHAPTER TWENTY-FOUR

Nora and Anne swatted at flies as they stood shoulder to shoulder with other female prisoners, watching the children's auction unfold. Three at a time, they had their shifts removed, and were prodded, naked, up the short flight of steps to stand cowering in front of a crowd that consisted of several dozen prospective buyers. The bidders were a conglomeration of men and women, English and foreign merchants, tradesmen, and plantation owners. Some were looking for cheap labor, others for "companions." A couple of sea captains waited nearby for the men's auction, hoping to pick up crewmen. Curious onlookers had also assembled, wanting to be part of the festivities.

Nora's heart felt like a stone as she watched a boy and two girls cowering before the crowd, attempting to cover their nakedness with their hands as spectators hooted and made ribald comments. Potential buyers hurried onstage to inspect the children. There was no thoughtfulness or consideration given as they were thoroughly examined for lice, oral health, signs of pox, open sores, deformities, and muscular fitness.

Nora said, "How can people be such beasts?"

"Those poor children," Anne said. "I can't imagine what's going to happen to them."

"The sad thing is, most have no family, and no one to care if they live or die. They are at the mercy of whoever buys their contracts."

"Like us."

"Yes, like us."

"All right, it's gettin' hot as Hades, ladies and gentlemen. Let's get this show started." The auctioneer was a heavyset, officious man in his mid-forties, who had been standing to the side of the stage while the children were inspected. He stepped to the front of the platform and shouted to the crowd, "These are fine Irish youngsters, healthy and sound of mind. The boy is ten, the girls eight and eleven." He gestured to the adolescent females. "Look at them, fit and strong. And one day, those flat little chests are going to start budding and growing. They'll make fine breeding stock."

The audience hooted and hollered.

"Monsters," Nora said.

"Opening bid is five pounds for this pretty little eleven-year-old lass," he said, pointing to a skinny, dark-haired girl with tears running down her cheeks. "That's for a five-year contract. If, during that time, any of the girls sold here today become pregnant, the baby as well as any other children they bear will belong to the man or woman who purchases their contract. At the end of five years, the mother can leave her child or children behind and go free or, if she so chooses, she can stay on with her child or children and remain an indentured servant for the remainder of her life. So, folks, remember when you are making your bids that you are buying a prospective mother with potential offspring, which will increase your investment many times over." He turned to the bidders on stage who were inspecting the girls. "All right. Finish up. After you own them, you'll be able to spend as much time as you like with them."

Rude laughter swelled from the crowd.

Nora said, "I can't watch any more of this."

"Nor I."

*****

An hour later, Nora returned to the bidding platform. The sun had risen higher in the sky. With its ascent, the stultifying wave of humidity increased, dampening the prisoners' shifts so that the material clung to them like another layer of skin. The children had all been auctioned off, and the male prisoners were now being brought to the stage two at a time. Breeches were removed and naked bodies inspected.

Nora glimpsed Billy Devlin on the platform as she and Anne inched forward in the crowd of women prisoners to be within earshot of the auctioneer.

"An' here we have a rare specimen, a young man who can read, write, and do math. Let's begin with an opening bid of fifty pounds."

Billy stood naked and proud. Nora knew she shouldn't be staring but found herself unable to pull her gaze away. Billy, despite whippings in Ireland and savage beatings on the *Goede Hoop*, looked, for all the world, like a drawing she had once seen of Michelangelo's Statue of David. His scars did nothing to diminish his appearance. In fact, they added to the powerful image of masculinity.

Nora had never thought in terms of a man being beautiful, but her eyes widened now as she accepted the notion that Billy, perhaps with the exception of his slightly bent nose, was indeed as close to being beautiful as any man she had imagined in her wildest musings.

She flinched. He was staring at her with those honey-brown eyes. His lopsided grin appeared, and she felt a quickening of her heart.

Embarrassed, she grabbed Anne's hand and they slipped back into the crowd of women, planning to move as far away as she could. But then she heard the auctioneer's voice, "An' not only can this man read, write, an' do math, but he is also an accomplished navigator."

Nora stopped in her tracks, her mouth agape. A navigator?

"A navigator, my friends!" the auctioneer repeated. "A man who can read the stars, sail the seven seas, an' return home to the exact port whence his journey began. This man is worth a fortune. Let the bidding begin. Do I hear fifty pounds?"

A murmur of excitement rose from the crowd.

How had Billy become so well versed in sailing while living in landlocked Athy? It was incomprehensible. Then it came to her that, had Billy been successful with his mutiny onboard the *Goede Hoop,* he would have been able to guide them to a safe port.

She cringed, feeling a wave of guilt. She had been so wrong about him. Other than having perceived him as a handsome scalawag, she knew much less about Billy Devlin than she had thought.

Two distinct voices, one Portuguese, the other English, clamored over each other in a spirited bidding war. Fifty-five pounds, sixty pounds, sixty-five pounds, seventy pounds, seventy-five pounds, eighty pounds, and then one hundred pounds! The Portuguese who had made the last bid glanced to the Englishman, who hesitated.

The auctioneer called out, "I have one hundred pounds. Do I hear 105 pounds?"

The Englishman shook his head in defeat.

"Sold to our Portuguese friend, Captain Diego de Almeida."

Billy had been purchased by a sea captain. Nora would never see him again!

Her heart contracted as if one of her life-supporting arteries had shriveled up and withered away.

*****

"We're next," Anne said apprehensively.

Nora's pulse quickened as she touched the pouch beneath her shift. She had to time this just right, or everything would be lost.

Only minutes ago, the female prisoners had been moved to the holding pen. An older guard had stood watch as the women removed their garments. Two at a time, with clothing in hand, they were urged up the stairs by the guard. As soon as the women stepped onto the platform, spectators began to murmur, commenting on their anatomy. Several prospective buyers clambered up on stage to inspect them more closely.

The auctioneer began. "Here we have two beautiful ladies in their early thirties. That means, gentlemen, they have years of good labor in front of them. As you can see, both are healthy and strong, and still of childbearing age. I'm asking for an opening bid of five pounds each. Remember, gents, these females come with a five-year contract."

Nora leaned over, feeling as if she had just been kicked in the belly. Even though she had heard of these contracts before, the reality of losing five, six, or seven years of her life hit home.

"Are you all right?" Anne asked.

"No, but I will be," she replied, straightening up. "This is all so sickening."

"I know," Anne said, shaking her head. "It's as if we've been caught in a never-ending nightmare."

"You two, clothes off," ordered the guard standing at the foot of the stairs.

Nora and Anne exchanged uncertain looks.

The auctioneer's voice boomed above them as the biding increased for the two women on the platform.

"Clothes off!" the guard repeated.

Nora reached beneath her shift and furtively began to untie the belted pouch. The guard frowned when he noticed her fumbling, so she pretended to massage a sore hip.

When the man kept staring, Anne whispered, "I have an idea." Stepping in front of Nora, she began to pull her smock up over her shoulders. She stopped, struggling as though the fabric were caught on her head, while at the same time exposing her voluptuous bosom. "Someone help me, please," Anne pleaded.

Bless you, Anne, Nora thought as the guard's eyes widened until they were the size of goose eggs. When Anne asked again for help, the man forgot all about Nora and hurried to Anne's side to assist her.

Nora, in one fluid movement, slipped the pouch and shift off and rolled them up together, hiding the bag.

"Thank you," Anne said to the guard who had helped her pull off the smock. The man stood speechless as he stared at the lovely young woman before him. Then, suddenly remembering his duty, he stepped quickly back as the previous women came down the stairs and into the possession of the winning bidders.

"Well done," Nora whispered.

"It was so easy," Anne replied.

"Next," the auctioneer called. "Hurry it up, ladies. We have anxious buyers waiting to give you new homes."

Nora swallowed nervously, hoping the bulge in her rolled-up shift wouldn't be noticeable as she followed Anne up the stairs. She immediately knew she didn't have to worry about the pouch being seen. All eyes were on her and Anne. Stepping forward, they maintained their dignity despite the lewd, unnerving catcalls. Nora wasn't bothered so much by the obscenities, as she had heard their like before. But the twisted, leering faces of the men—and women—sent a spasm of disgust through her.

How was it that ordinary people became such insensitive and lecherous animals when presented with female nudity? she thought. It was frightening! And how was it that Indian girls like the ones they'd seen when they disembarked could walk around bare-breasted without being harassed by the settlers? Perhaps the difference was anticipation. These disgusting beasts could purchase females, including young girls, and then do anything they wanted to them. It was horrific!

As the raucous comments continued, she and Anne covered their privates as much as possible with their hands and stared back defiantly.

"And here, ladies and gentlemen," the auctioneer said, "here we have two of the most gorgeous young ladies I have ever laid my eyes on. Look at those figures. You'd think we all died and went to heaven." He looked up and screamed, "Hallelujah! Thank you, Lord!"

The spectators guffawed and hooted. Several of them started for the stairs, but the auctioneer held up his hand. "No, no, no. With these two, there's no touchin' until you buy. Only after I have your money in hand can these two young beauties . . . be in your hands."

Groans and bawdy rejoinders were the loud response.

"Our first prize is Anne Smith. She's the shorter, buxom one. Anne can read, write, and do math. She will make any gentleman or gentlelady, merchant or tradesman, a proud owner. The opening bid starts at a very reasonable twenty-five pounds."

The crowd grumbled.

"Do I hear twenty-five pounds?"

"Twenty-five pounds!" yelled a muscular man in his fifties with small, black eyes and the brutish face of a brawler. Standing beside him, a head taller, was a man in his mid-twenties with long dirty hair, a full, unruly beard, and an oddly cherubic face. Both men studied Anne with eyes that made Nora's stomach crawl. Please, Lord, Nora prayed, don't let them buy her.

"Thirty pounds," countered a female merchant.

"Thirty-five pounds," the first bidder grunted.

"Do I hear thirty-six pounds?"

"Thirty-six pounds," a tall man in buckskins offered quickly.

"Rufus," the auctioneer addressed the brute, "do I hear thirty-seven pounds?"

Rufus barked, "Thirty-seven pounds."

"Do I hear thirty-eight pounds?"

"Thirty-eight pounds," the man in buckskins responded.

Nora noticed the brawler's face darken.

"Do I hear thirty-nine pounds?"

The woman bidder shook her head, dropping out.

Rufus stared hard at his competition, and growled, "Thirty-nine pounds."

Nora saw the man named Rufus say something to his companion. The wild-haired man's pale blue eyes fixated on the other bidder, and then he moved over to stand beside him.

Nora could see the two men exchange looks. The man with the cherubic face pulled out a long skinning knife and began to clean his fingernails. He grunted something that, from a distance, was inaudible to Nora. The bidder in frontier clothing blanched and stepped back as if he had been threatened.

"We have thirty-nine pounds. Do I hear forty pounds?"

Silence.

"Gentlemen," the auctioneer yelled, "look at this angel, this female goddess. What man wouldn't want to possess her? Think of the long, cold nights ahead. She is worth every shilling of forty pounds. If I could afford her, and I didn't have a jealous wife, I'd buy her myself. Who will bid forty pounds?"

Silence.

The auctioneer shrugged and threw his arms into the air. "All right. Going once . . . going twice . . ." He slammed his gavel onto the podium. "Sold to Rufus Pitt!"

"Oh, Nora," Anne said with a tremor in her voice. "He's so awful-looking. What will I do?"

Nora's heart went out to her friend as she replied sadly, "We will survive, Anne. Whatever it takes, we will survive."

The auctioneer motioned to a guard, who came up to Anne, allowed her to pick up the shift she had dropped at her feet, and then led her off the stage.

"I love you, Nora," were Anne's parting words.

"Be brave, Anne," Nora called after her.

Standing alone on the platform, Nora had never felt so vulnerable as she stared out over the heads of the crowd, determined to ignore the smirks and leers.

"Our last angel is Nora Smith," the auctioneer yelled. "Look at that figure—*unbelievable!* She's young, she's beautiful, and she's ripe for the taking."

The crowd howled.

"She's also intelligent. Nora can read, write, and do mathematics. She can take care of your books and your 'special needs' for years and years. You can breed her and produce a whole flock of little field workers. What you're looking at is value, real value, with a built-in pizzle warmer."

Hoots and hollers erupted from the crowd.

"Now, who can resist an opening bid of twenty-five pounds? Only twenty-five pounds to own this magnificent piece of womanly temptation?"

Nora closed her eyes and shut out the auctioneer's voice. She forced her mind to drift to Dublin and her family. Da, Ma, Brendan, are you alive? Please, be alive. I need us to be together again. John, oh, dear John!

Nora felt the auctioneer's hands settle on her shoulders, and her eyes opened. She was spun around for the customers to admire. As the bidding increased, her toes nudged her shift and the treasure hidden within.

How ironic it was that she was standing on documents that might very well assure her future, while men and women were bidding to take it away. Whatever happened to her during the next few weeks and months, she vowed, would not defeat her. Somehow, she would be free! Nothing would stop her from claiming what was hers by right of birth and inheritance.

"Thirty-five pounds." A man's strong baritone voice rose above the hubbub of the crowd. Nora's attention went to one of the few well-dressed men in the throng. He was of medium height with a slim physique. Wire-rimmed spectacles rested on a long, aquiline nose. His dark blue eyes seemed alive and intelligent. His hair, curling at the back of his neck, was brown turning to gray. She guessed his age to be late fifties or early sixties.

"Thirty-six," countered a heavy-set merchant.

"Let's raise the stakes by five," the well-dressed man said. "Forty-one pounds."

The crowd murmured. The merchant shook his head. "Too rich for me."

The auctioneer's gavel came down with a resounding smack, "Sold! Nora Smith, sold to Mr. Gerald Knox for forty-one pounds!"

CHAPTER TWENTY-FIVE

Sold for forty-one pounds as if she were an animal! Nora's stomach churned at the memory as she looked out over the crowd. Then a more pressing thought took precedence. Da's documents! She bent down and scooped up her smock with the hidden pouch, and prayed for an opportunity to replace it about her waist without being seen. Stepping down from the bidding block, she saw her chance. The closest guard was prodding two women up the ladder, momentarily ignoring her. Nora turned away from him and, as she slipped on her shift, fumbling with the material, she secured the pouch beneath the smock. Patting the fabric down, she turned back to the guard, half expecting to be called out.

He wasn't paying her the least bit of attention.

*****

Several minutes later, climbing up into the open carriage of her new owner and taking a seat in the rear of the coach, another worry began to gnaw at her. Who was her owner? Owner! What a foul thought.

"The first thing we need to do, Miss Smith, is to find you some decent clothes," Gerald Knox said as he climbed in and settled into the back seat, facing her.

Nora studied her new "owner" quietly, with a mixed sense of interest and relief. He didn't appear to be a lecher, and he was certainly not a brute. Poor Anne—the man who'd purchased her had seemed awful! Somehow, some way, she and Anne would reconnect and escape the circumstances that had so unjustly enslaved them. Da would be furious when he discovered their plight, and would certainly come to rescue them . . . if he was alive.

Finally, Nora turned her thoughts back to Mr. Knox. She assessed his expensive clothes: tailored black coat, white shirt, tan breeches, and black shiny boots. He was obviously well off, and handsome in an aesthetic way. And he had an air of importance about him. Something else caught Nora's eye. He seemed withdrawn, preoccupied, even somber. Yes, somber was the right word; there was a melancholy cast to his features. Curious. . . .

If appearances said anything, she ventured that Mr. Knox would be a formidable adversary in a business transaction. In fact, she thought with a start of surprise, he was a bit like Da. Only Da had a happier countenance, or at least he'd had before the troubles.

Nora's attention moved to the driver, whom Knox had called Mr. Nolan, as he climbed up onto his seat. He was a medium-sized, wiry man somewhere in his forties, with short, auburn hair, green eyes, and a hard-chiseled face. He carried a pair of flintlock pistols in his belt, along with a saber and a dagger, and he projected the cool self-confidence of a man who knew how to use them.

Mr. Nolan lifted the reins and slapped them on the hindquarters of a pair of dappled grays. As they pulled away from the auction yard and onto the main cobblestone street of Jamestown, Nora glanced from side to side, absorbing the environment. Jamestown was nothing at all like the villages and towns in Ireland. The buildings were relatively new—not one appeared to be much over twenty years old. Construction was going on everywhere. The streets and sidewalks were bustling with coaches, wagons, drays, merchants, shoppers, children, and more than a few half-dressed Indians.

As the newness of her surroundings began to fade, Nora again lent her thoughts to her owner, or at least to the man who thought he had purchased her, body and soul, for the next five years.

"Miss Smith," Knox said, startling her. "Nolan will drop me off at my office and then take you to purchase two dresses, one for every day and one for Sunday. You may also select one pair of shoes and any personal incidentals you may require."

"Thank you, sir," she said, rubbing her wrists where shackles had left scars.

"You will then be driven to my residence, where you will be shown your room and also my office, which is where you'll be working. You are to familiarize yourself with the staff. Besides Mr. Nolan, there is Mrs. Gibbs, my housekeeper, Ginny, the cook, Millie, the maid, and an assortment of children. Your position is to be my personal assistant. You will help me with correspondence and bookkeeping. My last accountant died of the flu three months ago, so I'm afraid my books are a frightful mess. You will have your work cut out for you, Miss Smith, I can assure you. And one more thing. You are not to leave the property without my permission."

Heat rushed to her cheeks. She was not to leave the property without his permission? His residence was to be her prison for the next five years? Well, she huffed in silence, we'll see about that!

On the verge of giving Gerald Knox her opinion on his ridiculous statement, she checked herself and replied with forced politeness, "Yes, sir." Frowning, she was aware that while Mr. Knox had mentioned the staff, he hadn't mentioned any members of his family. Was he a bachelor? Or had he a wife and children?

Her thoughts refocused when the carriage wheeled to a stop in front of the second largest building she had seen in Jamestown. The sign in front read:

House of Burgesses
Established: 1624

"Nolan," Mr. Knox said. "I'll take a horse from the stable and be home an hour before sunset."

"Yes, sir."

Knox descended from the cab and strode up the walkway to the imposing structure. After he entered, Nolan wheeled the buggy around, and they proceeded up the street.

"Mr. Nolan," Nora asked, turning in her seat to see the driver, "what would happen if I were to disobey Mr. Knox and go for a walk off the property?"

Mr. Nolan looked at her if she were a child. "That would be very stupid, and dangerous to boot. I think you'd better understand this. Mr. Knox owns you—*owns you*—for the entire time of your indenture. You are his property. He can do whatever he likes with you. He can beat you, whip you with a cat o' nine tails, brand you, or even bed you. And if you fight him, he can even have you hung—all legally."

Her hands curled into fists. "I'll murder him if he tries to bed me."

Nolan spat. "And soon thereafter, you'll be swinging from a tree. Young woman, you had better get used to the idea of being a servant. And remember this, the only thing that separates you from being a slave is that you work in the house. Slaves work the fields. Same people, different locations."

"I'll never be owned by any man!"

Nolan's green eyes seemed to soften when he said, "It's the way of it. Can't fault the system myself. There's no such thing as a civil society without social rules and laws. They have to be enforced."

Instead of arguing, which she knew would be fruitless, Nora asked, "What is the House of Burgesses?"

Nolan spat.

Rather an annoying habit! she thought. His spittle would have sprayed her if the wind had been blowing! To show her displeasure, she made an issue of brushing imaginary spit from her arm.

Ignoring her obvious vexation, he answered, "It's where English bigwigs gather to hold court and record deeds to the land they steal from the local Indians."

"They're stealing land?"

"They're English, aren't they?"

She gave him a second glance. *Interesting.* Yes, there was truth to Nolan's inference. The English had stolen a great deal of Ireland.

"Is Mr. Knox a bigwig?" she asked.

"I'd say so. He's a wealthy plantation owner, a Jamestown assemblyman, and he occupies a seat on the governing council." He added, "Not such a good occupation at the moment."

"Why is that?"

"They're all bloody Royalists."

Nora knew that Royalists were backers of the former king of England, Charles I, who had recently been beheaded by Cromwell and his followers, who now governed the English under the name Parliamentarians.

Nolan added, "When Cromwell's navy shows up, these Burgesses boys will all be scattering like a flock of sheep with a wolf at their heels." He spat. "I'm Irish, same as you. As you may ascertain, I don't like much about the Royalists, but they're a lot better than that bastard, Cromwell. I'd slit that one's throat if presented with the opportunity."

Nora cocked her head. Is the man serious? Probably not. Nolan was just mirroring the sentiment of most Irishmen. She certainly knew the feeling. Cromwell's army and his pernicious laws had decimated her family as well as the entire population of Ireland, leaving behind pain, misery, and death.

Curious to know more about the driver, she asked, "Where are you from, Mr. Nolan?"

"Dublin. You?"

"Portlaoise. Near Athy."

"I know it. Good people, mostly."

"How long have you been in Jamestown?"

"Arrived as an indentured servant in '40, after the English kicked our Irish asses during the rebellion."

"My da lost a leg in that fight."

He turned to her. "A leg, you're saying. Smith . . . I don't recollect any Smith that lost a leg. But I did fight alongside a good Irishman who did, name of Henry O'Lalor."

She almost blurted out, *That's my da!* But her survival senses went on high alert. She had to change the topic of conversation before she inadvertently revealed her birth name. "That was nine years ago, Mr. Nolan. Why aren't you a free man?"

"It's a long story." Nolan spat.

"Must you spit so much?" Nora complained, this time really wiping spray from her arm.

"Sorry. Bad habit."

"Why aren't you a free man?" she persisted. "Aren't there limits to indentured service?"

"Yes, there are limits, and I am a free man. I'm content to work for Mr. Knox for the time being. He pays well for an Englishman. I will say that for him."

"Do you have relatives in Jamestown?"

"You ask too many questions."

"Sorry." Nora frowned. She was curious to know Mr. Nolan's history, but since he was obviously reluctant to discuss the matter further, she pursued another topic. "Mr. Knox didn't mention having a family."

"It's not something he talks about. He had a wife, a son, and two pretty little daughters. They were murdered."

"Oh, my Lord. How did it happen?"

"Powhatans. They're the local Indians. The tribe finally grew tired of settlers stealing their land. They attacked us in '44. Slaughtered 500 men, women, and children, Mr. Knox's family among them. The colonists were finally able to organize and go after the bastards. Sorry to curse. They tracked them down and wiped out almost the entire tribe. Over 2,800 Indians were killed. That put an end to the hostilities." He spat. "Although there will never be an end to it until all of those heathens are planted in the ground. You can't blame them, I suppose, for fighting for their lands, but a savage is still a savage. If they should find you alone, they'll just as soon kill you as look at you."

"I'll try to keep my distance."

He gave her a lingering look. "Although, being as pretty as you are, they might just keep you for a plaything."

She blinked, unsure how to reply. His words had been both a compliment and a warning. Perhaps silence was best.

Nora's thoughts drifted to Mr. Knox. He must have been devastated by the loss of his wife, son, and daughters. She took in a deep breath; she knew too well the heartache of losing family.

CHAPTER TWENTY-SIX

"Again, Willie! Again!" Rufus ordered.

Anne's heart tightened as the dirty, longhaired man with the gentle features of a cherub slapped Trish across the face, knocking her to the floor. The thirteen-year-old rolled over, wiping blood from her trembling lips. She seemed to be struggling to maintain a brave face, but then her features crumbled and she began to cry.

"Stop it, please," Anne pleaded. "She's just a little girl."

"Not your concern," Rufus snarled. "She does what I tell her ta do. Ya better remember thet. Now keep yer mouth shut."

Trish's offense, Anne had learned, was that she had refused to be prostituted to the filthy trapper who stood nearby with wicked anticipation, chewing tobacco that dripped down his bearded chin. Trish was to be his bonus for selling a bundle of beaver pelts to Rufus.

Just hours after arriving at Rufus Pitt's home and trading post on the outskirts of Jamestown, Anne had discovered that Rufus not only traded in sundry dry goods and animal skins, but also in prostitution.

I'm to be living in a bordello/trading post! she thought.

Willie was Rufus's manager and disciplinarian. He presided over Trish and twelve-year-old Nell. Each girl had her own small room in the log structure, which consisted of an assortment of added-on log buildings with shingled roofs. The main trading room, where they now stood, was lined with stacks of smelly salt-cured hides, barrels of whiskey, clothing, tools, and traps for catching every kind of animal. A trestle table sat in the center of the room with an accompanying straight-backed chair. Four scarred leather armchairs encircled the stone fireplace, where low flames devoured split oak.

"You do what I tell ya, ya understand?" Rufus moved to hover over Trish. He grabbed the girl's hair and yanked her tear-streaked face back. "Ya belong to me, and yer ta do exactly what I say!" He motioned to Willie. "Or this one cuts yer ears off. That's the truth of it!"

Anne shuddered when Willie pulled a skinning knife from his belt and started to clean his dirty fingernails, the blade emphasizing the threat.

Rufus added, "Now git over there with Jeb!"

Trish's teary eyes sparked with hatred, but then the fire faded and her shoulders sagged.

"Ya give him a good time now," Rufus ordered. "Ya understand?"

Trish ignored him, wiping her face and staring at the floor.

Rufus grinned, displaying large, yellow teeth. He pushed Trish toward the trapper. "Jeb, if she gives ya trouble, ya jest let Willie know."

"Come 'ere, cutie." Jeb grabbed Trish, picked her up, and threw her over his shoulder, giving her a slap on the bottom. "Trish, I be thinkin' yer about ta fall in love." He chortled and left the room, slamming the door behind him.

Revulsion ran through Anne. She was owned by the devil, and she would be living in hell.

Rufus grabbed a jug of whiskey from the table, took a long swig, and passed it to Willie. Rufus turned to her. "Ya learn from thet. Yer ta do what I tell ya. It's my girls' job ta make my customers happy. Thet's how I make my livin', by tradin'. The trapper's git what they want, an' I git their business. Ya understand thet?"

Anne exhaled with a seething rage that simmered within. She quietly promised herself, *I will never be brutalized again!*

Nor will I engage in carnal activities with *any*one to make this horrible brute money.

Her sexual relationship with Pieter had been different. He had been one man, and their cohabitation had saved her life. Pieter had also been kind and gentle.

The thought of shagging filthy trappers made her physically ill. She stared at Rufus. He had threatened to have Trish's ears cut off if she didn't service the trapper. Would he threaten to do the same with her?

Anne glanced at little Nell, who stood by the fireplace. The eleven-year-old's eyes were as wary as an orphaned kitten. Had Nell gone to bed with men under threat of mutilation? The answer to both questions was obviously "yes." Rufus Pitt was a callous, immoral beast. The man's ugliness and overwhelming size were fearsome. But she promised herself, I will never become this monster's whore! On the verge of crying, she asked herself, What would Nora do? Anne knew the answer. She would be strong.

Easier said than done. Anne was not Nora. All she could do was try.

Steeling herself, she said, "Mr. Pitt, you may have bought my services for five years, but you do not own my body."

Rufus whipped around with the snarl of a bulldog.

Nell stepped back quickly, her eyes growing wide.

Willie, to the side of Rufus, grinned with amusement as he continued to clean his fingernails.

Heart thumping, Anne continued with tremulous defiance, "I will do your accounting for you, keep track of your inventory, and clean up this pigsty you live in, but I will not ever, *ever* prostitute myself for you!"

Rufus yanked his own skinning blade from its sheath. He stepped up to her and jammed it against her throat. "Is thet so?" he demanded, reeking of whiskey.

Anne recoiled, but it wasn't from the foulness of his breath. It was from the sensation of warm blood trickling down her neck. The bastard had cut her! On the verge of panic, knowing the blade might slice through vital arteries at any second, she realized she might die.

But, surprisingly, the terror that had been mounting suddenly waned, and an inner sense of calm took hold. She would not give in to this monster! With her new sense of strength, she realized she was fully prepared to let Rufus murder her if it came to that, but she would never, ever, acquiesce to any of his salacious demands.

Staring into Rufus's piggish black eyes, she raised a hand and slowly pushed the blade away. Mimicking his pronunciation, she said, "Thet is so."

Rufus's eyebrows shot up. Unexpectedly, he cackled. "Goddamn. This one's got fire in her belly, Willie."

The cherub-faced lout nodded, and something akin to respect appeared in his pale blue eyes.

Rufus chuckled again. "I like thet."

Willie spoke in a strange new voice, one as cold as ice, "Leave her be, Rufus."

The burly trader exchanged a long hard look with Willie. Finally, Rufus shrugged and sheathed the knife.

Anne's brow wrinkled. Why would this rough trader accommodate his employee?

"Yer lucky, little lady," Rufus said. "Lucky thet I be needin' a bookkeeper." He pointed to Nell, who looked as if she had just witnessed a miracle. "I can always git more like this one, but you, ya be somethin' special. Hell, ya'd better be. I paid a fortune fer ya." He peered straight into Anne's eyes. "Ya help me figure out my business, and I'll let ya be."

She'd done it! A wave of relief swept over her. She'd actually done it! Thank you, Nora.

"Anne Smith," Rufus continued sternly. "Ya never forget this. Yer mine fer five years. If'n I've a mind ta, I can do with ya what I likes. Ya jest remember thet."

Anne imagined Nora whispering in her ear, Stop him right there! Don't let him get away with that!

Anne leveled her gaze at Rufus. "If we're going to work together, Mr. Pitt, you'll treat me decently, without threats."

Rufus's mouth dropped open.

Willie guffawed.

Recovering, Rufus said, "Yer as bad as my old wife. The poor woman never stopped tellin' me what ta do till the day she died."

Anne had locked eyes with Rufus and was waiting for a response to her demand.

Rufus wavered, and then broke eye contact. Backing off, he took another swig of whiskey. The trader finally growled, "All right. Ya keep me happy *workwise,* and I'll treat ya jest like ya was one of my own family."

Anne suppressed a grin, even as she felt a smidgen of triumph.

But would the brute hold true to his word? She didn't know.

One step at a time.

*****

Don't people know how rude it is to stare? Nora thought, as pedestrians stopped to gawk at her flimsy prisoner's garb and bare feet while she followed Nolan along Front Street. Deciding to ignore the ill-mannered looks, she directed her interest to offices, shops, warehouses, and taverns on either side of the road. Most of the buildings were made of wood or brick, with glazed windows and slate, tile or planked roofs. The clanging of a hammer on metal drew Nora's focus to an open shed where a blacksmith stood beside a red-hot forge, shaping a horseshoe on an anvil as sparks flew around him.

Continuing on, they passed an apothecary, a tobacco store, a large livery stable, and a cooper's yard where wheels, wagon beds, and barrels were being fashioned from raw lumber. She marveled. Everything was all so new, so different from the centuries-old stone structures in Ireland.

One block later, they came upon a modest whitewashed wooden residence, surrounded by a picket fence. "This is Mrs. Miles's place," Nolan said. "She's a dressmaker."

Opening the gate, they walked up a garden path that was bordered by marigolds, bluebells, and white daisies. Nolan knocked on the front door, which was opened by a small, pleasant-looking woman in a seamstress's apron. Nora guessed her to be in her late forties.

"Good day, Mrs. Miles," Nolan said. "Mr. Knox would like you to make this young lady two dresses, one for every day and one for Sunday."

Mrs. Miles's nose wrinkled.

Oh, my, Nora thought with concern. I don't smell that bad. Or do I?

The dressmaker pulled a handkerchief from the pocket of her apron and raised it to her nose.

Oh Lord. I must.

Nora was on the verge of bolting when Mrs. Miles lowered the handkerchief. "Good day, Mr. Nolan. Yes, well, I can always use new business."

"This is Nora Smith, Mr. Knox's new secretary."

"Pleased to meet you, Nora."

"Thank you, Mrs. Miles. I'm so sorry that I'm not properly . . ."

"Pshaw," Mrs. Miles said, suddenly emanating sympathy. "I understand. You're just off one of those awful ships, are you not?"

"Yes, ma'am."

Mrs. Miles studied Nora's figure for a moment, and then nodded to herself. "Come in, come in, dear. This is your lucky day. I have just the dresses for you. You're almost the exact size of a customer who ordered two beautiful frocks and then moved away without paying for them. I believe you'll be very happy when you see them."

She turned and led them into a small but comfortable parlor. "Girls," Mrs. Miles called.

Seconds later, two young ladies, who Nora guessed were three to four years younger than she was, hurried into the room. Each wore a blue apron over a plain beige dress, and simple shoes. Their eyes darted from her tattered shift to her bare feet.

"Girls, this is Nora Smith. We are going to refit the two dresses we made last spring for Millie Burns for this young lady. I believe a few nips and tucks is all it will take."

As introductory nods were exchanged, Mrs. Miles turned to Nora. "But first, dear, you are going to have a bath. Mr. Nolan, you can wait here in the parlor or go for a walk, whichever you choose. Follow me, young lady." She turned to her seamstresses. "We'll need hot water for the tub. Come along, now."

Nora followed Mrs. Miles and the youngsters into the kitchen, and helped them as they began to fill a small tin bathtub. They used rainwater from a barrel at the back of the house and hot water from a large, steaming cauldron that hung on a bracket over smoldering coals in the fireplace.

As Nora slipped out of her shift, she noticed the girls eyeing the belted pouch secured about her waist. She said, "It's where I keep my personal things."

Her explanation seemed to satisfy their curiosity. They continued to busy themselves with filling the tub.

Nora stepped into the tepid water and sat. Oh, yes. . . . While the temperature could have been warmer, it was still heavenly! The seamstresses passed her a bar of soap and a washcloth. Nora raised the soap to her nose—lilac. She closed her eyes for a moment, inhaling the divine scent, and then smiled at the girls, who were staring at her with anticipation on their pretty faces.

Mrs. Miles turned for the door. "I'll be in the sewing room."

"Thank you," Nora said. "I promise I won't be long."

One of the girls offered, "Would you like your hair washed?"

"Why, yes. I would love that!"

When, Nora wondered, was the last time she had been so thoroughly spoiled? She recalled a time almost three months ago. Mam had been shampooing her hair in the kitchen, and they had talked about surprising Brendan for his upcoming birthday.

Mam . . . Da . . . Brendan . . . John. Her eyes welled as she washed up while one of the girls lathered her hair.

A few minutes later, Mrs. Miles bustled in. "Nora, you'll be needing something to wear while waiting for your new dresses." The woman gestured to a brown garment that she had draped over her arm. "You may have this. I believe it will fit you. It's seen better days, but it's clean, and it has a nice wool weave. It will do as an extra frock. A young lady needs more than two dresses."

"Thank you, Mrs. Miles," Nora said, feeling overwhelmed. "This is so very kind of you."

Her hair rinsed, Nora stood, picked up a nearby towel, and stepped from the tub. When the dressmaker glanced at Nora's shift and belted pouch lying on a chair, her mouth puckered. Ignoring the precious document carrier, she gingerly lifted the soiled garment with her fingertips, as if she were holding a dead rat. "This, my dear, we will burn. When you've dressed, come into my workroom and we'll get started."

*****

A short while later, Nora, wearing the brown dress, stood barefoot before Mrs. Miles, having her measurements taken. She smiled when the dressmaker showed her the two dresses that had been abandoned. One was a pretty gray cotton weave that would be more than suitable for every day. "Now for your Sunday dress. . . ."

Nora caught her breath as Mrs. Miles held the garment up for her to examine. "Oh, it's beautiful!" she exclaimed as she touched the light green material embroidered with petite flowers—yellow buttercups and white black-eyed Susan's.

Mrs. Miles smiled. "These dresses were costly, but since I won't be losing money on them now, I can give Mr. Knox a good price."

"Are you sure they're still not too expensive?" Nora said halfheartedly."

"Don't be silly. They will look beautiful on you, and after what you've been through, you deserve it." She placed her hands on her hips and added in a motherly manner, "You are not to worry about price, thank you very much."

Nora allowed herself to be coddled; it didn't really take much effort.

Once the measurements had been taken, Mrs. Miles, along with the two seamstresses, began the task of taking in a few seams.

To fill the time between fittings, Nora replaced the document pouch beneath the brown dress and wandered into the parlor, where Nolan, surrounded by samples of women's clothing, was looking as forlorn as a lost puppy. He glanced up and said in a pained voice, "How long is this going to take?"

"I would guess at least another couple of hours."

Mr. Nolan harrumphed. "Well, I can't wait in this place for two more hours." He stood and stretched. "Let's go for a walk."

"Where to?" she asked.

Nolan headed for the door. "To buy you a pair of shoes to cover those bare feet."

Shoes!

*****

Nora hurried to keep up with Mr. Nolan as they strode along Front Street. Looking past a gaggle of children playing on the boardwalk, she suddenly froze in her tracks. Oh, dear God!

Realizing Nora was no longer walking at his side, Nolan glanced back. "Nora, what's keeping you?"

Unable to speak, she stared at the far end of the street. An English officer and six soldiers were escorting three chained prisoners up the street. Bloodied faces and swollen, purple eyes were evidence that they had been beaten. She noticed that the two male captives were slightly older than she was, while the third, a young woman, was about her own age. They appeared to be Irish. Would Jamestown be like Ireland all over again? Did England have authority to arrest Irish in Jamestown merely because they were Irish? Or were they criminals?

As they tramped closer, Nora's lips tightened. There was pain and desperation on the prisoner's faces, yet a touch of rebellion shone through.

Nolan strode back to her.

"Irish?" she asked.

He nodded. "Indentured servants or slaves from the plantations, from the looks of them, runaways."

"What will happen to them?"

"Depends. If they're repeat offenders, or if they stole guns and sold them to the Indians, they'll be hanged as an example to others. The least punishment, I imagine, will be a good whipping, maybe fifty lashes, and having an "R" for runaway branded on their cheeks. They'll also have their contracts extended by three or four years. Any further trouble, they'll get the noose or be shot."

"It isn't right," Nora said, her temper rising. "Nolan, we're human beings, not animals. We have to try to help them. Please."

"Nothing can be done." Nolan spat. "It's the law. Without harsh penalties, the Irish would walk off the plantations and the colonies wouldn't survive another six months."

Nora seethed as the soldiers marched the prisoners past them. How long would it take before news of her "crimes" reached Jamestown? Two weeks, three? A few months? Would the English be able to figure out that she'd changed her name from O'Lalor to Smith? Not very likely, unless someone identified her. There was always that chance. It could happen any day.

Nora said angrily, "I don't like English soldiers."

"Nor do I," His green eyes narrowed at the intensity of her statement. "But certainly, they are no threat to you." When she didn't reply, he questioned, "Is there something you wish to tell me?"

"I don't care to discuss my life, if you don't mind."

He gazed at her for a long moment before he added, "As if anything that's happened in your young life could ever shock me."

Really, Mr. Nolan? she thought. You might think differently if you knew I was an escaped felon wanted for murder!

"Come along now," he said. "Let's buy you those shoes."

She didn't move until the soldiers and Irish runaways had disappeared around the corner of the livery stable.

Nolan spat. "You still want shoes, or not?"

"Of course, I still want shoes. You don't expect me to walk around barefoot all day, do you?"

*****

Nora's eyes lit up as she followed Mr. Nolan into the dry goods store. There before her, on racks, shelves, and tables, was a wide display of men's and ladies' clothing and accessories.

Surely, she thought with wonder, this merchandise hadn't originated in Jamestown. It must have been imported from Europe.

"Go on," Nolan encouraged. "Off with you. Enjoy."

"Oh, I will," she replied, putting thoughts of the Irish prisoners temporarily at bay. "This shop is heavenly."

The driver stood by the front counter as Nora began to browse. She couldn't help but grin as she inspected an assortment of female finery and toiletries. Finally, gaining courage, she began to charge incidentals—a bar of soap, a comb, a hairbrush, and a plain white nightgown—to Mr. Knox's account.

Oh, if only she had her own money, she could have such a grand time! No, she corrected herself. If she had her own money and *if* she were free—then she would shop like a Parisian countess and buy, buy, buy.

Sighing, lamenting the fact that that awful Dutch captain had stolen the family's money, Nora strolled down an aisle, gazing idly at this and that, until her eyes fell upon a frilly white item. Oh, my! She was staring at the loveliest white bonnet she had ever seen. It was so, so, pretty! She glanced around. Not a soul was watching her. She *had* to try it on.

She picked up the frilly cap, which was fashioned from the dearest lace, and carefully placed it on her head. Whirling about to face a small mirror on the wall, she saw her reflection. Her mouth curved into a smile. It was exquisite! She glanced hesitantly at Mr. Nolan, who had just turned to look at her.

He screwed up his face as if he were judging an artist's painting, then nodded brusquely.

Barely able to contain her delight, she almost danced as she moved to the next table to see what other gems she might find. Within minutes, she had selected not one, but *two* petticoats. She held each up to her chest. These, too, were divine! She bit her bottom lip and cast a sideways glance at Nolan, hoping . . .

He shrugged—and nodded.

She squealed with joy.

Mr. Nolan almost smiled.

As Nora hurried over to place the additional acquisitions on the counter, the driver, whose voice conveyed a touch of impatience, said, "Shoes?"

"Please, Mr. Nolan, I'm doing my best."

The shoe section was small, and carried only one style of ladies' shoes. Nora's nose twitched with disappointment. These weren't shoes—they were boots. She couldn't see any difference between the men's and women's clodhoppers. While reaching for a pair of the offensive footwear, she accidently knocked a box off the shelf. A pair of ladies' ankle-high, black leather shoes tumbled out.

Oh, good heavens! Or as Mam would say, Jesus, Mary, and Joseph! Nora was staring at the most beautiful pair of shoes she had ever seen! Speechless, she reached down and picked them up with care, as if they were breakable china. Unable to resist, she slipped them on her feet before another customer could arrive and steal them away.

Oh, Lord. They fit! They actually fit! As proud as a barn cat with a mouse between its teeth, she paraded between the aisles. It was like walking on pillows. Surely, by some miracle, they must have been made especially for her! Nora stopped and looked at the price.

Her mouth dropped open.

One pound, six pence! She groaned, experiencing genuine pain. They were much too expensive for an indentured servant. As she sorrowfully forced herself to take them off, she felt like she was parting with a treasured friend.

"Nice shoes," Mr. Nolan said. He had come up quietly to stand behind her.

"Yes, they are," she said dolefully. "But they cost one pound, six pence."

"Mr. Knox said to buy you a pair of shoes. He didn't say what I could spend, so if he doesn't know. . ." He lifted an eyebrow. "You are going to be doing his books, are you not?"

Nora's pulse quickened. What was Mr. Nolan suggesting?

"He'll never know the cost if you don't tell him," Nolan said. He leaned down and whispered in her ear, "They're yours."

Startled, she protested, "I can't. I . . . I simply can't."

"Simply can't?" he scoffed. "Bah! You're too good, you are. Hand them here."

Nora passed the shoes to Nolan and followed him, with a lump in her throat, as he strode back to the proprietor and plopped them down on the counter. "Add these to Mr. Knox's account."

Coming up behind him, Nora gasped. "Oh, Mr. Nolan, I can't..."

"Shh," he interrupted gruffly. "Does it look like you're the one doing it?" He paused to let his words register. He added, "I take full responsibility. And you'd better not tell a soul how much they cost, or you'll be getting me into a world of trouble." Nolan leaned in close, his green eyes locking with her blue ones. "And I'm telling you, I'm not one you ever want to be in trouble with."

Seeing through his stern façade, she had to hold back a giggle. This was a whole new side of Mr. Nolan! Beneath that stony exterior, there just might be an endearing rogue.

"Mr. Nolan, I would never say anything to get you into trouble."

*****

Nora, wearing her new bonnet and shoes, and carrying a small bag with the rest of her new possessions, was almost skipping as she and Mr. Nolan returned to Mrs. Miles's home.

The seamstress presented her with two new dresses. While Nolan waited in the parlor, she undressed, taking her pouch off, and quickly tried them on. She looked in the mirror. She could hardly believe her eyes. The workmanship was so fine, and they fit her figure like a glove. Amazingly, they had been tailored to fit her in just a few hours.

"Oh, Mrs. Miles, thank you, thank you. They are both so lovely."

"Hardly that," Mrs. Miles responded humbly, but Nora could tell she was proud of her handiwork. "But then, Nora, they're nothing to sneeze at, either. My little girls have become excellent seamstresses."

"I love these dresses." Nora hugged them to her chest. Her joy was suddenly tempered by the thought of her best friend. Oh, Anne, I have new clothes and a respectable household to go to. I hope and pray you are all right. Have faith, my dear friend. One day we will both be free.

"Time to get on the road." Nolan's voice interrupted Nora's thoughts as he called through the closed door to the parlor.

"You can come in, Mr. Nolan," Mrs. Miles said.

Nolan opened the door, took one look at Nora, and grunted. "Nora, you look as pretty as a flower in a hog wallow."

"Why, thank you, Mr. Nolan, I can't remember ever having had a more unique compliment."

*****

Nora had to grab for her new bonnet as a gust of wind swept by the carriage, sending leaves cartwheeling down the street. She laughed as she resettled it on her blond hair. Nolan, beside her on the driver's seat, tossed her a quizzical glance.

"I'm happy," she explained. "I feel like a young girl with a box of new ribbons."

Nolan spat. "Wouldn't make a boy happy."

No, most assuredly not, she thought. Her brothers were never giddy over clothes, but girls were different, and she hadn't had a new garment for so long! Nora glanced at her gorgeous new shoes. She felt like dancing for the first time in months! And, just think, in Jamestown of all places!

Nora ran a hand over the skirt of the brown dress she had donned before leaving the dressmakers. Now that she was about to be in the employ of Mr. Knox, she wondered—How many indentured servants had three changes of clothes? Not too many, she ventured, her cheerfulness tempered by the thought of others less fortunate.

Nora adjusted the bonnet in an effort to ward off the sun. Whew, it was so hot, and the air was thick as molasses. She suddenly wrinkled her nose. "Mr. Nolan, what is that *awful* smell?"

"Eau de swamp, we call it. The closer you get to the swamps, and they're all around us, the more you smell the rot. It's mostly decaying vegetation, sulfur, and dead things."

"Dead things?"

"Animals, critters, humans, too."

"Humans?"

"You'll get used to it. The first settlers weren't too bright. They founded Jamestown on the edge of marshlands."

Nora scrunched her shoulders as an insect buzzed her face. She swatted at it, missed, and swatted again.

"Mosquitoes," Nolan said. "They breed in the swamps. Annoying little shits."

*****

As the carriage left the wetlands, Nora noticed the topography gradually change. Open pastures and green fields began to appear. After a few miles, Nolan announced, "We're now on Mr. Knox's plantation."

"Mr. Knox owns all of this?" Nora asked.

They were passing through lush fields of tobacco where dozens of slaves—Irish men, women, and children—were harvesting green leaves that resembled elephant ears. Nora watched with interest as the workers rolled cuttings into bunches, tied them into bundles, and tossed them onto the ground, where they were picked up by children and loaded onto drays.

"Yes, it's one of the smaller plantations hereabouts. Just over three hundred acres."

Nora's thoughts drifted to her father's description of Running River Plantation: one thousand acres, four hundred of which have been planted with tobacco. The remaining acreage Da had planned to clear and cultivate. One day soon, she would have to find a way to visit the property. Claiming ownership would be another matter, a complicated one.

Nora leaned forward to gaze at a group of women cutting tobacco leaves by the road. They wore long-sleeved cotton shifts similar to the one she had been given at the auction yards. The children, who worked close by their elders, wore similar smocks. The men were dressed in long-sleeved shirts with breeches that ended at the knee. Men wore hats and women bonnets to help block the intensity of the sun. She noticed that the men's calves were crimson, as if they had been dipped in pomegranate juice.

"Mr. Nolan, why do the men have red legs?"

"Sunburn. You'll hear people refer to 'red legs.' It's another name for Irishmen who work the plantations."

"It looks painful."

"Overseers give them grease to protect their skin, but with all the sweating, it's not much help. And when the humidity gets unbearable, they throw off their clothes."

Nora slapped at a mosquito and gave Mr. Nolan a doubtful look. "They can't possibly work without a stitch on, can they?"

"That they can."

"The women, too?"

"Aye, all of them. But it doesn't help much." Nolan spat. "The sun makes them sick, and then they can't work. For that reason, Mr. Knox doesn't allow nakedness."

Nora felt the joy from her acquisitions dissipate as the carriage passed the workers. There were young and old, highborn and lowborn, working side by side among insects and certainly snakes, beneath the unrelenting sun and debilitating humidity. Her mood dampened further when she noticed two hard-eyed men on horseback, watching over the workers. Each wore a brace of pistols in his waistband and had a coiled whip hooked over his shoulder.

She shuddered. America was brutal beyond her imaginings.

"The house is just up ahead," Nolan said.

Nora turned to look for Mr. Knox's residence. All she could see were the tops of chimneys, which towered above a thick grove of oak and pine.

Nolan pulled back on the reins as the horses, knowing they were nearing home, suddenly broke into a faster trot. "Whoa. Whoa." When the grays settled down, he said, "Mr. Knox built his house and outbuildings in a meadow surrounded by trees. The greenery keeps the place considerably cooler in summer months."

A short time later, they came upon a clearing with a scattering of outbuildings. Nora spotted two large barns and several smaller structures. "Does all this belong to Mr. Knox?" she asked.

"Aye," Nolan responded.

"This is as large as some small villages in Ireland."

"Running a plantation needs barns for curing tobacco, for tools, carriages, wagons and livestock. We smoke and salt our own food." He nodded toward a low turf-roofed hut where smoke rose, curling into the blue sky. "That's our smoking and curing shed. The rest of the buildings are for carpenters. There's the farm manager and his wife's home and over there, and," he pointed to a double row of ten small houses facing each other across a dirt path, "that's where the field workers live."

Beyond well-tended pens that held a variety of fowl and farm animals, Nora spied a prolific vegetable garden and a small circular stone wall that appeared to be an enclosed well.

Her eyes widened when they drove up to a large two-story home with wings on either side. The middle section of the residence was constructed of pale yellow brick, while the adjoining structures, stretched out like welcoming arms, were sided with whitewashed oak. Dark green shutters framed tall windows along the entire façade. Patches of ivy crawled up the walls to the slate roof, where four dormer windows had been symmetrically placed.

Mr. Nolan reined the geldings toward one of the barns. As they passed the entryway to the house, Nora noticed that the front door had been painted bright red, and displayed shiny brass fixtures.

It's beautiful, she thought. Yet, so unlike any of the homes or buildings in Ireland. The plantation and its grounds, she had to admit, were even grander than the family farm in Ireland.

The buggy circled the house and stopped before the back door.

*****

Nora, carrying her purchases, followed the driver into the kitchen, where a group of servants and children were busily preparing dinner.

Mr. Nolan said, "This is Nora Smith, everyone, Mr. Knox's new secretary and bookkeeper."

As introductions were made, Nora studied each of the help in turn, attempting to ascertain their personalities. Mrs. Gibbs, the raven-haired thirty-five-year-old housekeeper, was of medium height with a round, pleasant face and large, intelligent brown eyes. She seemed friendly but reserved, as befitted her station. Beside her stood Mick, a handsome six-year-old, who turned out to be the housekeeper's son.

Next, Nolan introduced Ginny, the plump, red-haired, blue-eyed cook who appeared to be in her late twenties. Clinging to the woman's skirts were two adorable five-year-old auburn-haired twins, Cara and Colleen. Ginny, who stopped biting her lower lip long enough to throw Nora a hasty grin, seemed to have a cheerful nature. Nora liked her immediately.

Then she met Millie, the twelve-year-old maid. Small and frail, Millie had a delicate, sweet face framed by twin blond braids. She fidgeted nervously, like a hummingbird that might dart away at any moment. Recognizing the girl's vulnerability, Nora warmed to her as if she were a sibling.

The last of the help was a short, stout couple in their fifties, Angelo and Franny del Corso.

Nolan turned to Nora. "Angelo was a sailor for some twenty years before he gave up the sea to marry the Irish love of his life. They tend the livestock and the vegetable garden."

They remind me of leprechauns, thought Nora.

"Come along, dear," Mrs. Gibbs said, "I'll take you on a tour of the residence and show you to your room."

The housekeeper led her through the parlor, the formal dining room, Mr. Knox's office, four family bedrooms, the staff's quarters and, finally, to a bedroom upstairs in the far corner of the home.

"This will be your room," Mrs. Gibbs said.

The small chamber was painted a drab beige. The furniture consisted of a nondescript bed that had been pushed against a wall. Beside it was a battered table that held an oil lamp, a water pitcher, and a chipped washbasin. The only decent piece of furniture was a rocking chair that stood beneath the lone window.

Mrs. Gibbs said, "I hope you'll be comfortable here."

"Yes," Nora said, feeling a knot in her stomach as she noticed that there was no armoire for her new clothes—only three stubby pegs on the wall. She laid her new garments on the bed, realizing they would soon become as wrinkled as prunes. "It will be fine," she added halfheartedly.

"I'm glad you approve. You'll be sleeping here for the next five years."

Color drained from Nora's face. She had already known the length of her contract, but hearing it spoken in these surroundings seemed so very depressing. She felt like a captive bird that had been let out of its cage, only to find itself caught in a spider's web.

No! she thought, I cannot live in this house for five years —or even five weeks! I am a landowner. Somehow, I must find a way to prove my status to Mr. Knox and straighten out this whole misunderstanding!

Gathering her composure—the situation was not Mrs. Gibbs's fault—Nora responded, "Thank you, ma'am. I do like the rocking chair."

Mrs. Gibbs beamed. "Yes, it is quite nice. It belonged to Mr. Knox's wife. Now make yourself at home. You will be joining us for supper in the kitchen in an hour." She turned to leave but stopped in the doorway to direct a pointed look at Nora's feet. "Those shoes . . ."

Nora jumped, resisting an urge to scrunch down so the hem of her dress would cover her feet.

"Quite fetching," Mrs. Gibbs said in an odd voice that belied the compliment. She then left without another word.

Was the housekeeper jealous? Well, thought Nora, I suppose I might be if our situations were reversed.

She glanced at her pretty shoes. At least Mrs. Gibbs hadn't asked her how much they cost—a truthful answer would most certainly have caused a problem. So, what would she do if ever she *was* asked? Thoughtfully, she removed her frilly bonnet, gave it an admiring glance, and placed it on the side table. She would simply avoid an answer. No one could force her to say anything. So there. Mr. Nolan was safe, and so was she.

Satisfied with her little discourse, she let her hair down and gazed at the bed, where the two petticoats, her nightgown, and the two new dresses now lay. In spite of Mrs. Gibbs's reminder of her lengthy indenture, the excitement of having new clothes slowly rekindled her spirit.

She would think of her troubles at another time. Right now, she simply had to put on her dresses! Nora slipped out of the brown frock, draped it over the rocking chair, and then unbuckled the document belt. Where could she hide this? She looked around the room and frowned. There was no cupboard and no closet, only pegs on the wall for hanging clothes, but there was the chest of drawers. Nora waved the thought aside. That would be the first place a light-fingered filcher would look.

With so few options to choose from, she lifted the corner of the mattress and placed the pouch on top of the interlaced ropes that supported the bed pad. Lowering the mattress, she studied her handiwork. Good. Only the slightest bump.

Satisfied, Nora changed out of her everyday dress, and felt a chill on her bare skin. How civilized it was going to feel to wear a petticoat under her dresses again. But no time for that now. She picked up the new everyday dress and quickly changed into it. Adjusting the bodice, she ran her hands over the fabric and felt a wave of delight.

I have to see how I look, she thought.

Nora scampered over to the small mirror on the wall and gazed at her reflection. Her eyes fluttered with surprise as she stared at her image. The gray cotton frock, with its long skirt and high collar, was beautiful. Mrs. Miles and her young seamstresses were truly artists!

She breathed in, swelling her bosom, and beamed at her reflection as if it were a long-lost friend. The lilac-scented bath, the heavenly hair wash, the scrumptious new wardrobe. It had been so long since she'd felt like a human being—since she'd felt feminine!

Nora once again ran her hands over the material, appreciating the finely woven cotton as much as she would a rare silk. She glanced at her Sunday dress on the bed. Once again, it reminded her of a spring garden, with its muted shades of green sprinkled with tiny colored flowers. She unbuttoned the everyday dress and pulled it off over her head. After placing it carefully on a peg, she hurried back to the bed, where she stepped into Sunday's frock. Not waiting to do all the buttons, she dashed back for another look in the mirror.

Oh! It was exquisite!

She wanted to pinch herself, she was so happy, and would have, but for the sudden memory of her best friend, Anne. Where was she? Was she safe? Was she well? How she wished they were together! She had no idea if her friend was even in Jamestown, but she intended to find out—some way, somehow.

And Billy. Where was Billy Devlin? She would have loved for him to see her now, in the beautiful Sunday dress. But she knew her whim to be just that—a whim. Billy, in all likelihood, would soon be at sea with that Portuguese captain, and she would never see him again. She would miss him—his silly banter and that lopsided grin. A frown appeared, and with it a twinge of guilt. How she had underestimated him. Ever since she'd been a child, she had always thought of Billy as a buffoon of sorts—likable, but still a buffoon. She'd been wrong. He was smart and brave. She'd had no idea he had become a navigator.

If only we were given second opportunities in life, Nora thought sadly as she stepped out of the Sunday dress and carefully set it aside. Once again feeling a chill on her bare skin, she was picking up one of the new petticoats when she felt a presence, as if she were being watched.

She whirled around. Gerald Knox was in the hallway, peering in through the half-closed door. Oh, dear Lord! Blushing, she quickly pressed the petticoat to her bosom and thighs, covering her nudity. How long had he been standing there? Had he seen her without a stitch on?

The incongruity of her feelings made her question—Why was she embarrassed now, when dozens of men had seen her naked on the *Goede Hoop*, and on the auction block only hours ago? Attempting to calm the nervous flutter in her stomach, she reasoned—It was because being nude and alone with a man was much more intimate, and that made all the difference in the world.

"Excuse me, Miss Smith," Gerald Knox said, taking a gracious step backward. "I'm sorry if I'm interrupting. The door was open."

Oh, it's my fault! she chastised herself. Why hadn't she shut it when Mrs. Gibbs left?

Mr. Knox continued. "I thought I'd inquire if you and Nolan had a successful shopping trip." His eyes darted to her new clothes. "But now I can see that you did."

"Oh, yes," she said quickly. "I found everything I need— two new dresses, a bonnet, petticoats, and a pair of shoes." She realized the garment she was holding in front of her was quite sheer, and modestly readjusted her arms to cover more of her bosom. "Thank you, Mr. Knox."

"You are very welcome."

Gerald Knox lingered in the doorway, staring at her in a peculiar way, as if he hadn't really seen her before.

Nora's pulse quickened. Was he going to come in? If he did, what would she do?

"In the morning," he said, "after you've had breakfast, come to my office, and we'll get started. I'm somewhat behind in my correspondence and bookkeeping."

"Yes, sir," she said, relieved. "I'm looking forward to being of assistance."

"Good. I'll see you in the morning then." He turned and walked away.

Nora quickly slipped the petticoat on over her head, listening to his footsteps recede down the hallway. Letting out a breath, she thought: My employer is seemingly not a man who takes advantage of his female servants, even though he owns us and can do with any of us as he wishes— not that I'd ever let him seduce me.

Giving him his due, she allowed that he did act as a gentleman under circumstances where other men might have taken advantage of the situation. Perhaps, she mused with a feeling of relief, the Knox household would be a safe refuge for her until she could work out her vexing problems.

But, enough! Her eyes had already drifted back to her new clothes. There might be just enough time to try them on again before dinner.

She giggled and reached for her Sunday frock.

CHAPTER TWENTY-SEVEN

"What on earth is that?" Nora asked, entering the kitchen.

Ginny, the cook, had just opened the door on a two-by-two-foot cast-iron box that sat inside the fireplace atop a larger metal container. It was glowing red hot, warming the room. The apparatus took up a quarter of the hearth, leaving ample space for the moveable iron hook that held the cooking cauldron.

Using a towel to protect her hands, a pink-faced Ginny lifted a covered pot from the interior of the contraption and set it on a stone trivet on the kitchen table. Wiping perspiration from her brow, she plopped herself down, joining her twin five-year-old girls, Mrs. Gibbs and her six-year-old son, Mick, Nolan, and Millie, the young blond maid.

"It's called a Hammersmith oven," Mrs. Gibbs replied. "Mr. Knox had it shipped here from Massachusetts almost a year ago."

"Once I got the knowing of it," Ginny said, "I started baking all sorts of meats, breads, stews, and vegetables. It's a wonder, it is."

Mick said, "Makes good pies, too."

"How does it work?" Nora asked, somewhat awed as she stared at the contraption.

Millie said, "You place coal or wood in the fire box below and light it. The heat rises to the upper chamber and bakes anything you put inside. It takes a bit of getting used to, adjusting the temperature for what you're aiming to cook."

Nolan said, "The man who manufactures them must be making money hand over fist. Wish I'd thought of it."

Nora took her seat with the servants. "I've seen pictures of ovens, but I've never actually eaten anything that's been cooked in one."

"Well, you are in for a treat," Ginny said, taking the lid off the pot.

A delicious aroma rose up in a cloud of steam, revealing a roasted fowl.

Nora inhaled. Heavenly! She squinted at the bird. "Is that a goose?"

"It's not a goose," Mick said. "It's a turkey."

"Oh," Nora replied, remembering that wild turkeys were indigenous to the Americas. "It smells fabulous."

"Help yourself to the vegetables," Ginny said, passing a plateful of carrots, turnips, and long yellow cylinders covered with little pods in symmetrical rows.

"I've never seen anything like this," Nora said, as she lifted one of the yellow things. "What is it?"

"Corn," the twins said in unison.

"Corn on the cob. It's a native vegetable," Nolan explained. He grabbed a cob off the plate as Ginny began to carve and pass out turkey slices. "It grows on tall stalks inside green leaves, but these have been shucked."

"Slather it with butter, add a pinch of salt, and it's so good!" Millie said, reaching for the platter.

"Those orange things, are they potatoes?" Nora asked.

"Not ordinary potatoes," Mrs. Gibbs replied. "They be called sweet potatoes."

Ginny said, "I'd never seen their like in Ireland."

"No, I haven't either." Nora took a bite of turkey. "My goodness," she said, her eyes lighting up. "Turkey is delicious! Do you always eat like this?"

"Lord, no," Mrs. Gibbs said with a chuckle. "It's Mr. Nolan's birthday today, so we're celebrating."

"Happy birthday, Mr. Nolan!" Nora responded. "Mine was August first, just two days ago."

"Ah, another Leo," Nolan said with a twinkle in his eye. "I knew there was something special about you."

Never one to put much stock in astrology, Nora had to admit nonetheless that she shared a certain affinity with the brusque Irishman.

"This time of year," Mrs. Gibbs said, "we normally eat less. We start to ration our food in the fall. You don't want to be caught short when winter comes."

"People starve in the settlement," Ginny added, taking a bite of turkey. "We're lucky to be in Mr. Knox's employ."

Nora's eyebrows rose. "People have starved in Jamestown?"

"More than once," Nolan said, pouring cider into a cup and passing the jug to Mrs. Gibbs. "Most of the first settlers in Jamestown died of starvation."

"Good gracious," Nora said. A lack of food was the last thing she would have thought could occur in the colony.

Mrs. Gibbs used a small spoon to take a dip of salt from a bowl. As she sprinkled the salt over her plate, she explained, "We have droughts that wither crops, brackish water that kills seedlings, supply ships of food that are weeks late or never arrive."

Nora sputtered in disbelief. "But . . . but Jamestown is on the edge of the wilds and Chesapeake Bay. Game and seafood must be plentiful. Vegetables, fruits, and berries grow everywhere in the wilderness. I've read all about it."

"You can't believe all you read, Nora," Ginny said between mouthfuls. "There is game, like this turkey we're having tonight, but it's not that easy to come by. Most of the settlers don't want to farm, fish, or hunt. They make more money growing corn and rice, trapping furs, tanning hides, tailoring, carpentering, baking, and smithing. We don't have but a handful of farmers. Believe me, in the winter months, it's a struggle to keep food in the larder."

"Fortunately," Mrs. Gibbs commented, "Mr. Knox has purchased sheep and swine that see us through the lean months—if the Indians don't pilfer 'em.

"And we have lots of chickens and eggs," Mick said.

Nolan chuckled. "Mick's in charge of the coops.

"Nora," Mrs. Gibbs asked, "do you have family?"

"Yes. Yes, I do," said Nora. At least I hope I do, she thought. "My da, mam, and younger brother are . . ." She hesitated. It wouldn't be wise to mention the plague or, for that matter, her real surname. "They're still in Dublin. I'm hoping they'll arrive in the next few weeks. My younger brother, John, became ill and died on our voyage over."

"I'm so sorry for your loss," Mrs. Gibbs said.

Millie added, "My condolences, Nora."

"Thank you. I also came with a cousin, Anne Smith. She was auctioned off, too. I hope to be able to locate her one day. It's a worry."

"Lots of Smiths in Jamestown," Ginny remarked.

"They didn't all start off as Smiths," Mrs. Gibbs said. "Of that, you can be sure."

Of that, I am *quite* sure, Nora thought wryly.

"Anne Smith . . ." Nolan said contemplatively. "If you like, Nora, I'll nose around, see if I can find out where she ended up."

"Oh, Mr. Nolan," she responded, brightening. "That would be so very kind of you."

"My pleasure. By the way, I forgot to buy you something."

Nora lowered her knife and fork and looked at the driver.

"A warm coat for winter."

"And you're going to be needing one," Ginny said. "We get freezes that are long and hard."

"The snow reaches right up to your ears," Mick said.

"Not quite," Mrs. Gibbs said. "Well, perhaps *your* ears, Mick. But Mr. Nolan is right. Nora, you will need a warm cape or an overcoat. And, Mr. Nolan, those shoes you bought for Nora," the housekeeper added in an admonishing tone, "they'll never survive the winter. You should have bought her sturdy boots like the rest of us wear."

"It was my fault," Nora said. "I should never have . . ."

"Those fancy new shoes are completely impractical," Mrs. Gibbs interrupted, continuing her rant. "I don't know why Mr. Nolan ever bought them for you."

"Mrs. Gibbs," Nolan said evenly, "don't talk around me. If you have something to say to me, come out and say it. If not, I want you to know that what I buy is never a concern of yours."

Flushing, taken aback, the housekeeper mumbled, "That may be so, but the first time Nora steps on ice, she'll slip and break her neck."

Nora interjected, "I'll be sure to be careful where I walk."

With a harrumph, Mrs. Gibbs bowed her head and resumed eating.

Is she insinuating that I manipulated Mr. Nolan into purchasing my shoes? thought Nora. That isn't fair, or correct—not really. Or is she attempting to reprimand him for being influenced by a young girl's whims? In all probability, Mrs. Gibbs is comparing her clodhoppers to my pretty *shoes* and is, understandably, a bit peeved. Well, Nora continued to muse as she used her fork to push food around her plate, my new shoes may be impractical, but their loveliness makes up for it!

"Speaking of watching your step, Nora," Nolan said, "I would be remiss if I didn't mention another danger—our so-called *friendly* Indians."

Nora looked up.

Nolan took a swallow of cider and continued. "We trade with the Powhatan for seafood, game, hides, corn, and grains. But if a bad winter comes along, the savages stop trading with us, as they need the food for themselves. Since the settlers aren't about to let their families starve, they raid the Powhatan camps and steal whatever they can, killing whoever tries to stop them. Last winter was mild, so there wasn't much thievin', but there's still animosity on both sides."

Nora set her fork down. "I saw a group of Indians when we came off the boat. They were just standing around and talking like ordinary people."

"Them's the more peaceful ones," Nolan said. "There are others not so peaceful, who want your scalp and maybe something else, if you gather my meaning."

Yes, Nora thought, I certainly do.

Mrs. Gibbs blushed. "Mr. Nolan, please, not at the dinner table."

He ignored her. "A pretty thing like yourself can be snatched up and never be seen again. So, I suggest you stay close to home. Never go out walking alone. You have to be aware. There could be Indians watching you at any time."

This was a new source of trepidation. Was there any place on Earth where men were not fighting, killing, kidnapping, and raping?

CHAPTER TWENTY-EIGHT

Captain Dice drew his cape together and hunched down, shouldering his way against the ferocious winds that blew rain and sleet in off the English Channel. His feet slid precariously on Bristol's icy cobblestone streets, but he managed to stay upright by sheer willpower as he plodded resolutely up the hill, leaving the storm-lashed harbor and docks behind.

He grimaced as gastric juices ate at the lining of his stomach. Knowing that the agony was self-inflicted didn't help his disposition. The fiery disorder was spawned by hatred and bitterness—emotions he nurtured in his own private inferno.

One day, Dice vowed silently, this condition will disappear. All it will take is the death of one young woman.

Tiny, needle-like icicles prickled Dice's face, aggravating the scar tissue on his left cheek, an ever-present reminder of that same woman who had become his nemesis. He gingerly brushed an icy accumulation off of his black, zigzag stitches. It had taken him weeks to learn that when he ate or became too vociferous, a two-inch opening like a small mouth appeared in the stitched area. The lack of skin there presented horrified audiences a view of perforated gums and broken molars. He had learned to control the opening and keep it sealed, but drinking liquids was a constant challenge, as were the trickles of saliva that seeped out and dribbled down his jaw. As a remedy, he carried a large handkerchief in the sleeve of his tunic, which he withdrew when it was necessary to absorb spittle.

Only weeks ago, he'd had a countenance so handsome that strangers would stop him on the street just to admire his classical features! But no longer. He'd been a bachelor with a promising military career, one that attracted a bevy of fawning females who vied for his attention. All that had changed with that bitch's bullet. Now people recoiled at the sight of him. He had become an outcast, a pariah. Invitations to card games, dinners, and military functions had stopped as suddenly as if a guillotine's blade had chopped off his head.

Always a virile man, Dice hated himself for having to resort to cheap whores for sex, as no cultured woman would come near him. Shunned by old friends and comrades alike, he was well aware that the Admiralty would prefer that he be kept far away from the sophisticated military environment of London, where his disfigurement was an embarrassment. His future, he was broodingly aware, was to be assigned to distant locations for the remainder of his career.

During his convalescence, he'd had to learn to talk and eat again, like a damned infant. Unable to shake the festering anger, he quarreled and fought with old friends and strangers who had the misfortune to cross his path. His disposition was like a poisonous infection, gnawing at him day by day.

Dice angrily shook his head. That Irish *asp*! I will not let her infect me with her venom! No, he must compartmentalize her, place Nora O'Lalor in the far recesses of his brain, 'lest he go mad.

With effort, he refocused, bringing to mind his recent orders from Admiralty. Thirty minutes ago, he had been billeted in a warm, comfortable room in the army barracks situated by the waterfront. Then he had been summoned by General Meredith Chetwynd, vice-commander of England's Parliamentary navy. His orders—appear before the general within the hour.

Within the hour! It was bloody storming! Had Chetwynd thought to send a carriage for him? No! The inconsiderate swine!

Dice knew the general didn't care for him. The feeling was mutual; the man was a horse's ass and a stiff-collared prig. Dice yanked his scarf up, and nearly slipped on the ice. Recovering his balance, he swore, "Damn this slush! And damn you, General, for calling me out in this vile weather!"

*****

General Meredith Chetwynd, a heavyset man in his mid-fifties, gestured to Dice from his seat behind the room's large, mahogany desk. "Come in, Captain. Come in."

"Thank you, sir," Dice said as civilly as he could manage. Closing the door behind him, he brushed sleet and rain from his cape. He eyed the well-appointed naval command office with its dark wood-paneled walls, seafaring paintings, and other assorted nautical paraphernalia. A large window commanded a view of the bay, which was now partially obscured by the storm.

"Take a chair, Captain," the general said with a wave of his hand.

Dice crossed to one of two chairs positioned before the officer's desk and sat, fuming. Don't bother to stand and offer your hand, you coarse bastard, he addressed the commander in his mind.

"Captain, I have an assignment for you, one that I hope you will find pleasing. As soon as this inclement weather clears, you will assist Captain Robert Denis as his second in command while he assembles an armada of fifteen ships and an infantry of 2,000 soldiers. This force will sail for Barbados and Jamestown, Virginia by next May at the latest. That, Captain Dice, gives Denis and you well over half a year for preparations. Your specific assignment will be to reinforce our English troops in their efforts to put down seditious activities by Royalists in the West Indies and in our American colony."

Dice leaned forward in his chair, his annoyance forgotten. *Jamestown. . . .*

General Chetwynd's words were almost too good to be true, especially after the debacles that had occurred under his own command in Dublin. Dice's lips curled downward as he recalled being unjustly blamed for actions of the *Goede Hoop*'s captain, who had blown his skiff out from under him, resulting in the deaths of three soldiers. To Dice's horror, he had also been charged with dereliction of duty after the Dutchman had fired that devastating broadside into the *Sovereign*, leaving death and destruction in her wake. Fortunately, a military tribunal had recognized his past bravery and laudable service record, and had placed the entire blame on Captain Van der Root. Parliament had issued a 1,000-pound reward for the Dutch captain, dead or alive. No mention had been made of the shootout in the market square, where innocent people had been killed, and no one had questioned the escape of the three Irish murderers.

After the fiasco in Dublin, Dice had learned that the *Goede Hoop* had sailed to Jamestown, Virginia, along with the three criminals who had escaped him.

While recovering from his wound, Dice had written his superior officers, requesting transfer to Jamestown to pursue and bring the young criminals to justice. There had been no response—until now. His request might be the reason he was being given this assignment. Or perhaps it was just coincidence. Either way, it served his purpose.

General Chetwynd had grown quiet. The man was staring at him with a stricken look.

Dice was suddenly aware that the slit in his cheek had opened. Saliva was leaking out and dripping down his chin and neck. Dice did nothing for a moment, enjoying the general's discomfort. He then whipped the handkerchief from the cuff of his tunic and dabbed at the drool. "Sorry, sir. A bit of a bother at times."

A visibly distressed general turned to gaze out the window, where slush pelted the panes. "Captain, Barbados and Jamestown have steadfastly refused to come under the authority of our new Parliamentary government. These malcontents have sworn allegiance to the Royalists. It's sheer stupidity. With King Charles I executed and Charles II hiding out somewhere in Scotland, a monarchy will never again rule England."

I don't really give a damn who rules England, Dice thought bitterly.

"Oliver Cromwell," the General continued, "will be enacting an informal embargo on the colonies, which will stay in effect until they come to their senses and acknowledge Parliament as their sole governing body. We will be cutting off all trade and supplies going to and from the colonies. All ships attempting to run the blockade and trade with our enemies, Spain, France, the Netherlands, and Portugal among them, are to be destroyed."

Interesting.

"In the near future, we will also require all goods shipped to and from our colonies to be transported exclusively on English ships. All foreign vessels will be banned from trading in our ports."

Dice sat back, stuffing the damp handkerchief up his sleeve. That would not make the settlers happy, he surmised. It would deny them their best trading partners.

"We are attacking the problem from land and sea. It will be your duty, Captain Dice, to lead our ground forces, to see to it that no foreign ships use our docks or waterways. You will stop, arrest, and if necessary, kill any traitorous bastards who attempt to interfere with you or run the blockade."

"With 2,000 soldiers, that shouldn't be too difficult."

"It might be, if the settlers were to arm and lead the Irish slaves against us. These Irish number well over 40,000 in the colonies. A good many of them are former soldiers."

"That could be troublesome," Dice allowed.

"There was a rebellion of Irish slaves in Barbados just last year. Fortunately, a slave tipped off the authorities before it could get under way. Eighteen of the insurgents were caught. We had them drawn and quartered, and their heads placed on pikes as a warning to others. We were fortunate in Barbados, Captain. But if an uprising were to occur in Jamestown with able leaders to direct the Irish, it could be a much different story. We can't let that happen."

"I know how to handle these Irish. They simply need to be crushed into submission, sir."

"Good. I knew you were the man for the job. Your assignment is to put down any sign of insurrection and bring our misguided settlers back into the fold. The colonists must recognize Parliament as their ruling government."

"You can count on me, sir."

"I am, Captain. When you are successful, I'll personally see to it that you are well rewarded. You will receive a grant of land where you can retire and grow old, perhaps start your own tobacco plantation. You'd like to be a landowner, wouldn't you?"

"Yes, sir," he replied automatically, thinking, *Condescending bastard!* The General was banishing him from England, in effect. *Well, fuck you, you overstuffed piece of dung. I'll be happy to never see the likes of you again!*

"Good fellow. Dismissed."

Dice walked out of the general's office and strode down the hallway, feeling his rage ratchet down to a controllable burn as his thoughts turned to Jamestown . . . and to a young woman.

His grin was wicked.

CHAPTER TWENTY-NINE

Where am I? Nora thought, awakening with a start.

Heart pounding, eyes darting like a frightened fawn, she sat up in bed. The surroundings looked familiar. Then she sighed. I know. I'm in my bedroom, in Gerald Knox's home.

Regaining her composure, she recalled tossing and turning in her sleep with nightmarish visions: the prisoners chained in the hold of the *Goede Hoop,* surrounded by filth, sickness, and death, images of the mutiny that failed, of Billy and Anne strung up and severely whipped, and of John's body dropping into the sea.

Nora blinked away the disturbing tableau. As she said a prayer for the suffering and lost, she became aware of the sun's rays filtering through the window. Today was her first day of work! What would that be like?

She didn't know what to expect from Mr. Knox, having exchanged no more than a few awkward words with him. She stepped onto the cold floor and, after a glance to the door to make sure it was closed, slipped off her nightgown. She hung it on one of the three pegs where her clothes were draped, then lifted the water pitcher on the table beside the bed. After half-filling the chipped bowl, she picked up her new bar of soap and smelled jasmine.

Dipping a washcloth into cold water, she demi-bathed. Then, with goose bumps from head to toe, she dried off as quickly as she could with the towel Mrs. Gibbs had left hanging on one of the pegs. She reached for her new petticoat, wiggled into it, and put on the gray work dress.

It still fit perfectly! Not that she'd thought it would shrink. Nevertheless, it was satisfying.

Nora slipped on her lovely, impractical shoes and glanced into the small mirror on the wall. Her hair! It looked as if it had been struck by lightning! Alarmed, she searched for her comb and hairbrush and found them on the seat of the rocking chair. Combing and then brushing her hair, she began to speculate. Would her work please Mr. Knox? Nora stopped mid-stroke and studied her reflection. She didn't look very confident. Yet, she knew she was more than qualified to be a good secretary. She was an accomplished speller, excellent at grammar and math, and her calligraphy was neat and legible. So why the fretful expression?

Perhaps, she thought, it's because I'm a seventeen-year-old Irish girl wrongfully accused of murder, at a loss as to how to prove my innocence and claim my legal status as the rightful owner of my family's plantation.

Would Mr. Knox be open to hearing her story and helping her? Or would she discover a hard man who cared for little but himself?

As if those questions weren't enough to start her day off badly, another problem presented itself—the look in Mr. Knox's eyes when she had caught him staring at her while she undressed.

Had her nudity provoked lustful yearnings that were going to surface when she was alone with him? It was entirely possible. She grimaced. What would she do if he attempted to kiss her, or touch her, or even worse? What could she do to protect herself?

Stop it, Nora! she told herself, gathering her courage. There was a lot she could do! She could kick, bite, scratch, and scream.

But then reality asserted itself, and her bluster dissipated like a deflating bellows. She realized she hadn't the strength to fight off a man the size of Mr. Knox. And who could she turn to for rescue? The staff would not be likely to jeopardize their jobs to come to her aid.

She thought about Mr. Knox and the potentially perilous situation. Again, she tried to decipher the look she had seen in his eyes. Had it been lust? She bit her bottom lip with uncertainty. She wouldn't know the answer to that question until the two of them were alone together.

She released a sigh of frustration. Now, more than ever, she needed her mam and da to talk to, to seek the protection they had always provided. Nora silently said a prayer: Da, Mam, help me. Please. I need your wisdom and your strength.

In the moments immediately following, she *heard* an answer—not in words but in thoughts. *Nora, your imagination is running wild. Calm down, sweetheart. Mr. Knox is a good man.*

Nora had come to accept her inner voice as part of her habit of talking to herself. After all, who didn't talk to oneself? But the guidance she received, she was convinced, came from her parents.

Her stomach growled. Ah, a lack of food. Had that been stimulating her imagination? Quite possibly. The growl became more insistent. Yes, she had to eat. Food usually settled her emotions.

As far as Mr. Knox was concerned, she'd just have to wait and see if she was employed by a gentleman, as he appeared to be, or by a lecher.

*****

Having hastily taken a breakfast of porridge and cider, Nora hurried down the hallway to Gerald Knox's study, hoping to arrive before him. Breezing into the room, she stopped abruptly. Mr. Knox was sitting at his desk.

"Good morning, Nora," her employer said without looking up as he wrote in a ledger. "Did you sleep well?"

"Yes, Mr. Knox, thank you," she replied. He was wearing a long-sleeved white shirt and black breeches. A pair of round wire-rimmed spectacles balanced on the end of his rather long nose.

He finally looked up. "That's a very becoming dress." His tone was businesslike, and there was no hint of lust in his eyes.

"Thank you, sir. I like it very much, as well as everything else you purchased for me." She hoped he wouldn't look at her shoes.

"You are quite welcome."

Mercifully, his eyes returned to his correspondence. "You've had breakfast, I assume."

Still not the slightest hint of lasciviousness. She felt herself beginning to relax. "Yes, sir."

"Well then, it's down to work. Writing materials are inside that box on the table by the window." Knox pointed to a small refectory table, upon which sat a portable secretary's writing desk. "As previously mentioned, I am behind in my correspondence, and things at the House of Burgesses are in shambles. Our governor, William Berkeley, is extremely paranoid. He believes England is about to attack us at any minute."

"Begging your pardon, sir," she said, walking over to stand beside the table, "but I believe the English are very capable of any savagery to attain their ends."

Knox's hand went to his spectacles. Lowering them, he gave her a piercing look. "Oh, you do, do you?"

A warm flush crept up her neck. Why did she always have to say the first thing that entered her mind?

"Are you aware, Nora," he continued, "that I am English?"

Now she'd really done it! Flustered, she stared at the floor. "I am sorry, sir. I wasn't thinking."

Surprisingly, Knox chuckled. "No need for an apology. I respect an honest opinion. Although, understandably, I don't entirely agree with yours. Now please, Nora, be seated. We must get on with my correspondence."

Whew. Just as Mr. Nolan said, Mr. Knox was a good man —for an Englishman.

She sat at the table and lifted the lid on the portable desk. Her eyes lit up. The box contained a fine silver inkstand with a small glass jar of ink, along with a half-dozen feathered quill pens. She tentatively removed a few sheets of blank paper from the inside tray, set the inkstand on the table beside her, and closed the lid. Taking quill in hand, she opened the inkpot, dipped the nub, and sat up straight. She gave Mr. Knox a nod, indicating that she was prepared to write.

Gerald Knox hesitated. His brow furrowed in contemplation. Then he stood and began to pace around the room.

After a few seconds of silence, Nora couldn't help but inquire, "Sir, if I may ask, why would England attack one of its own colonies?"

Knox stopped in mid-stride to stare at her.

"Sorry, sir," she stammered. "It's not my place to . . ."

"No, no," he said, waving away her apology as he continued to pace. "That's perfectly all right, Nora. You've asked a very good question. And the simple answer is: We colonists support the monarchy, which we believe will soon return to power. Oliver Cromwell and his ilk have temporarily taken over England's Parliament, an illegitimate governing body that wishes to do away with kings and queens."

"Can they do that, sir?"

He stopped mid-stride, explaining, "In England, it seems to be a *fait accompli*. Here in Jamestown, we've been supporters of Charles I, who recently had his head chopped off by that very same Parliament. Now, to their consternation, we support his son, Charles II, and we await his return to the throne." Knox resumed pacing. "That's just one matter on the growing list of problems I'm dealing with at present."

On the verge of inquiring what those "problems" might be, she hesitated. No, don't ask, she told herself.

"Nora, as my secretary, it's important for you to know some of our history and our current state of affairs. Jamestown was built on a marsh. Subsequently, we are continually infested with mosquitoes, snakes, and all kinds of nettlesome biting insects. The House of Burgesses, of which I am a member, must raise money to fill in the surrounding wetlands in order to make life bearable. On top of that, Jamestown's water is brackish and unsuitable to drink. It is imperative that we build a piping system to transport fresh water to the colony. And then there's the matter of food. We have a shortage of farms on which to grow corn, wheat, fruits, and vegetables. Most of our indigenous Indians, the Powhatan, will trade with us, but in lean times they keep the fare for themselves. Some of them refuse to trade at all, because they hate us for settling on their land." He stopped walking to look out the window. "We must be wary at all times. The Powhatan have renegades among them who, ignoring our treaty, readily attack, kidnap, rape, and kill settlers." He turned to face her. "They do so whenever they believe they can get away with it."

Nora opened her mouth to ask a question, but Knox held up a hand, silencing her.

"They're not our only adversaries," he added as he began to pace again. "We have a number of escaped indentured servants who have set up illegal camps in the woods, from which they base raids on farms and plantations. The garrison of English troops in Jamestown is totally inadequate to deal with their lawlessness."

That may be so, Nora thought anxiously, but she was certain there were enough soldiers to arrest her as a fugitive, should they ever discover her true identity.

"And there are diseases: typhus, dysentery, yellow fever, pneumonia. You name the malady, we seem to be cursed with it. Mothers die in childbirth because we lack midwives and doctors. And, of course, there's the matter of religion.

We have zealots, Anglicans, mind you, who demand that settlers attend church fourteen times a week or they'll be whipped and fined. Nora, these are the very same people who came here for religious freedom. It's lunacy!"

Believing Knox had finally ended his discourse, she said, "Sir, I had no idea you had so many . . ."

"I'm not finished," he interrupted, throwing her a steely look.

Abashed, she nodded weakly.

"As my correspondent, it's important that you know these things so that my letters have the correct tone. Do you understand?"

She gulped. "Yes, sir. I do."

His features softened. "We have the additional challenge of getting colonists to pay taxes to support the settlement." He rubbed the back of his neck. "It's a tiresome endeavor, prying money from clenched fists. Everyone wants more cobblestone streets, along with repairs to our docks, but they want the funds for these improvements to come out of someone else's pockets. And it goes on and on. We have to build an inn with rooms for visiting guests, we need a sewer system, we need to cut and store a sufficient amount of firewood to last through the winter." He paused.

I'm not saying a word, Nora told herself.

"These are my most pressing difficulties, aside from the nasty rumors of England's plan to blockade our ports and cut off trade. That will, of course, strangle commerce! While I'm dealing with all of this, I have to persuade reluctant settlers who'd rather be growing tobacco or trapping furs to plant grain and vegetables."

Nora nodded, determined not to speak until after Mr. Knox had finished articulating his woes.

Knox finally returned to his desk and sat. He took off his spectacles. As he wiped them with a handkerchief, he asked, "Now, is there anything you wish to discuss before we get down to work?"

Overwhelmed by the immensity of her employer's problems, Nora knew that now was not the time to bring up her personal difficulties or to plead her case. But she mustn't wait too long. She couldn't be an indentured servant forever. She replied tentatively, "Perhaps there is something I would like to bring to your attention, sir, but I'll have to gather my thoughts first."

"Fine. I'm at your disposal. Now, let's get down to work."

Relieved and anxious at the same time—she did need time to plot her approach to Mr. Knox—she knew that once she revealed her story, her employer might offer to help secure her freedom and property. Or, as the Englishman and politician he was, he might feel duty-bound to turn her over to the authorities.

In which case, she would surely be hung.

CHAPTER THIRTY

"Where are you, my lovely?" Billy whispered, as the deck rolled gently beneath his feet.

His eyes were strained from hours of staring into the bank of dense fog, probing the opaque miasma for sign of the English galleon. The crew on the eighty-foot Bermuda sloop, *Lobo Do Mar,* had been tracking the elusive ship all night.

Now, with the orange glow of morning warming the air, the fog was beginning to lift in ghostlike wisps from the rolling sea. The buccaneers, armed with pistols, muskets, and cutlasses, stood ready on the main deck. They were alert, cautiously silent, listening for voices from their quarry above the sounds of sails fluttering and the gentle swish of waves rippling past the hull of Captain Diego de Almeida's pirate ship.

Yesterday afternoon, the lookout, high atop the main mast in his "birds' nest" had spotted the multi-deck 120-foot, forty-gun, *Lady of Dorset*, on the horizon. Captain Diego had quickly gathered his crew for a vote, to either attack the ship or sail on in search of smaller, easier prey. Billy had learned that it was customary among pirates that, after spotting a likely target, they would take a count of "yeas" and "nays" to determine their actions. The result of the impromptu ballot had been unanimous. Attack!

Billy had discovered the day after they'd sailed from Jamestown that Diego de Almeida was a pirate. Billy, who because of his course-plotting skills had been assigned the position of navigator, had asked the affable forty-year-old

Portuguese what had happened to the last man to occupy his position. Diego, who spoke passable English, told the story of a sea battle in which his crew had attacked a Spanish merchant ship. A bloody fight had ensued, ending in victory for the Portuguese, but his navigator had been fatally wounded. The Spanish galleon was pillaged of all her goods and sunk. The surviving seamen had been given a choice—swear allegiance to Diego or be executed. The men had opted for life, and were now part of *Lobo do Mar's* crew.

Diego had modestly informed Billy that, while in Jamestown, he'd sent the deceased navigator's share of the pirates' booty home to the man's family. After relating this story, the captain slapped Billy on the back, made him the new navigator, and promised to do the same for him.

*****

Never one to dwell on his mortality, Billy had laughed. But now, with a life or death battle only heartbeats away, he gripped a heavy cutlass in his hand and vowed: Billy Devlin, today is not your day to die!

Needing reassurance, he touched the two pistols that protruded from his belt, weapons he had carefully primed. He inhaled deeply, contemplating his new status in bewilderment. Within a period of two months, he had gone from being a free-spirited young man in Ireland, to a prisoner on a slave ship, to a commodity on an auction block in Jamestown, to a brigand, an outlaw, and a pirate—and all by the age of nineteen. Well, the good part of that was that he was still alive, at least for the moment.

He squinted, eyes probing the mist. Where are you, pretty lady?

Billy mumbled a prayer in Portuguese—and blinked. He was already speaking a foreign tongue. To his surprise, he had found Portuguese a beautiful language. With the help of several bilingual crewmembers, he had learned to speak rudimentary phrases, such as the short prayer he had just muttered. Dear God, let me live through this next battle, and I promise I will become a much better person than anyone ever thought I could be.

Realizing he was caught up in an adventure over which he had no control, Billy had made a pact with Diego: If he were killed in battle, his share of the pirates' booty would be sent to Nora Smith in Jamestown. A lopsided grin came to his lips. Maybe then, he thought, when I'm dead and gone, you'll know how much I loved you!

The weight of the broad-bladed cutlass in his hand was a reminder of how vulnerable his life would be in the next few minutes. He tightened his grip resolutely. He had no intention of dying! He would return to Jamestown, to Nora Smith or Nora O'Lalor or whatever name she might be going by, and he would marry her!

Billy was suddenly aware of a presence beside him. Captain Diego de Almeida had come up on cat's feet and now stood next to him at the deck's railing. With a glance to Diego, Billy recalled the man's plan of attack. It was simple, but daring—without using cannon, which would damage the valuable galleon. They would come alongside the larger ship under the cover of fog and, with the use of grappling hooks, latch onto the galleon's railings. Then, rapidly hauling the two vessels together, the pirates would leap onto *Lady of Dorset* and quickly subdue the crew.

Easier said than done, Billy thought. But he had no choice. He had been issued his weapons with the simple advice—kill or be killed.

"Hello, Irish," the captain said quietly. "How be your stomach?"

"A bit unsettled," Billy admitted. "It's saying it wishes someone had outbid you at the auction."

Diego chuckled. "Who else would have given you a chance to become a rich man?"

"Or so many opportunities to die."

"All of life, Irish, is a gamble."

"So, it is." And then he inquired, "How many battles have you fought?"

"Six, perhaps seven, but many times crews will surrender without a fight. Maybe we be lucky today."

I don't like maybes, Billy thought.

"There!" Diego whispered, pointing into the mist.

The multi-deck galleon had suddenly materialized out of the fog, her huge, square sails fluttering in the breeze.

That's a very, very big ship, Billy thought, apprehension grabbing onto him like the tentacles of a sea monster.

Diego squawked, mimicking a seagull, and motioned to his crew. Seeing the *Lady of Dorset,* they quickly made ready the grappling hooks. Some climbed the ship's rigging, carrying muskets, to shoot down on the English crew.

As *Lobo do Mar's* bow eased past the galleon's stern, Billy could clearly see two sailors on the galleon's main deck, engaged in conversation, unaware of the danger gliding up alongside of them.

The pirate crew, weapons ready, crouched silently beneath the railings—feral animals ready to pounce. When the sloop came abreast of the galleon with less than ten feet separating them, four pirates sprang to their feet, stepped back from the rail, and began swinging grappling hooks.

Captain de Almeida whispered to the helmsman, "Now!"

The whip staff was slammed portside, pronged hooks were let loose.

The hulls slammed together!

The English on deck whirled about, eyes widening as iron claws sailed over the railings and bit into wood. "Pirates! Pirates!" the men screamed.

As ropes were pulled, the two vessels were bound together as tight as a brutal kiss.

Portuguese muskets fired from the rigging.

Red blossoms burst on the Englishmen's chests.

"Board! Board!" Captain Diego de Almeida yelled.

Pirates leaped from *Lobo do Mar's* railings onto the deck of the galleon, swarming to meet half-dressed English sailors as they began to crawl out of hatches. The adversaries clashed head on.

"Come, Billy!" Diego yelled, leaping onto the enemy's deck.

Billy followed, heart beating wildly, to land on the deck beside his captain—just in time to parry the blade of an Englishman's sword that would have decapitated him.

"Mucho gusto, Irish!" Diego yelled, shooting his would-be killer in the face and turning to confront another opponent.

With no time to gather his wits, Billy swung his cutlass at a bloody-faced sailor who ran at him with an axe—and cut his arm off. Shocked, Billy froze, cutlass in midair.

"Behind you!" Diego shouted.

Billy reflexively ducked. The blade aimed at his head swished past his ear. Without thinking now, adrenaline pumping through his veins and fueling a rage he had never before experienced, he moved into the melee with its cacophony of screams, gunshots, and clashing sabers.

Blood splattered the decks from severed body parts. Men became beasts, snarling, fighting like rabid dogs. Cutlasses stabbed and sliced, fire spewed from point-blank shots from pistols and muskets. A cloud of gray-black gunpowder rose over the earsplitting combat as men fought valiantly and desperately, and died.

Time disappeared. Billy slashed left and right, cutting flesh and bone, opening skulls, slaying men as if they were cattle in a slaughter yard, until, finally, there was no one left to fight.

He found himself standing amidst piles of dead, surrounded by his victorious Portuguese mates. The few Englishmen who hadn't been slain dropped their weapons and raised their hands in surrender.

Splattered with blood and viscera, exhausted, gasping for breath, Billy checked his aching body for wounds that surely must be grievous. A laugh escaped him. He was still in one piece! He drew in great drafts of air and blew them out in an attempt to steady his pounding heart. Feeling that his knees were about to buckle, he grabbed onto the ship's railing and gazed out over the bloody carnage. His stomach lurched as he saw bodies with severed limbs and decapitated heads strewn haphazardly across the decks. Some, still alive, had entrails spilling out of their eviscerated bellies like giant steaming worms.

Billy's gorge rose. He leaned over the railing and vomited.

A hand came to rest on his shoulder, followed by Diego's voice. "Irishman, you fight like the devil himself."

Turning, wiping spittle from his face, Billy took one look at the captain and blanched. The hilt of a saber was protruding from the center of Diego's bloodied chest.

"It was a good fight . . . but my luck, it flew away," Diego gasped, his face as white as dried bones. He coughed and red foam bubbled from his mouth. He collapsed against Billy, who gently eased him to the deck and laid him on his side, careful that the blade didn't lodge against the deck and cause additional pain.

"O capitão é para baixo!" a Portuguese seaman shouted, repeating the declaration in English, "The captain is down!"

Several of the pirates, cut, bloodied, and battle-worn, rushed to Billy and Diego. Others stayed back to guard the dozen or more battle-scarred English sailors who had surrendered.

Diego grimaced as he fought to speak to those gathered about him. "Rodrigo, my first mate, I saw him die. I will soon follow. You must vote . . . a new captain and new first mate."

A chorus of voices protested, unable to believe that their formerly invulnerable captain was at death's door.

Diego held up a shaking hand, silencing the outcries. "My wound is mortal." He coughed, spitting up bright red blood. After wiping his mouth on his sleeve, he spoke slowly but with authority. "You need new captain. Billy. . . my vote . . . for captain Billy."

Me? Billy thought incredulously. Impossible!

Diego added, "Without you, Billy, they are lost. You navigator."

THE GIRL WHO WAS ME IS GONE

The crew was silent as they absorbed Diego's words—and his wish. Expectant faces waited for the captain to continue. A bloody cough gurgled deep within Diego. He was finally able to add, "My vote . . . first mate, Antonio."

A tall, thin man with a bleeding gash on his forehead stepped forward. "My honor, Captain."

"Vote now," Diego gasped. "Por favor."

Antonio turned and spoke rapidly to the crew. Billy listened as they mumbled among themselves and then took a vote. Antonio was voted first mate.

Billy was voted Captain!

He stared at the crew in disbelief. They had suddenly catapulted him from navigator to captain of a pirate ship!

"Por favor, Billy," Diego said, struggling to talk. "My wife, Mei, and my two little sons . . . See . . . papers, in cabin, our home, Lisbon. Give my shares to . . ." He stopped, unable to go on.

"Yes, Diego," Billy said, immediately understanding that the captain was asking him to take his shares of the booty to his family in Lisbon. "I will find your wife and sons and I will make certain they receive your shares. I promise you this on my honor."

Diego de Almeida's eyes fluttered. He attempted to speak once more, but words failed him.

He exhaled and died.

Antonio jabbed his bloodstained saber into the air and yelled, "O Capitão!"

To a man, the Portuguese crew cheered their fallen comrade. "O Capitão! O Capitão! O Capitão!"

Antonio, his bronzed cheeks streaked with tears, lowered the sword. He turned to Billy, his face hardening. He motioned to the surviving Englishmen. "Captain, the prisoners?"

Billy knew that, as their new captain, he was being asked to make a judgment. Should the survivors be executed or granted mercy? Billy studied the ragged group. Most of them, although bearing the marks of battle, appeared to be

260

fit. With two ships to sail, he would need all the crew he could get.

He said, "They will have the same choice Captain de Almeida would have given them. They can jump overboard and swim with the sharks, or they can join us and become pirates, with each receiving an equal share in all future prizes."

Antonio repeated the offer to the defeated sailors in a booming voice. The Englishmen readily accepted the opportunity to live and become pirates.

"Antonio," Billy said. "Have the men start cleaning up this mess. Once we are shipshape, you are to pilot *Lady of Dorset* and follow me. *Lobo do Mar* is sailing to Lisbon. There we will sell the galleon and divide the proceeds. That, I'm sure, will make the crew happy."

"Captain, we'll get a better price and avoid difficulties with Portuguese law if we sell *Lady of Dorset* in Barbados."

"I bow to your experience, Antonio. First we sail to Barbados, then to Lisbon. While we are there, I will find Diego's family and see that they receive his shares. Then we are going to Jamestown."

Antonio cocked his head quizzically.

"I have business there." That was all the explanation Billy cared to give.

Antonio scratched his chin. "We hunt along the way?"

"Yes, we will capture, loot, and destroy any English vessel that has the misfortune to cross our path. Are you with me?"

Antonio displayed a set of large, white teeth. "We are with you, Captain." He turned away and began issuing orders.

As the sailors begin the grimy task of throwing corpses overboard and swabbing up blood and body parts, Billy climbed the ladder to the poop deck and looked out over the sea.

The fog had dissipated. The sun's warmth was a welcome reminder that he had survived another battle. While the loss of Diego and other friends preyed heavily upon him, their deaths also brought to mind the dearness of life. Especially one life in particular—Nora's.

What was she doing right now? Had she thought of him even once since they had parted? Was the man who'd purchased Nora treating her well? Billy's jaw set. If any man hurt a hair on her beautiful head, they would answer to him!

Billy clenched the hilt of his cutlass, and then slowly released his grip. It would be a while before he would see Nora again. He would have preferred to sail directly for Jamestown, but his conscience wouldn't allow it, not after the vow he had made to Diego. Honor-bound to keep that promise, Billy knew the journey he was embarking on would take three to four months, and, with winter quickly approaching, the seas would be dangerous.

He looked up past the rigging and billowing sails to a clear blue sky.

I am coming for you, Nora.

CHAPTER THIRTY-ONE

Nora leaned back in the chair and glanced at the candle flickering beside her on the table. It had burned at least two inches since sundown. Mr. Knox had left the study hours ago.

Thankfully, she had finally finished his correspondence. Her employer, or more correctly, master—how she hated that word!—had dictated letters to the governor of Virginia, Sir William Berkeley, and to several other New England governors, as well as one to the new Parliament in England, to which he was vehemently opposed.

Yawning, she closed the lid on the secretarial desk and stretched her aching back.

"You're up late."

Spinning around she saw Mr. Nolan had entered the room. "I'm after a bit of tobacco," he said as he came forward, gesturing with the pipe in his hand.

"Good evening, Mr. Nolan."

"No 'Mister,' please. Just Nolan," he said, reaching for the cedar tobacco caddy on Mr. Knox's desk. "Enjoy your first day of work?"

"Yes. It's been very informative. Mr. Knox is certainly an important man."

"Aye, that he is."

She frowned as she watched Nolan open the container. Should she try to stop him from stealing her employer's tobacco?

"Don't you worry," he said in response to her unsettled expression. "Mr. Knox allows it."

"Oh, I wasn't worried at all."

Fibber, she admonished herself.

"Best tobacco in Virginia." Nolan proceeded to pack the bowl of his pipe. "Grown right here on the plantation."

A question had been bothering Nora ever since she arrived. "Nolan, how many Irish work for Mr. Knox?"

"I would say there's a bit over fifty in the fields, plus the household help."

Good Lord! "Mr. Nol . . ." She quickly corrected herself, "Nolan, how on earth does one man have over fifty Irish servants working for him?"

"Slaves," he corrected her. "Slaves work the fields. Servants work in homes and businesses. 'Indentured servants' is the name the English would like us to call all Irish so they can pretend they're not slave traders, which they are. However, the English are no different from most of the other nationalities in the world. They all deal in slavery, one way or another. They have since the dawn of time."

Nolan closed the tobacco caddy's lid and crossed to the fireplace, where he pulled a long taper from a basket. "Have you any idea how many Irish have been murdered or sold off to be slaves in the West Indies and the American colonies?"

"No, I don't."

He touched the stick's end to smoldering logs. When it caught fire, he brought its tip up to the bowl of his pipe. He drew in a few puffs to make sure the tobacco was burning, and then tossed the taper into the hearth. "I can give you a fairly accurate count. I have an educated cousin, a dirty Anglican by the way, who teaches at Trinity College in Dublin; they do not allow Catholic students or professors these days, as you may already know. My cousin takes perverse pleasure in writing me letters relating the latest horror stories. He has estimated that the English have killed approximately 500,000 Catholics in the last decade, and over 300,000 more have been deported and sold off as slaves. If you include another 100,000 for emigration, Ireland's population has fallen from 1,500,000 to 600,000. In Barbados and Virginia alone, 80,000 Irish are working on sugar and tobacco plantations. On some islands in the West Indies, Montserrat for example, over seventy-five percent of the population are Irish slaves. Jamestown and the American colonies were settled with the muscle, sweat, blood, and tears of the Irish. Don't let anyone ever tell you differently. Oh, we have a few German, Italian, Slavic, and African indentured servants, but that's all going to change. Black slavery is just beginning. Within the next few decades, they'll replace the Irish, who are much too troublesome for the overseers." He shrugged. "It can't happen soon enough for me."

Nora stared at Nolan. She recalled overhearing Captain Van der Root and Pieter mentioning that they were sailing to Africa to purchase blacks, as they too believed the next market for slavery would be Africans.

"Nolan, I don't know what to make of your cousin's information, but those numbers are so incredible they're hard to believe."

"Believe it, it's a fact."

"Can't some God-fearing people stop slavery? It's so wrong."

"It won't happen in our lifetime. Massachusetts legalized slavery in 1641, and Connecticut did the same this year. There are already fugitive slave laws in Plymouth and New Haven. The House of Burgesses, as well as other assemblies in New England's colonies, have now proposed laws that make children born to slaves the property of their employers."

"I thought that was already the case."

"It's been common practice among many plantation owners, but now the bastards are making it legal."

"It's inhuman. It makes me sick."

"It all comes down to man's oldest sin—greed. My advice to you, Nora, is to not have children." Puffing on his pipe, Nolan walked out the door.

Was Nolan daft? Children? She had no intention of having children at her age! Besides, she hadn't met a man she would even contemplate marrying.

An image of a lopsided grin flashed in her mind's eye.

And most particularly not Billy Devlin!

*****

Could those figures be correct? Anne was barely aware of the candle sputtering beside her on the table, casting wavering shadows across her account's ledger, as she pondered the profit and loss columns.

Willie, resembling a bearded bear, dozed in a chair before the fireplace, ever on call to protect and oversee Pitt's interests.

Anne sat back in her chair and turned to gaze at the hearth, where burning logs kept the night's chill at bay. Willie's snoring brought to mind the strange relationship between the cherub-faced man and Rufus. Willie, while never acting subservient to Rufus, nevertheless did his bidding—unless he chose not to, in which case Rufus would simply accept Willie's decision and ignore him. It was an odd association. Was Willie an employee or a business partner?

Anne lifted her pen and tapped its feathered stem against her cheek. That was an enigma for another time.

Returning her attention to the ledger, she attempted to comprehend the numbers she had just rendered. Two hundred-and three-pounds profit! "Good Lord," she whispered. "It's a small fortune."

A large part of that sum, she had ascertained, came from prostituting Trish and Nell in exchange for trappers and merchants bringing business to the trading post. For two men who could barely read and counted numbers on their fingers, they were uncannily astute when it came to negotiating for furs and hides or, for that matter, with anyone who had influence or valuables to peddle in exchange for access to the girls. Trish and Nell had become virtual doxies, subject to carnal encounters at any time of the day or night.

Upon moving into Pitt's compound over two months ago, Anne had been shocked to discover the man's degenerate business methods. Since then, she had begun to formulate a plan to locate Nora and escape with the girls. That course of action presented many risks, but anything would be better than staying in Pitt's bordello.

She blinked in dismay as she recalled broaching the subject with the girls.

"We're not goin' anywhere!" Trish, the feistier of the two, had stated. "Rufus an' Willie are awful, smelly pigs, but they give us things we never had before—good food, all the whiskey we wants, pretty clothes, perfumes, an' even scented soap."

Nell had added, "An' we have our own tin bathtub! If we left, where would we go? Who would take us in an' take care of us an' give us pretty things?"

Before Anne could recover from the girls' shocking responses, Trish had added, "We would starve to death, we would! No one would be wantin' us. Certainly, none of Jamestown's Christian families."

"An' besides, if we ran off an' Willie caught us," Nell added with a shudder, "he'd beat us half ta death an' cut off our ears, too."

"We don't wants to leave. The work is easy, an' sometimes it's even pleasuresome."

"Though sometimes it's not," Nell said, clearly remembering less-than-pleasant experiences.

"Anne," Trish had said. "Rufus pays us two pounds every month. A girl can't make that money anywhere else. Last week, a man gave me a whole pound an' I didn't do hardly nothin' fur it. Nay. We's goin' nowhere, is we, Nell?"

Nell put her hands on her hips. "Stayin' right here, we is."

That discussion had been eye-opening. In spite of Willie's occasional beatings and mistreatment, Anne realized that Rufus had been shrewd enough to persuade the girls to remain as prostitutes by offering them gifts that were simply too tempting to turn down. He had also brought in a doctor, who gave Trish and Nell instructions on how best to avoid pregnancy by either having a man withdraw before climaxing or achieving the act without penetration. The last thing Rufus wanted in his establishment was babies. They would not only take time away from the girls' carnal activities, but more importantly, they would cut down on his profits.

Rufus had recently bought a third Irish girl at auction, Addie, aged fourteen. When they arrived home, Rufus introduced Addie to Willie, and the bearded young man had explained in plain words what was expected of her. Addie had balked—until she heard about receiving rewards of clothes, money, and other gifts. Addie had since become an active participant in Pitt's stable.

While never approving of their actions, Anne could not blame the girls. They had all come from poor backgrounds, and the rewards of prostitution without criticism from priests, family, or friends to dissuade them, had been too seductive. All three girls were now in their bedrooms, where they would remain with customers until morning.

The smoldering logs cracked and popped. Willie stirred but didn't awaken. Anne's thoughts returned to the dilemma that was never far from her mind—how to escape.

Rufus was at a friend's house, where he went three nights a week to play cards, drink, and gamble. His behavior reminded Anne of some hard-drinking Irishmen she had known back at home. Sober, they were amiable enough, but when inebriated they became different people, mean and dangerous. The thing that scared her most about Rufus was that he was half-drunk most of the day, and completely inebriated by nightfall.

How long would it be before he came staggering home, besotted and mean, to break into her bedroom and rape her? Who could she call for help? Certainly not Willie. That lout wouldn't lift a finger to help her.

Anne stared at Willie as he snored before the glowing logs. His lurking presence was strangely reassuring, and yet frightening. Although he offered security from outside dangers, she felt ill at ease whenever he was close by. She had caught him staring at her when he thought she was not aware of his scrutiny. She was unable to read his intentions, which scared her, as the unknown often did.

She had to get away from this place. Leaving the compound would not be that difficult, but even if she were to be successful, it would place her in the same predicament as the girls. She had no place to go and no one to turn to.

Where are you, Nora? she thought. Are you even in Jamestown?

Anne tapped the quill on the inkpot. The first two months had flown by, and she was no closer to escaping than when she'd first arrived. She lowered the pen and closed the ledger. It was late, and she had better be in bed before Rufus returned home and Willie awakened and started leering at her in that way that made her skin crawl.

Voices and giggling came from the back bedrooms. The girls' morals weren't for her to judge. She had been doing what she could to protect and care for them, on occasion persuading Willie to turn away the dirtiest and most troublesome individuals without Rufus's knowledge. She realized she had, in effect, become the girls' older sister, or, as Willie referred to her—Miss Madam.

A madam at seventeen!

What would Nora say? Or even Billy?

*****

Earlier, despite fetlock-deep snow and bitter cold, Mr. Knox had ordered his carriage and the larger barn wagon brought around to the front of the house. He had ushered the entire household staff and their children, all bundled in warm capes and scarves, into the vehicles. After having heard numerous reports of marauding Indians over the last

269

few weeks, he'd made sure all the men were armed. In a festive mood, they had traveled through windblown snowdrifts to St. James Anglican church in Jamestown for a late afternoon Christmas service.

Nora had enjoyed the liturgy, finding it similar to the Catholic masses she and her family had attended in Ireland. She had prayed for her family and for Anne and Billy, and that one day she might assume her rightful ownership of Running River Plantation.

Later, they had all returned home and Mr. Knox led them to a set of double doors leading to the formal dining room. When he opened them, Nora gasped, "Oh, how beautiful!"

The staff, crowding in behind her, echoed her words. They were astonished to see that the room had been decorated with freshly cut greens: boughs of laurel, holly, ivy, and mistletoe.

Nora smiled happily. "Mr. Knox, this is so kind of you."

"Oh, no, I don't deserve any credit. This is all Mrs. Gibbs's doing. It's her Christmas present to you all. Now everyone, please be seated."

He nodded to Ginny, who rushed off with Millie in tow.

Mr. Knox took his seat at the head of the long, polished mahogany table as the staff sat, for the very first time, in the formal room. He seemed pleased as the servants, murmuring appreciatively, first gazed at and then cautiously touched the fine china, cutlery, and crystal.

Watching their reactions, Nora felt a wave of nostalgia. Memories of her childhood in Ireland came to mind, with Da, Mam, John, and Brendan sharing meals together in the family dining room. It had been so long ago . . . and she missed them all so terribly.

Ginny and Millie soon returned, carrying platters of food. The servants "Ooh'd" and "Ah'd" as the two women laid out dish after dish.

Ginny must have been secretly preparing all this for days, thought Nora. There was roasted ham and a baked goose, fried clams and oysters, which Nora politely refused, striped bass, sweet potatoes, corn cakes, string beans, and peas, along with warm hard cider and cookies for dessert. It was a culinary miracle!

After dinner, they all retired to the parlor to listen to Mrs. Gibbs play her ancient harp while Ginny enthusiastically accompanied her on a three-holed fipple flute.

Nora was feeling a little more than pleasantly full when she raised a steaming mug of the fermented cider to her lips. She closed her eyes and inhaled the aroma. Divine! She took a Christmas cookie from the plate that was balanced on her lap and nibbled contentedly as the ladies entertained them with familiar carols: "O Come All Ye Faithful," "The First Noel," and "God Rest Ye Merry Gentlemen."

How quickly time had flown, Nora thought. She found it difficult to believe it was almost the New Year, 1651! And still, she lamented, she was no closer to being free than when she'd arrived last August. Mr. Knox's meetings, business transactions, and correspondence had kept her so busy that she hadn't been able to find an opportunity to present her case—as a free woman and a property owner—to Mr. Knox.

Well, that wasn't entirely true, she ruminated. She'd put it off because she was afraid of how he might respond. Once she revealed that she was wanted for murder, she might never get as far as demonstrating her ownership of Running River Plantation. Mr. Knox might feel compelled to have her arrested on the spot—or he might not. Not knowing how he would react was the most worrisome dilemma of all. Could she trust him with her life, and Anne's, too?

Mr. Knox began to sing along with the carolers, his melodic baritone interrupting her reverie. Nora was delighted. This was the first time since they'd met that Mr. Knox seemed to be actually enjoying himself. It must be the hard cider, she concluded. She, too, felt a little tipsy from the strong brew.

As the carol ended, Mr. Knox called out, "One more, Mrs. Gibbs, if you would be so very kind. Play one for our dear friend, Oliver Cromwell, 'Ding Dong Merrily on High.'" They all cheered.

Nora grinned, fully aware of the mockery in her employer's toast, as the puritanical Cromwell disdained religious music, especially any carol that might be considered frivolous and fun. As the women played, she sang along, tapping her feet, enjoying the rambunctious rhythms. The children, unable to contain their exuberance, jumped to their feet and danced, bouncing around the room like marionettes at a street fair. Millie followed soon thereafter, her long blond braids twirling. Nora found herself rising and joining them as they all capered about.

Nora bumped into one of the children, lost her balance, and almost fell—but an arm reached out and encircled her waist. She had been rescued by Mr. Knox, who was dancing and laughing right along with the rest of them.

"Having a good time, Nora?" he asked cheerfully. He released her, but not before she felt his hand briefly squeeze one of her breasts.

"Oh, yes, sir," she said, flustered. Had his touch been intentional?

"A wonderful Christmas, is it not?" he said, his blue eyes sparkling.

"Yes, sir," she replied, deciding that, surely, the contact had been accidental.

When the carol finished, they all laughed and applauded, all but Mrs. Gibbs, who was staring at Nora with a strange look. Why, Nora wondered, was the housekeeper suddenly looking so bereft? Perhaps, she allowed, she had overindulged a bit and was beginning to feel ill.

Mr. Knox, flushed with bonhomie and alcohol, lifted the cider pitcher from the table and refilled his mug. Seeing Nora, he stepped over to her and said, "A little more?"

"Oh, no. I'm fine, thank you, Mr. Knox."

"It's Christmas, Nora," he insisted as he began to refill her cup. "It's so seldom we have anything to celebrate."

Before she could protest further, the mug had overflowed. With a laugh, he turned to the crowd. "Has anyone seen Nolan?"

"Not since early afternoon," Mrs. Gibbs said. "Unusual for him not to be here."

"Probably enjoying the evening with a lady friend," Mr. Knox said.

"He'd better not be," Ginny replied with a possessive grin that prompted guffaws from the merrymakers. Nora began to realize that there were undercurrents within the Knox household of which she was not aware.

"Well, this old man is off to bed," Mr. Knox announced with a yawn. He downed the last of his cider. "I hope you've all had a jolly time this evening. I know I have. Merry Christmas to one and all." With an exaggerated bow, he added, "And to all, a good night."

Everyone chimed in with good nights as their employer left the room.

"Can you believe that?" Ginny asked. "Mr. Knox danced!"

Franny added, "I've never seen him enjoy himself so much."

"He surprised me, too," Nora said.

"Yes, Nora, Mr. Knox surprised us all," Mrs. Gibbs said as she rose from the harp. She added pointedly, "I think we can all thank *you* for that."

Nora froze. Had she heard correctly? Was the housekeeper implying that she was flirting with Mr. Knox? Yes, Mrs. Gibbs must be thinking she'd fallen into his arms on purpose. The idea was so utterly preposterous that she almost laughed. Even if she had, why would Mrs. Gibbs care? Then it hit her. Mrs. Gibbs was jealous!

"Why thank me, Mrs. Gibbs?" she asked in an attempt to confirm her suspicion.

"Your secretarial work, dear, has lifted a heavy burden from Mr. Knox's shoulders. He told me just the other day how much he has come to appreciate your *many talents.*"

Nora bit back an acerbic response. She realized she was dealing with bruised feelings, and that it would be best if she corrected any misconceptions. "I am happy to have helped alleviate some of Mr. Knox's business worries. He is a nice, elderly man. He reminds me a bit of my fiancé's grandfather."

Of course, Nora didn't have a fiancé, but a harmless white lie might help ease the housekeeper's ridiculous jealousy, she reasoned.

Mrs. Gibb's features softened. "You have a beau, then?"

"That I do." Nora nodded, crossing her fingers behind her back.

"You shouldn't keep those things a secret, dear." Mrs. Gibbs had brightened perceptibly. "Aye, Mr. Knox is a nice, elderly man at that." She smiled. "Ah, to be young again, and in love. I'm pleased for you, Nora. Is he anyone I might know?"

"No, he's presently at sea," she replied, and then caught herself. Why had she said that? It wasn't true at all.

"Let's hope he returns safely." Mrs. Gibbs turned to the others. "Now, everyone, let's clean up. It's way past bedtime, especially for the wee ones."

The children moaned, but upon seeing Mrs. Gibbs direct a stern face in their direction, they scampered from the room like wild kittens.

Ginny laid aside her flute-pipe, picked up two empty cookie plates, and leaned close to Nora. She whispered, "You handled that quite well." She grinned and headed for the door. "Millie, there are more dishes in the kitchen. I could use your help."

"I'm coming," Millie responded. On her way out, she gathered up the remaining mugs and plates.

Nora, sipping at the final dregs of her cider, pondered the growing complexities of life in the Knox household.

She was just about to follow Millie when the front door opened. A tipsy Nolan stumbled in, followed by a swirl of snowflakes. "Nora! Ah, I see I've missed the Christmas party," he said, brushing snow from his cape. "That's all well and good as I've had one of my own, and a fine one it was."

Nolan's grin reminded Nora of her younger brother Brendan's expression whenever he was caught consuming a forbidden treat. "Somehow, I can tell you had a *very* good time."

With an elaborate bow, Nolan said, "So now I'm off to bed." He staggered for the hallway door, but stopped before reaching it and pulled a small packet of letters from his pocket. "Almost forgot. Mail arrived for Mr. Knox, and there's one here for you, too."

"For me?" she asked, her heart suddenly aflutter. It has to be from Da with news of Mam and Brendan. They had survived! She rushed over and took the bundle from Nolan, "Thank you," she said breathlessly.

Nolan turned once again for the hallway as Nora sorted through the mail. She came upon a brown envelope. A message had been penned on it in black ink.

> Please contact Jamestown auctioneer for current address of   N o r a   S m i t h , arrived in Jamestown end of July 1650 on the Dutch ship, *Goede Hoop*. Auctioned off in early August as indentured servant to party unknown. Deliver as soon as possible.

A chill smothered her expectations. Da would not have known the date of the *Goede Hoop's* arrival or the subsequent auction.

She turned the letter over and read: Billy Devlin.

She ripped the envelope open, withdrew a one-page letter, and began to read:

My Darling Nora,

My Darling Nora? Her eyebrows rose as she read on:

THE GIRL WHO WAS ME IS GONE

I hope this letter finds you in good health and spirits in spite of your current circumstances. Many changes have occurred since we parted. By a stroke of fate, I am now captain of a pirate ship on my way to Portugal.
I will explain, God willing, when I arrive in Jamestown sometime next year. I am now in possession of a small fortune—enough to buy your freedom, along with Anne's. If your contracts are not for sale, I will simply steal you away, as I intend to make you my wife—if you'll have me. I can't imagine you saying no, as you must still be madly in love with me and missing my handsome, charming self.
Ever yours,
Billy.

Make me his wife? Still madly in love with him?

Billy Devlin, she thought, you are the most conceited man I have ever known—and the most amusing. Imagine thinking I would marry you—and that I love you! You are indeed daft. I may care for you a bit, as I would any old friend from Ireland, but my feelings certainly don't come to more than that. As for you having enough money to buy my contract, that's certainly wishful thinking. Billy, I admit you've always had good intentions, but they're seldom associated with reality.

About to toss the letter into the fireplace, Nora hesitated. She would keep it as a memento. After all, Billy's ship could be lost at sea, and this message would be the last evidence that he'd ever existed.

She felt a moment of despondency. Why was she feeling sentimental? She didn't really have an answer.

MICHAEL BROWN

Unwilling to delve into feelings she was sure would amount to nothing, Nora blew out the candles and went to bed.

CHAPTER THIRTY-TWO

Nora's eyes flew open. Someone was in bed with her!

About to scream, she froze when the intruder whispered in her ear with breath smelling of sweet cider, "It's all right, Nora. It's just me."

Mr. Knox!

"Sir, what are you doing in my bed?!" she gasped. Rolling over, she felt bare skin up against her. He was naked! "Sir, you must leave at once!"

He propped himself up on an elbow and peered down at her. Flickering light from a candle on the side table mottled his features. He must have brought the taper with him to light his way.

"Mr. Knox, please, you can't be here. You must leave at once."

"I was lonely. I thought we could talk."

His slurred words told her all she needed to know. Her employer was inebriated. "Sir, we can't talk in my bed." Pinned between him and the wall, she attempted to suppress the fear welling up inside her by trying to reason with him. "We can talk in the morning, in your office. Now, sir, if you'll please leave."

"I know I shouldn't be here, Nora, but I . . . I couldn't help myself. It's been so long since I've been with a woman, since my wife . . . If you would really like me to go, just say so."

I definitely want you to go! she thought. She said, "Yes sir. I think it would be best." She gasped—every muscle in

278

her body tensed. His hand had slid beneath her nightgown, and was resting on her bare thigh!

Fighting an urge to cry out for help, she spoke as calmly as she could manage. "Sir let us have our conversation in your office tomorrow. Right now, I am very tired, and I would like to go to sleep. If you would please just leave." She flinched. His hand was moving! "Sir, you must stop. You must not touch me like that. You said you would leave if I asked you. Now, I am asking you to go. Take your hand away, please, and go!"

"I will," he said huskily. "In just a few moments."

Shocked and embarrassed by his fondling as it became more and more intimate, she squirmed to the edge of the mattress, where it met the wall. She was trapped, on the brink of panic.

"It's all right," he said. "I'm not going to hurt you." He raised the back of her nightshirt.

Scream! her inner voice yelled. But who would dare come to her aid? Nolan? Perhaps, but he slept on the other side of the house, and wouldn't be able to hear her. Ginny? Millie? Neither of them would interfere. And Mrs. Gibbs would be furious to find them together.

"Mr. Knox, sir, please stop! You must not do this," she said, all the while trembling from his touch. "Sir, you must leave my bedroom at once."

He ignored her. His breathing had become increasingly ragged. She had heard stories of plantation owners having their way with the help. But, she thought angrily with tears welling, she was not going to become one of those Mollies. If that was what Mr. Knox was thinking, she would set him straight!

"Sir," she said, trembling with fear—and then his hand slid up to fondle her breasts. "No! Please, sir, stop!" She raised her arms protectively to cover her bosom. "Please, sir, you shouldn't . . ."

"Nora, be still," he commanded. "I promise you, I won't do anything you don't want me to do."

"Sir, I don't want you to do *anything*."

He chuckled softly. "Wait and tell me that in a few minutes. Then, if you still say *no* to me, I promise you I will leave."

Cornered, feeling more vulnerable than she'd ever been, she didn't know what to say or do. Would he really leave if she said no?

Then she gasped. His hand was sliding below her midriff!

Heart thumping as if it might burst through her chest, she demanded, "Sir, please, you can't touch me like this! I am asking you to leave, now, this instant! You said you would . . ."

"Nora, calm down."

Shivers rippled over her torso as she felt his hand move *down there*. His fingers began touching, exploring, moving in a slow, circular motion. Oh, God. What was he doing? No man had ever touched her intimately before.

Suddenly he lifted her up and pulled her nightgown off over her head!

Gasping, completely naked, she attempted to curl away, to escape, but he grabbed her and pressed her shoulders onto the mattress—and straddled her!

She let out a wail. "Sir, no! Please stop! You can't do this! Please, I've never lain with a man. I don't wish to . . ."

"Shush," he said as his hand caressed the side of her face and then her breasts. "You are a treasure, a beautiful treasure, one I will cherish, but *only* if you wish it."

Only if she wished it?!? Grasping at a thread of hope, she pleaded, "Sir, I *wish* you to get off of me! I do not want you to . . ." Her words were stifled as his lips pressed harshly against hers! *NO!* Struggling, she pushed his face away. She tried to fight him, to buck him off, but he had her pinned to the mattress. She realized with a growing sense of terror that he was too strong for her. She suddenly cried out—he had wedged himself between her thighs!

"Oh God! Stop! You said you'd—owww!" A searing pain tore through her.

He was inside of her!

Thrusting, thrusting. Thrusting.

Beaten, broken, she lay motionless as tears rolled down her cheeks.

Finally, she felt him shudder, and then he gasped, "I'm . . . I'm sorry, Nora. I couldn't stop. I couldn't . . ."

His voice faded as a deep sense of loss flooded Nora's senses and her world drained of *oh, so many dreams.*

*****

Weepy-eyed, unable to sleep, Nora lay alone, curled up on the mattress like a wounded fawn.

For the last few minutes, she had been vaguely aware that dawn had crept silently in through the window to chase the shadows away. If only sorrow and pain could dissipate as readily as the night, she thought. A deep soreness within prompted the reoccurring question that had been tormenting her all night.

How could she have let it happen? How could she have let him violate her? She should have yelled and screamed. Surely, that would have scared Mr. Knox away. Yet, she hadn't. Why not?

She finally had to admit that she had been too frightened, and that she was no match for his physical strength. And, if she had yelled, no one would have answered her pleas for help. Was it her fault that she'd been raped? She hadn't done anything to encourage Mr. Knox. No matter what Mrs. Gibbs might have thought, she had not been flirting with him. She hadn't fallen into his arms and pushed her bosom into his hand!

Outside her window, the first chirping of birds began. How was it possible for sparrows to be happy when she was so miserable?

She rolled over to stare at the wall. Although Mr. Knox had been gone for hours, she couldn't stop recalling the shock of his unsolicited touches and intimacies, which all added to her growing sense of incredulity and embarrassment.

Still struggling with her loss, she couldn't shake her self-incriminating thoughts. I didn't fight him as hard as I could have. I should have scratched and bitten him, and gouged his eyes! Why didn't I? Was I too frightened? Or was it because I knew that further struggle would have been futile? Mr. Knox must think I have no virtue, that I'm a girl of easy morals. How is it possible for a moral person like me to have allowed myself to be taken advantage of? It is inconceivable! And yet it happened.

Nora threw back the covers and slipped out of bed. She winced as the ache in her groin caused her to curl over. Tentatively, she straightened up. The pain was more pronounced, but not as bad as she thought it might have been. Then she saw the bloodstain on the sheet. What was she going to do? How could she explain? Well, she thought with a grain of hope, if anyone saw it, she would just have to say it was her time of the month.

Nora stripped the sheet from the mattress and carried it to the washbasin. Lifting the water pitcher, she soaked the fabric, and then glanced at her reflection in the mirror above the dresser. Did she look any different? Would people be able to tell she was no longer a virgin? Nora turned her head this way and that. Oddly, she looked remarkably the same.

Relaxing a bit, she washed herself thoroughly. She then lathered the sheet with soap and rinsed it, all the time wondering how she would be able to face the man, almost a stranger, to whom she had lost her virginity. She knew that the next time she saw Mr. Knox, she was likely to flush with humiliation.

Her eyes widened as she stared again at the mirror. How can I be alone with that man? she thought. How should I respond? Oh, if I could just go back to bed and stay there forever. Or maybe I can run away.

Knowing those were not viable options, Nora lifted her petticoat from its peg and began to dress.

She didn't know how she would be able to face him, yet she had no choice.

Caught in a web of uncertainty, her chest tightened. How would Mr. Knox react? Would he give her a smile or a hug? Or would he ignore her and act as though nothing had happened? What could she do if he wished to come back tonight? Or every night?

Nora shuddered. She was at the mercy of her owner.

*****

Nora walked down the hallway with feet as heavy as lead. As she approached Mr. Knox's study, she stopped short of the door to gather her courage, and then she went in.

Mr. Knox looked up from his desk and took off his glasses.

Oh, Lord, what must he be thinking?

Before she could venture a guess, he rose and came to her, taking her hands in his. "Come, Nora, sit down with me. Please."

Nervous as a lamb in a wolf's lair, she allowed him to lead her to one of the two chairs before his desk. As they sat, she was surprised to notice that he seemed ill at ease, quite unlike the Mr. Knox she had first met.

"Nora, I must humbly ask that you accept my apology for last night. I don't know what possessed me to act in such an ungentlemanly manner. My behavior was abhorrent. I really shouldn't drink, as it lowers my sense of propriety. I am so terribly embarrassed. Can you find it in your heart to forgive me?"

Encouraged by his unexpected expression of remorse, she was searching for a proper response when he added, "I am really not the horrible kind of person you must think I am. And, believe me, none of what happened last night was your fault. I wish to heaven that it had never occurred. Please, Nora, forgive me."

Relief flooded through her. He didn't think she was an awful person after all. Mr. Knox was taking full responsibility for last evening, and he'd asked for her forgiveness—as he should!

She inhaled. "I don't know what to say."

"Will you forgive me?" he repeated.

Her worries regarding future harassment melted as she looked into his pleading blue eyes. He was sincere. She nodded. "Yes," she said, "as long as you never come into my bedroom again. You must promise."

"I promise," he responded with a shake of his head. "It will never happen again. I can assure you of that."

An errant thought came to her from out of nowhere. He didn't like being with me. Nora blinked at the outlandish notion. What is the matter with me? Am I crazy? Stop it, Nora!

She nodded to Mr. Knox and said, "I am thankful for your apology."

"I hope we can put this ungentlemanly act aside and resume our relationship, as I am sorely in need of your valuable services."

"I'll try."

But you did rape me.

"Nora, please, you must promise that you will never say anything about last night to anyone. I have a close relationship with someone, and the last thing I want is for her to hear about my lack of judgment. It would hurt her deeply."

He had a relationship with someone, perhaps in the house? If so, who could that be?

"Nora?"

He was waiting for an answer. She nodded. "Yes, I promise, Mr. Knox. I assure you, I don't wish for anyone to hear about it, either."

He smiled. "Bless you. Now, let's put this behind us and go to work. We have several letters to get out today."

So easy for you to say, she thought. As if my virginity was nothing!

Mr. Knox rose and went around to his desk while Nora proceeded to what had become her secretarial table. Shaking off her disappointment at how little her employer had valued her virginity, she realized how callous men could be—even after the fact. Simply put, he got what he wanted . . . and that was that. Any emotions that might be troubling her had not even been considered. How convenient for men.

Sitting in her chair, purposefully pushing aside further thought on the subject, she picked up quill and paper. As she glanced to Mr. Knox waiting for dictation, she wondered who he could be in a relationship with. Ginny? Possibly. Mrs. Gibbs? Perhaps. Millie? No, far too young. Some lady in the township?

Interesting. Who was Mr. Knox's lover?

CHAPTER THIRTY-THREE

"Ya seen Rufus?" Willie asked as he shuffled into the trading post's great room, scratching his unkempt beard. "He ain't in his bed."

Anne and the girls were huddled in their shawls around the fireplace, attempting to ward off the cold that seemed to come right through the log walls.

Anne replied, "Haven't seen him this morning."

Willie grunted, picked up a mug, and filled it with cider. "Then, I 'spect, he's probably still playing cards at Murray's. Can't drag him away when he's winnin'." He sipped his drink, then added, "He was supposed ta help me slaughter a pig this mornin'. One of ya want ta give me a hand?"

Trish's eyebrows rose in disbelief. "Us slaughter a pig? Ha!"

Nell scoffed, "Not me. It's snowin' outside." She pulled her shawl closer around thin shoulders.

"We're whores," Addie said as she rubbed her hands together and held them out to the hearth. "Not butchers."

Willie responded, "Ya girls ain't pullin' yer weight 'round here. Least ya could do is help me out once in a while."

"Willie," Anne said, "as soon as the snow lets up, Trish, Nell, and Addie will be bringing in more money per month than you and Rufus combined. And besides, slaughtering animals is not a ladylike endeavor."

"Work is work," Willie said with a dismissive wave of his hand. "Don't matter if it be man or woman."

"Try tellin' that to one of me mutton mongers," Trish said.

As Nell and Addie laughed, Anne studied Willie. If it weren't for bad hygiene, tangled hair, and matted beard, he might be half-decent looking. There was a cherubic face beneath all that hair. His features belied a fiery temper that could be sudden and frightening, although at times she thought it was an act he put on for Rufus. He seemed to enjoy the role of bully and enforcer.

It was a pity he works for Rufus, she thought. Their association was destroying a person who otherwise might have some redeemable qualities.

Willie drained his mug, set it down, and shrugged into a heavy sheepskin cape. "Guess I'm gonna have ta gut thet sow all by meself." He added sarcastically, "I appreciate all yer offers fer help, ladies."

The girls giggled.

Anne said with a twinkle in her eye, "Stay warm, Willie."

Willie hesitated as he reached the door. "When yer eating pork chops tonight, ya can all thank me." He pulled the latch open. As snow blew in, he grabbed a musket from beside the door and shouldered his way out. Before he had the door closed, he stopped abruptly. "Sweet God almighty."

"What is it?" Anne asked, alarmed that he had let the door blow back open and was standing stock still with his back to her.

"Rufus," Willie groaned.

Anne and the girls hurried to the door, watching as Willie approached Rufus, who lay on the snow only steps away.

"Indians!" Trish exclaimed.

Nell and Addie cried out in horror. Three arrows protruded from Rufus's still form. One had pierced his throat, two others were buried in his chest.

Anne shivered. Lifting her shawl over her head, she glanced warily around the front yard for a sign of the savages. Seeing none, she stepped out and walked up to

Willie, who was kneeling beside Rufus, checking his torso for signs of life.

Anne noticed snowflakes falling on Rufus's open eyes. "Is he dead?"

"Yeah. Been dead fer awhile." Willie raised the flintlock and checked to see that the firing pan was dry. Satisfied, he took a piece of cloth from his pocket and covered it, protecting the gunpowder. Cocking the hammer, he eyed the grounds, searching. . . .

Anne followed his gaze. The livestock corrals had been knocked down. A few pigs and sheep loitered on bloodied snow, but most of the animals had been stolen or had run off.

"Goddamned Indians!" Willie swore. "Anne, get back inside with the girls. Make sure all the windows an' doors are barred. The savages are likely still around. An' if they're not, I'm gonna track 'em."

"Willie," Anne said. "You can't go after them by yourself!"

"Yes, I can. I'm gonna kill every one of them murderin', thievin' devils." He stomped off to shoo the remaining livestock back into the broken corral, and then began raising the fallen rails to secure the animals in place.

Anne knew Willie was referring to the Powhatan Indians, who were known to steal food and kill settlers, especially during the lean winter months. "Girls," she said, hurrying back to the doorway. "Let's make sure all the windows and doors are barred."

The girls, plainly frightened, backed into the trading post. Nell asked, "Are we gonna be attacked?"

"I hope not. Hurry on with you, now. And don't open the door unless you hear a friendly voice." Anne grabbed a musket from inside the doorway and ran over to the corral, where Willie was doing makeshift repairs. She said. "I'm coming with you."

"No, yer not! This is my fight."

"Rufus is my fight, too."

"Why? You hated him."

I didn't hate the man, she thought. I hated his drinking and his rudeness.

She said, "That's only partially true."

"Ya'd only slow me down."

"If I slow you down, you can leave me." To strengthen her argument, she added, "Two muskets are better than one."

His eyes narrowed. "Can ya shoot?"

"Not very well," she admitted. "But I can reload your rifle while you shoot mine."

Willie cocked his head, staring at Anne as if he were seeing a new side of her.

A voice called, "Yo, Mr. Pitt!"

Anne and Willie spun around to see a mounted English officer followed by a dozen infantrymen double-timing it up the road.

"Looks like we might be getting' some help," Willie said.

Anne's stomach twisted into a knot. In the distance, the English officer looked familiar. She raised a hand and pressed knuckles against her lower lip to stop it from trembling. Moments later, Anne let out a sigh of relief. The officer's face was young and unblemished.

The military group advanced upon them at a steady pace, moving past the corral that was tainted with patches of blood. The officer's face hardened when he saw Rufus's arrow-riddled body.

He reined in before them. "Mr. Pitt?"

"Thet's me," Willie answered.

Anne stared at Willie with surprise. Why was Willie assuming Rufus's surname?

"I'm Lieutenant Hastings from Fort Jamestown. I am sorry for your loss." He glanced at Rufus's body. "A friend of yours?"

Willie nodded. "My uncle."

Anne's eyebrows flew up. Willie was Rufus Pitt's nephew! Well, that explained Rufus's deferential attitude toward him.

"Any idea how long ago the Powhatan attacked?"

"I'm guessin' it was late last night. My uncle woulda been comin' home from playin' cards when he came across the murderin' savages. Looks to me like he tried ta make it ta the front door." He raised his musket. "Anne here, and I are just about ta go out after 'em. Yer welcome ta come along."

"Please, Mr. Pitt, leave the savages to us. It's our job. It's best if you and the young lady stay here and protect your property."

Willie's mouth set stubbornly. He wasn't happy. Willie wanted to avenge his uncle.

"Please, sir," the officer said, noting Willie's defiant expression. "It would be best. The Powhatan are starving. They're marauding the settlements for meat and grain. Another group could come by at any time. Your place here is still in danger."

"All right, Lieutenant," Willie said reluctantly. "I'll see ta my uncle."

The officer nodded. "I'll let you know when we've eliminated the savages. Good day, sir." He touched spurs to his mount, and the small column started off in pursuit of the Indians.

Anne's glance fell to Rufus's body, as snow pelted his unseeing eyes. She asked, "What should we do about your uncle?"

"Bury him. Good and deep. I don't want him comin' back."

CHAPTER THIRTY-FOUR

I have to stop believing that Mr. Knox will dismiss my claim, Nora thought, but dare I trust him with my story?

Preoccupied with the concern that had lingered unresolved for far too long, Nora paused in the midst of writing a letter to the House of Burgesses regarding Jamestown's need to lengthen its main cobblestone street.

She twirled the quill pen between her fingers as she weighed the pros and cons of her employer's character. He *is* English, she thought, and he believes in the letter of the law. I know he's fond of me, but is "fond" enough of an incentive to offer aid in solving my problems?

She tapped the tip of the long feather against her chin. If I tell him I'm a wanted criminal, will he offer to help me, or will he have me prosecuted?

She stole a glance at Knox, who sat at his desk reading correspondence that had recently arrived. It related to England's latest insult to the colonies, an embargo on all imported or exported goods that made it against the law to trade with any country other than England. It was a proclamation that would be financially ruinous for Jamestown's merchants, and an outrageous move that would punish the settlers for not acknowledging Oliver Cromwell's Parliamentary government.

Was now a good time to approach him? Nora had discovered that there was no appropriate time to broach the subject of her personal dilemmas, as Mr. Knox was busy with assembly business from dawn to dusk. Nevertheless, time was flying by, and she had to do something, or she would die. Would he listen to her story and offer assistance, perhaps feeling indebted to her for his night of weakness?

With her heart thudding against her ribs, she finally mustered the courage to say, "Sir?"

Gerald Knox looked up. "Yes, Nora?"

"If I might have a word with you, sir?"

"Certainly," he replied, lowering the papers. "What is it?"

Not knowing where to begin, she finally asked, "Are you happy with my work?"

"Of course I am," he replied, sitting back in his chair. "You wouldn't be here if I were not. You have been a tremendous help to me, more so than I could ever have imagined."

Wavering in her commitment to proceed, Nora glanced out the window. It was snowing again today, and it was only mid-November.

Quit procrastinating!

Nora braced herself, knowing how much the next few minutes would mean for her future. She carefully placed the quill pen on its silver tray and turned to face Mr. Knox.

"Nora," he prompted before she could say anything, "what is it?" He suddenly looked annoyed with himself. "Oh, of course. Forgive me. I should have spoken to you about this earlier."

Taken aback, she watched with curiosity as Mr. Knox rose from his desk and came forward hesitantly, as a penitent might approach a confessional. "I want you to understand that if you are with child, you and the baby will have no financial worries. It will be my duty and honor to care for both of you, and to see to it that our child has a proper upbringing and education." He shook his head as if to shed a memory. "Nora, I am still so ashamed of myself."

She blushed. The man standing before her had never tried to say, as some men might, that it had been her fault. On the contrary, he had taken full responsibility. Would she ever be able to forget that night?

Nora stared into earnest blue eyes. Even though the loss of her virginity had been a horrific experience, Mr. Knox's previous heartfelt apology and his courteous behavior since then had convinced her of his innate goodness.

She might eventually forgive him, but she would never be able to forget. However, she acknowledged, losing her virginity could have happened under far worse circumstances.

She knew it was time to address her employer's concerns. "Mr. Knox, I have had my monthly cycle. I am not pregnant."

"Thank God," he said with relief. "I must admit that the possibility had me a little worried. Well, what then is it you wish to speak to me about?"

Fighting an urge to retreat from the subject, she barreled ahead. "Might I ask for a favor?"

"Of course, you may," he replied with the hint of a smile.

Where to begin?

"I have a friend who traveled with me on the *Goede Hoop*. She was auctioned off on the same day as I, and . . ."

". . . and you wish to know what became of her?" he asked, anticipating her inquiry.

"Yes."

"I believe I may be able to assist you," he said, turning to his desk. "What is her name?"

"Anne Smith."

"A sister?"

"No. Anne is my friend."

He sat in his chair and picked up a quill pen. "I will see if I can locate this Anne Smith for you," he said as he wrote the name down. "Although, you know, she could be anywhere in the colonies."

"Yes. It's just that if I know she is of sound mind and body, I will feel so much better."

"I'll get on with it first thing tomorrow. Now, anything else?"

"Yes, there is . . ." Dare she tell him?

"Please, Nora, continue."

"Well, first of all, my surname is not Smith. It's O'Lalor. I am Nora O'Lalor."

He blinked with surprise.

"I should explain."

He nodded. "Please do."

"My family was preparing to emigrate to Jamestown when my brother and I went to say goodbye to my friend, Anne, at her family's farm. When we arrived, we found English soldiers there. They had killed Anne's da and brother. We ran to the back of the house and opened the door, looking for Anne. Two English officers were inside. They had raped and murdered Anne's mother, and were raping Anne before our eyes. When the officers saw us, they drew weapons with the intent to kill us. My brother and I shot first, wounding one and killing the other."

Mr. Knox lowered his spectacles in shock.

"It was self-defense," she added quickly.

He finally asked, "Were there any witnesses?"

"Only the wounded officer. But he's in Ireland, if he's still alive."

Knox lifted a hand to massage the back of his neck. "That may or may not be a problem, depending upon circumstances. Were murder charges filed?"

"I don't know."

"Time will tell," he said. "To your advantage, we are a long way from Ireland."

Nora swallowed and continued. "After the shooting, when I told my da what had happened, we left for Dublin immediately. My father had booked us passage on a ship to Jamestown under the assumed surname of Smith, which we were using for protection from the authorities. The ship we were scheduled to board wasn't in port, so, with the English in pursuit, my da arranged passage for us on a Dutch frigate, the *Goede Hoop*. Before sailing, my mam and little brother came down sick with the plague, which was rampant in Dublin. Da insisted that John, Anne, and I sail on without them, saying that the family would follow when they recovered. Unfortunately, I have heard no word from them."

"I am sorry for you," Mr. Knox said sincerely. "That's quite an ordeal you've been through."

"There's more."

Mr. Knox sat back in his chair. After studying her for a moment as if she were another, far more complicated person, he nodded for her to continue.

"The English officer I wounded followed the family to Dublin. He caught up to us as we were boarding the *Goede Hoop*. Captain Van der Root, who hated the English for his own reasons, saved us by shooting several soldiers, and then, as we were sailing from Dublin Bay, he ordered his crew to fire a broadside into the *Sovereign*."

Knox's eyes widened. "England's man-of-war?"

"Yes."

"Good God!" he exclaimed. "That captain must be insane. Tell me. This English officer you wounded, did he live?"

She shrugged. "The last I saw of him, he was swimming in Dublin Bay. His boat had been shot out from under him."

Knox said, "Odds are he drowned or died of his wounds. Even if he lived, the chances of this officer locating you are very small, especially since you have changed your name to Smith. As far as that Dutchman goes, I wouldn't want to be in his shoes. The Admiralty will hunt him to the ends of the earth. Nora, this is quite a surprise. You've experienced some very distressing incidents in the past months."

"There's more."

"More?!" Mr. Knox stared at her in disbelief. He folded his arms and nodded for her to proceed.

"Onboard the *Goede Hoop*, after I had paid Captain Van der Root the money owed for our voyage, he kidnapped us and put us in chains with the prisoners who were being transported to Jamestown to be sold at auction."

Mr. Knox steepled his fingers. "Are you claiming that you, your brother, and your friend were sold under fraudulent circumstances?"

"Sir, Anne and I are free Irish citizens. Unfortunately, my brother passed away on the voyage."

"I am sorry to hear that, Nora." Knox lowered his hands and shuffled some papers on his desk. "Well, that's quite a story. If you and Anne can prove what you've just related, then you are indeed free citizens, and I will have to deal with that. It's complicated. Money that has changed hands will need to be recovered."

"Sir, once I am free, I believe I will be able to obtain funds to repay you."

"I am not worried about being compensated. These claims of yours will have to be presented before the assembly. You will also have a case of kidnapping against the Dutchman. In our colonies, that's a serious crime. Of course, the fact that this Dutch captain ordered the deaths of English soldiers and fired a broadside into the *Sovereign* has already made him eligible for the gallows. I doubt he will live out the year."

"Yes, sir."

"The first thing you and your friend will have to realize is that the courts will need proof of who you are, and that your father purchased tickets for your voyage."

"I have no receipt of ticket purchases, but I do have papers that prove who I am." Nora hesitated, feeling as if the floor beneath her were turning to quicksand.

"What is it, Nora? You've lost your trust in me so soon?"

"I, like you, sir, have many problems."

Knox rose from his chair and came to stand beside her. "I am fairly good at problem solving, at least when it's a problem that's possible to solve."

Mine may not be, Nora thought miserably.

"Have you heard of Running River Plantation?" she said.

"Yes, I know it. A valuable piece of property. A man by the name of Malcolm Butler runs the place for a foreign investor, I believe. What of it?"

In for a penny, in for a pound. "Sir, my family owns the plantation."

Knox's blue eyes narrowed behind his spectacles.

"I possess my father's last will and testament, which states that if all my family should pass on, I am granted full ownership of the Running River Plantation. While I pray they are still alive, I hope to assume ownership as the sole heir until, God willing, the remainder of my family arrives in Jamestown."

Mr. Knox removed his spectacles. "You say you have legal documents that will substantiate your claim?"

"Yes, sir. Upstairs. Would you like me to show them to you?"

"Yes, eventually, but first things first. Number one, since you have no proof of purchase for the voyage, you must remain an indentured servant until your claim as a landowner can be verified."

"But, sir . . ."

Knox held up a hand. "Nora, I really don't want to lose you. You've become invaluable to me. But, that said, I *will* help you."

Relief coursed through Nora. She settled back in the chair.

"I will look over your father's last will and testament and the deed to Running River Plantation. If what you claim is true, then you are obviously a free Irish citizen who has been badly mistreated. Give me a few months to. . ."

"A few months!"

He nodded. "I know it must sound like a long time to you, but that's what it will take to clear up my schedule so that I can begin the process of authenticating your claim. It may take even longer, but I *will* help you. All I'm asking for is patience."

Patience?

She fought to withhold a scowl as she thought, Yes, I can be patient, even though it isn't one of my more outstanding attributes.

"That will be fine, Mr. Knox," she said, attempting to show some enthusiasm. "I've waited this long. I can certainly wait a little while longer."

"Nora, out of curiosity, why didn't you mention this earlier?"

"You've been so busy, and I was afraid of what you might say. I know this doesn't show that I have much faith in you, sir, and I apologize."

"No reason for an apology. Trust is something that has to be earned," he said. "And I'm gratified that you've confided in me. It shows that I've regained a measure of your trust. That means a great deal to me."

A knock sounded on the door.

Nolan entered. "Mr. Knox, there's an emergency meeting assembling at the House of Burgesses with Sir William Berkeley. They are gathering to devise a plan to circumvent England's pernicious trade edict."

Knox rose from his desk. "I will go at once. Nora, be patient. I will help you."

"Thank you, sir."

The two men hurried out, leaving Nora alone. A thrill tingled up her spine and brought a smile to her lips. She'd done it! Her dreams were about to come true. She would soon, or fairly soon, be a free person and a landowner!

CHAPTER THIRTY-FIVE

Finally, back at sea.

Captain Billy Devlin stood at the helm, operating the whip staff, adjusting the long handle that passed through the hole at his feet to the deck below where it attached to the rudder. While many ship builders located the whip staff in a covered cowling on the poop deck, Billy preferred the *Lobo do Mar*'s design without the cowl, as it gave him an unrestricted view in all directions.

He glanced at the compass—south by southwest. Satisfied that he was on course, he turned his attention to Antonio, who was climbing the ladder from the main deck. His lean, ponytailed first mate came to stand alongside him as the Bermuda sloop passed through the mouth of the Targus River, leaving the colonial port of Lisbon, Portugal.

"Captain," Antonio said, "we're steady at nine, ten knots. Weather permitting, we'll reach Jamestown in six weeks, unless we find a loose sparrow and decide to give chase."

Billy grinned. *Loose sparrow*, he had come to learn, was pirate jargon for a ship to be attacked and looted. While he was anxious to return to Jamestown and locate Nora, he knew he had to keep the crew happy. In all likelihood, there would be more battles and booty to take before he reached Chesapeake Bay.

"Antonio, I'm sure you and the men will inform me as soon as you see a loose sparrow."

"Aye," his first mate replied. "That we will, Captain."

Billy marveled at *Lobo do Mar's* speed. She cut through the sea like a new ship. The sloop had been in dry dock at the city's shipyards for almost three months, where her barnacles had been scraped off, her leaky planks re-caulked, sanded, and painted, and the configuration of her deck reengineered. Billy had seen to it that unnecessarily high bulkheads be lowered, and all hand-carved adornments removed. The main deck was de-cluttered for ease of movement. An additional four gun ports had been added, making her a twelve-gun ship. Finally finished with repairs and restructuring, Billy had been confident the vessel was ready for any encounter at sea. With a fair wind blowing, *Lobo do Mar* could reach speeds of slightly over twelve knots. All elements equal, she could outrun most, if not all, of the ships presently afloat.

Billy breathed in deeply. The fresh salt air filled his soul with optimism.

I'm on my way, Nora. The world will be ours for the taking.

Overhead, seagulls circled and soared in the cloudless, blue sky. The tall main sail rippled in the blow as seamen scampered up and down rigging, securing lines and releasing the jib sail.

When Billy was in Lisbon, word had reached him that British Admiralty had branded him a pirate and placed a price of 1,000 pounds on his head.

A mere thousand pounds, was that all?

Billy had had his first laugh in ages.

Shortly after selling the galleon, *Lady of Dorset,* Billy had located Captain de Almeida's wife, an attractive woman in her early twenties, and had relayed the sad news of Diego's death. He had also left a large amount of silver and gold with her, the captain's portion of the pirates' booty. It was a fortune, enough to support her and her two young sons in style for the remainder of their lives.

Lobo do Mar had been made ready to sail just in time, as, somehow, the crew had managed to spend all of their money on gambling, women, and drink, and were now broke and growing more ill-tempered by the day.

Nothing like empty pockets, Billy mused, to spur blood lust for pirating and fresh booty.

CHAPTER THIRTY-SIX

"Mmm," Anne murmured, inhaling the fragrance of apples as she sipped from a cup of warm cider. Opening the kitchen door, she stepped out into the garden.

Early morning, before the little doxies awoke and business began, was her favorite time of day.

Strolling through the small meadow bordered by marshland and dense forest, she enjoyed the changing scents of pine, tupelo, and maple, as well as the more pungent, yet pleasantly musky odor of moss-veiled cypress, whose gnarly knees protruded from dark, placid pools of water. Shielding her eyes from the rising sun, she followed the flight of an osprey to its nest of jumbled sticks high atop one of the enormous cypress trees.

This morning, the wetlands seemed more alive than usual, with birds chirping, frogs croaking, insects buzzing, and a flock of wood ducks splashing to a landing only a few yards from her. Rare treasured moments. . . .

Her thoughts drifted back to her arrival in Jamestown, the humiliating auction, and the move into Rufus Pitt's Trading Post. The first eight months, while Rufus had been alive, had been purgatory. A virtual prisoner, she had not been allowed to leave the house. But since Willie had taken over for his deceased uncle, she was given small liberties. She now had time to read, sew needlepoint, and take walks in the garden. She was still forbidden, however, to leave the property.

Sipping cider, she strolled through ankle-high grass, on the lookout for snakes and the ever-present poison ivy. Aside from these inconveniences, she marveled at the wild berries and swamp flowers, which seemed to have bloomed overnight since the cessation of winter.

Her thoughts turned to Trish, Nell, and Addie. They had all recently celebrated birthdays. Now at thirteen, fourteen, and fifteen, they were becoming young ladies—not in the proper sense of the word by any means, but physically.

How had Anne, at soon-to-be seventeen, become their adoptive mother, or their "madam," as Willie liked to call her?

"I am no madam!" she remembered protesting.

Yet Willie had insisted. "Yer ta watch after 'em like a mother hen. Thet's what ya are, Anne, a madam."

While there was no comparison between a mother hen and a madam, she'd had to admit that she did take care of them. So perhaps Willie was right.

She not only managed the girls' sessions, but also ran the store and tallied the inventory of assorted dry goods, clothes, trapper's pelts, and paraphernalia. She was fast becoming an expert in the art of bartering. To her surprise, Willie, who couldn't read or write and who had shown no prior interest in business, had suddenly shown a facility for numbers. Where that talent had come from was a mystery.

Thinking of Willie, she recalled that he had risen at dawn and left for Jamestown. Why? She had no idea, but waking early, let alone going anywhere before noon, was unusual behavior for the lazy oaf.

Anne idly stopped by a rosebush to pluck a small blossom. She smelled its perfume, then smiled and tucked it behind her ear. Watching a blue heron fly above her with slow, deep wing beats, long legs trailing, she contemplated the change in Willie. Ever since Rufus's death, he had seemed more and more human. Heretofore, the unkempt lout had displayed as much interest in business as a slug, but lately he had begun to pay attention to inventory, costs, and balances.

Yes, now that she thought of it, Willie *had* changed. He had gone from being a nonentity under Rufus's domineering and mean-spirited influence to a young man who showed signs of intelligence.

But, although he had become more bearable, he never let Anne forget she was an indentured servant—*his* indentured servant. He had said, "With me uncle's passin', yer me property now. An' ya'll do what I say. Ya understand? I'm yer master!"

Master—a hateful word! No man owned her! At least not mentally.

Willie's words had sent revulsion flooding through her, especially when she recalled his relentless ogling. Willie wanted to bed her, she had concluded. To her relief, she soon learned that he hadn't been after carnal pleasures; he had the girls to take care of his physical needs. It became evident that his close scrutiny was an attempt to learn what she was doing and how she was doing it.

Turning to retrace her steps through the garden, her eyes fell upon the earthen mound that covered Rufus Pitt's grave. Oddly, it had been dug only a few yards from the combination trading post/bordello. Nothing grew on the churned earth; it was as barren as the day Rufus had been buried. She half-smiled when she remembered asking Willie why he had buried Rufus so close to the structure. "Makes it a short walk ta piss on 'is bloody grave," he had replied.

That explained the lack of vegetation.

When the breeze changed direction, rustling the leaves in the trees, Anne inhaled, tasting salty air as it blew in from Chesapeake Bay. Jamestown, with its fort, its homes, buildings, and docks, was less than two miles away. But to Anne, property bound, the distance between settlement and trading post seemed as vast as the distance between the Earth and the moon.

A horse neighed in the distance. Anne turned to look at the road that wound past the trading post. Willie was cantering up on his powerfully muscled chestnut stallion. The wild-haired, unshaven young man rode into the yard and dismounted. Anne walked over to him as he was opening his saddlebag.

"I got somethin' ta show ya," he said with subdued eagerness. He pulled out three books. "Here, take 'em."

She blinked. Willie was giving her books?

Accepting the tomes, she glanced at the titles: *The King James Bible, Romeo and Juliet,* and an English translation of *Don Quixote.* "Why, thank you, Willie."

"They're not just fer you, they be fer *us.* Fer ya ta learn me ta read an' write."

Anne almost dropped the books.

Willie's hairy face scrunched up with concern. "Ya *can* teach me, can't ya?"

To conceal her shock, Anne lowered her gaze and stared at the books.

"Thet's all I could git. Will they do?"

"Well, they're a little advanced."

"I can learn," he said with grave intensity. "An' thet's not all."

"Not all?" She looked up, not knowing what to expect.

"I also need ta speak like you." He nodded, confirming his intent. "Yer ta teach me ta talk like educated folk."

Anne gawked at Willie as if he were a different person. This was the antithesis of the Willie Pitt she had come to know. Gazing into his eyes, she could see resolution. He was dead serious, and he was waiting for an answer. Quick to realize that an opportunity had fallen into her lap, Anne thought: Maybe, just maybe, I can work something out for the both of us.

"All right," she said cautiously. "I will try to help you, but on one condition."

He tugged suspiciously at his shaggy beard. "What thet be?"

"If I'm successful, it's going to change your life. You'll be a new man. And for that, you are going to have to pay me—a lot."

He replied slowly, "How much is *a lot*?"

"I want you to give me a percentage of the trading post, and I also want my indenture time dismissed, so I can be a free person. I don't like being owned."

Before he could open his mouth to protest, she added quickly, "And I want fifty percent of everything."

He growled like an angry bear that had just stepped into a trap.

Jumping a step back, she was reminded how much he did resemble a bear. She hastened to support her requirements. "Willie, I do all of the trading post's inventory, the adding, subtracting, and multiplying of costs and figures. I keep this place running. I also take care of the girls' schedules, their needs, and their wants. You can't do it alone. And the plain fact is, Willie Pitt, you can't do it without me."

Willie's face contorted. He pawed through his unruly mop of hair and scratched at his furry jaw.

Did he have fleas? Anne wondered.

Willie finally blew out a breath that could have snuffed a dozen candles. His eyes crinkled and narrowed to cagey slits. "I'll give ya ten percent. Nothin' more."

Hallelujah! Anne wanted to shout. Instead, she jutted out her jaw. "Fifty percent."

His nose twitched as if he had just smelled a skunk. "Twenty percent. An' thet's me final offer. Ya can take it or leave it!"

On the verge of accepting the offer, she hesitated. What could it hurt if she were to . . ? She steeled her eyes. "Willie, it's fifty percent *and* my freedom, or no lessons." To emphasize her conditions, she handed the books back to him.

His mouth dropped open. His gaze fell to the books, and then came back to her. Finally, he nodded curtly. "Here it is. Yer to stay until the rest of yer indenture time's up, 'cause I need ya. If ya agree to thet, then I'll give ya an additional ten percent a year till ya have forty percent." He leaned in close, eyes flaring. "Now ya can take thet, or ya'll git nothin'."

Oh, my God! Anne blinked with astonishment. With the exception of her immediate freedom, Willie was giving her almost everything she'd asked for, even if it was in installments! But he was shrewd. The agreement would keep her at the trading post for the remainder of her allotted time, but then she would be free—and own forty percent of everything!

William stuck out his beefy hand. "Deal?"

Dare she push for fifty percent? She vacillated—it was tempting—but then she placed her small hand in his paw and shook it. "Deal."

"An' one more thing."

Uh-oh.

"I'm not ta be Willie no more. From now on, yer to call me by me Christian name, William."

Anne almost laughed, but he had such an earnest look in his eyes that she couldn't hurt his feelings. "Pleased to meet you, William."

CHAPTER THIRTY-SEVEN

"Those damned colonists!" General Meredith Chetwynd said as he gazed out at Bristol Bay from his Admiralty office's window. "Governor Berkeley has openly defied our embargo! This is sedition. We must retaliate!"

He turned to face Captain Dice, who sat in a chair before his desk. "Captain, there are only six naval vessels in the harbor. Your assignment was to assemble a fleet of fifteen ships of the line and 2,000 infantrymen by the first of May. It is now the end of June. Kindly explain yourself."

It had been an impossible task in the first place, and the general knew it. The horse's ass! That was how Dice wanted to reply. Instead, he waited a few heartbeats to cool his temper. He said, "I'll have the additional nine ships and the troops within the next three months and . . ."

"Three months?" the general interrupted. "The fleet was supposed to be leaving this month, not in September!"

Dice clenched his jaw. Months of festering infections had required the extraction of three more teeth, and still the pain, a constant reminder of that Irish slattern, persisted. He said, "Sir, Oliver Cromwell has been steadfastly holding onto the ships that I requested."

"I don't like excuses, Captain Dice. We have a blockade to put in place, and we have ships all over the world that you can . . ."

"That's the problem, sir."

"Don't interrupt! The uprising in Ireland is coming to an end. Ships and troops will be coming home. As they appear in Bristol Bay, you are to requisition the vessels and troops needed to fulfill your assignment, and set sail for the West Indies and the Americas. If you can't accomplish that relatively simple task, I will find an officer who can. Do I make myself clear?"

Dice replied tightly, "Yes, sir, but when additional ships return, they'll have to be overhauled, their hulls cleaned and painted. I doubt we can be ready to sail much before mid-July or early August, and then it would be prudent to delay the armada's voyage until after the winter months, as hurricane season runs from . . ."

"I know when the hurricane season is! You are to follow my orders, Captain. You do understand orders, don't you?"

Dice might have argued for a later voyage, but the fact was that he had been chomping at the bit to leave England. Delays were eating at his soul like a malignant disease. He wanted his revenge, one that had become an obsession, and it couldn't come too soon.

"Yes, sir," he said.

"Dismissed."

*****

Nora sat at her desk, the quill idle in her hand. A half-smile played upon her lips as dreams danced in her thoughts. God willing, she would soon have her freedom! Although it had taken almost five months for Mr. Knox to clear his schedule, he was now ready to take up her case. Enthralled, she placed a hand to her bosom.

My heart is pounding so, she thought. Oh, I feel like jumping and dancing!

Then, inexplicably, she shivered. This was odd, as the room was quite warm. The skin on her arms prickled. Unable to quell a growing anxiety, Nora rose to look out the window. The grounds were peaceful and quiet. But, wait! A flicker of movement caught her eye.

Angelo and Franny had stepped from their cottage, an added-on extension of the barn. Angelo seemed wary. He drew his pistol and said something to Franny, waving her back.

Nora's pulse began to race.

Angelo walked cautiously toward the pigpens.

Suddenly, an arrow flew out of nowhere and pierced his neck!

Franny shrieked! A split second later, another arrow struck her in the chest, knocking her to the ground!

Angelo dropped to his knees. Two additional arrows struck his shoulder and belly! His flintlock discharged into a mound of hay. The fodder immediately ignited, sending up a wisp of smoke.

Terrified, Nora couldn't move.

Indians were racing out of the woods.

Suddenly, a yellow and red painted face leaped in front of the windowpane!

Nora screamed.

The Powhatan raised his tomahawk.

Adrenaline spiking, Nora whirled and bolted from the office. The sound of shattering glass rang in her ears.

"Indians!" she yelled at the top of her lungs. "We're being attacked! Indians!"

Mrs. Gibbs ran from the kitchen into the hallway, followed by Mick, Millie, Ginny, and the twins. "How many?" Mrs. Gibbs cried.

"I don't know. A dozen at least. Angelo and Franny have been shot, and one of the savages is breaking into the office!"

"Quick, into the parlor," Mrs. Gibbs ordered. "Lock and block the windows and doors! Loaded muskets are in the gun rack!"

Rushing after the servants, Nora slammed the door behind her, but there was no lock on it. Nora placed her shoulder against a tall, heavy sideboard and attempted to push it to block the door. Struggling with all her might, she could only get it to move a few inches.

"Millie," Nora yelled to the servant girl who stood frozen in the middle of the room. "Help me with this!"

The girl jumped to life and ran to her.

The two of them pushed on the cabinet. It slid across the door.

Mrs. Gibbs had two muskets in hand that she had taken from the rack, along with powder horns and accompanying shot bags. She instructed, "Prime the pans. These're ready to shoot!" She jammed flintlocks, powder horns, and shot bags into Nora and Ginny's hands, and then opened a drawer to retrieve two pistols.

She offered one of the flintlocks to Millie, whose eyes flew open. "I . . . I can't," the maid stammered, nervously twisting one of her long blond braids. "I don't know how to shoot."

"Then grab a poker from the hearth. You can use that."

Thud! Thud! Thud! The door, blocked by the heavy cabinet, was reverberating with powerful blows.

Mrs. Gibbs led her son quickly to the back door. Opening it, she peered out, searching the woods behind the house. "This way is clear!" Without wasting another second, she leaned down and said, "Mick, you have to run for help!"

"Yes, Mother," the boy said bravely, as tears welled.

"Go to the House of Burgesses. Tell Nolan and Mr. Knox we're under attack. Spread the alarm! Go now, and God be with you, my darling." She kissed the top of her son's head and pushed him out the door. "Run, Mick! Run like the devil is after you!"

Mick dashed off.

Thud! Thud! Thud! The heavy cabinet in front of the door was beginning to give way. Nora breathed in deeply, her hands shaking as she raised the flintlock.

The door splintered. The cabinet was thrown aside. The painted monster leapt through the opening, obsidian eyes blazing with blood lust. Tomahawk in hand, he charged.

Nora squeezed the trigger. A bloody hole appeared in the Indian's forehead a split second before he collapsed at her feet.

"Reload!" Mrs. Gibbs shouted.

Heart racing, Nora tipped the powder horn into the musket's barrel. She chased the gun powder with a lead ball, which she jammed down with the ramrod.

"Oh, God no! Mick's been hit," Ginny screamed, looking out the window as her twin daughters clung to her skirts.

Nora, Mrs. Gibbs, and Millie rushed to her side.

Mick was on the road, running, but now he had an arrow piercing his left upper arm. One of the Powhatan was sprinting after him, rapidly gaining ground.

No, you don't! Nora thought. She broke the window with her weapon and brought the musket up. Harkening back to memories of her youth in Ireland, she prayed, "John, dear brother, I need your steady aim." Nora pulled the trigger.

The savage fell like a mass of disjointed bones.

"Thank God!" Mrs. Gibbs cried.

With a sigh of relief, Nora saw that Mick was still running. She said a hasty prayer, "Thank you, John, for teaching me how to shoot."

Glass shattered. The housekeeper grunted.

"No!" Millie cried.

An arrow was buried in Mrs. Gibbs's chest. She collapsed on the floor. Cara and Colleen, crying hysterically, scampered out of the way.

Bloodcurdling cries raised the hair on the nape of Nora's neck as she hastily tapped a measure of gunpowder onto her musket's flash pan.

Savages smashed away at jagged shards of glass in the window frame. Behind her, a blue faced brave burst through the door. He lunged at Nora, but tripped over his dead companion.

Before he could regain his footing, Nora swung the butt of her musket. It glanced off his skull, stunning him. She staggered back, raising the flintlock to shoot, but quicker than a striking serpent, the monster rolled over and sprang at her. Knocking her weapon aside, he straddled her, pinning her to the floor.

With her heart in her throat, she watched as his features twisted with triumph. He raised his tomahawk. There was a flash of movement as Millie struck the back of the Indian's head with an iron poker. The savage collapsed on top of Nora.

Struggling to push him off, she saw a black-and-red-faced Powhatan crawl through the window, armed with a knife in one hand and a tomahawk in the other.

He slashed Ginny's throat with the blade. As the cook collapsed, the garishly painted Indian turned to Millie, who panicked and dropped the iron poker. He leaped at her, grabbing her by her blond braids, and held her in place as he swung his club. He smashed in the side of the girl's head, spattering blood and brains.

Panting like a rabid wolf, the fiend then turned to Nora. A rush of panic coursed through her as she pushed out from under the dead Indian and came up with rifle in hand. Black-and-red Face let loose a piercing cry and charged. Nora jammed the barrel of the flintlock into the brave's chest and pulled the trigger. BOOM! To her horror, the ear-splitting discharge came an instant after he had knocked the barrel aside.

Nora's mind froze. The savage grinned hideously as he swung the tomahawk.

Everything went black.

*****

"Sirs! Excuse me!" Nolan yelled, bursting through the assembly hall's double doors, interrupting the meeting at the House of Burgesses. Mr. Knox, a dozen elders, and Sir William Berkeley, Governor of Virginia, turned with alarm at the intrusion. "Mr. Knox," Nolan explained, "there's been an Indian attack at your home! Mick ran all the way here to alert us, even with an arrow in his arm."

"Good God!" Knox jumped to his feet. "There's only Angelo there to protect the women and children."

"Angelo and Franny are dead. The women have armed themselves and are barricaded in the parlor."

Knox turned to Sir Berkeley and the assemblymen. "Gentlemen, alert the militia. Have them rush mounted troops to my home. Speed is of the essence."

"Go, Gerald," Sir Berkeley said in his booming voice. "We will be right behind you."

Nolan and Knox rushed down the hallway to the front entrance. "How bad is Mick's wound?" the assemblyman asked.

"The arrow went halfway through the fleshy part of his upper arm. If there's no infection, he'll recover."

"I pray there is no contamination," Knox said. "That boy means everything to me."

Outside, Nolan and Knox dashed down the steps to the waiting carriage. Nolan leapt onto the driver's seat as Knox climbed up beside him.

"We have two muskets," Nolan said. He reached behind him to retrieve the flintlocks, which he handed to Knox. "And two pistols apiece."

Knox said, "Hopefully, we'll get close enough to those savages so that even I won't miss."

Nolan slapped reins to the backs of the geldings. "Yah! Yah!"

The carriage raced away.

*****

Where am I? Nora wondered groggily, awakening to a haze of darkness accompanied by waves of pulsating pain that relentlessly attacked her skull.

Slowly, as her brain began to function, she became aware that she was moving—but not of her own volition. She opened her eyes to images of hooves splashing through a brackish swamp and tall cypress trees heavy with moss. Frogs croaked and other living things slithered through reeds and muck. Everything reeked of decay and dead animals. She attempted to move, but her hands and feet were restricted, bound. She realized she was tied to a horse.

She had been taken prisoner!

The memory of a swinging tomahawk flashed before her. That accounted for her throbbing skull. She wondered if any of the others were still alive. She twisted her neck to investigate and instantly regretting it as darts of pain pierced her head. Grimacing, Nora saw she was tied to one of two horses being led by a group of war-painted Powhatan who jogged beside them. She caught glimpses of Ginny's twins, Cara and Colleen, sitting astride the second horse. They were also tied hand and foot.

The poor things, she commiserated, to witness so much violence and death.

Besides human cargo, the horses carried an assortment of pilfered bear and deer hides. One of the bearskins had been thrown over Nora's back. There were also sacks of grain, several dead piglets, and at least two dozen squawking chickens dangling from ropes. Mosquitoes hovered around prisoners and Indians alike, biting, drawing blood.

The small party climbed out of the swampy wetlands and proceeded up a pine-covered knoll, where they followed a narrow, rocky path. The horses stumbled and almost fell several times before they came to the top of a promontory, where the party stopped. Nora spotted a trail that led down to a river a hundred feet below. Two canoes had been pulled up onto the bank and partially hidden in underbrush.

Her hopes sank. Rescuers, if they were coming, would never reach them before the Indians loaded them into canoes and they all disappeared into the wilderness. She wondered, did Mick make it to Jamestown? Was help even on the way? Were they going to be murdered? Probably not. The savages had had the chance to kill them, but kidnapped them instead.

The black-and-red painted heathen who seemed to be the leader of the Powhatan carried a musket stolen from Knox's home. He motioned to his yellow-faced companion, a scrawny boy not more than fifteen years old, and said something in their native language. The youth had a bloody scalp attached to his breechcloth that was covered with greenish-black flies. Nora moaned when she recognized young Millie's blond braids.

Yellow Face trudged back to the horse that carried the children, and pulled them to the ground.

"Nora," Colleen called, "what are they going to do to us?"

"I want to go home," Cara cried.

"You're going to be all right, girls," Nora replied, hoping it wasn't a lie. "The militia will be coming after us."

"But what if they can't find us?" Colleen asked.

"They have excellent trackers," she said, not knowing if it was true. "They're sure to find us."

Black-and-Red Face grabbed the bearskin covering Nora and threw it onto a pile of pine needles beneath a tree. The other braves began unloading the horses and carrying their booty down the path to the canoes at the river's edge.

Yellow Face picked up Cara and threw her over his shoulder while another brave lifted Colleen. The braves carried the twins down the trail.

If help was coming, they'd better hurry, Nora thought as she glanced over her shoulder to the lowlands and swamps they had traversed on the trek from Knox's residence. A lone hawk circled high over the vista. The only other sign of life, a distant smudge of smoke on the horizon, was coming from the plantation. Her heart sank. There would be no rescue.

Black-and-Red Face stepped over to Nora and pulled her off the horse. Looking past him so as to avoid eye contact, she noticed the other braves were staring at her and making lewd gestures. Black-and-Red face roughly spun her around and slapped her buttocks, to elicit howls of delight from his companions.

Nora turned on him like a wildcat. "Turn us loose! You can't kidnap a woman and children, and expect to get away with it. You'll all be arrested and shot. Your only chance is to let us go. Climb into your canoes and go home, all of you.

Otherwise," she added for emphasis, "you'll be killed. The soldiers and militia will never stop hunting for you!"

Black-and-Red Face's mouth curled into a cruel smile. He grabbed onto her arms, his fingers digging painfully.

"Let go of me!" She twisted, attempting to wrestle away, but the Indian's vice-like grip made it impossible.

The savage edged closer, his eyes black, mercilessly black.

Trembling, she pleaded, "Let us go. You can still escape."

The Indian responded with Powhatan gibberish.

He doesn't speak English, she thought with a sinking heart. He hasn't understood a word I've said.

Suddenly, the heathen picked her up, carried her over to the bearskin that lay on the pile of pine needles, and threw her down on the hide.

Nora rolled over, her heart thumping wildly as she grasped his intention. No, this was *not* going to happen! Spotting a fist-sized rock only inches away, she lunged, grasped it, and turned on her assailant.

She recoiled. The monster had dropped his loincloth!

His companions yowled like coyotes as the beast began to flaunt his manhood.

Come any closer, you filthy beast, and I'll kill you! she thought.

With terror and rage burning through her veins, she raised the rock, baring her teeth and snarling as if the bearskin beneath her had suddenly burst to life with all its primitive ferocity.

I'll split your skull open like a melon!

Heart thundering, prepared to fight to the death, she was waiting for the naked Powhatan to lunge when one of the braves fell on her from behind and, with Black-and-Red Face's aid, pressed her to the earth.

Nora screamed, bit, and kicked as tears burned her eyes. "No! No! You savage beasts! Damn you! Get off of me!"

A blow to her face stunned her. Barely conscious, she felt the gray dress ripped and pulled off. Hands clawed at her petticoat and tore it away.

THE GIRL WHO WAS ME IS GONE

Naked, helpless, she clenched her eyes as the yipping, howling savages closed in on her like a pack of wolves after a bitch in heat.

*****

"Yah! Yah!" Nolan shouted, whipping the sweat drenched, foam-streaked team to a full gallop. The carriage slid from side to side as its wheels fought for traction on the narrow road. Gerald Knox held tightly onto the bench seat while gripping the muskets between his knees.

Nolan's green eyes narrowed as they focused on a plume of dark smoke swirling in the air above a copse of trees. "Fire!" he announced.

"Damned savages," Knox replied. "God willing, we'll get there in time to kill the bastards!"

"Yah! Yah!" As they rounded a curve, the road became a straight line. Nolan spat. "Dead Indian ahead."

Knox nodded grimly. "One less for us to kill."

They swept past the body.

"Yah! Yah!"

The geldings raced on, charging through the thicket of trees that surrounded Knox's residence and farm buildings. Nolan yanked back on the reins, abruptly bringing the lathered team to a stop in the forecourt.

The men were speechless. Yellow-orange flames shot out of the barn like an erupting volcano. The wood crackled and popped as the fire consumed dry siding, engulfing the structure. Horses trapped inside the barn neighed in terror. Fiery embers, caught by the gusting wind, showered the yard with burning sparks.

"Angelo and Franny!" Knox exclaimed.

The Del Corsos's arrow-riddled bodies were sprawled close to the barn beside a burnt, smoking pile of hay.

Nolan glanced quickly around. No sign of the savages—or anyone else. His eyes followed windblown embers to the west end of the residence—the wood-sided wing was also afire.

"The house!" he yelled, grabbing a musket from Knox. He checked its flash pan, leapt from the carriage, and ran for the front door.

Knox, his face full of anxiety, tightened his hold on the second musket and jumped to the ground just as a half dozen field hands ran into the yard and stopped to stare in shock at the burning structures.

The shrill whinnying of terrified horses inside the barn spurred Knox to order, "Half of you, try to save the animals. The rest of you grab buckets, fill them at the well, and get moving!"

Without waiting to see if his commands were obeyed, Knox dashed after Nolan, who was already sprinting up the front steps two at a time.

Upon entering the parlor, Nolan stopped short. Mrs. Gibbs, Millie, and Ginny's bludgeoned, arrow-punctured, mutilated bodies were lying on the floor in pools of blood. Millie was the only one who had been scalped. Probably because of her long blond hair, Nolan surmised. It would be a valued trophy.

"Dear Lord!" Mr. Knox exclaimed as he rushed in, recoiling at the sight of the arrow protruding from Mrs. Gibbs's chest. Glancing quickly to Millie and seeing her staring eyes and scalped head, he blanched and then went to kneel beside the housekeeper. He placed a hand on her neck, feeling for a pulse.

Nolan, eyes and ears alert for danger, crouched beside Ginny, who had a bloody gash on her throat. His stomach clenched.

"Mrs. Gibbs is gone," Knox said with a pained voice as he stood.

Nolan nodded, knowing how much the housekeeper had meant to Knox. Then he saw Ginny's chest rise and fall. "Ginny's alive!"

Mr. Knox rushed to his side. "Thank God."

Nolan touched Ginny's throat, inspecting the wound. Her eyes fluttered open. "Nolan . . ."

"I'm here, Ginny," he said. "You're going to be all right. You have a gash to the side of your throat, but there's little bleeding and no cut arteries."

"Cara and Colleen . . ." Ginny gasped.

Nolan's head jerked around, eyes ablaze.

"Where's Nora?" Knox said, casting a glance toward the door.

"I didn't see . . . Nolan, the girls," Ginny moaned.

"Stay with Ginny," Nolan told Knox, already dashing from the parlor.

*****

Nolan's gut twisted tighter and tighter as he ran from room to room and found each one empty. He hurried to the servants' bedrooms. They, too, were empty.

Nolan burst into the parlor, where Knox was securing a cloth around Ginny's bloodied neck. He announced, "Nora and the twins are missing. The savages must have taken them hostage. I'm going after them."

"I'm coming with you," Knox said, rising to his feet.

"No, take care of Ginny," Nolan said.

"You can't go after them alone," Knox protested. "There will be others here soon. Wait for them. We can form a . . ."

"There's not a minute to spare," Nolan interrupted. "The Powhatan will be running for the James River. They'll have canoes waiting. I have to catch them before they load and push off, or we'll never see the twins or Nora again." He knelt beside the cook. "Ginny, I'll bring our girls home, I promise."

Tears welled in the cook's blue eyes as she murmured weakly, "There are so many more of them than you."

"Have faith in me, Ginny-girl." He kissed her forehead. "Get well."

As he stood, Knox handed him his musket and said, "Take this. Go with God, Nolan."

With two flintlocks in hand, Nolan said, "I'll be taking the geldings."

Knox nodded. "No quarter!" he said, with fervor.

"None given." Nolan raced from the room.

*****

Oh, dear God, I hurt everywhere, Nora thought as she lay curled in a fetal ball. What have they done to me? What *haven't* they done to me?

The tip of her tongue touched her lips. She flinched. They were split, swollen, bloody. Like the rest of her, she reflected bitterly, beaten and violated.

She raised tethered hands to wipe vestiges of dirt and tears from her cheeks, and grimaced. The slightest movement elicited pain. She lay still, barely breathing in order to ease the ache from possible broken ribs. The pine needles beneath her were damp with perspiration and other bodily fluids that she didn't want to think about. The bearskin partially covered her nakedness. She was in too much agony to make the effort to pull it above her waist. Her disheveled clothes lay on the ground a few feet away.

The aroma of roasting fowl prompted her to shift her gaze to the small campfire where three of the stolen chickens had been killed and spitted. Yellow Face was tending to the birds. It seemed the Indians were not concerned about being followed. Or, more likely, they were starving and considered the rising smoke a risk worth taking.

Nora noticed the horses were gone; the Indians must have released them as they prepared to leave. A stab of fear pierced her heart. Where were the twins? Then she remembered. They had been carried down to the canoes.

Nora's thoughts turned to her mortality. Da, Mam, I came so close . . . so close. It's going to be up to you now to claim the family plantation. I'm sorry I won't be at the wharf to meet you when you arrive with Brendan. I'm afraid that when these savages tire of using me, I'll be murdered, as they have murdered my friends.

THE GIRL WHO WAS ME IS GONE

She tentatively stretched her legs, and winced. Curling back into a ball, she considered Cara and Colleen. What was to become of them? Their odds of survival weren't good. Thankfully, they'd been by the river when she was molested, thereby spared the horrors of witnessing her torment. That was a blessing, the only blessing in a day of revulsions.

And as for her? Would the savages kill her quickly or . . . Nora shuddered. She couldn't bear to think of the additional tortures the savages might have in store for her.

Had all of her life been lived to end like this? Everything she'd dreamt of, only hours ago so close to being attained, had been decimated by the Powhatan attack. A tear rolled down her cheek. There would be no freedom and no Running River Plantation.

A squirrel ran past her and scurried up the trunk of a pine tree, followed by the noisy chirping of birds. It's odd, she thought, but when I die, the flora and fauna of this world will continue on existing as if I had never lived. The loss of my life won't even cause a ripple in a pond. Actually, I suppose that's fair. I haven't mourned the death of many of nature's living creatures.

Gazing heavenward, she realized, I am not afraid to die. I'll accept death when it comes, not at all willingly, but with resolve. Lord, I have a favor to ask of you, not for myself, but for the twins. Please spare them. They are so young and innocent. Please save them from being ravaged by these heathens. Please, Dear Lord.

Something in her subconscious whispered, *Nora, help might never arrive. You must attempt to escape with the twins.*

Nora's brow wrinkled. How? I am trussed like an animal.
You must try, Nora.

Gritting her teeth, she cautiously uncurled. That wasn't as bad as I expected, she thought, with a slight grimace.

Furtively looking about, she saw that the Indians were coming back up the path. They straggled up to the campfire, their attention on the sizzling chickens.

Nora surreptitiously began to pull at the bindings on her wrists. She flinched as the rope cut into her flesh, drawing blood. Ignoring the pain, she continued twisting and pulling. The restraints wouldn't give.

Raucous laughter prompted her to turn to the painted devils who were now pulling the roasted fowl from the spits and, screeching like children, tossing the hot birds back and forth until they had cooled. Then the braves tore the carcasses apart and began to devour the meat like ravenous animals.

Black-and-Red Face, chewing on a thigh, glanced over at her with a lascivious grin.

Nora grabbed the edge of the hide and pulled it up to cover herself. The Powhatan laughed at her attempted modesty. The way they ogled her sent a clear message: We're not finished with you.

Looking away from them, a flicker of movement caught Nora's eye. She squinted, attempting to discern the faraway object. Her heart jumped! A man on horseback was approaching, with a second horse on a lead line! They were heading in her direction, galloping across the wetlands. The rider slowed to a canter, obviously searching the ground.

He must be following our tracks! she thought.

A yell pierced the air. Black-and-Red Face had also spotted the tracker.

The savages rose in unison, quickly gathering up the two stolen muskets, bows and arrows, tomahawks, and knives. Their faces twisted into hellish masks as they eyed the approaching threat. Then, seeing there was only one man, they shrieked with coyote-like yips and yaps. Black-and-Red Face spoke harshly to the youngest heathen in his native tongue. Then he and the other three savages raced off.

Nora's breath caught in her throat as she watched the rider gallop out of the marshland and take the rocky trail up into the hills. As he drew closer, she recognized him. Nolan! Oh, Lord! Four against one—impossible odds. Nolan was going to be murdered!

THE GIRL WHO WAS ME IS GONE

Yellow Face, the young man who had been left behind to guard the captives, hunkered down beside Nora. Munching on a piece of chicken, he watched as his tribesmen swept down the hill, closing in for the kill.

*****

"Yah!" Nolan yelled as he whipped reins from side to side, urging the gray to a faster, near-killing gallop, followed closely by the second gelding on its lead line. Steam rose from hot, white-lathered chests, nostrils flared, and iron-shod hooves struck rocks, spewing sparks as they thundered up the narrow, tree-lined trail.

Earlier, Nolan had found the war party's tracks in the swampy earth. He had counted two horses and five Indians. He knew instinctively that Nora and the girls would be riding, as the Powhatan shunned horses.

Traveling by foot put the Indians at a disadvantage, one Nolan had been counting on to catch up to the war party. He knew that the Powhatan, the Creek, and nearby Iroquois tribes had foresworn the riding of horses for more than one reason. The tribes lived in close proximity to rivers and had historically used birch bark canoes to travel from one village to the next. The ancient paths they trekked while inland were steep, narrow, and rocky—for the most part unsuitable for horses. These reasons, as well as the fact that they steadfastly refused to cultivate feed for livestock, had left them without the advantage of equestrian travel.

Nolan's green eyes darted to movement in the distance. He reined in. As the gray trembled beneath him, blowing hard, he observed four war-painted Powhatan running downhill toward him. They were darting around trees, leaping over rocks, and closing the distance between them.

Nolan spat.

He sat still for a moment longer, studying the Indians as they suddenly divided, now coming at him from different directions. Looking past the savages, he spotted a wisp of smoke at the hilltop and a lone Indian guarding the campsite, but no sign of Nora or the girls.

He hastily pulled the geldings into a thicket and tied them to a sturdy branch. Then, with both muskets in hand, he loped into the densely treed area, where large rock outcroppings and boulders vied for space among long-armed, gnarly branches.

Nolan skirted a small meadow and scrambled up a rocky ledge. Breathing heavily, he climbed to a natural pocket among the boulders and stopped to check the flash pans on the muskets along with those on the brace of pistols in his waistband. Satisfied that the flintlocks were primed and ready, he pulled a plug of chewing tobacco from his pocket, bit off a piece and, beginning to chaw, settled down to wait.

The wind whistled softly through the trees. Pine needles drifted down, silent as falling feathers. An occasional pinecone dropped to the earth with a *thump*. Birds tweeted and wings fluttered.

Suddenly, song and movement ceased. Stillness. . . .

Even the breeze had fallen off.

Nolan spat. He breathed in and out to calm nerves that had been roiling his stomach. Steady, he whispered to himself. He knew he couldn't afford to miss a single shot. A bird on his left chirped. Nolan tightened his grip on the musket.

Chirp! Chirp!

Those calls came from his right.

He gently pulled back the hammer on the first musket, cocking it. He set the weapon aside, lifted the second flintlock, and repeated the motion.

Chirp!

That one had come from a copse of trees behind him. He was encircled.

He spat.

Suddenly, a brave armed with bow and arrow darted between two trees fifty paces away. Nolan raised his weapon and aimed, but checked the urge to fire.

He would not shoot until the black-eyed devil came closer.

Chirp! Chirp!

Two Indians burst from the foliage, one to Nolan's left, the other to his right, not fifty feet away. The first savage nocked an arrow and shot. The arrow hissed past Nolan's head. The second brave fired a musket. The bullet ricocheted off a rock behind him.

The Indians, screaming fiercely, whipped tomahawks from their waistbands and charged!

Nolan calmly took aim and pulled the trigger, hitting the first brave in the throat. As he fell, Nolan picked up the second musket, swung around, and, when the charging savage was within twenty feet of him, squeezed off a shot.

The musket ball slammed into the savage's chest. Blood erupted like a gusher. The painted face registered shock a millisecond before he hit the ground.

Discarding the musket, Nolan yanked pistols from his waistband. Two down.

The Indian in the meadow had disappeared.

A blood-curdling yell!

Nolan spun around. A red-faced brave was sprinting toward him! The heathen stopped not fifteen feet away, raised the flintlock, aimed, and fired just as Nolan squeezed his trigger.

Simultaneous shots!

Nolan winced as a bullet tore off the lobe of his left ear, then watched the savage fall, his brains spilling out of his half-blown-away skull.

Whizz!

An arrow grazed Nolan's neck. He whirled around. The fourth Powhatan, ten paces away, nocked another arrow to his bowstring.

Nolan aimed his second gun.

The Indian yanked back the feathered barb.

Nolan pulled the trigger.

The savage, hit between the eyes, cartwheeled backward as his arrow flew harmlessly into the air.

The twins! Nora!

Ignoring his bleeding earlobe, Nolan gathered up the muskets and started off at a run for the Powhatan encampment.

CHAPTER THIRTY-EIGHT

Had Nolan been shot? Nora worried. Was he wounded—or dead?

Six gunshots, echoing one after the other, had shaken her as if the bullets had thudded into her own rapidly beating heart.

Out of the corner of her eye, Nora watched Yellow Face. He carried a bow with an arrow nocked on its string as he paced at the edge of the encampment. He was mumbling nervously, pulling the arrow back and forth as he searched for his companions.

Had he been one of the Indians that raped her? Nora didn't know, but she did know one thing. If she could somehow overpower him and then release the twins, they could run off and hide before the others returned.

The probability of Nolan surviving a fight with the odds four-to-one against him was doubtful. Nora, who had surreptitiously been chewing on the bloodied wrist bindings, gritted her teeth and yanked. They parted! Gasping with surprise, she bent over and, with cramped, shaking fingers, struggled to untie her ankles while keeping a wary eye on Yellow Face.

The savage suddenly stiffened. Whatever he had seen made him turn and run. He darted past Nora and scrambled down the path toward the canoes.

Moments later, she heard, "Nora?"

She whipped around to find a bloodied Nolan jogging up the hill.

328

Reaching her, he immediately assessed her situation. "The twins?"

She pointed to the path. "Below, on the river. Canoes. Hurry!"

"Take this." Nolan unsheathed his knife and placed it in her hands. Without another word, he disappeared down the trail.

Nora sawed the bindings off her ankles, snatched up her petticoat and dress, and ran after Nolan. Hurrying down the slope, she saw Nolan standing over the twins, talking to them. Beyond, in the river, Yellow Face was rapidly paddling away.

Nolan stepped to the edge of the water, eyed the escaping Indian, and raised his musket. He squeezed off a shot.

The back of Yellow Face's head exploded. He toppled over the side of the canoe, his body quickly vanished beneath the surface of the river.

Nora dashed over to the twins and, still holding the knife, began to slice through their restraints.

"Where are your clothes?" was the first thing Cara asked.

Oh, Lord. She suddenly realized she was carrying her garments, but hadn't stopped to put them on.

"Yes," Colleen chimed in as if Nora's nudity were the most shocking part of their ordeal. "You are supposed to wear clothes."

Nora cut through the remaining ropes. "I was just going to get dressed, but I thought you'd like me to cut you free first."

"Thank you," Colleen said, as her bindings fell away. "You can get dressed now."

Nora's half smile twisted as a stab of pain shot through her lower belly. Turning away to hide her discomfort, she slipped into the torn petticoat and pulled the ragged dress over her head. The clothes barely covered her, but they were better than nothing.

"Mr. Nolan saved us, didn't he?" Colleen asked.

"Yes," Nora said, suddenly realizing they were free. The terror was over. A wave of relief swept over her. "Yes, he certainly did."

"Nora, are you going to be all right?" Nolan asked with concern as he walked up to them.

"I believe so. I'm a bit damaged, but I'm alive, thanks to you."

"Daddy!" the twins yelled as they ran to Nolan. Smiling broadly, he scooped them up into his arms.

Daddy? Nora felt her eyes misting as she registered the similarity between the little girls and Nolan—the auburn hair, those green eyes, and the smiles. Why hadn't she seen that before?

Nolan, after hugging the girls, focused on Nora. He said sincerely, "Nora, whatever happened up on the bluff, we need never talk about it."

"Thank you," she replied, overcome by his thoughtfulness.

*****

Nora winced, aching from the abuse she had endured. Riding astride the gelding wasn't helping, but Cara asleep in her lap somewhat mollified the pain.

The important thing, she thought, is that we're all safe! After what we've been through, it's so difficult to believe.

As if to reassure herself, she glanced at Nolan, who rode a horse-length ahead, cradling Colleen in his arms. Nora couldn't help but give a whisper of a smile at the sight of him. She had torn a strip of cloth from the hem of her ruined petticoat and wrapped the makeshift bandage around Nolan's head to stop the bleeding from his wounded ear. He reminded her of the fopdoodle knight she had read about in the English translation of one of her father's books, *Don Quixote*. It was almost impossible to believe that the slim, taciturn man with no outward signs of strength or bravado had singlehandedly killed five savages.

MICHAEL BROWN

In my wildest dreams, she marveled, I could never have imagined it.

Nolan was not only bringing them all home, but he had also retrieved the pilfered muskets, hides, grain, pigs, and chickens before kicking holes in the remaining canoe and pushing it into the river to sink. He had left the bodies of the Powhatan to rot. He had spat—nasty habit—and then remarked, "It's a fitting end that wild animals devour their carcasses."

When Cara stirred in her lap, Nora said, "We're almost home, sweetheart. Almost home." The little girl settled back to sleep.

The warmth of the young girl, so innocent and vulnerable, prompted Nora to wonder, will I ever have children of my own? Could the molestations have caused permanent damage? Worse, could I be with child? She groaned, once more in the realm of uncertainty.

The thought of having a baby fathered by one of the savages sent shivers of revulsion through her. She clenched her eyes, only to have images of the carnage at Knox's residence flash before her. Mrs. Gibbs, Angelo and Franny, Millie—all murdered! Wonderful people, gone forever, never to experience the joys of life.

Why, God, she silently entreated, why do you allow evil to exist?

God didn't answer.

The mysteries of His ways were indeed confusing.

Well, she thought as she gave up attempting to find a reasonable explanation behind the actions or inactions of her Creator, in spite of all the suffering and death over the last few months, a few things had worked out positively. In the near future, she would be a free woman. She would verify her claim to the family plantation and, despite what had happened to her, she would recover, and start her life anew.

While there was some consolation to be gained from those thoughts, she knew that her circumstances didn't help the dead. But for her, in spite of God not answering her questions, it was still worthwhile saying, Thank you, Heavenly Father.

As they neared Mr. Knox's home, Nora recalled that Nolan, while loading the horses, had related the story of Mick arriving at the House of Burgesses to announce the Indian attack. Nolan had also told her that Ginny would recover.

Now that Nora knew who the twins' father was, she wondered why Nolan and Ginny hadn't married. After all, that would have been the proper thing to do. The twins, she assumed, must be the reason Nolan, a free man, had never left Mr. Knox.

Nora frowned with annoyance. An image of Billy Devlin had wiggled its way into her thoughts. He was dressed as a pirate, wearing his silly, lopsided grin. Why had his memory invaded her private musings? She couldn't think of one good reason. Billy had been gone for months. She recalled his Christmas letter, how he had become a pirate and captain of his own ship, and his most audacious line, . . . *that he intended to make her his wife, as she was surely madly in love with him!*

Ha! she huffed as she thought, Billy, you have always been delusional, but you have since crossed the line to insanity! I am not in love with you . . . And, Billy Devlin, never take a woman for granted, especially me. Besides, by now, you have probably met the fate of most pirates, having either been killed in battle or captured and hung.

Her heart suddenly squeezed so hard that it hurt. She placed a hand on her chest. Why was she feeling this way? Certainly not because of Billy. Nora blew out an exasperated breath, chasing away her thoughts of Billy as one might shoo a tomcat out of a chicken coop.

With his image gone, Anne came to mind. Where are you, Anne? Will we ever see each other again?

Nora desperately hoped so. If ever she needed a friend, someone she could talk to and confide in, it was now.

Nora crinkled her nose. Smoke! A moment later, they rode into Mr. Knox's forecourt. Nora's eyes widened with shock as they came upon the smoking ruins. The barn was a total loss, as well as the Del Corso's cottage; both had been burned to the ground. At least a dozen men on horseback, armed and ready to ride, were milling about in the yard while plantation workers filled buckets at the well and ran to the smoldering structures, splashing water on dying embers.

Nora drew in a quick breath. There were two bodies on the ground, wrapped in sheets.

"Cara! Colleen!" she heard Ginny yell from the side of the house. The cook, holding her bandaged neck, ran toward them with tears streaming. "My twins! My little darlings!"

The crowd of men cheered and congratulated Nolan as he brought their little procession to a halt beside Ginny, who eagerly reached for Colleen and took her in her arms.

"Nolan, thank you!" Ginny cried. "Thank you, Nolan! God bless you! I'll love you forever!"

The cook turned to Nora who, holding onto Cara, slipped gingerly to the ground while gritting her teeth to suppress a jolt of pain.

The little girl awoke, saw her mam, and wiggled out of Nora's arms. "Mommy!" Cara called. She ran to her mother and sister. The threesome hugged and cried.

Mr. Knox hurried over to Nolan, who had come up beside Nora. Knox looked tired; his face and clothes were smudged with ashes. "Nolan, I can't imagine how you . . . How did you ever manage to free Nora and the children from those savages?"

"Got lucky," he replied simply.

"Lucky! Good Lord, man, you're going to have to tell us all what happened. Seeing you ride in with the twins and Nora is as close to a miracle as I'll ever see."

"God was on my side," Nolan said simply.

Was He? Nora wondered. Why was the Lord on his side and not on Mrs. Gibbs's, the Del Corso's or Millie's side? While Nora knew she shouldn't be disrespectful, she also thought that, had it been left up to God, she and the twins might still be in the hands of savages.

Or, she questioned her thought with a rush of guilt, was she being unfair? Maybe Nolan had been acting as the instrument of God. Maybe it had been fated that the others were to die. Was that possible? She sighed. It was all too much to contemplate.

"We were just about to come after you," Mr. Knox said as the horsemen began to dismount around them. "Come inside the house and join us for drinks. I'm sure there's more to the story."

"Go on without me," Nolan said. "I'll be right along."

Knox nodded, but before he turned away, his eyes flickered as he assessed Nora's cut lip and disheveled appearance. "Nora, you're hurting. That lip needs some tending to."

Nora exchanged a quick look with Nolan. "I had a fall. I'll be fine," she said, forcing a weak smile as she pulled her tattered dress together. "The savages didn't harm me, if that's what you're thinking. Thank you for your concern."

He stared at her with unsettling blue eyes, obviously judging her response. Then, glancing past him, a jolt of alarm transfixed her—the west corner of the residence was blackened and smoldering.

"The house . . ?" she asked, with rising panic.

"Yes," Mr. Knox replied. "Fortunately, we were able to put out the flames before the entire place went up. I'm sorry, Nora, but a good portion of your bedroom was destroyed, although I did manage to save your clothes and a few things."

Momentarily paralyzed, a disastrous thought raced through her brain. Her room! Nora ran across the yard and, ignoring as much as possible the throbbing in her groin, hurried into the house and up the stairs.

Throwing her bedroom door open, Nora stopped short, almost keeling over with pain from her exertion. Leaning against the doorjamb for support, she stared at the room. The walls and furniture were black with soot.

The bed! Oh, dear God, no!

Her heart pounded as she stepped across the wet floor to the grimy, soggy mattress, where water had been splashed to douse the fire. With shaking fingers, she lifted the edge of the burned mattress.

The pouch had fallen through the rope supports and was lying on the floor. It was blackened by the fire's heat, but the canvas seemed to be intact.

Catching her breath, she reached through the ropes and carefully retrieved the slim bag. It felt brittle to her touch. Fearing it might crack and fall apart, she gently pried open the flap. The pouch crumbled in her hands!

Nora gasped with horror as the charred remnants of her father's will and the deed to Running River Plantation fell like dead leaves through her fingers. She collapsed to the floor crying as she had never cried before, knowing that all of her hopes and dreams for the future had turned to ashes.

CHAPTER THIRTY-NINE

"You're not going to believe this, Miss Anne!" Trish exclaimed as she, Nell, and Addie burst in through the front door of the trading post.

"Not in a million years," Nell added.

"Come on, you've got to see," Addie said breathlessly.

"What is it?" Anne asked as she rose from the desk, where she had been tallying the week's receipts.

"Come on!" Trish grabbed her hand.

The girls, all in proper dresses that gave no hint of their occupation, tugged on Anne's hands.

"Girls, just tell me," Anne said, resisting.

"It's William," said Trish. "Come on!"

Perplexed, Anne allowed the girls to pull her out the door and into the front yard. She stopped short when she saw William dismounting from his horse.

William extracted four packages from his saddlebags and turned to them with an uncertain look on his face—and what a face it was!

Anne stared in astonishment. William's long, straggly hair had been cut short, and his food and tobacco-stained beard had been shaved off to reveal surprisingly handsome, albeit paler than the rest of his face, features. He was wearing new clothes—a clean, white linen shirt and buff cotton breeches stuck into knee-high brown leather boots. Topping off the apparition was a fancy new hat!

The girls clapped and cheered.

William's face flushed. He stepped hesitantly up to them. "Ya think I look all right?"

Anne stammered, at a loss for a response. She chose to correct his grammar. "*Do you* think I look all right?"

His brow wrinkled. "Well, do you?"

"Yes," she admitted, still staring at the transformation. "William, you look more than all right. In fact, you look quite fine."

He beamed.

Anne lifted an eyebrow. William had straight, white teeth, which had been previously hidden beneath an unkempt mustache.

"I got some . . ." He quickly corrected himself. "I *have* some presents for ya . . . *you* all."

William ceremoniously handed each girl a package. "Anne, this is for helping me ta . . . *to* learn to speak proper English. And I especially have to thank you for your patience as a teacher."

"William, you did most of it yourself. You're a very fast learner," she said in truth. "It's hard to believe you've progressed this far in just five months."

"Rufus always said I could be smarter than a solicitor if I wanted to be."

Anne nodded happily. After all, she was responsible for his learning metamorphosis. The physical transformation, however, was entirely his own doing. "I'm pleased that you decided to join the human race," she said.

"Oh, thank you, William!" Trish exclaimed after she had opened a little carton containing six bars of soap.

"Hold them to your nose," he said proudly. "They smell of violets."

Nell and Addie opened their containers, which also had little bars of soap. They held the bars to their noses and swooned with pleasure.

"I got . . . I *bought* the same for everyone, except for you, Anne. I have something special for you."

"Oh?" she replied. She couldn't imagine what William had brought her. She tore off the wrapping, revealing two rather used books.

William nodded anxiously and said, "I bought them off an English officer."

Nora read a title. "*All's Well that Ends Well* by William Shakespeare." She looked up at his expectant face. "I'm happy you like Shakespeare. He's a wonderful writer."

William grinned.

Anne looked at the second book. "*'Tis Pity She's a Whore* by John Ford."

Trish, Nell, and Addie jerked up their heads.

William said quickly. "These were the only books I could find. I didn't mean anything disrespectful."

"That's all right, William," Anne said. "The girls *are* whores and I *am* a madam. Maybe you would read to us a little later, now that you are literate?"

He grinned. "I just might, if you keep making me money."

"Oh, we will," Trish assured him.

"Yes," Nell said. "We like money."

"And clothes, lots of pretty clothes," Addie chimed in.

"Anne, you're going to need a new dress," William said. "I'm taking you to a party next week."

Anne couldn't believe her ears. "A party?"

"Yes, a party."

*****

People who think there's a time limit for grief have never lost a piece of their heart. Nora would always remember those words her parish priest in Ireland had spoken over the grave of a neighbor's child, who had died from tuberculosis. The message, she felt, not only applied to people but to material loss, the loss of one's dreams.

Losing her father's will and the deed to Running River Plantation had been devastating. The fire had eradicated all of her hopes for the future and for her family's fortunes. She thought, When Da, Mam, and Brendan arrive from Dublin, if they ever do arrive—another worry—they will discover they are paupers, and it's my fault! I should never have kept valuable documents in my bedroom.

Nora sighed. Some part of her knew she was being unduly hard on herself.

While clinging to the hope that her family would eventually turn up, each passing month diminished Nora's expectations. She knew they could have been arrested and hung, or succumbed to the plague, or their ship could have been lost in one of the hurricanes that sank an untold number of vessels every year. All were possibilities. How many more pieces of her heart could she lose before she simply curled up and died?

Nora stared myopically at the correspondence she had been drafting for Mr. Knox to the House of Burgesses, protesting England's embargo on the colonies, and considered, was this to be her lot in life, to be a secretary?

True, she had been content to work for Mr. Knox when there had been a rosy future to look forward to, but now with that prospect literally in ashes, she felt as if she had fallen into a bottomless pit. She wasn't ungrateful for the position she occupied. She had been fortunate—so many indentured servants were working as slaves in the fields. And, she allowed, Mr. Knox had been kind to her and had remained a gentleman, except for that one night of indiscretion. It's just that she had expected so much more out of life!

Nora sighed, dipped the quill's nub into the inkpot, and began to write. She paused in midsentence, unable to concentrate. Frustrated, she set the pen down, thinking, I can't do this for four more years! I can't be any man's property! What are my options? To run away?

"Excuse me, Nora."

She turned to see Mrs. Latimore standing in the doorway. Mr. Knox's new housekeeper was a pleasant older woman whose full figure beneath a black dress stretched her white apron.

THE GIRL WHO WAS ME IS GONE

The housekeeper continued, "If you have a moment, Mr. Knox would like to see you in the parlor."

"Thank you, Mrs. Latimore. I'll be right there."

*****

"SURPRISE!"

A chorus of voices greeted Nora as she walked into the parlor. Mr. Knox and the staff merrily called out, "Happy birthday, Nora! Happy birthday!"

Nora raised a hand to her cheek in bewilderment. She had entirely forgotten today was August 1st, her eighteenth birthday!

Ginny picked up her fipple flute and began playing. Nora glanced to the ancient harp, sitting untended in the corner. Poor Mrs. Gibbs! If only . . . Enough! she admonished herself, this is a party!

Nora blinked away the moment of sadness. "Thank you. Thank you all so very much."

"Are you surprised?" Cara asked.

"Completely."

"Mommy made a cake just for you," Colleen said.

"And we got to lick the icing spoon," Cara added with a giggle.

Grinning, Nora turned to her employer. The party must have been his idea, or if not, it certainly had to have had his stamp of approval. "Mr. Knox, thank you so much."

"You are welcome!" Mick answered for his father.

Mr. Knox laughed. "All right, everyone," he said, pointing to a table laden with an array of appetizing victuals. "There is plenty to eat, and mulled cider to drink. Go at it, one and all."

Nora looked at the faces surrounding her—Mr. Knox and Mick, Ginny and the twins, Cara and Colleen. She had known them for almost a year. The new arrivals since the Indian attack were Mrs. Latimore, Oona, the thirteen-year-old African maid, and Derby and Fiona Sweeney, the new livery and garden caretakers, who lived in the rebuilt Del Corso cottage attached to the new barn.

Nora frowned. Someone was missing. Nolan. Where was he?

Before she had time to ponder the driver's absence, the front door opened, and Nolan ushered in a smartly dressed young couple.

Nora's heart tripped. "Oh, dear God, Anne!! Is it really you?"

"Nora!"

Squealing with joy, Nora and Anne ran into each other's arms.

Nolan turned to the man standing beside him. "William, I'm starved. Perhaps a bite to eat?"

"A grand idea."

The two men walked over to the table where the group was cheerfully filling mugs with cider and piling plates with roast pork and vegetables.

"Oh, let me look at you!" Nora said, taking a step back from Anne and gazing at her best friend, who was dressed in a lovely white bonnet, a high-necked blue cotton dress, and pretty black shoes. "You look wonderful! I cannot tell you how happy I am to see you. I've thought about you every day since that awful man bought you at the auction. I've been so worried about you."

"Nora, I've also thought about you every day and wondered where you were and if you were being well treated." Anne stared at Nora and added, "You look positively marvelous. Mr. Nolan was telling us on the ride over that you are now Mr. Knox's personal assistant. That's a wonderful position. He's an important assemblyman."

Nora wasn't quite listening. Her mind was churning. How had Nolan located Anne? She had an idea, but it needed confirmation. She turned to the driver, who was passing with a mug and a plate of food. "Nolan, how did you find Anne?"

"It was Mr. Knox's idea."

She had guessed as much.

"Mr. Knox suggested I go to the auctioneer's office and have them review the records, to find the name of the person who purchased Anne Smith. It turned out to be Rufus Pitt, William's uncle. And here we are. Nice coincidence that it happened on your birthday."

"You are an angel, Nolan."

He gave her a wry look. "That's the first time anyone has ever called me an angel, but my good Mother, God rest her soul, would have loved to hear it." He lifted his cup in a toast. "To your health, and to yours, too, Anne."

"Thank you, Mr. Nolan," Anne said.

"You're a remarkable man," Nora said after she had taken a sip of cider.

"Shh. Don't be passing those rumors around. I won't be able to keep the ladies away." He winked and walked off to rejoin the others.

Nora turned to Anne, her brow crinkling. "You're free, are you?"

"Yes and no. It's, well, it's complicated."

"You have to explain 'complicated,' but first I need a word with Mr. Knox before he leaves. Be right back."

"Mr. Knox," Nora said, approaching her employer, "I want you to know how grateful I am to you, not only for my birthday party, but for all the time and effort you put into locating Anne, and for inviting her here." She kissed him on the cheek, thinking, I don't care if it is inappropriate.

"It's my pleasure, Nora. After the loss of your father's papers, I wanted to do something special to lift your spirits."

He was so perceptive, so thoughtful. "You have certainly done that," she said. "You are the kindest man."

"Not always, but I try. Now go back to your friends and enjoy yourself."

Nora flashed a smile of gratitude and hurried back to Anne, giving a sideways glance to William, who was at the table with the staff. "Anne, tell me about William and how you are free, but not free."

"As I mentioned, it's a bit complicated. William is the nephew of Rufus Pitt, the man who purchased my contract. Rufus was killed by Indians a few months ago, and William inherited his property." Anne scrunched up her face. "That included me. Don't you just hate being a man's property?"

"From the top of my head to the tips of my toes," Nora said, shaking her head gloomily. "Four more years. . . ."

William stepped over to them, carrying two plates. "I brought you beautiful ladies something to eat."

"Thank you, William," Anne responded, accepting one of the platters. "I'd like you to meet my best friend in the whole world. William Pitt, meet Nora Smith."

"Pleased to meet you, Miss Smith," he said. "Anne's told me you were friends in Ireland." He offered Nora the remaining plate. "This one is for you."

"Thank you, William. It's nice to meet you, too," Nora responded as she took the serving. "This is very kind of you."

"May I get you something to drink?" he asked.

When the girls demurred, William said, "You two have a lot to catch up on. Enjoy. I'll be sitting with Nolan."

"William seems very nice, and a gentleman," Nora said as he sauntered off.

"Thank you," Anne replied, "You wouldn't have thought so in the beginning."

Nora cocked her head inquisitively.

Anne glanced around. "Is there someplace we can talk privately? I have so many things to tell you. Some of them are going to be quite shocking."

*****

"Oh, my goodness!" Anne exclaimed, "and I thought my life was complicated."

Nora and Anne sat on the four-poster in Nora's restored bedroom, with their plates between them. Nora had been relating her experiences, beginning with the day they parted at the auction, becoming Mr. Knox's secretary, up to and including the loss of her virginity. Anne, of course, had to know all the details, which Nora related in a candid, straightforward manner, acknowledging her employer's subsequent heartfelt apology.

"How do the two of you get along now?"

"It's as if it never happened. Our relationship is purely platonic."

"In a way, you are fortunate," Anne said. A pained expression shadowed her face. "There are far worse ways of losing one's virginity."

Nora knew Anne was recalling her experience at the family farm in Ireland, when she had been brutally raped by the English officer. And then, there was Pieter on the *Goede Hoop*.

Nora decided to continue with her story. "Mr. Knox hasn't been the only one. Some vicious savages . . ." When her friend gave her a searching look, she continued, "Weeks ago, the household was attacked by Indians, and the twins and I were kidnapped. To make a long story short, five of them took turns violating me."

"Oh Nora, I am so sorry. How did you . . . how did you ever get away?"

"I have Mr. Nolan to thank for saving my life. He killed the Indians and rescued me and the children."

Anne's eyebrows rose. "Nolan? The same Mr. Nolan who brought us here tonight?"

"Yes. He can be surprising at times."

"I would say so. Good Lord, five Indians!"

"Anne, just so you know, I've haven't told anyone other than you about the rapes. And I really don't want my ordeal to become common knowledge."

"What about Nolan?"

"He'll never say a word," she said with confidence "and the girls didn't see anything." Nora dropped her gaze to stare at her hands for a moment and then looked back into Anne's eyes. "I believe there are some things, private things, that people just don't need to know."

"I completely agree. I've told William about the officer who raped me, but not about Pieter. Too much information muddles a man's mind, and I don't believe it helps a relationship."

Nora nodded in agreement.

"Thank you for having faith in me, Nora. I promise you, I will never tell a soul."

"There's more."

Anne blinked with surprise.

"After Nolan brought us back to the house, we found that most of the staff had been murdered, and a fire had destroyed the barn. The flames also burned a portion of the house, including this bedroom. You'd never know by looking at it now. The repairs were just finished a few days ago." She paused, unable to go on, as an imaginary weight fell like a heavy cloak upon her shoulders. Taking a breath, she concluded, "My father's will and the deed to the plantation were destroyed."

"Oh Nora! After all you went through to save those documents, I can't tell you how sorry I am."

"I'm alive. And for that I am thankful." Nora reached over and gave Anne's arm a squeeze. "It's so good to be with you again. Now, enough of me. Tell me about you."

"First, if you don't mind my asking, do you think the rapes may have resulted in . . ."

"No," Nora said. "That's one blessing. I had my time of the month last week."

Anne reminisced. "I'll never forget becoming pregnant with Pieter and then losing the baby when Billy and I were whipped." She reached to her plate, picked up a small piece of cake, and plopped it in her mouth. "Well," she said, "now get ready for even more revelations. I haven't been living what one might call a very moral life."

Anne related her story, beginning with her arrival at Rufus Pitt's Trading Post, the young girls he had whored out in exchange for pelts, and how Anne had come to look after the trio's welfare. Then she explained how, after Rufus's death, she had taken Willie under her wing and taught him to read and write and speak proper English. Lastly, she told Nora how she was now managing the girls' appointments.

Wide-eyed, Nora managed to ask, "You run a brothel?"

"More or less, along with the trading post," Anne replied sheepishly. "I *manage* three young ladies. Well, they're a far cry from being ladies, but they are young and they're smart enough to learn that there's no real future in being a whore. I've convinced them to start saving a bit of their income for their futures."

Nora could hardly believe her ears. "Don't tell me you give yourself to men for money!"

"Me? No, no, I don't do that. Occasionally, I've held hands with a customer and talked with a lonely man who just wanted a woman's companionship for an hour or two. My main work is setting up appointments for the girls every day except Sunday. Importantly, since Rufus's death, I've seen to it that the girls are allowed to turn down any customer they don't wish to spend time with."

"How do you manage?" Nora asked, still a bit flabbergasted. "Are the girls locked up?"

"No, not at all," Anne said. "They are as free as I am, which isn't completely free, but they are certainly not locked up or forced to do anything they don't wish to do. Believe it or not, they are happy little whores."

"I am speechless."

"I would be, too, if I were you."

"You manage the girls and the trading post?"

"William and I are doing it together. He's become quite the businessman. To be honest, I had no idea he was so smart. You would have had to meet the man a year ago to understand."

"All I can say is I hope he appreciates you."

"He does. He really does. He's made me his junior partner. I think, eventually, I may be even more that."

Nora knew her friend could only be hinting at marriage. "Oh, Anne, really? You think so?"

She smiled and then shook her head in wonderment. "Miracles do happen. Nora, I wish you could be as happy as I am, that you had someone." Anne searched her face and gave her a questioning look. "Have you heard anything from Billy?"

Billy? Nora thought. Why is Anne equating my happiness with Billy? She replied, "I did hear from him last Christmas, a letter, but nothing since. He's become a pirate."

"A pirate? That doesn't surprise me. He always was after a bit of adventure."

"He wrote that he had made some money and was planning to buy our freedom or, failing that, steal us away."

"That's typical Billy, a dreamer with good intentions. I do miss him, though. He certainly made life interesting."

"That, he did," Nora said, remembering him with more fondness than she cared to admit. "I do hope he's alive, but pirates aren't known for their longevity."

CHAPTER FORTY

Billy ducked. The cutlass's blade swished past his head, carrying with it a tuft of his hair. Losing his balance, Billy slipped on the bloody deck of the Spanish galleon as the Iberian rushed in for the kill, sword slashing down. Billy rolled away a split second before the blade cut into planks where his head would have been. Turning swiftly, he thrust his sword up. It entered the Spaniard's belly just below the sternum, penetrating the heart. Gasping, the man collapsed to the deck, which was littered with his dead companions. Billy sprang to his feet, cutlass already swinging, cutting into flesh and bone. The *Lobo do Mar's* crew fought like wild men, shooting and savagely hacking at the Spaniards, who were being decimated. Billy kicked a severed head out of his way as he made his way to Antonio's side.

"Excelente, meu Capitão!" the first mate yelled as he impaled a sailor.

A chorus of Spanish voices sang out across the decks, "Nos rendimos! Cedemos! Cedemos!"

Billy knew those words. "We surrender! We yield! We yield!"

The bloodied Spanish seamen—those who could still stand—threw their weapons down.

Feeling the rush of exhilaration that came from surviving a battle with life and death in the balance, Billy lowered his bloodied blade and stood with chest heaving, surveying the damage.

The *Lobo do Mar* had caught up to *Santo Domingo* as dawn was breaking. Although vastly outnumbered, the pirates had the advantage of surprise. They had grappled onto the galleon's railing, pulled the vessels together and boarded swiftly. Moving like shadows, they had surprised the crew and shot, stabbed, and beaten the luckless Spaniards into submission.

I did it! Billy thought. Well, my crew and I did it. We captured one of Spain's great treasure galleons. If only Diego had lived to see this!

*****

Shortly after leaving Lisbon, *Lobo do Mar's* crew had voted to hunt *sparrows* in the shipping lanes off the coast of Cuba, where Spanish vessels passed on the long voyage home to Seville, laden with New World treasures to enrich the Spanish crown.

Later, when they had filled their coffers with pirated gold, the crew had assured Billy they would sail to Jamestown. With no recourse, he had agreed.

It had been slim pickings—until now.

Santo Domingo was reputed to be a treasure ship.

"Shall we have a look and see what this beautiful lady has in her belly?" Billy asked his first mate.

Antonio's eyes sparkled with anticipation. "Si, meu Capitão!"

As Captain Billy's crew began throwing the dead and the hopelessly wounded overboard, Billy followed Antonio and a small contingent of pirates down two flights of stairs. A Spaniard, happy to be among the living and wishing to remain so, guided them with a lantern through the expansive hull to a locked compartment. Antonio broke the lock and made the gallant gesture of allowing Billy to be the first to enter.

Billy's pulse quickened when he saw a dozen iron-bound crates, all bearing the royal seal of Spain.

"Holy mother of God!" Billy exclaimed when the crates had been broken open.

"Mãe de Deus!" Antonio responded.

The pirates stared in astonishment at the treasures before them—gold, silver, rare gems, pearls, spices, sugar, tobacco, and silk.

"Capitão, Feliz Natal!" Antonio exclaimed.

"Merry Christmas?" Billy questioned.

"Sim!" his second in command said. "Yes! Today surely must to be Christmas!"

The booty was equal to a king's ransom. Billy was rich! Every crewmember was suddenly wealthy beyond their wildest dreams.

*****

"If I could get my hands on that bastard, I'd have his useless ass keelhauled!" Captain Dice cursed the memory of General Meredith Chetwynd. He stood, bracing his legs on the frigate's poop deck as sleeting rain lashed and stung his scarred face. Overhead, black windswept clouds discharged a steady deluge, swelling the white-capped sea. Dice yanked at his gold rimmed bicorn, pulling the hat down firmly. He cinched the belt on his oiled black cape against the cold deluge.

Every sailor worth his salt knew that fall was peak hurricane season, and few captains were foolish enough to tempt fate by making the Atlantic crossing at that time of year. Yet General Chetwynd had ordered him to set sail!

And sail they did—with an English force of fifteen ships carrying 2,000 infantrymen. Dice's assignment was to reinforce the English blockade of the colonies and subdue the rebellious inhabitants who had sided with Monarchy Rule.

The armada had traversed the Atlantic without incident from Bristol to Barbados, where they had planned a six-week stay to suppress Royalist rebels. Unfortunately, the colonists weren't at all interested in being suppressed. It had taken an almost unbearable four months to beat them into submission. The armada then sailed for Jamestown—and was hit by an unprecedented series of brutal storms. The cost to ships and men had been shocking. Admiralty's fleet, which Dice had worked for months to assemble, had been almost totally demolished. Eleven ships plus their crews and 1,500 infantrymen had perished. The once mighty armada had been reduced to four frigates and 500 soldiers.

A historic disaster, the blame for which fell directly on General Chetwynd's head. The colonies, the general had said, had to be blockaded at all costs.

Utter crap. As if the colonies were a physical threat to England!

The real motivation for the expedition, Captain Dice surmised, had been purely financial. English merchants and ship owners had demanded Admiralty stop the colonies from trading with foreign countries.

Why?

So that English investors could cut out their competition and reap huge financial gains for themselves.

Does anything ever change?

Dice lifted a hand to shield his eyes, gazing up to a flapping topsail that was ripping loose from its yardarm. As he watched, the canvas unfurled and winged away as if it were an ungainly albatross.

While pulling his scarf tighter, he inadvertently brushed his left cheek. A stab of agony instantly reminded him of his nemesis. The continual torment from rotting teeth and gums, and the incessant drooling were relentless reminders of Nora O'Lalor.

She was an abscess, one that he had to cut out and destroy. Once he reached Jamestown, he would find her and eliminate her, finally ridding himself of his burning, all-consuming obsession.

*****

Nora breathed in January's cold air as she stepped through the front door. Early this morning, Nolan had arrived with the message that Mr. Knox was in need of her services at the House of Burgesses. Nora assumed the master of the house had received documents that needed immediate attention. She had placed her writing materials in a small, protective box and safeguarded them in the deep pocket of her cape.

Descending the porch stairs, she crossed the short distance to the carriage, where Nolan waited, reins in hand. As she reached for the buggy's door, she hesitated. No, she thought, I will sit beside Nolan this morning. Having him all to myself will be a rare opportunity, one I intend to take advantage of.

She moved to the front of the coach, placed a foot on the L step and pulled herself up onto the bench seat.

"All ready?" Nolan asked.

"Ready as I'll ever be."

He flicked the reins. Nora had to grab onto the side rail as the geldings lurched forward, white frost streaming from their nostrils. The carriage wheeled out of the courtyard and Nora settled in for the short ride to Jamestown. Gathering her cloak against the cold, she saw patches of snow blanketing the ground in shady spots beneath the oak and pine trees that surrounded the compound.

"Nolan, do you mind if I ask you a rather personal question?"

He gave her a bemused look. "Rather personal?"

She caught an errant curl that had fallen from her bonnet and wrapped it around her finger. "Fairly personal."

He shrugged. "Ask away."

"Why haven't you married Ginny?"

Nolan coughed as if he had swallowed a dust ball. Clearing his throat, he said, "That's between Ginny and me."

"But you have two little girls who need a father."

He leaned over the side of the carriage and spat. "They have a father. That's me, and they know it."

"But shouldn't you be married for their sakes?"

"Nora," he responded with a tone of exasperation, "I stay on with Mr. Knox for one reason only—to be close to Cara and Colleen. I love my daughters dearly, but their mother and I are not in love, and we never have been, although we do like each other. That's enough for the both of us."

Nora's forehead creased. "Really?"

He glanced at her troubled face. "It's not just that." He struggled with his next words. "Men and women . . . we have needs." Nolan was obviously referring to sex. A muscle twitched in his jaw.

"Please, don't spit again."

He continued without spitting. "Sometimes satisfying those needs with a little companionship is all there is to a relationship, as it is with Ginny and me." He spat. "Ginny sometimes riles my better nature, as I do hers. We like things the way they are."

"But what if Ginny secretly loves you?"

He gave Nora a dubious look. "She might think so at times," he allowed. "But she also loves being her own person." He paused and then added, "Ginny and I had this discussion years ago."

Nora thought, it doesn't seem right that two people could be so close, have children, satisfy each other physically, and yet have no desire to be married. She sighed. Well, I still have a lot to learn about relationships.

But Nolan, by touching upon the subject of friendships, had prompted another question. "Were Mr. Knox and Mrs. Gibbs ever in love?"

Nolan spat. "That was a different situation entirely."

When Nolan remained quiet for a length of time, Nora prodded. "How was it different?"

"You're a persistent one, aren't you?"

She raised her eyebrows inquisitively, encouraging him to continue.

Nolan hesitated, and then said, "When Mr. Knox's first wife and children were murdered by the Powhatan, he took it very hard. We thought he might die as well. Mrs. Gibbs helped him back from the abyss, and along the way, they fell in love. Mick is the result of their union. But you have to understand, Mr. Knox is upper-class English, while Mrs. Gibbs is—*was*—not. As you can guess, it was an insurmountable obstacle, a barrier that ended any thought of marriage. But still, that didn't stop them from loving each other."

Nora sat back and stared ahead as she thought, I have been so blind to the goings-on beneath Mr. Knox's roof! If the walls could talk, they would have many stories to tell.

"Nora, I'm not wise enough to have answers as to how the human heart works. I just mind my own business and live day to day. I do know this—be careful who you give your love to. We humans bruise easily."

Startled, she responded, "Me? I'm not even close to being in love."

Nolan chuckled. "One day, it's going to happen, and that person will either be wonderful or hurtful. My advice, don't give your heart to a scoundrel."

Billy Devlin flashed in her mind's eye. How very appropriate! she thought. Yes, Billy was certainly a scoundrel.

The dirt road the carriage had been rolling over gave way to the cobblestone streets of Jamestown. They were passing the wharf when Nora noticed a British frigate anchored in the bay, along with another naval vessel approaching in the distance, a huge man-of-war.

"Is the blockade still on?" she asked.

The driver nodded. "In its second month. That first frigate arrived earlier this morning. The Brits are here to reinforce England's presence in Virginia. The bloody swine have forbidden foreign vessels from trading in American ports, denying us our best trading partners. It's a power play by that ass, Oliver Cromwell. Shame we can't get the French to help us kick those bastards out of our territories."

As the man-of-war drew closer, Nora could see crewmen crawling on yardarms, rapidly reefing sails. The large vessel, slowly drifting now, was pulling close to the frigate's stern. A pair of anchors splashed into the bay, halting her progress. The two ships, bristling with cannon, effectively created a blockade of the docks. A longboat was lowered from the man-of-war, and two naval cadets followed by a fancy uniformed officer climbed down a ladder and stepped aboard. They took their seats and the crew began rowing toward the smaller frigate.

Nolan spat. "Mr. Knox and the assembly will have their hands full negotiating with those bloody bandits. If it were up to me, I'd set up a dozen cannon on the wharf and blow every damned one of them to hell."

*****

Seagulls screeched overhead as Captain Dice stood on the frigate's deck watching the longboat approach. Seeking relief from his throbbing jaw, he retrieved a small flask of brandy from the pocket of his cape, uncapped it and took a swig. He immediately flinched as rotten teeth and raw nerves burned. Yet he persisted in having another swallow, knowing that after the first jolt, the alcohol would help numb the pain. Dice recalled, as he always did at these moments, having bits of broken teeth removed by the ship's surgeon. But there were still shattered pieces entrenched in his gums, which had been impossible to extract without cutting away part of his jaw.

Continual anguish had driven his once charismatic personality into depths of darkness he could never have imagined. He existed now on the edge of madness. That, combined with a military career in shambles and his abominable disfigurement, had driven him to thoughts of suicide. The single driving force that kept him alive was revenge. Now that he had arrived in the settlement where *she* most certainly still lived, it was time for retribution.

The longboat knocked against the frigate's hull. Seconds later, Dice joined his superior officer, Captain Robert Denis, aboard the boat. After cordial pleasantries were exchanged, they were rowed toward the pier. Dice and Captain Denis were to reinforce the blockade of Jamestown until they could negotiate a treaty with the settlers that granted England sole rights to trade with the colonies.

Having arrived a few hours before the man-of-war, Dice had sent his first lieutenant ashore to call for an emergency meeting with the Jamestown assembly members at the House of Burgesses. He was now accompanying Captain Denis to assist with negotiations. The meeting, he had figured, should not take more than an hour at most. Once his task was accomplished and he had time on his hands, he planned to scour the settlement for information on Nora O'Lalor. After locating her residence, he would place her under arrest. But he wasn't planning on a public apprehension. No, he had other, far more private plans. An eye for an eye was a biblical example. She would suffer as he had suffered. The Irish bitch's final hours would be hell on earth.

Then, and only then, would he finally be at peace.

*****

"Thank you, Nolan," Nora said as she descended from the coach in front of the House of Burgesses. "I don't know how long I'll be."

He nodded. "I'll be over at the stables, giving these beauties some oats and a rubdown." The driver slapped reins on the geldings' flanks and the carriage rolled off.

Nora dashed up the steps and entered the building. Hurrying down a long hallway floored with rough-hewn wooden planks, she came to a door with a plaque that read:

MICHAEL BROWN

Mr. Gerald Knox
Jamestown Assembly

Nora knocked lightly.

"Come in," came Mr. Knox's response.

She entered to find her employer sitting at a desk across from a well-dressed, gray-haired man in his fifties, who immediately rose, offering a pleasant smile.

"Nora," Mr. Knox said, "I only have a few minutes before I must join the assembly, but I thought it important that you meet Mr. Malcolm Butler this morning."

Her eyes widened. Da's overseer. What in the world was this about?

"Miss O'Lalor," Mr. Butler said, "it's a pleasure."

"Thank you," she said, aware of the usage of her real name, but still not certain where the conversation might be heading.

"Please, take a chair," Butler said. "I have some documents I've been holding for some time in the hopes that we would one day meet. I also have correspondence for you from your father."

"From Da?" she exclaimed as she sat down. "He's alive?"

Mr. Butler replied somberly, "I received a letter from Henry several months ago." He opened a pouch to withdraw an envelope and a thin package, both sealed with a small circle of red wax impressed with the O'Lalor family crest. He passed them to her.

Nora recognized her father's handwriting, even though it was scrawled, as if he had labored over the text.

> To be opened only by my daughter, Nora
> O'Lalor, and my son, John O'Lalor, in
> the presence of a solicitor and at least
> one other witness.

"My brother, John," Nora said, "died on the slave ship, *Goede Hoop*."

THE GIRL WHO WAS ME IS GONE

"I am sorry to hear that," Mr. Butler commiserated.

With shaking fingers, she broke the seal on the envelope and withdrew a single sheet of paper.

> My dearest Nora and John,
> It is with a broken heart that I must tell you your dear mother and beloved Brendan have passed away. They put up a valiant fight to the end, but the plague showed no mercy. I, too, have contracted the disease and will surely be dead within the next twenty-four hours. I am writing you not to tell you that I love you—you already know that. We have loved you, and nothing, not even death, will ever change our love for each other!

Nora had to stop reading—the writing had become blurred. She wiped her eyes, let out a long breath, and began to read again.

> Enclosed with this letter is a packet containing the original document of my last will and testament, as well as the deed to Running River Plantation.

Nora's heart jumped! Taking a moment to digest the shock, she then continued reading, even as the pounding in her chest continued.

> You and your brother, John, are now my sole heirs. I have also enclosed the inked imprints you and your brother made that will prove beyond any doubt that you are my children and rightful heirs.

358

May God bless you, and always look
after and protect you!
Your loving father, who so wishes he
could see you and hug you both one last
time,
Henry O'Lalor

Nora was shaking as she lowered the letter and began to
sob unashamedly.

Mr. Knox rose and came to her side. She felt his hand on
her shoulder. He passed her a handkerchief. After a few
moments, she released a ragged sigh and attempted to gather
her composure.

"I am sorry," she said, gaining control.

"No need to be sorry, Nora," Mr. Knox said. "We
understand."

She nodded, sniffling, and finally put to words the
thoughts she had been unwilling to accept for so long. "I
feared they might have died. This just makes it so . . . so very
final."

As the import of the letter struck her again, she gazed at
Mr. Knox with incredulity. "Mr. Knox, I can hardly believe
this. My da's will and this deed. How . . . how did this all
come about?"

"After hearing your story, I took the liberty of
investigating your claim. Malcolm will explain the rest."

"Nora, I believe you should open the packet," Mr. Butler
said. "Gerald is a solicitor. I will bear witness to the
documents and verify their contents. That is, if you would
like us to be your witnesses."

"Oh, yes!" she said. Wiping her cheeks, she fumbled with
the seal on the package. Breaking away the small circle of red
wax, Nora withdrew several pieces of paper. Her hands
trembled as she recognized the three ink-stained sheets. She
stared at the palm imprints, and was overwhelmed by
memories of that final gathering in Dublin. She recalled that
Da had been sitting with her and John and Brendan at the

small parlor table as they each placed an inked palm upon these very same pieces of paper. Nora blinked. Even as the image faded, she could still feel Da's presence, as if he were alive and in the room with them.

"Nora," Mr. Butler said, interrupting her reverie. "Could you let us compare your palm print with the one from the packet that has your name on it?"

"Yes, certainly."

Mr. Knox set an inkpot and a blank piece of paper on the table in front of her. "A few drops should suffice."

Nora poured a small amount of ink onto her palm and used the fingertips of her other hand to rub the black liquid over her skin. She raised her inked palm above the paper and held it there for a tantalizing moment, then pressed it upon the sheet. Lifting her hand, she passed the sheet of paper to Mr. Knox. He laid it beside the original and, noticing the ink on her hands, said, "Please use my handkerchief to wipe your hands."

She rubbed the ink away as she watched the men study the two imprints.

Mr. Knox looked up and exclaimed, "Identical! The prints are identical. There's no doubt about it. You are indeed Nora O'Lalor, heiress to Running River Plantation—a vested landowner who certainly should never have been auctioned as an indentured servant."

"Oh, my Lord!" she shouted joyfully as her eyes welled. She jumped from her chair and gave Mr. Knox a kiss on the cheek and then a big hug. She turned to Malcom and gave him a happy embrace.

Tears streamed; she could hardly contain her happiness. "I don't know how to thank the both of you. You have erased my worst nightmare. I am so very grateful! Mr. Knox, how can I ever repay you for all you have done for me?"

"Your happiness is my payment," he said, wearing a contented grin. "You owe me nothing."

"But I must repay you for the money you paid the auctioneer."

"I would never accept a penny from you, Nora. You have been invaluable to me. And now you are free, free as a bird."

Nora suddenly gasped, the blood rushing from her face.

"Nora, what is it?" Mr. Knox asked, witnessing her startling loss of color. "Are you ill?"

She stammered, "I . . . I just realized that this will and the deed are worthless. My name, the O'Lalor name, makes it impossible for me to claim Running River Plantation. Nora O'Lalor is a criminal in Ireland, even though the crimes I am accused of are baseless. Since I am Irish, I am automatically guilty. I would have no juried trial. And, even if there were one, it would be a farce. The English will certainly have warrants out for my arrest. All they have to do is connect my name with the plantation, and I will immediately be apprehended and hung from the gallows."

Knox frowned. "Yes, the O'Lalor name isn't a common one. But you can't possibly give up on this, Nora."

Malcolm Butler said, "Miss O'Lalor, the plantation is rightfully yours. It's worth a substantial amount of money."

"But how can I take possession with the threat of death hanging over my head?"

Mr. Knox rubbed his chin pensively, and then walked back to his desk and reclaimed his seat. "Nora, as you are aware, a lot of what I do as an assemblyman is solve problems. I see your situation as an interesting challenge, one I would like to pursue."

"Why?" she asked as a sense of depression enveloped her. "Why would you do that? You're English. You should turn me in to the authorities."

"We English, once we stop fighting those we have differences with, are the most law-abiding people on the face of the earth. We respect civil laws, and we hate injustice." He must have seen her skeptical expression, for he added, "Granted, not all of us, but most. That's part of the reason I'm going to help you. The other part you know." He gave her a whisper of a smile.

Yes, she thought, he is fond of me, I do know that. The fondness that began with a carnal act has since transformed into a bond of platonic friendship.

"Besides," he added, "it's the thing to do. If you want an old Englishman's help, that is."

"Mr. Knox, I would sincerely appreciate your help," she said, though still at a loss. "But how? How could you possibly stop the courts from ordering my arrest?"

He made a steeple with his fingers. "Here is what we're going to do."

CHAPTER FORTY-ONE

Captain Dice strode alongside Captain Denis, followed by the two uniformed sailors who had rowed them to the docks.

"Captain Dice," said Denis, "when our meeting begins, I will do the negotiating. If you have any ideas, please tell them to me as an aside. It's best if one man runs the show."

"Yes, sir," Dice replied, not in the least bit interested in talking to backwater provincials. The sooner negotiations were completed, the sooner he could begin investigations into the whereabouts of the O'Lalor bitch.

Walking up to the House of Burgesses, they were approached by two English officers, a young, heavyset lieutenant and a tall captain. After introductions were exchanged, Captain Denis nodded toward the impressive building and asked, "What's the current situation?"

"Stubborn is a good word," the tall officer replied. "Governor Berkeley and his assembly want us to believe they'll fight to retain their right to support free trade and the monarchy."

Captain Denis harrumphed. "Don't they know that Charles I had his head chopped off? And that Charles II is hiding like a rat in Scotland?"

"They are aware of that, sir. But they believe that when Charles II returns to England, the country will rise up and support the monarchy again."

"That will never happen. These people must be made to swear allegiance to the Parliamentary Republic."

The tall officer shrugged. "As I said, sir, they're stubborn."

"Fools is what they are," Denis said. "Can they rally an army?"

"Possible, but highly unlikely. There aren't enough settlers to put up a good fight, but they could enlist slaves from the tobacco fields. The slaves number in the thousands, and many of them are former Irish rebels. They can fight. But the last thing the plantation owners and merchants want is an armed Irish populace who could turn on them and take away their possessions. So I don't think Sir William Berkeley and his assembly are ready to declare war on England, or even to try to send us packing, although you can be sure they will threaten to do so."

"Well, then," Captain Denis said, "it is up to me to make these backcountry bumpkins see things realistically. They will accept English rule, or we will tighten the blockade and squeeze every last drop of blood out of their economy."

"They are squeezed already," the tall captain said. "I believe, sir, that with the weight of Parliament behind you, this standoff will end in a matter of days. A word of advice, if I may?"

"Please."

"As the Chinese say, allow them to save face, and this matter will soon be resolved."

"Thank you for that, Captain. Good day to you."

As the officers bid them farewell and walked off, Captain Denis said, "Shall we go inside and meet the pilgrims?"

Walking up the steps, Dice passed a young woman who had just left the building. He stopped in his tracks, causing the sailor behind to collide with him.

"Sorry, sir," the confused sailor said, regaining his balance.

Dice ignored him, squinting at the back of the woman as she walked away. She was familiar—*very familiar.* He felt his throat constricting. He was about to run after her when a voice severed the impulse.

"Come along, Captain Dice," Denis said impatiently. "We have business to conduct."

On the point of rebelling, Dice stared after the young woman, who was quickly distancing herself from them. His companions were giving him curious looks. Dice watched her enter the stables across the street.

Had he just seen Nora O'Lalor?

"Captain Dice," Denis said with exasperation. "What is holding you up?"

"Coming, sir," he said reluctantly. "For a moment, I thought I saw someone I knew."

*****

Nora felt her excitement growing as she approached Nolan, who stood beside the carriage with Toby, the pimply and rather smelly young stable employee. Toby was helping Nolan unhook empty grain bags from the geldings' bridles. "You're not going to believe this," she said.

"Try me," Nolan said as he set the feedbags aside.

"My da sent original legal documents, including his last will and testament, to Mr. Butler, proving I'm the legal heir to Running River Plantation!"

"Well, I'll be!" Nolan replied with surprise. "Congratulations."

"That's not all," she said. She had fully intended to inform Nolan how Mr. Knox and Mr. Butler had managed to circumvent the legal problem of the O'Lalor name on the deed, but one look at the stable boy cautioned her to keep that information to herself. She continued, "Mr. Knox said I could move to the plantation just as soon as I am ready."

Nolan cocked his head. "Oh? And just when will you be ready?"

"I'm ready now!"

Nolan laughed. "And I suppose you'll be wanting me to drive you?"

Her eyelids fluttered beseechingly. "If you wouldn't mind." When Nolan hesitated, she added, "It's a bit far to walk in the heat of the day, although I suppose I could, even though I've been told it's a bit more than five miles past Mr. Knox's."

"What do you think, Toby? Shall I give Nora a ride?"

"If ya don't, I will," Toby said with an eager grin, displaying a missing front tooth.

Nora had to fight back an inclination to cringe.

Nolan stepped up onto the carriage's bench seat, and said, "Nora, if I'm going to take you to your new home, we'd better hurry, as I suspect you'll be wanting to stop by your room first to pick up your clothes and things."

"Oh, thank you!" she said with relief, hurrying around the coach to climb up onto her seat. "I am so grateful."

Nolan flicked the reins and the carriage rolled out of the stable onto Jamestown's cobblestones. A buxom woman who was hurrying across the road in front of them reminded Nora of Anne. "Nolan, I have one more little request. Would you please stop off at Pitt's Trading Post? I'll only be a few minutes."

The driver's eyebrows shot up.

"I want to visit Anne," she explained. As Nolan had located Anne, he was certainly aware of her place of employment. Nora added, "I know it's also sometimes a bordello."

He sat back and eyed her. "She told you, then?"

"Yes. Will you take me?"

"As long as it's kept between the two of us."

"I promise."

*****

I know I'm smiling like a silly dolt, Nora thought, but I don't care.

When Nolan reined the gray geldings to a halt in front of Pitt's Trading Post, she leaped from the carriage, calling back to Nolan as she hustled toward the store. "I'll only be a few minutes, I promise."

Inside, Nora stopped abruptly to allow her eyes to adjust to the dim, almost windowless room.

"Nora!" Anne rose from her table by the back shelves. "What on earth brings you here?"

Nora hurried over to her friend and they hugged. "I have some wonderful news . . . and some sad news." Quickly, she told Anne the story of her father's last will and testament, along with the deed to Running River Plantation. Still overcome with astonishment, Nora released an exuberant laugh. "Can you believe that?"

"No. I can't believe it. Yes, I mean, I can! I am so thrilled for you." Anne gave her another quick hug. "Does this mean you're going to be a free person?"

"Yes," Nora nodded happily. "Absolutely."

Anne's smile suddenly faltered. Nora watched as her friend began to rub the back of her neck in a troubled manner.

"Anne, I believe I know what you're thinking. If Nora 'O'Lalor' assumes ownership of the plantation, she will soon thereafter be dancing a jig at the end of a rope. Right?"

Anne's eyes were worried as she bobbed her head.

"Well, listen to this." Nora cautiously lowered her voice, which didn't diminish her excitement. "Mr. Knox is brilliant! He came up with a solution. He and Mr. Butler witnessed the sale of the Running River Plantation from Nora O'Lalor to Nora Smith for an unspecified amount of money. If the sale is ever questioned, the story will be that Nora O'Lalor took the money and left for parts unknown. Nora Smith is the new legal owner! Isn't that grand?"

"It's brilliant!" Anne said. "Do you realize that now that we both have new identities, we can finally forget arrest warrants and all those terrible times. Oh, this is such good news!"

"And now for the sad news. Mam and Brendan died soon after we left Dublin, and Da, too." Nora's lips trembled as she added, "I had so hoped they would survive, but somehow I knew . . ."

Anne reached out and took her friend's hand.

Nora continued. "Life is so confusing. Here I am, ready to break down and cry, while at the same time I'm incredibly happy that I've been given the chance to make my father's dream come true."

"We have to make the best of what the good Lord gives us. We both miss our families. That will never change." Anne squeezed Nora's hand. "Now it's up to you to make the most of the legacy your da left you."

"I will," Nora replied fervently. "I'll make the plantation a success for my da and for the memory of my family. A day doesn't go by without my thinking about them. It may sound odd, but I believe they're still with me in spirit, watching over me, guiding me."

"You're not alone," Anne nodded. "I believe my parents and brothers are with me, too."

A sudden thought hit Nora and she released a spontaneous chuckle. "Wouldn't Billy be surprised if he could see us now?"

"I don't think there's much chance of that. Let me show you something." Anne picked up a poster from a nearby table and handed it to Nora. Prominently displayed on the sheet was the sketch of a rakish pirate aboard a ship, with the skull and crossbones flag flying beside him. A caption read:

REWARD!
1,000 £ sterling offered by
England's Parliament for information
leading to the capture or death of the
Irish pirate, Captain Billy Devlin.

"That not Billy's likeness," Nora scoffed as she looked at the sketch. "That man's face looks more like Attila the Hun."

Billy Devlin, Nora thought. Are you alive? Will I ever see that lopsided smile again?

*****

Captain Dice and Captain Denis walked out of the House of Burgesses. The two sailors who had been waiting outside the main door fell in behind them as they walked toward the wharf.

"That was a good hour's work, Captain Dice, if I do say so myself," Denis said. "I believe Sir William Berkeley and his motley assembly are beginning to see that they have no options. They either accept Parliamentary Rule or the blockade remains in effect until the ship owners and merchants of Jamestown are destitute. I predict we'll hear promising news by the end of the week."

Dice, whose thoughts had never left the woman he had crossed paths with earlier in the day, said, "Yes, sir. You were quite persuasive in your arguments. As you say, they really have no choice but to capitulate."

"Thank you, Dice. Yes, I enjoy a good debate. Although, considering the ineptitude of my opposition, I really shouldn't take too much credit."

"Sir, if you won't be needing me for the rest of the day, I thought I'd hire a horse and see the countryside."

"Thinking of becoming a settler, are you?" Denis said.

"Yes, sir. I have thought of it. It's a new land with fresh opportunities."

"And not a bad choice for you, Dice. By all means, have a look around. You might find civilian life more accommodating under your current circumstances. Not a lot of room at the top, you know."

Withholding a biting retort, Dice turned his attention to the stables several yards away. "I'll leave you here then, sir," he said. "I'm off to hire a mount."

"Excellent, Captain. We'll talk in the next few days."

"Yes, sir."

As Captain Denis and the sailors continued toward the wharf, Dice crossed over to the stable. He peered through the open double doors and called, "Anyone here?"

"Can I help ya?" a voice responded. A moment later a scrawny, unkempt young man appeared, carrying a bucket and pitchfork.

"Yes," Dice said, becoming aware of the pungent smell of horse manure and the buzz of flies. "I thought I saw a friend walk over here a bit earlier in the day—tall, slim, a very pretty young lady."

"An' who are you?" the stableman inquired.

"Captain Dice," he replied, noting with irritation that the stableman's eyes had shifted to his weeping scar.

"I'm Toby." The boy kept staring as he placed the pitchfork and bucket down beside a water trough. "Only one lady fits that description, Nora Smith."

"Nora *Smith*, not Nora O'Lalor?"

"Nora Smith," Toby confirmed.

Dice digested this piece of information as he swatted at a cloud of horse flies attracted to his cheek by oozing saliva. "Her name may have changed, but she's my old friend, of that I am quite certain. Now, where I might find Nora?"

"If she's yer friend, why don't ya know where she lives?"

"Toby," Dice said evenly, "we were friends in Ireland, and I've just arrived in Jamestown. I'd like to reacquaint myself."

"Most men would," Toby said, leering. "I'll tell ye this. She ain't no molly, if'n that's what yer after."

"Listen to me, you shit shoveler, Nora Smith is a friend, no more." Dice placed a hand on the hilt of his sword. "Now, where the devil does she live?"

Toby's smirk fell away.

"I asked you a question!"

The stable boy buckled. "I heard her mention Running River Plantation. It about five or six miles straight out. Follow the river. Ya can't miss it." His eyes narrowed shrewdly. "If yer goin' there, ya'll be needin' a ride. I'm the only stable in the settlement thet has mounts fer hire."

CHAPTER FORTY-TWO

Billy had adjusted *Lobo do Mar's* whip staff a few degrees, keeping the sloop on course as her bow sliced through the choppy waters of the James River like a cutlass's blade. The mainsail's white canvas rippled in the breeze and, as the swells glided past, Billy estimated they were sailing along at just over ten knots. If the clock inside his head was correct, and it almost always was, it was just past noon, and Jamestown would soon be appearing around the next bend in the river.

Antonio, his first mate, crawled out of a hatch and made his way forward, carrying a steaming mug. "Hot cider?"

"Yes, obrigado." Billy gratefully wrapped his fingers around the warm cup.

Antonio motioned him aside.

Billy stepped back readily, allowing the first mate to take the helm.

After a few moments, Antonio asked, "Your woman, what if she says *no*?"

Billy spit out a mouthful of cider. "Ha!" he said, wiping the front of his jerkin. "She loves me, you idiot. Nora's going to be my wife."

Antonio shot him a look dripping with skepticism.

"Go to hell. Or shall I say, vá para o inferno!"

"I understand 'Go to hell.' I see you there, minha amigo."

Billy grinned and sipped at his mug.

"Women," Antonio said philosophically, "are like água-viva, jellyfish, pretty, even beautiful, but you get too close, picada—sting."

"You don't know a damn thing about women, Antonio."

"I know much. How do you think she waits for you?"

"I wrote a letter. I told her I was I'm coming for her." Antonio scoffed.

As *Lobo do Mar* tacked around a curve in the river, Billy suddenly warned, "English."

The first mate raised an eyebrow. "Fragata and homen de guerra. Man-of-war."

"Devils have blocked the wharf." Billy scanned the shoreline on either side of the wide river. He spotted a finger of land jutting into the current a mile from where the two ships were anchored. "Antonio," he said with a gesture, "head for that point and bring us about on her lee side."

"And then?"

"I'm going ashore. I'll pay a visit to the auctioneers and find out who purchased Nora and Anne. When I find that out, I'll gather them up and be waiting back on the point a few minutes after dawn tomorrow."

Antonio laughed and pushed the whip staff to its new course.

"What's so funny?"

"Você, you esta louco."

"Me, crazy? That's a matter of opinion."

"Inglese soldiers see you, they shoot you. They be very happy. Collect one thousand pounds." Antonio added with a glint in his eye, "You lucky I rich already, or I would kill you and collect reward myself."

"Obrigado," Billy responded sarcastically.

As they drew close to the shore, Antonio called out to the crew, "Reef a vela maior!"

When the seamen scrambled to the task of lowering the main sail, he added, "I go with you. Find su amigas. Then we cut Ingleses throats and make escape. Bem?"

"No. It is not good."

"Then I bring crew. They like to fight, kill English. Bem?"

"No. One look at our group of cutthroats would scare the hell out of the entire settlement. My plan is a little more subtle. Once I locate Nora and Anne, I'll offer their owners a small fortune for their freedom. Then I'll bring them back here, where you will be waiting for us. Then, my friend, we sail to French Jamaica. There, you and I part company. My days of pirating will be over."

"Bah! Estúpido!" Antonio said derisively. "Giving up pirating is like giving up women. I'd rather cut off my own head."

"Keep pirating long enough and someone will do that for you."

The sloop, with her main sail temporarily reefed, used the jib to power it to shore. Once within a hundred feet of the spit of land, the small sail was lowered, and a skiff thrown over the side.

Antonio's eyes narrowed. "What if ladies not for sale? Have you thought of that, meu amigo?"

Billy shrugged. "Then I will free them with lead and sword."

Antonio laughed. "For that, you will need me, no?"

"No, Antonio. I'm alone on this one." Billy checked the brace of pistols in his belt, adjusted his cutlass, and started for the railing. "If the women and I aren't waiting here tomorrow morning, you are to leave. No argument. Divide my shares among the crew."

"Shh," Antonio said with feigned caution as he followed Billy. "If crew hear that, they hogtie you, deliver you to English. They get reward and your share of booty."

"If you didn't all have rewards on your heads, I might worry."

Antonio grinned as Billy reached the railing. "Go with God, meu amigo."

"Obrigado," Billy responded. He climbed down the rope ladder to the skiff.

THE GIRL WHO WAS ME IS GONE

The oarsman began rowing toward shore, leaving a worried Antonio to watch after them.

*****

Minutes later, Billy leaped from the skiff and onto the sandy riverbank. Pushing the small craft back out into the current, he thanked the crewman who had rowed him ashore. Finding a well-worn trail, he strode toward Jamestown, carrying two pouches of coin in his pockets. He had brought along enough gold to ransom a prince.

Nearing the settlement, Antonio's worrisome question came to mind: Your woman, what if she says no? A frown creased his forehead. Was it possible that his letter had never reached Nora? And, even if she had received it, what if she weren't inclined to marry him and sail off to start a new life in French Jamaica? What then?

Unsettled, he trudged on. He would know that answer soon enough.

*****

"Nora, your property begins at this tree," Nolan said from the seat of the carriage as he pointed out an ancient oak with a huge gnarled trunk and heavy branches. A large, flat boulder sat at the foot of the tree. An inscription was carved on its stone face:

RUNNING RIVER PLANTATION

Clasping her hands together, Nora withheld an urge to ask Nolan to drive faster. She replied with contained excitement, "What a beautiful tree. It must be three or four hundred years old."

Shortly thereafter, the carriage turned onto a long lane lined with stately cypress trees. As they passed beneath a canopy of branches, Nora was delighted to catch fragmented glimpses of a large home.

By the time the coach came to the end of the drive, Nora's heart was beating like a hummingbird's. Before her was an elegant two-story red brick house with a gray, slate roof. A white stallion was tethered to a hitching post. Beyond the main structure were a handsome barn and several outbuildings.

Nora turned to Nolan, who had just reined the carriage to a stop in front of a flight of stairs that led up to a wide veranda supported by stately columns. "Are you sure this is the right place?"

"Yep. I am sure."

Nora alighted from the carriage and inhaled deeply. Home. . . .

"Enjoy your new place," Nolan said.

"Aren't you coming in?" Nora asked, disappointed.

"I must be getting back. Another day."

"I know you went out of your way to bring me here. Please, when you have time, come back with Ginny and the twins. We can all explore the plantation together."

"We'll do that." Nolan slapped his reins and the carriage headed back the way they had come.

The front door opened, and Malcolm Butler stepped out onto the veranda. He was followed by a thin, diminutive gray-haired African woman who wore a white cap and apron over a plain black dress, along with sturdy black shoes. Her friendly face lit up with a wide smile.

Nora blinked with surprise at seeing the plantation manager, who said, "Welcome to Running River Plantation, Miss Smith. I live just up the way, and since I was passing by, I thought I would stop in and tell your housekeeper to expect you. Maisie, this is Miss Nora Smith, new owner of the plantation."

Maisie curtsied. "Miss Smith."

A housekeeper? she thought. She hadn't even considered having help. Of course, it must take staff to run such a large home. Remembering her manners, she said, "Nice to meet you, Maisie."

Gripping her carryall, Nora bounded up the stairs to the veranda, where Maisie took the bag from her hand.

"Miss Smith," Mr. Butler said. "There's only Maisie here at the moment. With no one in residence, I've kept help to a minimum. As you'll see once you go inside, Maisie has done an exemplary job of keeping the house in order. I will see about hiring additional staff in the next few days, but until then there will be just the two of you."

Nora raised an eyebrow. "Can I afford staff?"

"Oh, yes," Mr. Butler said, sounding pleased. "Your father left a good sum of money on deposit. Now I must be off. Maisie will show you around. You can see, it's all quite lovely. I'll return the day after tomorrow. We can then go over my duties as your manager and the plans your father had for developing the remainder of the plantation."

Nora frowned. "Will that entail purchasing slaves?"

"Yes," he replied, looking a bit surprised by the question. "Servants for the house, and laborers for the fields."

"Mr. Butler, are there alternatives to hiring Irish?"

Her manager looked out over the courtyard, seeming to mull over the question. He said, "A few plantation owners have started to bring in Africans, but they're quite a bit more expensive. Then again, in the end they might adapt better than your compatriots, and they will probably be less trouble. The Irish can be a vexing lot, if you'll excuse me for saying so."

"Of that I am quite aware."

"Now, I must bid you good day. Congratulations on your inheritance, Miss Smith."

"Thank you for everything, Mr. Butler."

"Please, call me Malcolm."

"And you must call me Nora."

"Nora, it is." The plantation manager strode down the stairs and crossed to the stallion at the hitching post.

Nora glanced at Maisie. She had never seen an African up close before, and she certainly had never talked to one. It was curious, the pigment of Maisie's skin. Were African babies born with black skin? There was so much she didn't know about the culture, but she would learn.

"Maisie, since it's only been you in this big house, have others come in to help you?"

"Just me, Miss Smith. I clean, wash, polish, and cook pretty good."

Nora smiled and then thought how vulnerable the little African must have felt living in the residence all alone. "Maisie, weren't you frightened, being in this big house all by yourself?"

"I weren't alone, ma'am." The housekeeper pulled two flintlock pistols out of her side pockets. "Primed and ready."

The little woman was a veritable walking fortress!

"My goodness, you certainly are a surprise," said Nora. "I feel I'm in good hands." She glanced to the open front door. "Shall we go inside? I can't wait to see the house."

Maisie pocketed the flintlocks and gestured for Nora to enter.

Nora passed into the foyer and stopped mid-step, gazing into the parlor. Oh, my! The room was large, but not too large, with oak-paneled walls, heavy crown moldings, and tall windows that let in the sunlight. Sofas and easy chairs, upholstered in various silk floral brocades, fronted a large fireplace encased in carved limestone that depicted an array of game birds. Above the mantel was an oil painting of an English countryside. Polished chests with shiny brass fittings and inlaid wood lined the walls, along with a red, lacquered writing desk and matching chair that seemed to beckon Nora to come closer. Moving forward, she crossed a Persian carpet woven in colors of blue, russet, and gold.

She stopped before the desk and felt its pull even more strongly. How strange, she mused. It felt as if the desk was asking her to sit down and write! She ran her fingertips across the lacquered finish and smiled, thinking, You and I are going to become fast friends. Turning to observe the parlor in its entirety, she shook her head in wonderment. It was obvious that the original owners had had exquisite taste. The room simply took her breath away.

"You like, Miss Nora?" Maisie asked as she padded up beside her.

"Oh yes, Maisie. I like very much." Nora touched the top of a highly polished chest. "You've done such a wonderful job of keeping everything dusted and spotless. Who taught you to be so thorough, and to speak such fluent English?"

"The former owners, Mr. and Mrs. Egan. Mrs. Egan was a very strict housekeeper. Did you know that your daddy bought this plantation from their estate after the Egans died?"

"I didn't know who he bought the property from, but I'm thankful that Mrs. Egan took you under her wing. I doubt there's a better housekeeper in all of Virginia."

"Thank you," Maisie responded humbly.

"How did you come to work for them?"

"Two pigs and a keg of rum."

"I beg your pardon?"

"That's what Mr. Egan paid the Spanish sailors for me."

"Really? How did that happen?"

"Dutch slavers kidnapped my people, twenty of us, in Africa. Then the Spanish captured the Dutch ship and brought us to Jamestown."

"My goodness. How long ago was that?"

"1619. Thirty-three years ago. Mr. Egan said we were the first Africans to come to the colonies. And now, you own me."

"I don't want to own you!"

"Well, you do, and that's that."

Nora blinked with surprise.

"And you have to feed and clothe me, too. It's the Christian thing to do."

"You're a Christian?"

"Yes, ma'am," Maisie said proudly. "The old gods did nothing for me. I pray to Jesus now."

"You pray for your freedom?

"No. I want Jesus to find me a good man for my bed."

Nora coughed to stop herself from laughing.

"I had a good one once, and a family, too, but that was in Africa. I'll never see them again."

"I am sorry, Maisie."

Maisie looked at her with dark, serious eyes. "You have a husband?"

"No, Maisie, I don't. You and I are in the same boat."

Maisie smiled, displaying white teeth. "Well, we better hurry an' catch us some. Folks around here die fast, here one day, and then, *phfft*, gone the next."

"Why do they die so fast?"

"Many reasons. Tuberculosis, yellow fever, dysentery, plain old accidents, infections, pneumonia, bites from poisonous spiders and snakes, owners killing slaves, then slaves killing owners, and there's hangin' for stealin', and of course Indian murders, and even starvation."

Nora let out a long breath. Virginia, she was still learning, was a far cry from what she had imagined.

But at the moment, all that mattered was that she was home at last!

*****

Leaving the path at the edge of Jamestown, Billy walked into the settlement. New homes and buildings were going up as carpenters and brick layers labored on structures. Wagons and carts rolled by, delivering lumber and building materials. As he strode along, heading for the auction area, he was relieved that no one paid him the slightest bit of attention. This lessened his worry that some colonist might connect his face to the image on the wanted poster.

Memories returned like an ill wind as he came upon the pens where he, Nora, Anne, and the other prisoners from the

Goede Hoop had been corralled prior to being auctioned off, all those months ago. They were empty now, but the stink of raw sewage from open latrines still lingered.

"Help you, mister?" a voice asked.

Billy turned to see that he had reached the auctioneer's shack. The man who had asked the question stood in the doorway staring at him. He was fiftyish, bearded, and heavyset. He wore a tan shirt and dirty brown trousers. Fortunately, there was no sign of recognition in his dark eyes.

"I'm looking for the auctioneer."

"That would be me."

"I'm trying to locate two young ladies. They were auctioned off in August of 1650. I'm hoping you keep records of your sales."

"We keep records. What's your interest with the women?"

"They're my sisters," Billy said. "I'd like to contact their buyers and see if I can purchase their contracts, as I've come into a small inheritance."

"I hope it's not too small. That information will cost you a pound sterling."

Billy reached into his pocket and withdrew a gold Spanish doubloon, equivalent to slightly more than five English silver pounds. "This is yours if I can have the information within the next few minutes."

The auctioneer's eyes brightened. "Follow me."

*****

Billy strode toward the public stables with a jaunt in his step. The auctioneer had given him the names and locations of Nora and Anne Smith's owners. His plan was to hire a horse, ride to the Knox residence, and surprise Nora. After she agreed to come away with him, which she surely would, he would buy her contract. No sane man would possibly refuse twenty-five gold doubloons. And even if Mr. Knox did refuse the gold, Billy intended to simply steal her away—and let the devil try and stop him! Then, returning to Jamestown with Nora at his side, he would purchase Anne. They would all meet up with *Lobo do Mar* at dawn. Yes, he thought confidently, life is good, and it is about to get even better.

Coming upon the stables, he spotted a stringy-haired young man grooming a fine-looking mare in the building's open doorway.

"Good afternoon," Billy said. "I'm looking to hire a horse for the day."

The young man threw him a sideways glance and kept grooming the horse. "I only had one animal ta rent," he said, "an' she's been taken."

"What about this one?"

"Nope."

"You must have another horse available." Billy took a gold sovereign from his pocket and held it out in the palm of his hand.

Toby dropped the brush, his eyes widening in astonishment. "Ya offering thet ta me?"

Billy nodded. "Or I can always find a private owner to . . ."

Toby snatched the coin from Billy's hand and pocketed it. Then, acting as if he thought his new customer might change his mind, he saddled the mare in record time and handed the reins to Billy. "Don't ride her too hard."

Billy swung up onto the saddle.

"How long will ya be? The mare belongs ta me father, an' he'll be needin' him ta ride home tonight."

"I'm riding to a plantation six or seven miles west of here. I expect to be back by sunset."

Toby cocked his head quizzically. "Goin' ta Runnin' River Plantation, are ya?"

Billy gave the man a look. "What makes you ask that?"

Toby scratched his head. "That be about the distance yer travelin'. Ya goin't to see Miss Smith, too?"

"What do you mean, *too?*"

"Rented a horse ta an English officer. He was goin' ta visit Miss Smith."

"An English officer?"

"Yeh. Ugly cuss. Face all scarred an' dripping. He left a bit earlier."

Billy frowned as he remembered a story Nora's brother, John, had told him aboard the *Goede Hoop*. Back in Ireland, Nora had shot an English officer in the face, disfiguring him. The man had sworn to track Nora down and kill her.

"Move aside!" Billy ordered. Toby scampered out of the way as Billy wheeled the horse about, dug his heels into the mare's flanks, and raced off.

Toby yelled after him, "Go easy on thet horse, ye blithering idiot!"

CHAPTER FORTY-THREE

Dice rode at a canter, slowing only when he could no longer stand the jarring that set his jaw afire.

Looking out over passing fields, he reviewed his plans for Nora O'Lalor, plans that had obsessed him with malevolent anticipation for many months. His first step would be abduction or, barring that, isolating her from any chance of rescue. Once that had been accomplished and she had been immobilized, he would shoot off the side of her face as she had shot away his cheek. He would be sure that the bullet shattered her back teeth and gums, leaving a gaping exit wound that mirrored his own. Yes, she had to experience the same agony she had wrought upon him! From that point on, and while she was still alive, he would begin slicing her flesh, cutting her up. Yes, there would be body parts. Finally, when she expired from shock and loss of blood, he would transfer her remains to a remote area and bury her where she would never be found. For those who mourned or missed her, her disappearance would remain a mystery, although many would think Indians had kidnapped her, which was not an unusual occurrence in the colonies.

Yes, he was finally about to get his revenge, and Nora O'Lalor would soon disappear off the face of the earth.

Spotting a large boulder that bore a chiseled legend, he read:

RUNNING RIVER PLANTATION

A surge of venom shot through his veins. Riding on, he looked ahead. There was no sign of a residence, but he presumed all he had to do was continue on the road, which would lead him to his destination.

Minutes later, coming out from under a canopy of cypress limbs, Dice glimpsed an impressive two-story brick home. His gut tightened as rode into the courtyard. It was oddly vacant, which pleased him. He dismounted in front of the home and tied the gelding's reins to the hitching rail. Adjusting his sword and pistols, he climbed the stairway to the veranda and knocked on the front door.

A small African woman opened the door. Her eyes widened at the sight of his scarred face and English uniform. "Yes, sir," she said somewhat hesitantly, "may I help you?"

"Fetch a servant to feed and water my horse, then tell Nora Smith that an officer of Parliament is here to see her."

"No servants here but me. You can find grain in the barn and water at the well out back. Who may I say is calling?"

"I want it to be a surprise," he said. "We're old friends."

"I will need a name," she said stubbornly.

"I'll just come in. Step back."

When the housekeeper didn't move, Captain Dice pushed her aside and entered the foyer. "Where is she?"

"Stop! You wait here. I will tell Miss Nora . . ."

Dice grabbed the front of Maisie's dress and lifted her off the floor. "Don't make me repeat myself!"

"Put me down," Maisie replied defiantly.

"Or what? You'll call for help?"

"No help, just me, I enough!"

He scoffed.

"Let go!" Maisie demanded.

Dice threw her against the wall. "I'll find her myself."

"No!" Maisie pulled her pistols from the pockets of her apron. "Leave this house now!" She cocked the flintlocks.

Dice stepped back in surprise, then snarled, "I can have you hung for this. Lower those pistols at once."

"I told you to leave!" Maisie raised her weapons.

Dice's eyes shifted to the gun barrels and then back to Maisie. He shrugged. "I will wait outside. Tell your mistress to meet me on the veranda." Dice suddenly grabbed onto the gun barrels and, holding one in each hand, yanked them down, simultaneously slamming Maisie into the wall.

One of the flintlocks discharged, plowing a lead ball into the floor.

Dice wrested the guns out of Maisie's grasp and used the butt of one to savagely club her over the head, again and again.

Pausing to catch his breath, he heard a gasp and whirled around.

Nora, having heard the gunshot, had run to the foyer and was now staring in horror as Maisie crumbled to the floor. Her gaze rose. She blanched at the sight of the horribly scarred face. It was the officer had she had shot! How had the beast found her? Nora's inner voice yelled, *Run! Escape!*

Her eyes darted to the petite African woman lying on the floor in a growing pool of blood. Outright fury shot through her. No! I will not flee! I am going to kill this murdering monster or die trying!

Dashing into the parlor, she sidestepped sofas and chairs until she reached the large stone fireplace, where flames licked up the flue like devil's tongues. Grabbing the handle of an iron poker, she yanked it free and spun around.

Dice, only steps behind, pulled up short. Wolfish yellow-brown eyes flicked to the weapon in her hand. "That won't help you," he said. "No one on this earth can help you!" He edged a step closer. "It's taken a long while to track you down, Nora O'Lalor. But I'm going to make the most of it." He sneered at her cringing expression. "That's it, take a good look. You did this to me!"

"You raped and killed innocent friends of mine!" Nora managed to respond. "I'm just sorry my bullet didn't blow your brains out!"

His skin flushed the color of a ripe plum. Wiping a trail of saliva from his jaw, he said, "Do you remember the biblical phrase, 'an eye for an eye, and a tooth for a tooth'?"

Nora heart was thumping so hard, she could feel her whole body shaking. Gripping the iron rod tighter, she thought, I'll only get one chance. . . .

Looking for an opening to strike, she began to circle to Dice's left.

He followed her, step by step, gesturing at his disfigured cheek. "You created this! After your bullet tore through my mouth, there wasn't enough flesh left to sew the skin back together. See the slit? It never closes. It drips night and day. Don't keep backing away from me! I want you to smell my saliva, to see my broken teeth, my ruined gums. I'm going to do the same to you. It's God's law. Do unto to others as they do unto you."

Nora recoiled as he continued to rant, and his spittle sprayed her face.

"I'm going to place the barrel of my pistol against those pretty lips of yours and pull the trigger."

Raw terror almost stopped Nora's heart. The man was insane!

"Nora, you have to understand how cathartic this is going to be for me, how I long to rid myself of the vile hatred you have contaminated me with." Dice ranted on, but Nora could no longer hear the words. She was concentrating on his movements, praying to find an opening.

His steps halted as he pulled a pistol from his waistband.

Now! Nora lunged, whipping the rod at Dice's head.

He jumped back, avoiding the blow.

Frustrated, furious, she swung again. He ducked away, reaching for his saber. The *hiss* of steel sent a chill through her as the blade appeared. He maintained his grip on the flintlock in his other hand.

Heart pounding, she knew her only chance was to attack. Nora leapt at him, swinging the iron rod again and again, driving him back in an attempt to bash his brains out. To her growing frustration and panic, he easily parried the iron poker with his saber.

Backing off to wipe sweat from her eyes, she noticed Dice's almost casual attitude.

He'd been toying with her. Well, two could play that game.

She lunged to his right, tripped on purpose, and fell to the carpet.

Dice moved in quickly.

Nora whipped the iron poker against Dice's knee.

Crack!

The captain screamed and began to crumble, but before he hit the carpet, he lurched forward and fell on top of her, pinning her beneath him.

"Rotten bitch!" he seethed.

Panicked, Nora swung the bar, attempting to strike Dice's injured knee, but he dropped his pistol and grabbed her hand, holding it in a paralyzing grip. He brought the sword that was still grasped in his free hand up between them until its edge was pressed against her throat.

"Stop moving. Stop!" he demanded as he adjusted his body to straddle her.

Refusing to surrender, Nora kicked, attempting to buck him off, but froze when the blade's edge cut painfully into her neck. Trapped, unable to move, just inches from Dice's demonic eyes, she inhaled the man's vile odor and gagged.

He discarded his saber and pried her fingers from the poker. She watched helplessly as he threw it across the room. Nora's eyes darted to a second pistol in his waistband. Her hand shot forward. She was yanking it free when his fist hit her face, stunning her.

The next thing Nora knew, Dice had trundled her onto her stomach. He grasped her roughly, tied her hands behind her back, and then rolled her over again. He stood and stared at her with such malevolence that her body locked with fear. Paralyzed, she watched as saliva dripped from his hideous face.

He grimaced, displaying broken teeth as he snarled, "After I blow away your face, I am going to gut you and then begin to cut you up—slowly. Then, after I decapitate you, I'll bury your body parts along with your African maid in an area where no one will ever find you. It will be as if neither of you ever existed."

It's over, she thought miserably. I'm dead.

Her eyes widened as he picked up the pistols and saber from the floor. He sheathed the blade and placed one flintlock in his waistband while cocking the other. Straddling her once more, he leaned forward and pressed the tip of its barrel hard against her lips. Tasting blood, she shook her head violently from side to side.

His eyes glistened as he taunted, "Think, you rotten bitch, think what is going to happen when I pull the trigger, when the lead ball rips out your molars and gums . . ."

She clenched her eyes, waiting for the unimaginable.

Silence . . .

He had stopped talking. Was this part of the maniac's sick, demented torture? She opened her eyes. He was staring toward the courtyard.

The barrel slid from her mouth.

He leapt up off her and ran to the window.

Then she heard hoof beats, pounding, approaching fast.

Dice snarled. "God damn!"

Whatever he had seen had prompted him to rip a drape from the window, tear it into strips, and dash back to her. Continuing to curse, he rapidly gagged her and bound her feet.

Running for the door, he said, "I'll be back."

*****

Billy reined in the foaming, sweat-drenched mare beside the horse that was tied at the hitching post and vaulted from the saddle, just as a scar-faced officer in shirt sleeves, trousers, and black boots strode out the front door. Billy immediately assessed the cocked pistol, as well as a second flintlock in his belt and a saber.

"What the hell do you want?" the officer demanded. "Who are you?"

The man had one of the ugliest countenances Billy had ever seen. The officer's hostility told Billy all he needed to know.

"I'm a friend of Nora Smith's." Billy responded in an almost civil tone as he strode toward the veranda, climbing the steps two at a time to confront the officer. "Who are you?"

"Captain Dice of Oliver Cromwell's expeditionary force sent to Jamestown to enforce England's blockade. I have placed Miss Nora O'Lalor, Nora Smith's real name, under arrest for murder. You would be wise to leave at once."

"Murder, you say?"

"Don't fuck with me, Irish," Dice said, his feral eyes narrowing with menace. "Leave the premises immediately or you, too, will be placed under arrest."

Billy's lopsided grin flashed. "That would reward you handsomely, Captain. One thousand pounds sterling."

Dice blinked in confusion.

Billy said, "Does the name Billy Devlin ring a bell?"

Dice's face twitched.

"Pirate, scourge of English shipping. I might be a little behind the times on my current value, but apprehending or killing me would give you more than enough silver to hide that hideous mug of yours for years."

Blood drained from Dice's face, leaving a pale, deformed mask.

Billy added, "Perhaps you would like to try to collect the reward? All you have to do is arrest me—or kill me. What are you waiting for?"

A growl erupted from Dice's throat as he whipped the pistol up. Billy knocked the weapon aside, grabbed Dice by the front of his shirt, and threw him off the veranda. The captain hit the ground, rolled over and came up with flintlock still in hand. He aimed.

Billy drew his own firearm.

Two shots rang out simultaneously.

Dice's slug nicked Billy's scalp, while Billy's bullet sliced through Dice's good cheek, knocking him to the ground. The Englishman's eyes flew wide with horror. He raised a shaking hand to the newly shredded cheek, and a *scream* erupted as if from the depths of Hades. He whipped out his second flintlock, cocking it . . .

Billy, who already had his other pistol in hand, squeezed the trigger.

The slug struck Dice directly between the eyes. He was slammed backward to the ground. His gun went off harmlessly in the air.

Billy heard a noise from behind and spun around.

A small African woman with a bloodied head staggered out the door with a gun in her hand. She looked down at the dead English officer, then to Billy, then back to Dice. Raising the flintlock, she aimed at the captain.

"He's dead," Billy said.

The woman grunted and pulled the trigger. The bullet plowed into the officer's white shirt, directly over his heart. "Devil needs to be shot in the heart," she said.

*****

Gunshots? Who had fired them? With rising hope, Nora struggled to free herself from her restraints.

A man sprinted into the room.

"Billy!" she exclaimed. "How is it possible?"

"Hello, my darling," he said, hurrying to her side and kneeling. "Don't worry, the scar-faced devil is on his way to hell." He grimaced at her bloodied lips as he removed her gag and bindings. "You're going to be fine, sweetheart."

Nora fell into his arms. Unable to speak, she held him tightly, not daring to let go. She felt Billy's kisses caressing the side of her face.

He whispered, "There's nothing to worry about. I'm here to take care of you."

She pulled back to gaze into his eyes. "Billy," was all she could manage.

When that lopsided grin curved his lips, she cried out and hugged him once more.

Finally, she asked, "How . . . how did you find me?" Before he could answer, she added, "That madman, he was going to . . ."

"Shh, shh. You're bleeding."

"He cut my neck and . . ."

Billy inspected the wound. "It's superficial. You'll be fine." He then gingerly inspected her mouth. "But your lips . . . they're not going to be kissable for at least a week."

Yes, she thought, Billy is back.

"I take it that officer was the one you shot in Ireland?"

She nodded and shuddered. "Billy, if you hadn't shown up . . ."

"Shh, it's over," he soothed. "And I won't let anyone harm you, ever."

Ever? Her heart fluttered. She wiped her cheeks and attempted to regain her composure, then suddenly pulled away. "Where's Maisie? Billy, have you seen a little African lady?"

"I be here, Miss Nora," Maisie said as she limped in.

"Oh, Maisie! You're bleeding!"

The little woman wiped blood from her face, touched the top of her skull, and flinched. "It stings a bit."

Nora rose to her feet with Billy's help, and hurried over to the housekeeper. "Oh, you poor thing," she said. "You're going to need stitches."

"I have needle and thread," Maisie offered.

"And I can stitch you up better than any seamstress," Billy said. "I was taught to sew by the best sail maker in Wexford County, Ireland."

Maisie said, "You bleeding, too."

He touched his scalp where a grove of brown curls had been shot away. Wincing, he said, "Just parted my hair a bit."

Nora said, "You're both going to need your wounds cleaned with beer and honey, and I'll mix a . . ." She hesitated, suddenly overcome by their near brushes with death. "I am so sorry the two of you had to go through all of this because of me. At the same time, Billy, I'm so very grateful you showed up. I have no idea how you managed."

"Nora, are you saying that after all these years you are finally beginning to appreciate me?"

"It's possible," she allowed.

"As my good mother would say, 'I think I'm beginning to see white blackbirds.' But it's not going to do us any good if someone finds a dead officer in the yard. I'd best be off to dump his English ass into a fitting hole in the ground." He glanced around the room. "Is there something I can use to cover the corpse?"

Nora ripped the remaining drape from its window frame and handed it to Billy. As an afterthought, she retrieved the discarded sashes the captain had used to bind her. "Take these, too. You can use them to tie him across his saddle. But before you go, perhaps you should let me put some ointment on your scalp and shoulder. They're still bleeding."

"'Tis nothing. Let's me know I'm still alive." He leaned over and placed a gentle kiss on her cheek. "I'll hurry back."

"Wait," Maisie said. She shuffled over to a corner and retrieved an Indian bow and a quiver of arrows. "Last owner collected these." Maisie pulled a handful of shafts with sharp flint arrowheads. Jabbing the arrows into the air, she added, "Stab. Stab. Push into dead devil's wounds, yes?" A conspirator's gleam twinkled in her eyes. "Everyone will think Indians killed the soldier."

Nora and Billy exchanged a look and laughed.

"Maisie," Nora said, "you're a genius."

Billy took the arrows. "He's going to look like a pin cushion. Ladies, I'll be back in less time than it takes to make a pot of tea."

Billy hurried out the door.

"Miss Nora," Maisie said, "I will fetch beer, honey, needle, and thread."

Maisie left the parlor as thoughts drifted into Nora's head. *My darling, Nora.* That was how Billy's Christmas letter of over a year ago had opened. It contained outrageous phrases such as, *I intend to make you my wife.* Billy, as usual, had been so full of himself that he had simply assumed she was *madly in love with him.*

At the time, Nora had thought Billy wildly presumptuous, conceited, even amusing, but now thoughts of his declarations puckered her brow. Do I wish to be Billy's wife? Am I in love with him?

*****

Maisie is a tough little bird with the courage of an eagle, Nora thought as she watched Billy carefully sew together the last of three cuts in the housekeeper's scalp. His stitches were uniform—he really could sew. Nora kept a cloth pressed on the side of Maisie's head to absorb the trickles of blood that had all but ended. The wounds she had seen varied in length from one to two inches. During the entire process, the African housekeeper had not cried or uttered a word.

Nora studied Billy's face as he sutured. His unusually serious demeanor brought out a studious, compassionate side of him, enhancing his features with confidence and maturity. Billy no longer looked nor acted like the wild youth she had known. As she stood beside him, their shoulders touching, his body radiated heat, reminding her of a warm blanket on a cold night. Her eyes drifted to Billy's lips, which were pursed in concentration as he pushed the needle and thread in and out.

She thought, I want to kiss those lips—after mine heal.

The idea startled her, as her feelings for Billy had been ambivalent in the past. I liked him, and then I didn't. I may even have loved him—a little—and then I didn't. Perhaps I've never allowed myself to love Billy, because I believed that his wild nature and my more down to earth temperament could never be compatible. But I don't know any longer. Could they be?

Billy had returned in less than an hour after riding off with the captain's body. The corpse and the officer's horse had been left in a well-traveled area several miles away. To anyone discovering the captain, it would appear as if the arrow-pierced body had been the outcome of a deadly encounter with Indians.

Nora's eye flicked to Billy's scalp and the plaster she had pasted to it. She had washed the wound with ale, an ingredient she had also used to clean Maisie's scalp. The poultice had been made from her mam's recipe for cuts and open sores. The necessary components had been found in the kitchen—egg whites, honey, oil of rose, and turpentine. After gathering a small handful of straw, Nora had ground everything together to form the plaster.

Maisie's nose twitched as Billy tied off the final stitch.

"There you are, Maisie. The stitches should come out in a couple of weeks. You're going to be good as new."

"Thank you, Mister Billy."

Nora spooned up the remainder of the poultice and applied it to the housekeeper's stitches. "This will make you heal faster, but for a while I'm sure you're going to have a headache. You are to take the rest of the day off and lie down. No work at all. Understood?"

"Yes, Miss Nora," the housekeeper responded. She gathered up needle and thread before shuffling out of the parlor.

Billy raised a hand to his forehead. "I believe I'm going to have a headache, too. Is there someplace I might be able to lie down?"

Before Nora could reply, Billy swept her up in his arms. "Where is your bedroom?"

The warmth of his embrace set her heart to pounding. "Upstairs."

Billy bounded up the stairs, hesitating on the upper landing as he looked at the hallway with its many doors.

She whispered, "Last one on the right."

As he strode down the hall, her thoughts ran wild. Do I want this? For years, I have struggled with my feelings for Billy, even denying some heartfelt yearnings. But, oh Lord, oh Lord! I cannot deny them anymore! I am about to burst with happiness and desire! My soul has finally come to the place it has always belonged, beside Billy—one with Billy! Billy Devlin, I love you to the ends of the earth!

He kicked her bedroom door open. Her heart was in her throat as he carried her to the four-poster bed and plopped her down on the mattress. As he gazed down at her, breathing hard, amber eyes sparking, she thought, My wildly handsome pirate!

"One question, my darling, that begs an answer."

She raised an eyebrow.

"You haven't gone off and married while I was away, have you?"

"No, you silly oaf. And there was good reason. I just realized I've been waiting for you all my life."

"And I, you."

Billy fell onto the bed beside her and drew her close. "Nora, you are the most beautiful lass I have ever known, with a bonny taste in men."

"Oh! You insufferable egotist!"

"Aye, one who knows how lucky he is to finally be in your arms."

She closed her eyes. Thank you, Lord. Thank you. Thank you. . . .

Hungry kisses, tenderly avoiding split lips, rained down upon her, filling her heart with joy and happiness. Before she completely lost herself, she was overcome by a truth that had to be spoken. "Billy, I have to tell you something."

"What is it?" Billy asked with surprise.

Oh, Lord, she thought, how can I say this? Am I about to destroy everything?

"Billy," she said with trepidation. "I have to let you know. Something happened to me. Something truly awful."

Concern furrowed his forehead.

Have faith in him, her inner voice said.

Nora drew in a ragged breath and said, "A few months ago, Mr. Knox's home was attacked by Indians. They set fire to the house and barn and killed many of the staff. I was knocked unconscious and kidnapped, along with the cook's two little girls. They took us to a remote area, and while the girls slept, they . . . they . . ." Tears welled in her eyes. "There were five of them, Billy. They got on top of me, one after the other. I couldn't fight them. I couldn't stop them."

Tears kept streaming, and Nora's throat constricted every time she tried to speak. She saw Billy's face lose its color.

Oh, what have I done?

Then he smiled gently and pulled her into his arms. He whispered, "Nora, things happen in life that we have no control over. Please, you must never think badly of yourself. I surely won't. I love you. Nothing, nothing will ever come between us that could change my feelings for you."

With that, her heart swelled. She added cautiously, "There is something else."

When his eyes met hers, she hesitated, remembering her conversation with Anne: Too much information muddles a man's mind, and I don't believe it helps a relationship.

Yes, she had agreed, some things should remain unsaid. Mentioning her night with Mr. Knox would accomplish nothing, while it might cause unwarranted pain.

She came out of her reverie to hear Billy's soft words. "Nora, there is nothing you can say, nothing you've ever done, that will change my feelings for you. So say no more, unless you feel you absolutely must."

Relief flowed through her as if a fresh spring had suddenly burst free from the earth and inundated her with life-giving waters. She decided that her one night with Mr. Knox would remain a secret.

"Billy," she said, wiping her cheeks. "You never stop amazing me. I only wish I could have saved my maidenhood for you."

"Shh, shh," Billy said, lightly touching a finger to her lips. "We mustn't let things from the past worry themselves into our future." He offered his lopsided smile. "I, myself, am a long way from being a virgin. I have done things I'm not at all proud of, things I will never discuss. From this moment on, you and I will make a new beginning. For me, today is going to be my first time. I will be your virgin. Will you be mine?"

Nora choked back a sob. "Oh, yes. Yes, and yes."

Billy took her face in his hands and pressed his lips ever so gently to hers, a mere feather of a touch, with such love and tenderness that Nora felt she was about to start bawling.

"I love you, Billy Devlin."

"I adore you."

Moments later, their clothes strewn on the floor, they were lost in each other's arms. There was no resemblance between their coming together and the rapes she had experienced.

Truly, Nora thought, I am making love for the very first time.

CHAPTER FORTY-FOUR

Later, too exhausted to speak or move, Nora delighted in the feel of Billy's weight on top of her, his slim hips on hers, his muscular chest pressing warmly upon her breasts, his breath close to her ear, his fingers entwined in her hair.

This is what everyone makes so much fuss about, she thought. This is why lovers have that glow I never understood—until now. Billy, I want you to stay here with me forever.

He opened his eyes. "How long have you been awake?"

"Not long."

"I've been half awake, thinking about us and our future, making plans."

"Tell me."

About to respond, he blinked as he looked at the window. The dark of night was turning gray. "Oh, my Lord, it will be dawn in just a few minutes," he said, sitting up. "How soon can you be packed?"

Startled, she asked, "Packed? Heavens, Billy, what for?"

"To find a place for us to live, of course, a new home."

Nora's stomach knotted. "A new home? What are you saying?" She sat up straight, looking completely puzzled. "I have a home—*we* have a home—here at Running River Plantation."

"Nora, we can't stay here. I've arranged to meet my crew at dawn this morning. We'll have to wake Anne on the way. Hopefully, she'll join us. But we must hurry."

Leave Jamestown! Shocked, unable to speak, she listened in startled silence as Billy rolled off the mattress and began to dress, talking excitedly. "Sweetheart, we have a grand life ahead of us. I have become wealthy beyond anything I could ever have imagined. And," he said pulling on his breeches, "if plantation life is what you want, I will buy you one! You can have anything your heart desires. We can live anywhere, Spain, France, Italy, or any island in the Caribbean or West Indies—wherever the English flag doesn't fly."

Nora's heart was pounding; tears welled. "Billy, I don't know what to say. I've never dreamed I would live any other place but here, on this plantation. It's my home. As for Anne, I don't believe she'll wish to go. She's involved with a man."

Billy's face drained of color. "Nora, we can't stay here. Don't you understand? I'm offering you the world."

"Billy, this is my world, my land. It's all that's left of Da's legacy. This plantation was his dream, and now it is mine."

He shook his head in consternation as he buttoned his shirt. "We have to build our own dreams. Come away with me, and I promise you, you'll never be sorry."

The love in his eyes was unmistakable, as was the pain.

"Oh, Billy, I want to live with you, to be with you, to be your wife, more than anything on earth, to be partners in life together, but . . ." It was difficult for her to go on; a sense of loyalty to her father's legacy had a viselike hold on her conscience. "I can't leave. It would be like turning my back on my family. Abandoning Running River Plantation would be like deserting everything my family ever strived for." She placed a hand over her stomach, feeling as if she might be ill. "I could never forgive myself." She stared into his eyes, begging him to understand. "I can't possibly leave. I can't."

"And I can't stay." His features were now a mask of torment as he pulled on his boots. "I'm a pirate, a wanted man, with 1,000 pounds on my head."

"Oh, Billy," she cried, rising from the bed and embracing him as if she would never let him go. She knew the dangers he mentioned were real.

"I know, I know," Billy said. He placed his hands on either side of her face and pressed a kiss on her cheek. "Nora, you and I are like ships at sea, being pulled apart by wind and tide."

"I am so sorry, Billy. I love you so much, I hurt. I feel I might die without you."

He flashed his lopsided grin—and it brought even more tears to her eyes.

"You'll not die, Nora Smith. You'll live and you'll prosper." He paused as if searching for words. Finding none, he continued, "Fate is not with us, lass. I wish to God it were. I would stay and prosper with you but . . ." He paused before adding, "Nora, you will always be in my heart, as surely as I am flesh and blood." Placing a hand beneath her chin, he once again kissed her cheek. The warmth of his lips sent a longing through her that ached. He leaned back. "Ah, Nora, Nora, Nora. We were meant to be, just perhaps not in this lifetime." Reaching to the bed behind her, he lifted a sheet and placed it around her shoulders. "My ship will be waiting, but not for long. Will you see me off?"

"Billy, there has to be some way . . ."

"Not unless the English leave the Americas, and I don't see that happening any time in the near future."

With sorrow seeping into her soul, she cried out, "Hold me, Billy. Just once more."

They fell into each other's arms, embracing with the strength of lovers.

Moments later, Billy was gone.

*****

On the verge of being sick, Nora threw on a robe and ran down the stairs to the front of the house.

He was still there, mounting his horse.

"Billy, wait!"

He gathered the reins and looked into her eyes as she came up to stand beside him. Her heart faltered. She took his hand to steady herself. He leaned down and kissed her forehead. She closed her eyes. Oh, Billy. . . .

"Nora, if you like, I'll let you know where I end up."

Fighting back tears, she said quietly, "Yes. Yes, please. I would like that very much."

Billy's hand pulled away, and she felt as though her heart had broken.

"Goodbye, Nora."

"Billy . . ."

The finality of their parting hit her. Was she making a terrible mistake? Could she actually let this wonderful man ride out of her life?

Billy reined his mount around. As the trees rustled in the rising wind, he touched heels to the mare and cantered out of the yard into the pre-dawn.

She watched after him as her inner voice cried, *Don't let him go!*

Feeling a wave of depression inundate her very soul, she gazed to the east. The sun would soon be rising over the tobacco fields, where her Irish would soon be tilling the soil for next season's crop. A sense of possession, of belonging to the land, began to temper the pain of impossible love.

Her family's land. The O'Lalors's plantation. It would always be their land. Her Da's dream.

The wind picked up considerably, blowing thousands of leaves from the trees. It stirred her hair, whipping her blond locks about her sorrowful face. A faint, melodious refrain began to whistle through the branches.

Nora cocked her head. What was it? Narrowing her eyes, she concentrated. There—sounds were forming, fragments of a melody. They were familiar. . . .

The hair on the nape of her neck rose. She felt a presence. The melody increased in tempo. Now she recognized the tune. It was the plaintive song Da used to hum when he was feeling melancholy. Was it a message? Was Da telling her she was making a mistake?

THE GIRL WHO WAS ME IS GONE

Nora looked quickly to the road. Billy was barely an image, a mere shadow, on the main road now.

Billy! Nora's hand flew to her bosom. No! Oh, Lord. Billy, stop! Don't leave me! I've made a terrible mistake. I'll give up the plantation. I'll give up everything!

Nora began to run. She ran as fast as she could, shouting, "Billy! Billy!" Her voice echoed down the lane—which was now empty.

Billy was gone.

Nora came to a halt, chest heaving, gasping for breath. Even if she dashed back to the barn for a mount, she knew she would never be able to catch up to Billy before he turned off the road to meet his ship, and the location of his rendezvous was unknown to her.

Crushed, devastated, a great sadness overwhelmed her. As if anguish itself had melted her bones, she collapsed to the earth and sobbed.

I've made such a dreadful mistake, she thought. I've lost you, Billy, and it's entirely my fault. How could I have been so stupid? Oh Lord, I've lost you forever!

With tears streaming down her cheeks, she inhaled deeply before gazing out over the shadowy land—her land—and for the first time, it seemed alien to her.

EPILOGUE
One year later

"Thank you," Nora said to the young man, one of Anne and William Pitt's employees. He had handed her a mug of warm cider on his way through a crowd that had gathered to celebrate the opening of Pitt's Mercantile Store. There was more cause for celebration—the end of the blockade on the American colonies. Virginia had voted to acknowledge England's Parliament.

The cup in Nora's hands brought welcome warmth as she strolled past a table laden with cookies and cakes baked for the occasion. Nora glanced up to see seagulls soaring in the cool February sky, and she inhaled salt-tinged air that blew in off the bay. Only yesterday, storm clouds had passed overhead, dusting Jamestown with two inches of snow. By noon, the snow had melted, and cobblestones glistened in the sunshine. Her gaze drifted to a sleek sailing vessel in the harbor, and she thought of Billy. The "if onlys" in her life.

She had heard of Billy's death in September. The *Lobo do Mar* had been sunk in a fierce battle with an English man-of-war. All aboard were lost.

Taking a deep breath, Nora remembered how the news had completely debilitated her. It had taken months before she'd been able to function normally again.

Time helps the healing process, she thought, but regrets linger, especially when I'm alone at night. In the sleepless hours, significant events emerge from my past to make me cry, or perhaps smile, or even laugh. Memories, good and bad, never completely leave us.

The breeze heightened, and with its new fervor came a malodorous stink. Wrinkling her nose, Nora spotted the source of the odor—a large frigate moored at the opposite end of the wharf. It was a slave ship, the type used to transport Irish to the American colonies. Her stomach churned when she saw the poor souls, dressed in rags, who were being herded off the vessel to the dock, where armed men waited to lead them to the auction pens.

Nora shook her head, knowing from firsthand experience the inhumane treatment those people had already suffered, and had yet to endure.

She recalled last November's news of the Van der Root's demise. A cyclone had destroyed the *Goede Hoop*. Her entire crew, as well as three hundred Africans, had gone down with the ship. Nora had mourned the loss of the Africans, but not the Van der Roots.

The *Goede Hoop* was only one of dozens of ships carrying hundreds of crew and slaves lost annually to Atlantic storms. That didn't stop the trade in human cargo. More were arriving every week. Several months ago, African slaves had begun to replace the Irish. It was said that Africans, with their darkly pigmented skin, were better able to withstand the searing sun and humidity of Virginia.

Moving to the edge of the crowd, Nora noticed a weather-beaten WANTED poster tacked to the wall of an adjacent building. She stepped closer and stared at a very bad drawing of Billy Devlin. Surprised that it had survived the elements, she pulled the tattered paper down and gazed at the drawing.

"Good riddance to that one. He was nothing but trouble, I'm told."

That voice! Nora's hand flew to her bosom. It wasn't possible! When she turned, the first thing she saw was the lopsided grin. Billy Devlin! He was standing behind her, as large as life. Nora couldn't believe her eyes.

"Have you missed me, my darling?"

"Billy," she choked, barely able to speak, "I was told you were dead."

"Billy Devlin *is* dead, at least as far as the English know."

"How?" she asked.

"Perhaps we should take a few steps away from this crowd." He took Nora's arm and, as they began to stroll, he explained. "When *Lobo do Mar* went down with no survivors, I had, just weeks before, given up pirating. I was in Havana, purchasing a merchant ship. The English didn't know that, and subsequently the pirate Billy Devlin has been legally declared dead."

"Does that mean . . ?"

"Yes, I am no longer a wanted man. I did, however, take the precaution of changing my name. I am now known as Billy Smith."

"Smith?" Nora laughed.

"Why not? If it's good enough for you and Anne . . ." He raised his brow. "By the way, you haven't married in this past year, have you?"

"Lord, no! No, Billy, I haven't."

"Then a little hug might be in order?"

Nora fell into Billy's arms. Their lips met, and she lost herself in a whirlwind of passion that had been dormant for far too long.

Suddenly realizing there were people about, she gently pulled back. "Billy, I have so many things to tell you."

"And I, you."

"The day you left, I ran after you, but I couldn't catch you. Ever since then, I've prayed to have the chance to see you again, to let you know that I would give up the plantation, everything I have, to be with you. Then, oh God, when I heard you were dead, I almost died. Oh, Billy!"

His arms comforted her once more. "And I, my darling, in spite of circumstances, have always believed we would be together. By the way, I'm the proud owner of a grand ship. I've become a merchant trader—but not in slaves. That I'll never be! The best thing I've ever done was to let Billy Devlin die. Now I can live here in Virginia as Billy Smith, without fear of arrest. That being said, I might even be willing to try plantation life."

She searched his eyes. "Billy, you don't have to do this for me, and I won't ask it of you. I'll be an absentee landlord. I'll go anywhere with you, anytime. All you have to do is name the place." Unable to contain her emotions, she burst into tears and held onto Billy as if she were grasping an impossible dream. "Is it really you, Billy?"

Nora and Billy turned to see Anne and William hurrying toward them, each carrying a baby in their arms. "I can't believe it!" Anne said as she came up and hugged Billy with her free arm. "You're alive, you scalawag!"

"Yes, it's me, himself, living and breathing."

Anne motioned to her companion. "Billy, I want you to meet William Pitt, my husband. William, this is Billy . . ."

". . . Smith," Nora interrupted. "Billy *Devlin* died when his ship went down." When confusion furrowed Anne's brow, Nora added, "I'll explain later."

"Not necessary," Anne replied with a grin. "We're all someone else, aren't we?"

William offered his free hand to Billy. "Good to meet you, Billy."

"Pleased," Billy replied, shaking hands. "Congratulations on your . . . twins, are they?"

"Let me take him," Nora said, reaching for the infant William was carrying.

Anne hoisted the child she held in her arms. "This little one is Keela. I named her after my mother."

"Billy," Nora said, turning the baby she held to face him, "what do you think of this little fellow?"

"A fine-looking lad if ever I saw one."

The baby grinned. No, it wasn't a grin. It was a lopsided smile.

Billy's eyes almost popped out of his head. His jaw dropped. His face blanched, reddened, then blanched again. Almost choking, he asked, "Nora, is he . . . my . . . our . . ."

"Meet Billy Jr., your son."

"Jesus, Mary, and Joseph!" Billy exclaimed. "Oh, my God. Nora, may I hold him? Please, I promise I won't let him drop."

Nora passed the infant into Billy's arms. She watched Billy's face. He was spellbound, completely in awe. An impossible dream, she thought, that has miraculously come true.

"He's so tiny," Billy marveled, touching the child's hand. "Look at these perfect little fingers and the miniature nails. Ah, and such a handsome little fellow he is."

"He's the spitting image of my da," Nora teased.

"Oh, he is now, is he?" Billy replied, smiling broadly as he scrutinized the cherubic face. "If you were to ask me, I would say he has his father's good looks." He glanced quickly to Anne. "Keela is beautiful, too."

"Thank you, Billy," Anne said, exchanging a smile with her husband.

"William," Billy said, "let's you and me take our wee ones for a stroll along the wharf. We should show off our youngsters to the world."

"Aye," William replied. "A grand idea. Ladies, come along."

Nora took Anne's hand in hers, and they followed several yards behind their men.

After a moment, Anne said with incredulity, "Not in my wildest dreams."

The last three years flashed before Nora in milliseconds. And then she made a choice—to embrace the good and let the bad fade into obscurity.

She squeezed Anne's hand. "Nor in mine!"

The End

ABOUT THE AUTHOR

MICHAEL BROWN

Michael Brown is a retired Hollywood film editor who has won three Emmy Awards and an ACE Eddie Award, as well as a Career Achievement Award as a film editor. He is a member of the American Cinema Editors Guild, the Writers Guild of America, and the Directors Guild of America. He is also a member of the Academy of Television Arts and Sciences and the Academy of Motion Picture Arts and Sciences. He has sold numerous TV scripts to NBC, ABC, and CBS. His first novel, *William & Lucy*, won the 2012 Global eBook Award for Best Historical Novel of the Year (era 1500-1940). He lives in Austin, Texas with his wife, Holly.

OTHER BOOKS BY MICHAEL BROWN

Three short quotes from *William & Lucy* by Michael Brown that appear on the back of the book cover:

"Sensitively written with a foot in two centuries, this book provides the kind of retreat from contemporary problems the Romantic era embodied."
US REVIEW OF BOOKS

"A strong pick for any historical fiction collection. Highly recommended."
THE MIDWEST BOOK REVIEW

"If you love history, read this book. If you love brilliant writing, read this book. If you love romance, read this book. If you love a page-turning ending, read this book. Yes, even though it's based on historical facts, *William & Lucy* delivers an ending that will have your heart pumping.
"Excellent job, Michael Brown. Not only did I enjoy your novel, I believe I learned a thing or two along the way. I can't rate this book highly enough. I'll say five stars because that seems to be the norm, but it's worthy of ten."
CB REVIEW

Penmore Press
Challenging, Intriguing, Adventurous, Historical and Imaginative

www.penmorepress.com

CPSIA information can be obtained
at www.ICGtesting.com
Printed in the USA
LVHW030816311021
702017LV00001B/64